HINTERLAND

CHRIS DIETZ

HNS Publishing | Bisbee, Arizona

ISBN: 978-1-7335729-0-3

HNS Publishing
Bisbee, Arizona

for Billy & Tami

CHAPTER 1

"Up, down, charm, strange, top, bottom."

How many quarks do you know?

What's the name of a particle of action?

The small, plump female with odd red spectacles cringed at the table in the bed and breakfast's dining room, mouthing off to her mother. Suddenly she was India. India...subcontinent of tropical deciduous forest and Hindu monkey temples. India chanted her way aloft—

You know when you close your eyes, and you see colors or shapes, maybe shadows. Light and darkness. You can't stop seeing—

She knew all that jazz about perception, and had downloaded the history of the tools, those senses, those systems that pretended to stand for the normal way of seeing. Then, she discovered Charles Fort, who was defiant, and saw all sorts of things normal people didn't see.

She recited to herself, "A world or a vast super-continent hovered over India—" She knew the next part, too: whales in the sky attacked by celestial swordfish!

Who was this guy, Charles Fort? Turns out, he was a blob of a man at the turn of the Century with incredible research skills. He documented sightings, spills, disappearances, cracks, holes, and creatures. Something 19th Century about his prose?

Charles Fort said things are not things but relations, the great merging into some other else. So the threat is entropy. Why resist. Sew it back together. Make entropy earn its keep, useful and essential.

She felt clear, then phony. She pictured her dad. She twitched in her seat missing her items...the electronica—

Her mother was stalking her now, like a lioness. Medea asserted, "You're mad because I made you leave your toys. You have your books and notebooks. Come on, don't be this or that. A-roar! You can be away from the wired world a few days. This is our time." She sighed dramatically, went "Up!"

Quickly, the girl replied, "Tidbit." She muttered, "Down."

Her mother pondered prettily, then popped: "Gyp!"

"If they're toys, then what am I?"

Her elegant mother, sitting opposite her, was the life of the party. Every eye in the dining room eventually took in her delightful hiking outfit. She had big leather boots on her dainty feet, khaki shorts with big pockets, a tank top. She was wide-eyed—azurite...shivering her mane of brown hair in tangential cascades...then mommy dearest disrupted the antiphony: "My angel! Where is she now? Bad mood? Hello, sky flower! Good morning, my little subatomic particle."

"Strange. Strange—try it."

Her mother puckered, then chimed: "Only if you sit up. You look like you're collapsing into a black hole."

Right away, more cringe, more crouch. Her mother said, "Le Petomane. And I say that only because he is as vulgar and crass as you are being."

"He was an artist."

"Of farts?"

"Frank Lentini, the three legged man."

"Dord! You and your freaks. Freaks aren't necessarily strange. Are they?"

"Quiz. You and your negotiations."

"My sweetie pie! Flesh of my flesh!"

"Moods are ways of moving through the world. That's what you tell me. That's what you say all the time. As though you could choose."

"Youth is a world view, my frabjous tortilla chip. You try on all the outfits in all the sizes. And you're an artist too: that makes it worse. Better? My luminous one. Because you can get away with anything. What—am I being harsh? I can't do it—move between worlds the way you do. You know quarks, you know the first 3 minutes. I barely keep up. I have to be professional. Adult. Ha! Numinous one, are you there?" She smirked. "Corona of conflagration, you're an artist!"

"Words are toys. We're just playing. I haven't individuated enough to be objective," the girl murmured.

"Maybe you're feeling an excess of protons this morning? Maybe it's a bit of spoiled cyclotron? I'm kidding. Don't go away! Ma petite microchip. Where are you? Stay with me!"

"Dark matter!"

Mother snorted—she was so animated, life force spewing, from her. She couldn't resist, whispering huskily, "The light! Go towards the light! Move to the light!"

Lethologica: ubluxulation. The girl was word drunk. The names, the naming...her names...every word collided with a word next door that was standing too close... appellations...nomenclature. Everything pointed to something else. Nothing was still. All was movement and imagination.

She knew she was coming in for a landing. She did miss electronica: letting go by letting it out which was letting it in. Every everybody everyone electrifies. Online or texting and she pretended evidence. Validation volition. Wasn't it always about proof? Establishing authority? All she needed was a good link. But she hated electronic connection acting like human connection. As though they might mate? The data fog...the cloud...the big connectors coupling. Electronics did little for humans but occupy them. She hated social media as much as she hated RPG's. She hated Redditt. She hated shareware. She shared and blogged and tweeted. She knew kids who texted 800 times over a weekend. She hated that her mother was right about it being good for her to get away from 'the toys'.

She wanted to go to Los Alamos. The birthplace, the cauldron of fabulosity! that changed the world. That's what the Southwest meant to her: Oppie and the boys. But her mother knew a better Southwest, she said. The Southwest of astronomy and geology, the Southwest of Native peoples and incredible light.

She hated how her mother had convinced her to spell her name 'Aurora' at school. She had to or they wouldn't be able to pronounce it. She hated that extra 'a'. Her name was Aurore. French, not Spanish or Basque. Her mother didn't want her to have anything to do with Spanish or Basque. She admired 'Aurore' as in Aurore Dupin, also known as George Sand...whose grandmother had been Marie-Aurore. George Sand's mother's name was Sophie. A very nice name. George's daughter was Solange.

That was a name of intention. Solange.

Maybe, she should take her cue from Dupin and change her name to a boy's, Cuthbert Cunning.

Fort said that if one knew the initial state of bodies precisely, then the position of those bodies at any given later moment should be predictable. The girl with bad hair at the dining room table in the bed and breakfast in Arizona in late May predicted the future. School let out 2 weeks ago. Next year she'd be in high school, but not just any high school, art school. Prep school. The academy beckoned.

Futures were easy. Present was hard. Pasts could be selected. She recalled another initial state when she and her mom and her dad were tight. She had put everything she knew, everything she was, into play back then. She loved forts, bug hospitals. Her parents did too. Play meant pure attention. She knew it depended on the security the family provided. Family, like an infrastructure. The continuum from which the atom emerged.

She missed her dad. She missed her old mom. This famous mother wanted to get away with her before her next show. How had her family become so pony pony phony? Who would have predicted the family fail? Continuum discontinuous.

Medea—that was her mother's artist name (Aurore had promised never to use her former name again), beamed with health in her flattering hiking outfit. Big boots. She looked ready for adventure. Her eyes were all over Aurore, like her daughter was scenery. Aurore kept her eyes away. She could tell her mother was antsy. Probably needed a cigarette, though she'd quit 3 times in the last year...this time for good.

"My angel floating in prana," she taunted. Medea shifted, then: "That dreadful book you made me read said the first 3 minutes of the universe were incomprehensible. Density and pressure and temperature changed in ways we can't understand. Basic forces like gravity glitched." She sighed, like it was a lot of work.

"The Planck wall. I know it well." She tried not to giggle or smile. "I think of it more as a Lovecraft wall. Behind this wall, gelatinous creatures pustulate. These forces, density and pressure and temperature, still occur. Which means little big bangs are going on all the time, all through the universe. Mini-big bangs. When scientists think about the Big Bang it's already over."

"Which means what? There're no mini-big bangs.

You're messing with me now."

"First 3 minutes like a trigger on a windup toy."

"Physicists label anything they don't understand 'quantum flux'. Right? Artists label anything they don't understand, style. That's funny. I made a funny!"

"You don't care about physics."

"You're titillated by big brains. Those physicists are big brains, right? But do they know there is more to life than quarks? Art exists because there is a lot more to life than quarks. We love each other. Where does that fit? There wouldn't be any art without love. Quarks need love. I need love. You need love. I trust your love. Uh-you're getting that look?"

Aurore went, "The look. The look!" Then: "Tautology. Da needs love, too."

"You look like your father when you get pensive. That way."

Her father was Arana, the New York City, Basque artist. While his ex-wife's career skyrocketed, his struggled, fabricating sculptures from found items. Organic bits he dug up. Junk he found on the street. He lived in Brooklyn. Aurore had visited twice since the divorce. She signed her name Aurore Arana. Medea didn't like it. She said he was not Basque. She forbid him from teaching Aurore Basque. She learned 'jingo'—

"Brooklyn Bridge—bones of a dinosaur," Aurore said.

Her mother humphed, said, "Come on, please try."

"Top, bottom. Top: lillypilly."

"Bottom: unceremoniousness."

"Overnervousness."

"I like that," said her mother.

Aurore blurted, "You didn't read that book on the first 3 minutes. You scanned it. Like you do everything. You're humoring me."

"Don't be mean."

"Strange! Dog-Faced Boy!"

"Uhh, Human Caterpillar."

"Lion-Faced Man!"

"Puppet Woman!"

"Good, Mama. You've learned your lessons well. Okay, that was mean."

Sarcastic...sardonic...withering...derision. Let the gibes flow! She was logosphile! 'Bibliobibuli'! Philtrum...feck. She announced, "I don't know what I want to be when I grow up. All these words around art. All these words around 'dark matter'. Around the first 3 minutes. They stand for what's not. Maybe I'll draw. But I'm not that good. Maybe I'll play a musical instrument, but I'm not good at that either. Maybe I'll be a poet. You would like that, wouldn't you, Mama? It's not me who's so impressed with big brains. You want an honest to goodness prodigy child."

"I'd settle for a respectful daughter."

"Suppose I became a physicist? Would you shun me?"

Medea's eyes went to twill. Her mouth was moist as she said, "Why do you do this to me?"

Aurore continued, "Lumpy probabilistic. You decided to play momma bear for the weekend. All probabilities point to that. 'Come on' yourself."

Her mother gasped. The speech had been delivered head down. Then Aurore couldn't tell whether she'd actually said it. But it didn't matter, her mom knew her so well she received the bump, understanding the way Aurore held herself in her chair. Aurore was resisting. Medea took a sip of coffee, stared at her oatmeal. The dining room was sleepy. Were they the only ones talking? Bickering? Their table like a bee hive in a dining room of still. Families around, at their own tables, having their own breakfasts. No one acting out, out loud. Medea didn't grin fast. Calmly, she smiled, went, "You can play musical instruments. You are gifted. Let's have fun. This is silly. I know, words you can play on a musical instrument. I got one, baggage."

"Feedbag. Shift, sift: shields down, phasers on stun, hover mode—"

"Double ha! Now you're being obtuse. I'm going down to the river to photograph. Come with me. You can help. You said you wanted to learn photography. Now's a good time. Maybe you will get in to film next year...let's see what happens. Okay?" She scanned the room, evaluating timbre, then nodded and: "Very exclusive B and B."

One of the bed and breakfast people came over with a coffee pot. "Need a fresher upper?" the young woman perked. She was tan, sleek, in her 20s.

Medea nodded. Aurore slumped.

The young woman smiled, said, "Birdwatchers? Birdwatchers come from all over the world to check out our river."

Medea said, "Of course. My daughter knows all the birds. She knows everything."

Aurore kept shrinking.

The server giggled, "There was a sighting today. Like an exotic kingfisher. A real beauty. That's what Tom said." She gave a brief nod and pursed her lips as though she had shared a secret. "Tom knows all the local birds." She kept nodding. "Good energy." She walked away.

Medea said, "Good, it's settled. We'll go to the river. Look for kingfishers."

"Halcyon," said Aurore. Then: "Film sounds flim flam. Yes, maybe film. Three minute long films."

"That would be perfect!"

"Words that you add one letter to that make a new word. Lien, like with leases and stuff, add an 'a'."

"I'll buy you a camera!" Triumphantly, she asked, "This is a new one? Let's see. How about photo?"

"Rode. Add an 'o'. Rodeo."

"Boa constrictor. Add a 't'. Boat constrictor."

"Very funny."

"Beautiful words! Tell me beautiful words! Like...like dawn and oriole. Hush. Flush. Asphodel!"

"Gonorrhea."

Inforrhea...like diarrhea...those weird double 'R's'...like freaks with 2 heads. Covered in hair: Hypertrichosia. Doppelganger. Bifurcate. Antinomianism... antimony.

She still had her notebook. She touched her notebook beside her setting at the table. Eventually, a full notebook—complete, filled in. Not so fast. Insert time warp, ascend the sky. Filling up a notebook was recording what she did to herself. No one must know.

Medea was grimacing prettily. She went, "Gross."

Aurore mumbled, "James Joyce said the most beautiful word in the English language was 'cuspidor'."

Aurore would take her notebook with her. She would open the cover, turn to the exact page. Wherever she was. She would write in long hand...as opposed to short hand.

Aurore spluttered, "I am trying."

"Give me a break!"

Aurore thought of thinking. She was complicating again, making everything happen at once. Chaoplexity. She thought of Krao, from Laos, who was famous the world over as 'Darwin's Missing Link'. She thought of the Voynich manuscript. She loved secret codes. Vaults of the brain unleashed their overflow: patterns, contingencies. 'What do I know?' Of value? What matters? A quantum of communication was a qualcum. She thought of 'India'! Could water catch fire? Could gravity be repelled? For now, she reported directly to Charles Fort. She smiled and said, "Don't want to go to the river. Jet jet. I mean just yet. I mean I'll work my way down my own way."

"Finish your breakfast. Oatmeal, yummy."

Gruel...solder and treacle...dodder. Aurore did not do glutinous wads, mucilaginous clumps that had already been eaten. She drank orange juice. Fresh squeezed—tasted like trees.

The book they'd been talking about was *The First Three Minutes* by Stephen Weinberg. Aurore liked to check out books that summed things up. She liked check lists. She liked Venn diagrams. The pictures from the Hubble discounted Weinberg, proved he needed a big dose of metaphor therapy. If things could change so drastically, so fast, in her lifetime, everything turned topsy-turvy, south side up, lillypilly—then

First.

Three.

Minutes.

From right now! For my notebook. GO! What happens in the next 3 minutes? What is sensed? What is seen? If these were the first 3 minutes, starting right now!

If she'd added a 'u' to age, she'd have had ague.

First three minutes.

She saw herself.

Aurore Artemisia Arana.

She liked the A's. A was the most architectural of the letters.

'My candle burns at both ends—'

What did she see?

First 3 minutes!

She collected words. She read to distraction. She knew the best sites on the Internet where things like giant bot fly larvae being removed from a baby's eye could be found. She was fond of teratology, anomalies like rainfalls of blood or frogs, and she cherished Princess Caraboo.

She was Meja! But no one knew that name. She focused. Her 3 minutes were ticking. What did she see? What was happening? Besides her mother and her at their table, two other tables had people. Families. By their looks, normal as could be. Aurore would not stare. She would not peek. She would be aware—

The girl with the coffee pot fluttered among the tables, dispensing hot joe and smileys. Everybody had already been served his or her oatmeal and juice. The nearest table had two parents, mom and dad, then little brother, middle brother, and older sister. The older sister seemed to be slumping into her center of gravity. She was pretty in a trashy way. Aurore knew she'd have tattoos all over her clavicles by the time she was 18. The middle boy plunked down his oatmeal spoon and folded his arms in front of himself. He was tough, arrogant, cute in a jock kind of way. Little brother got the idea, hesitated, then changed his mind and dug his spoon into his oatmeal. He ate up. Kindergarten? A bedroom chest full of Teenage Mutant Ninja Turtles?

The table at the end of the dining room, before the picture window, had two parents, one girl. They were black, African-American. The other table's patrons were white. In front of this girl, her oatmeal bowl off to the side, a plate, and on this plate a heap of orange. A pile of glow. At first Aurore thought the bright orange mass was some kind of mysterious fruit. They were pumpkin orange oblongs, shiny and waxy. Such a bright, piercing orange, as though everything around them got bleached to monotones. She liked the girl right away!

Her mother followed her gaze and said, "Habaneros, hottest chiles in the world."

"They look radioactive," said Aurore.

Both the black girl and the middle boy were about her age. She liked looking at the boy so moved her eyes back to the chiles in front of the girl. What could the girl be thinking? What would she do with them? Now the girl folded her hands over something on her lap—a book, with a library sticker on its binding.

No one was talking at the other tables. Did they do moods? Did they travel between worlds? Both tables, serene as hell. The boy's parents were baby boomers, 60's generation people like her mom. His father worked at an electronics company that specialized in domestic robots.

The mother was a community college administrator. They were Catholics. The boy had an X Box 350, liked sports and Heavy Metal. *Beastie Boys. World of Warcraft.* He wore jeans and a blue t-shirt without a slogan—a good sign. The black girl's parents wore lycra work out suits. Hoity toity, upscale outfits for sweating. They jogged. Had mountain bikes. The father was a research chemist for a pharmaceutical firm. He liked to camp. His wife, the mom, didn't like to camp. She was a technical writer at the firm. The girl was a math prodigy and could calculate 6 digit numbers' square roots in her head. She'd learned to read at age 3. She had on safari pants and a light jacket, hair in corn rows.

The boy had an old bulldog he told his secrets to...Aurore could see it...juddering jowls...while the girl in her fancy bedroom in the suburbs conducted genetic experiments on crustaceans ...beakers and Bunsen burners jostled for space atop her dresser.

Aurore had learned to read at 2.

Were her 3 minutes up?

Now her mother would try to win her over. Aha! she was starting—

"What were the names of Emperor Norton's dogs?"

Aurore met her mother's eyes, smiled wanly. "What do I get, if I guess?"

"You win a prize! You come to the river right now, and you have fun with me the rest of the day."

Aurore said, "Maggot and Foreskin."

"Vulgar!"

"It's not fair if I can't win something I want. Reciprocity."

Medea said, "I want to get down to the river! Now is the best time for the light. Have you noticed the photons around here?"

Aurore glanced away from her mother to the picture window. Distant mountains painted on a Chinese screen.

Her eyes came back to Medea, and she was rewarded with a beaming scintillation of pure mama bliss. Grownups were so easy, it was scary—

"Every place," Medea went on, "has a soul. All the souls that ever lived here in this place, in this light."

Aurore nodded. "This is going to be part of the Goddess series?"

Medea pushed away from the table. She stretched out her scrumptious legs. "Ishtar, Belilli…Virgin of Guadalupe. Tonantzin."

Aurore wiggled her face the way her mother hated to make her glasses set more comfortably. "Go on!" she said. "I'll be down in a split—"

"Watch out for rattlesnakes. Pay attention where you put your feet. You can't go down in flip flops."

Aurore waited for everyone to leave. She sat hunched over, open notebook in front of her, favorite pen in her left hand. Even though she was right handed. She had written 2 words on the blank page: 'newt cellar'. With her left hand, it looked like an EEG. The family with all the kids took off in a flurry of discussion bordering on chaos. Some argument. The youngest kid said his sister was acting like a baby. Aurore saw the middle boy's eyes slide past her. No peeking! The other family left in an orderly manner, the girl having packed her pile of habaneros into a plastic sandwich bag. The server came over and asked Aurore if she needed anything. Aurore had to snort. Still…brightness visible through the picture window. Or: pouring through the window, a ton of photons. Mother was right again. Aurore said, "I don't need anything."

The server was already slipping away in search of good vibes. Aurore closed her notebook and put away her pen. Outside? Not yet. Jet—

Until she was alone in the dining room. When she got outside, the black man and his wife were jogging down the desert road that meandered from the bed and breakfast to the paved county road. They smiled at her...a little wave. Further on, the other family was piling into their humongous SUV. It was metallic blue and looked like a space pod. Except! for the middle boy...where was he?

Aha! the plot thickens!

* * *

Aurore went around the buildings. Gardens, patios, bird feeders. Hummers at the feeders. Quail calling. Towhees and thrashers running by, checking out every nook and cranny. Rakes leaned against the adobe wall. The wrens investigated tines for spider webs. Potted geraniums could have larvae. What kind of hummers? Anna's? She couldn't see them very well, so wasn't sure. Where were her binoculars? She felt funny. She always felt funny. Why were her senses so acute? What was she looking for?

Cute! One letter!

She found the trail to the river. Not too far. Trees— green giants made a living, breathing wall above the river...not too far at all. Their crowns of leaves seemed to be puffing, respiring in and out, like they were giant green lungs. The trail cut across a broad field of white gold grass. Mesquite in clumps. She got on the trail, paid her toll. Checked her TripTik. Distant mountains made perfect skylines. Vista. Was this scenery? She'd seen it on the web. She couldn't help being snide, as she taxied in for a landing. She wanted to locate every assumption. She'd only been out west once before, when Medea had the Beverly Hills show. Now, as she walked and scanned, she saw she was realizing she was moving through a wide, wide bowl surrounded by mountains. This river sliced down the middle of the bowl, made the valley between mountains. She stayed on the trail, hoped for the best.

Two men on horseback came plodding up the trail.

Aurore got out of the way of the horses. Big as mountains, with packs tied at their sides. So close, she could smell them. The horses breathed in chortling gasps. The 2 men, maybe in their 30s, nodded and smiled to her. They didn't look like cowboys. Their hats—helmets, were all wrong, or funny, like those oddly dainty ones polo players fancy.

One of the men said, "Is this the right way?"

The other man laughed. They pulled on their reins, the horses' heads went up and down.

Aurore said, "Depends." She looked away fast, studied her little feet in blue flip flops.

The same guy said, "Fair enough. I'm Jakes. This is Graves. We're on an adventure."

Aurore looked up. "At the B and B?"

The men laughed. The second man, who had not spoken, said, "We're doing a re- enactment. Do you know what that is?"

"Creative anachronism. It's like D and D for grownups." Her shoulders went up, braced for the rebuttal.

The first man yelped, "Whoa!" to his horse that had started side stepping, eager to be on its way.

But these weren't cowboys. They were L.L. Bean adventurers. Aurore beamed at them, noticing how the horses' bizarrely thick heads were attached, like maybe with Velcro, to the grotesquely huge torsos.

The first man got his horse under control. He called back, "We're re-enacting Coronado's expedition through the Southwest on horseback. The whole way on horseback!" He clicked his jaws, making a smacking sound, and he and his horse made tracks.

The other guy bid Aurore, "To adventure!"

Aurore knocked her notebook against her side. Horsies! She remembered playing horsie with her dad when she was 8. He'd get on all fours and gallop about insisting in his whinnying that she call him Ibon, a good

Basque name for a horse.

Child's play. We grow up. Horsies! Emerging from the continuum to a new—attention! Watch for rattlesnakes! What was that wasp doing? It looked all mecha, like a Guyver, in its plated chitin shields. What was its secret? Wasp world. Ant world. She felt hypnotized when she was really focused, but that was when it was best, and that was when she was vulnerable.

Big ants made bare gravel circles around their nest's opening. Red and black ants. Did they war? What if the queen escaped? What if the mother breached the caissons? If you stay off the ants' trails, they won't get stuck between your toes.

She felt vulnerable because Aurore Arana was a fake. Aurore Arana was not a prodigy. She had a good memory and a noggin for words. She just liked weird stuff like every other kid her age. She was embarrassed. She felt guilty. She'd be discovered by her mother sooner or later. She hadn't read as much as she claimed. She knew the tips of a lot of ice berg topics. She was a phony. Masked. She knew a smattering of this and that. To be found out! The curtain pulled back...but then about a year ago the epiphany had come: her half assed scan of the first 90 pages of a book gave her enough ammo to outshine her...colleagues' best efforts. Peers like pears. Her show-offy scam juggled priorities expertly for the 8th grade milieu. Her mother would *not* find out. What a Poindexter! Her intuition guided her feet along the uneven trail.

It was so stupid about girls her age and horsies. *Just wuv dose ponies!* She twittered, hurried, flip flops flapping. Little birds snapped and bumped through the grass and brush. Sparrows. What kind? Sparrows hard to tell apart. Black throated? She should have brought her binoculars. No, they were finches. She needed a good field guide. She stepped around a horse pile, still steaming, and wondered if the 2 adventurers had seen Medea. They'd been relatively calm so evidently not. She remembered what happened in Beverly Hills, where she first understood the power her mother had over men.

The white gold field of grass was traversed. Much more brush then. The trail branched. The main part blatantly continued straight to the river. The smaller branch took off to the left, southward, towards Mexico. Mesquite—tall, bristly beasts. Tumbleweeds, thorny clots big as refrigerators, plastered against the mesquite. She took the smaller branch. It was narrow, too. A corridor of pokers.

This trail dampened the sprites she had bursting from her chest like baby aliens. Moods, worlds, mothers—then, now, she was outside, so she unpacked them. Zwiebel, cebolla, l'oignon. Maybe it was the light...outside...maybe it was the air. She felt outside. Sprites pfft-ed out. She saw a duck go over. Must be close to the river. Closer to the big trees, too. She didn't know her ducks. She'd learned birds in a book. So a beaky quack.

Diffuse? Was that the right word? Oh, this was chillin'. As the kids said. Diffusion...delusion...prism...prison. She sighed herself to adventure and slowed, deliberate where she put her feet.

Speculate...speculum. She walked on tiptoe, proceeding curious. Onieric? Adventure needed new words. She did it as good as she *could* do it. (That came direct from Medea.) Right now, what she did best was stealthy steps down a spiny trail, moving her body, bending her body like a cartoon Ninja. Flip-flops slapping—

The trail, a tunnel...passage...corridor...abruptly opened. Before her, a circular area at the edge of the trees. Aurore pulled back like she'd been struck at by a cobra! But she didn't think she'd been seen. In the clearing the black girl and the middle boy were kneeling. They were looking down at something between them. Aurore held her breath, wished herself invisible, slowly withdrawing into the mesquite thorns. Her muscles vibrated. So this was arms and shoulders' excitement? She craned her neck to a vantage that allowed a peek. She checked for rattlesnakes. She dared not giggle. Funny, how the feeling of aloneness was so different when she was spying. They hadn't glanced her way. She was near them, but to the side, in the brush—

Between the 2 kids was a pile of those pumpkin orange habaneros. The hot peppers. The girl was talking in a disgusted voice to the boy: "They're the hottest peppers known to man or woman. They rate 450,000 units on the Scoville scale. A jalapeno rates about 150,000 units."

The boy muttered some reply Aurore couldn't hear.

The girl pulled back, went from her knees to her heels. "No way!" she cried.

The boy picked up one of the peppers. He thought he'd never seen such a funny looking, beauteous thing. He twirled it a little on its thin stem. He waved it before him, eyes flickering over it, searching for a clue to the orange glow. Then, in an official sounding voice, he proclaimed, "We'll each eat one at the exact same moment. And we can't spit it out. No matter what."

The girl said, "Absolutely not! That's crazy!" but she extended an arm and took a pepper. She lowered her head and whispered, "You know that girl is watching—"

The boy shrugged, said dramatically, "Aaaabbbra—"

And the girls said simultaneously, "cadaver."

Aurore knew they could be friends.

They bit down on the habaneros, then crammed the whole things into their mouths. The pile between them instantly melted. That's what it looked like to Aurore. The pile's faint glow changed to an intensifying smear of burning white hot that hurt her eyes. The pile had become a small white circle too bright. An orange glow expanded outward from the white circle. The glow suggested a sphere, enveloping everything around. Bubble of glow.

The 2 kids held their hands to their mouths, but they would not spit. They were holding it in. Eyes squeezed shut. Did they know what was happening? Their heads quivered. They were inside the sphere or bubble of glow. The boy's hands in fists shot up. Tense! The girl growled. Now the boy's hands came down, opened, and he wiggled his fingers in the glow. Eye wide, he studied the effect. The girl pointed to the habanero pile. So they knew. They could see it! But their jaws were locked. The boy nodded vigorously. What was going on inside the kids' mouths? Mouthful of lava? The 2 kids remained kneeling and squatting above the pile which was now a tiny sun grenade.

Wrapped in photonic Saran Wrap.

Orange light...odd light...damn light...damn desert, dumb desert... outside light. Outside sucks. Arizona light, Arizona stuff happens chaos.

Reflection? Refraction? Redaction?

The 2 kids were inside the light.

How do chiles glow? Could chiles melt? Was the glare coming in? Or going out? From where? From the pile of habaneros?

Aurore screamed, bursting from hiding. She yelped, "Target!"

The kids looked at her. They were there. Then they were gone.

The glare broke. They were—

They were gone.

They were back. They were different. They looked different.

The chiles were gone.

No glow.

No glare.

Some other else—

CHAPTER 2

The undifferent ones saw 2 white giraffes hiding their heads in clouds. They couldn't be that tall! Maybe they only came out at night—

The boy imagined they would look wonderful striding across the desert in moonlight.

With every fiber of her being, the girl cried, "Impossible!"

The boy snapped his head to attention, focusing on her. She was standing up. He got to his feet. But he couldn't focus on her for long as his gaze insisted on scanning their surroundings. This was different. Pure astonishment felt like this.

"What happened?" asked the girl. "Those are giraffes. White giraffes. Everything's different. What happened?" Her head kept moving back and forth, eyes wide. She stopped her eyes on the boy. "Do you see giraffes? Am I going crazy?" Her eyes were fiery; her mouth was open. In a calmer voice, she said, "Something happened when we put the habaneros in our mouths. Hey! My mouth isn't burning at all!" She spat, spluttered her lips. "Nothing in my mouth at all."

The boy gazed at her intensely, a worried expression slowly crinkled his eyebrows and forehead.

"Look!" she cried, spinning around in place.

"I am...so—"

"Where did the cottonwoods go? Those are giraffes. They can't be giraffes! It's so green."

"Do you have something against giraffes?"

"Look at the river. It's all marshy. Where did the giant cottonwoods go?"

The boy stared about him. He seemed unsure, anxious. "Well, the dealio is I'm kinda interested in history. We live north of here in Glendale, but I know a little about this area. There weren't that many cottonwoods, back in the day. And the thing is—see that grass. Sacaton. And look at this." He stomped his foot against the ground. Thud soft sound. "That's soil. There hasn't been much sacaton or soil around here for 100 years. It got eaten & blown away."

The girl stomped her foot on the ground. She hummed with it, her arms and shoulders rising and falling. "So you're saying—"

The boy interrupted: "I don't know your name. I'm Tyler Gack."

"Sophie Rose. Gack?"

"Yeah, like you're clearing your throat."

"So you're saying what?"

"I'm not sure. We're at the exact same spot but suddenly like it was 100 years ago?"

"We took a bite of habanero and went back in time? That's ridiculous!"

"Impossible is what you said. Those bushes the girl was hiding in—the girl's gone. The bushes are gone. Something happened."

"I don't know. I hope the girl is okay. Why did she yell 'target' at us? This *can't* be—"

He shook his head, glanced around nervously. "I don't know what, I don't know what happened. Those bushes were mesquite. Now, no mesquite. See, there weren't mesquite bushes back then either. This was all high desert grassland."

Sophie gasped. Maybe she was in shock. But if he was into history, then he'd know something. Maybe he was in shock. Weren't you supposed to lay down, head up, force fluids in shock?

She couldn't remember. Everything seemed scrambled up. She said, "Something happened when we bit down on the habaneros. I felt—"

"What? What did you feel?" encouraged Tyler.

Sophie said, "I don't know. The habaneros! Is your mouth on fire?" She glanced at her feet where they'd been kneeling and exclaimed, "They were right here! Between us. Where did they go?" She pushed her hands in her pockets and pulled out from the right one, a grocery store plastic bag. "This is the plastic bag for the habaneros. Did you bring your phone?"

Tyler bent down and used his left hand to feel around the ground. He was mumbling. She could barely make out: "Family time, no phones. Where are they? They gotta be—"

Sophie yelled, "You think they're hiding? They're gone! The light, the light changed. There was a glare, then—"

"I saw something."

Sophie was looking wildly around for anything familiar, for the landmarks of just a moment ago. She said, "What did you see?"

"Like you said, light, a glare. Then a white, super white, orb or sphere or something, where the peppers had been."

Sophie thought before was painted pale earthy hues of bare sand, dried grass, with the occasional weathered gray, broken down farm with collapsing fence. Now all replaced with a green valley, a marshy river, no fence or farms in sight. Sophie exclaimed, "I don't have my phone either. My parents also announced family time." They both snickered. Then, she added, "What if that girl that was hiding blew up or something? We don't know."

Tyler said, "You know what? My mouth's not on fire at all. Just like yours." He spat. "Nothing. Another thing: are habaneros the hottest chiles in the world? What about the fabled ghost peppers of Thailand?"

"Are you kidding me?" Now she thought she'd start screaming.

Tyler nodded. "My mouth was really on fire."

"We're in shock. It's impossible. The fire is capsicum molecules. Right? So for the fire to just suddenly be gone would mean every single one of those molecules was gone. Right?"

Tyler said, "Unless *our* molecules shifted…or moved away from those molecules. Only stuff in the glow or glare moved or shifted—I don't get it, wouldn't that mean rocks and dirt too? How far down does it go? Where did the peppers go? How come they didn't show up here with us?"

Sophie groaned. "You're not some kind of *Star Trek* nut are you? Forget how we got here, how do we get back?"

"To the place without white giraffes? They're gone. Did you notice?"

"Come on."

Tyler raced around gaping and pointing. "In the blink of an eye! It happened just like that." Suddenly, Tyler almost looked happy. He went, "Whoa!" Circling away from their spot, going off at a lope to look around, he could find no giraffes. Perhaps they had blown away? Taller trees nearby, but none as large as giant cottonwood. Sacaton came down to the wide, wide river, but stopped when it got muddy. Then low banks, thick with green growth, turning mushy. Little stagnant pools along the shoreline. Some places had no bank and the river seemed to merge with the land in a soupy, sloppy, muddy quagmire. Tyler realized it was the banks that were throwing him. The river banks were drastically different.

No deep walled banks at all…like in the before—

Sophie came up alongside him. She said, "You okay? I have no clue. Do you? Everything's changed. There's nothing here that's ours."

Tyler kept on with his reconnoiter, swinging around sacaton clumps, avoiding mud.

Sophie said, "The mountains are the same."

Tyler said, "Maybe we should mark the exact spot where the habaneros were. I'll get some rocks." He scrambled around, bent over, grabbing at stray stones.

They found their spot, where it had started. They saw where they had been kneeling.

Sophie had to say it: "Are we dead? Seriously, nothing could have changed everything like this. It's impossible. A physical impossibility. And time travel is silly, Einstein proved that. So it's not physical: we must be dead?"

"You're smart—"

"For a girl? For a black person?"

"I didn't mean that at all. You're smart." Tyler kneeled down to drop his rocks in the spot where the habaneros had been. "Whatever happened, I'd hate to be stuck here with some dumbass." He grinned. "Should we head back to the B and B?"

She looked at him like she might scream yet. Slowly, she said, "You can't see it from here. It's just down the path. Right? Well, where's the path?"

Tyler finished with his rocks. Sophie kneeled beside him, correcting his arrangement with stones of her own— the rocks in a cairn they would recognize.

Tyler said, "You don't think the B and B is—"

From behind them, over by the river, a deep booming voice yelled, "Yoiks! Reach for the sky!"

They hustled to their feet, but kept close to each other, slightly crouched, tensed, ready to spring away. Their eyes pored over a thick stand of willows and horsetails at the river. They searched for the source of the voice. They couldn't see anyone. But it was pretty lush—

—and out of the green wall of plants erupted a beast as big as an SUV. This huge head! Right out of Greek mythology! Black, and bull like, with small eyes and a short beard. Giant, forward pointing horns. Quickly, it sized up the two, young people's threat, and started sniffing in loud explosions of snot, while slurping through the green, churning up mud. Maybe a bull? More like a mountain of muscle held together by a heavily scarred hide. Another voice, this one to the side, smooched in: "If you want to live, hop on, you lumpies."

They skittered around to this fresh invasion. At least the second voice was generous, something about its pitch promising easy laughter. The man was in Davy Crockett get up—that's what Sophie first thought. Tyler thought, buckskins. The man in buckskins stood on a two wheeled device, holding on to a central T bar in front. Tyler thought, 'Segway'. But, no, the device bumped along in an odd manner no Segway could. The device bore down on them. The machine made no sound, released no smoke, and didn't roll so much through the sacaton clumps as *crawl over and around and through* them. Tyler realized what was wrong with this picture: the wheels did not go round and round, they did not seem to be hard or stiff...the wheels appeared to be flowing, stretched out smears of motion—

But their immediate concern was the bull!

If it were a bull—

They jerked back and forth in place, from massive mountain of a beast idling in the mud nearby, to oddly leathered fellow on 2 wheeled device.

Sophie blurted, "It's David Bowie—I mean Davy Crockett! on a Segway!"

The man pulled up on his T and the device slowed, stopped right beside Tyler and Sophie. The man smiled warmly. "One on either side. Vite! Your feet beside mine.

It's not like you haven't done this before. Why looking so prismatic? I caught you two! Those are wild duds!"

The kids clambered on board and they lurched forward. They grabbed at the man's arms to steady themselves. But instead of heaving away from the animal in the mud, they moved towards it. The deep voice that had called first resounded again from the greenery: "If this isn't a rosy pickle, I don't know what!"

The beast huffed loudly, then got interested in some yellow flowered plants, moosching towards them in a tidal wave. Behind the huge head was a hump. The beast's hide was dark in places but mainly tan colored. A man appeared behind the bull, slogging his way through the mud and plants. He, also, was in buckskins. He strode right over to the beast and slapped it a good one on the rump. He made 'tsk tsk tsk' sounds to get it moving.

The kids gawked as the man between them gave a hearty laugh. But the other man pointed to something behind them and said with that same deep voice, "If you don't believe me, I don't know what. We're surrounded."

The riders on the 2 wheeler glanced behind and saw Indians coming in from the grassland at a gallop. Sophie immediately gasped. Tyler swallowed, tittered: "All right! Centaurs!"

Their pilot said, "Tyler, you know well as me, they eschew that terminology. Crots the name they prefer. For Johnny's sake."

Sophie whispered, "Has everyone gone mad?"

Now, the bull was sidestepping away from the mud, heading back towards the river. The man on foot stayed with it, offering encouraging 'tsk-s'. He called, "Meet you at camp!"

The driver of the 2 wheeled device pushed the T forward and angled it around to face the oncoming Indians. Sophie and Tyler assumed they were Indians, as they had long, thick black hair held back with headbands of red cloth. They had dark skin the color of pecan, with aquiline faces. The one out front held a bow. Another had what looked like a club. A mace? The rest all appeared to be holding sticks...lances?...spears? Normal hands and arms, heads and chest, then just below their belly buttons, the great merging with a horse's body.

The leader of the Indians, or Crots, clattered up so close they could smell his heaving breath. It smelled of grass. But the kids' eyes went to the long, heavy scabbard tied to his side. "Graves," he said and nodded. His breath slowed, eyes staying on them. "That auroch bull is ours by rights."

The driver said, "Okla, good morrow to you. It's a darn fine bull. You know that. We know that. It's a darn fine bull. So this is what we're gonna do. When your heifers need servicing, bring 'em on by. Share the wealth. How's that?"

The Crot leader's front hooves stamped at the ground in high stepping excitement. But he turned to his fellows, mumbled something to them. They talked for a moment but the kids couldn't understand what they said. The leader turned, said, "Graves, we have no quarrel with you."

"We each have our story," said the man on the 2 wheeled device. Was his name—it must have been Graves!

The Indians took off.

Tyler said, "Graves—is that your name?"

"Graves," said the fellow, nodding at each of them. "Let's go!" He pushed the T and they sped forth, moving north, up the river, following the edge where the sacaton met the mud.

Sophie called out, "What just happened?" in a strained voice, tiptoeing towards panic—

Tyler quickly announced loud enough to hear: "I'm Tyler. This is Sophie. How did you know my name?"

Graves said, "I know a cozy place to cross. Sweet little ford. As though I'd forget you—"

Sophie burst, "You know us?"

They kept going. Tyler scanned the landscape. Where was the Bed and Breakfast? No telephone poles. No fence. Sacaton grassland mounded away from the river in gentle sweeps. Then the wide marshy river itself.

Sophie couldn't stand it: "What's happening?" she cried. No one responded. She muttered so only Tyler could hear, "I don't believe in centaurs. I don't believe in Arizona giraffes."

Graves pulled back on the T and they slowed. "Sophie," he said, "why you acting like this? Why you talking so funny? Where'd you get those clothes? Are you in some kind of trouble with your folks? Is that what this is about?"

Sophie fell away from the 2 wheeled device, stumbling backward, landing on her butt. Graves stopped the device. Tyler jumped off, hurried to Sophie. He said, "It's okay, Sophie. Take it easy. Come on." He extended a hand to her and she took it. He helped pull her to her feet, sliding his head in close to hers, near her ear, where he quietly said, "Easy! Don't say much until we know more."

Graves said, "Your parents know where you are?"

Sophie and Tyler got back on the device, settled their feet, leaned in. Graves felt Tyler's t-shirt sleeve between his fingers. "Plastique cotton?" he went.

Tyler said, "I don't know what you mean? But you know us?"

Sophie said, "Our parents are here?"

Graves chuckled. "You lumpies! Pranksters all the way! Wish Jakes were here to hear this. He'd know how to handle you! What the right come back would be."

Tyler stuttered out, "We're confused. Aurochs, the giraffe. What happened to the river?"

Sophie added, "What happened to the habaneros?"

"Now, Tyler, you know well as me, that me and Jakes just brought down those giraffes for your folks. You help me tend 'em most every day. Maybe every other day. MeSop and BoRop—you named 'em!"

Sophie said, "I have no idea who you are. I don't think we've ever met. I think you have me mistaken for someone else."

"Sophie I know don't wear her hair like that, that's for sure. How the hell your ma do that? You always have such short hair."

"If our parents are here," said Sophie, "we should go to them."

"We'll make camp, check with Jakes, then I can see you back to your folks. Sophie, I know your folks too. I met you and your folks when you all first came in from St. Louis. Your folks got hired by the collective to do some plastique work. Remember?"

Sophie said, "My parents are insurance executives. We do live in St. Louis. What is 'plastique'? You mean like explosives?"

"There you go again," said Graves. Then: "Here we go, there and back again."

Here was a spit over the river where logs and brush had piled. Water surged below the tangle, but it presented a flat enough surface...even for a 2 wheeled device.

"How deep is the river?" asked Tyler.

"How deep you want it? Depends on where you're looking."

Sophie said, "Do our parents wear different clothes?"

Tyler said in a whisper, "You're smart!"

Graves said, "Funny thing happened on the way to the world, I met a man without a name, I met a name without a man, I met a man without a frame, I met a man without a game—" He roared with laughter and pushed the T forward. They jerked, got their grip, clambered over the makeshift bridge.

CHAPTER 3

Aurore finished shouting, "Target!" and launched herself to the center of the clearing where different kids stood. They looked like the same kids but—Aurore was filled with oceans. Something big had happened, that none of her words or freaks prepared her for. Bye bye, mood sprites! Hello, outside! Because these kids were dressed totally different in lumpy, leather regalia with fringe, plus plain cotton shirts and pants. Their hair was different. *They* were different. They also were gurgling and spitting fiercely, while jumping up and down, which had to mean they had a mouthful of habanero. But besides the clothes— when had they changed clothes? In the glow? The white glare? The girl's hair was different. The boy's was longer.

The intense white had gone out. The glow was gone. Not a flicker now. New clothes now. Where were their other clothes? Why did they break the rule about spitting? The habaneros! The orange pile of them was gone! How could the kids have changed in that momentary flicker? Magicians' prestige was hard, requiring identical twins. But the girl's hair was cut short now. Gone were the corn rows. When did she do that?

Strange had happened. The fabric of her life had a gash: emergence posited transcendence. A process was at work.

Where would it take her/ Metamorphosis. Caddis fly. Axolotl. Neoteny. New trajectories. New physics. She was outside the big bang. Entropy be damned. The chiles were still in their mouths, ergo that was impossible, because they were different mouths? Right? Different kids? That didn't make sense. Explain didn't work here. Whatever had happened, the chiles stayed here! Which means the kids from here went there without a mouthful of chile, and the kids from there came here to a mouthful of chile? Here—where? There was another 'here'?

The new kids caught their breath. They wiped their mouths with the backs of their hands, then rubbed their hands across leather leggings. They kept looking around. Their heads were camera jacks, scanning all frequencies. What did they see? What did they know? wondered Aurore. She thought the leathery fringe looked like lichen. Parasites?

The girl's eyes settled on Aurore and she smiled. "Ça va?"

The boy faced Aurore. "'Scuse us'n for making such expectoration!" He nodded his head—was it a little bow? Now, he looked at the other girl. "Sophie," he said, "I take it same dang thing happened to you happened to moi? One minute we're minding aurochs, then I've got a mouthful of fire. Still burns." He shuddered, then started spitting again. He managed, "Where are we now?"

Aurore went, "'Now'? I hadn't thought of that. A different 'now'? A different time?"

"Maintenant," said the girl. "What do you mean? Who are you?"

Aurore said, "I saw the whole thing. I was standing back there in the mesquite."

Sophie said, "'Mesquite'? Mosquit-o...oui? You speak English with an American accent. I don't think you find acacia here, around—"

Suddenly the boy shouted, "The trees! Look at the

trees!"

Sophie scooted around in a circle, with her mouth open, wide eyes. Like she was seeing this place for the first time. Which, Aurore thought, might be true. Sophie said, "Les arbres sont tres joli, mais how could this be—"

The boy cried, "Incroyable!"

Aurore said to the girl, "What happened to your hair?"

Sophie laughed. "Chapeau?"

Aurore went, "Gateau."

Sophie smiled, went, "Bateau." So that was that!

The boy extended his hand to Aurore. "I'm Tyler Gack. What is this place?"

Aurore took his hand, held it for a second, let go. She said, "This is the San Pedro River. Birdwatching? Bed and breakfast? You two don't happen to have identical twins, do you?"

Sophie shook her head, her eyes still moving over the terrain. She said, "Sophie. My name is Sophie Rose."

Tyler, too, shook his head. "Don't savvy this at all." He moved closer to Sophie. "What happened, Sophie? How could this be?"

Sophie said, "Bed and—'"

Tyler said, "Le petit dejeuner." Then, fast, he pushed in close to Aurore. "You saw it happen? You saw what happen?"

"I'm Aurore," said Aurore. Her cheeks were pink. Her heart beat fast. Of all the things in all the world that could happen, for this to happen to her, because assuredly the rule book rubric of experience had been tossed aside. She was no longer standing on the shoulders of giants. She said, "You were kneeling around a pile of habaneros. I don't know where they went. They were right here!" Aurore put her foot on the spot.

"Your sandals are blue?" said Tyler.

Sophie said, "What...what are these ha-ba-neros? Iberian?"

"Chile peppers. You were kneeling by the habaneros, and you each took a bite of one, but you couldn't spit it out. That was the rule. Then it got all Twilight Zone on you…an amorphous ball of glare around you. Like a glow? You were there. You were gone. Real fast. Then you were back. And spitting out chile pepper. Now you're dressed in animal skins, and you got a haircut."

Tyler stacked a few rocks by Aurore's foot. He touched her flip flop with an extended finger. "Huh. Not leather at all. Plastique? My moccasins are leather. Voila."

Aurore didn't answer.

Tyler said, "So we'll know where this pile of chile peppers were." Then: "Morpheus, huh?"

Sophie exclaimed, "We dreaming? C'est reve!"

"Everything is so different," said Tyler.

Sophie reached over and pinched Tyler's arm.

"Ow!" he yelped. "Que-ce-sais?"

Sophie whispered, "It looks like the Castor but it's not." Her eyes stayed on the big cottonwoods, their tall, fluffy crowns of radiant green. Her hands came up, palms forward. "Our world has switched. Switched? Is that right? How you say it? Shift. Changed? Then change back. Yes? Change back? We go back?

"Reve, dream, reverie," said Tyler. "No, we're not dreaming," said Tyler.

"What happened?" said Sophie.

Aurore said, "Something happened. I saw it. I can't explain it. As soon as you put the habaneros in your mouths—"

"We don't know nothing about them habaneros," insisted Tyler.

Aurore went on: "Well, something happened. That has never happened. Maybe you 'switched'? Maybe some other kids identical to you bit into the habaneros? So where are they? But what do I know? I mean, you look identical. Do you have twins?"

"What is this 'something'?" asked Sophie.

Tyler said, "Twins? No twins."

Aurore said, "We should go back. You can talk to your parents."

"Our parents are here?" said Tyler. "What about the aurochs?"

Sophie now looked said and scared, like she might cry. Her voice trembled: "We've gone mad." She nodded at Tyler with a sad expression. "Like the stories of the Athabascans? Those seekers who eat of the winter night cactus—then the monsters come."

"No monsters so far," said Tyler.

Aurore said, "What's a 'auroch'? Or ox? Like a mastodon or griffon? Like a basilisk? Right?"

"Basilisk, here?" went Tyler.

Sophie turned, moved away from them. Her arms came up. She swayed, her back arched. She moved slowly. Was she dancing? Was she meditating? She said, "The aurochs are not here. Mais les arbres! The trees! Poplar?"

Aurore stomped her feet. "They're cottonwood." She hesitated, then blurted: "Are you guys the same kids who were at the bed and breakfast dining room a little while ago? Tell the truth! Come on, you're not pulling some prank, are you? Like a hoax?" She raised her head, smooched her glasses up with her wiggly nose. She met their eyes. She could tell—

Sophie slowly said, "I don't understand and you talk so...vite! So fast! What is this 'come on'? Your spectacles—they are red."

Aurore said, "Come on. Let's head back. The trail's over here."

They filed onto the trail through the thick brush. Sophie promptly got too close to a poker and squealed.

Aurore said, "Watch for thorns. You have to be careful."

Sophie snorted, "Oh, that helps." She rubbed at her

arm, as they continued down the trail.

They reached the main trail that opened into the fields of white gold grass. They hesitated. Sophie and Tyler looked scared as they glanced around. Aurore didn't know what to say. She realized those weren't scared looks, they were terrified looks. Her head was quiet though, as though she knew what to do in the face of entropy. She was trying on one second at a time. Tyler got down on a knee to get closer to the grass.

"Que?" went Sophie.

Tyler shook his head and stood up. "I don't this grass. I know all the grama." He shrugged with a despairing look.

They walked on in single file. Sophie and Tyler sighted the B & B beyond the field. They seemed stunned, like they'd never seen anything like it. But they didn't freak like regular kids might have. They didn't babble about it or jump up and down, pointing wildly. The vaguely ranch style, brick and wood frame structures seemed fairly innocuous to Aurore.

Tyler said quietly, "What is that place?"

"That's the B and B."

Tyler said, "The grass is alien. Strange buildings. Tres tres."

"Nous sommes les etrangers!" said Sophie.

Aurore said, "You guys haven't tried to Tweet or text at all." They looked confused. "Oh, you don't have...devices? Now I know you're not from around here. Unless your parents forbid you, too."

Sophie said, "Aurore," (she said it perfectly) "your spectacles are daring."

Aurore rolled her eyes, so she happened to catch sight of the Kraken approaching from behind them on the river. Here comes Medea! Camera around her neck, with a small backpack pressed between her shoulders.

"There you are!" she called. "I got tired waiting for you, but I see you've made friends."

"Medea," called Aurore, "tache!" Would her mother remember the signal? No, her face had the cute quizzical look of a kitty, as she sauntered to them. She would barge in. They would all get a gander as she took over. Everything would change yet again. More people involved, more impossible to resolve. Basic lesson of entropy!

Sophie and Tyler watched her approach with fascination.

Tyler said, "Mucho gusto," and extended his hand but Medea didn't take it. "Bonjour," went Sophie.

Medea looked from Sophie to Tyler, then back again. She smiled, her eyes sparkly. Sophie and Tyler couldn't take their eyes off of her. Her eyes came to Aurore. She said, "Regalia!"

Aurore said, "Tache! Momma! These kids are not the same ones we saw at breakfast. I saw it happen."

Medea was still. Slowly, she moved her eyes off Aurore. She went back to studying Sophie and Tyler. She wanted to say something. Aurore bit her tongue and waited for the punch line to be delivered.

Tyler said, "That machine around your neck. What does it do?"

Medea guffed, her hands going to the camera, caressing it. "It's a Hasselblad."

Sophie said, "Deutsch? Ici? Aqui?"

Aurore said, "Here."

"You guys!" guffawed Medea, going into a little wiggle, her hand coming up to offer a wagging finger. "So it's freak out the lame mom routine, is it? I'm going back to the B and B for supplies. You guys coming?"

The kids fidgeted.

Medea blurted, "Well, Ms Borealis, aren't you going to introduce me to your friends?"

Tyler stuck out his hand more firmly this time. "Tyler Gack, ma'am. You're a tech?"

Medea took his hand, shook it. "I saw you at breakfast with your family."

"Frühstück," said Sophie.

Medea put out her hand to Sophie. "I'm Medea, Aurore's mom."

"Medea?" nodded Sophie. "I am Sophie. My parents, too, are techs, in plastique. We're from St. Louis. Came here for the aurochs breeding." She held onto Medea's hand, and Medea let her, smiling sweetly.

Medea said, "What did you do to your hair? Where'd you two get these outfits? You guys are re-enacting San Pedro colonial history? Like mountain men, and mountain girls? Back in the day? Beaver trapping?" She broke into a laugh. "Ha! 'Auroch'—that's one of Aurore's critters, isn't it? She put you up to this!"

Tyler mumbled, "Castor. Castor. En Anglais."

Medea said, "You guys are really into character! So, my crispy Academy Award winners, are we going back to the B and B?"

Aurore said, "Medea! They're not the same kids. They look like them, the kids that had breakfast with us. But they're not the same. Look at their hair? How could Tyler grow his hair this fast? It's not a wig! How could they have done that? I saw it happen. Momma, believe me! They had those habaneros. The ones we saw at breakfast, that you named for me? They had them in a little pile. Then, they each selected one from the pile and put it in their mouths, then they bit down. The habanero pile started to glow. I swear, Mamma! I am not making this up. A tiny ball of glare, glow all around that. They flickered. Gone! Flickered back in these clothes, with this hair."

Medea stared at Aurore.

Aurore went, "Take a picture, it'll last longer."

Medea raised the camera, made some adjustments without looking, doing it by feel. The front of the camera accordioned out. Medea looked down its view finder. She snapped. Snapped again. She turned to Sophie. Snap! Then to Tyler. Snap!

Tyler asked, "This snapping of the mech? What is it doing?"

Medea said, "We'll call them *Twilight Zone* at the B and B."

Tyler said, "This *Twilight Zone*, did it cause the trees?"

Sophie said, "Madame, you know what happened? You know how to get us back?"

Medea rolled her beautiful eyes. "It's a luminous day! Glorious! I'm gonna go to the room, get some more film, and head back to the river. Wanna come, Borealis? Or, are you going to stay with your friends?"

"I was taking them to their parents," said Aurore.

"Our parents, here?" said Sophie.

"You were with them this morning," said Medea.

Tyler said, "Yes, we were."

"Momma," moaned Aurore, "I think I know what's happened."

"Tache," went Medea. "Tell me as we walk."

They headed down the trail single file, behind Medea. Aurore held back her explanation, as it pivoted and flexed about her brains. Sophie and Tyler were all eyes, gesturing, ooo'ing and ah'ing.

Sophie's parents were back from their run. They were looking for her at the patio in the back. They found her and her mother screamed!

"What have you done!" she cried, her hands covering her mouth, as the four approached.

Sophie said softly, "Momma?"

Tyler said, "Plastique delight makers! Look at their clothing!"

Sophie's mother scolded, "Hundred dollars for those corn rows. What did you do? Did you let these kids cut them off? You're shaved!"

Sophie's dad had a big grin. He said, "I think she looks

adorable. Where'd you get the duds?"

Sophie pulled at Aurore, stopping her. Medea saw what was happening and stopped too, gliding over to the two girls.

Sophie whispered, "That's not my mother!"

Tyler came over to the huddle, breathed or gasped, said, "Where are my parents?"

Aurore whispered, "I saw them drive off in the SUV."

"What is S-U-V?"

Medea took Sophie's hand. "Come," she said. "Fun is fun but let's not push it."

Sophie pulled out of Medea's grasp.

Aurore went, "Tache!"

Sophie's mother said, "Well, come on over here. Let me see."

Sophie burst, "Comment t'allez-vous?"

Sophie's dad laughed. "Well, at least she knows her French."

Sophie's mom looked worried. Her brow was knit, her eyes boring in. She rubbed her hands together, then held them to her bright blue running pants. She said, "Something's wrong. Sophie!" She hurried across the distance between them, threw her arms around Sophie. Sophie hugged back.

Her mother sobbed, "What is it, baby? What's going on?"

Sophie's father said, "You're scaring me, honey! So she cut her hair and got some wild clothes! I mean—"

Sophie's mother pulled away from Sophie but held her shoulders in her hands. "You don't even smell the same. Who are you? Where's my Sophie?"

"You look like ma mere. You are. Mais you're not. You don't sound...sound?... the same. Momma, I'm scared!"

Sophie's mother said, "I know you are, baby. So am I." She hugged her, then: "Alan! Something's going on."

Tyler said, "Where are my parents?"

Alan strode forward. Sophie turned from her mother and gave him a hug. "What's up, baby?" he said. "This isn't because we took away your cell phone, is it?" Sophie looked confused. He said, "We can still go up to Flag to check on NAU just like you wanted."

Sophie pulled back, fingering his sweatshirt. "What is this material? Like glass?"

Sophie's mother screamed.

"Winona! Winona!" cried Alan going to her, holding up her melting form.

Medea said, "Enough! Aurore, what's going on? You guys are scaring these poor people."

Aurore said, "Mother, I been trying to tell you—"

Alan nodded for her to go on. Winona, still in her husband's arms, gasped, "Who are you? Where's my Sophie? How can this be?"

Aurore said, "Things are not things, only relations. These kids are not the same kids we know."

Alan looked stunned. "You people aren't in some cult, are you? You haven't been trying to convert our child?"

Medea said, "Of course not."

Tyler said, "Aurore, you sound like a nature philosopher. You are a student of John Chapman? Swedenborg?"

Aurore spluttered on, as though she were lashing Medea, "Sophie had those habaneros at breakfast. You saw them. You told me their name. Sophie had them piled on a plate in front of her. Then, she and Tyler went down by the river and dared each other to eat one. They had the whole pile of habaneros between them. At their feet, on the ground. They each took one. They couldn't spit them out. They bit down. It got all blurry around them. I swear! They flickered. They were there. They were gone. They were back. But with new clothes. New hair. But the pile of habaneros was gone. But the habaneros they had bitten into stayed here, at least in these kids' mouths. When these 2 flickered in, they were in their mouths. Right?"

Medea said, "Maybe we should all go back to our rooms. Sophie, go with your parents. You need to talk. Tyler, you come with us until your family gets back."

Alan nodded. "You're right. We need to slow it way down and have a family confab."

Winona left his arms and returned to Sophie. She clung to Sophie and Sophie clung back. Their departure seemed strained, as though they were trudging off to some painful duty. Tyler stepped on to the patio. He stomped his buckskin moccasins onto the surface, then shuffled his moccasin back and forth over it, feeling the material with his feet. "Lime?" he ventured softly.

Medea said, "Tyler!"

Aurore went, "Mom, you don't believe me? This is not a joke! Something big has happened right here, right now. I think we need to call in the authorities. The state physicist."

Medea glared at her, then burst out with a giggle. Aurore would not meet her mother's eyes but followed the retreating shadows of the entangled family members. Medea said, "I don't think there is a state physicist."

Tyler blurted, "I am sorry, Medea. I meant no disrespect. I was wondering about the fabrication."

"I suppose you're a big Charles Fort fan, too?"

"No, ma'am. Don't know the man. Nor the name. My people are merchants, furriers. Oh, we read, we keep up with international reports. But pelts have their own story out here."

Medea made Aurore face her. She said, "You win. I admit it. I concede. I give. Is that what you want to hear?"

Aurore shook her head fiercely.

Medea said, "I'm not getting this at all. You have me stymied. Heal me! Cleanse me! Tell what the heck is going on!"

"Thwarted. Thwarted bellicose!" went Aurore.

Tyler jumped in with, "You speak poetry. I write poetry. On the side when I'm not chasing aurochs." He smiled shyly. "Or working at the tannery. I believe my life has poems in it. That I may tell."

"Please do," said Medea. "Let's go sit over there." She motioned to some lawn chairs.

Aurore sat with a flourish and a bump and a collapse. Medea flowed into hers. Tyler stood next to his lawn chair, then reached out an arm to touch the plastic weave. "Glass?" he said.

Medea said, "Tyler, sit."

Tyler sat. He fidgeted as though he were uncomfortable. He began: "I think I love the days when the riverboats come the best. They usually arrive at dusk, tie up. Four men usually, sometimes 4 women, but 4 people to tend the boat. More of a barge, really. No keel. They run shallow, Castor so shallow. Bundles under tarps tied on top. My mom makes a feast. We talk, tell stories. Gossip is exchanged. Sightings. Premonitions. Then, after the feast, we have poetry and music. War path cimarrons."

Medea said, "Tell me a poem."

"'Sleeping lightly
a deer is watching me dream,
the deer is tiptoe, living in the wood.'"

Medea went, "Mmmm, like a haiku." She nodded, smiled. Then: "That's nice. Very Asian."

Aurore said, "Steam?"

Tyler shook his head. "You make me dizzy. 'Hi-coo?' 'Steam'? What?"

"It was nice," said Medea. "Very 'be-here-now'."

Aurore humphed. "Is the barge, your riverboats, powered by steam engines?" asked Aurore.

Tyler looked confused. Shocked or appalled. "'Steam engines'? I don't know what you mean. What are you talking about?"

Medea said, "Go on. You were telling your story."

Tyler breathed out, gulped in. "My parents were from up north. They came here to establish their own business. 'Susan Vincent Fine Furs'. That's the name of the outfit, on account of my mom's name is Susan and my dad's is Vincent. I have an older sister, Lise, who is studying to be a medic. And a little brother, Campbell, who is 6. I think."

Aurore tried again: "What powers the boat?"

Tyler shrugged. "Inertial drive. What did you think?"

Aurore said, "Do you have radio?"

"Broadcasting? Of course," said Tyler. "And receptors."

Medea said, "Tyler, what year is it?"

"The date?" asked Tyler.

Medea nodded, breathless, her hands on her camera. She leaned forward in her seat, her pack keeping her at the edge of her seat. She snapped a photo of Tyler.

Tyler said, "Primavera 36, 612."

"Six twelve, what?" went Aurore.

"What 'what'? What are you asking?"

Medea said, "Six hundred and twelve years from the birth of Jesus?"

Tyler smiled. "Jesus lived more than 2000 years ago. What do you mean?"

Aurore said, "Six hundred and twelve, counted from when?"

"Oh," said Tyler, nodding. "Since the Singularity."

Medea and Aurore sat quietly. Occasionally, their eyes left staring at Tyler to nervously glance at each other.

"Wait, wait, wait," went Tyler. "What date is it for you?"

"What's the 'Singularity'?" asked Aurore, quivering with joy.

Tyler said, "Aurore, every pupil your age knows that. From the time children start kindergarten on, teachers are declaiming on the Singularity."

Aurore and Medea waited for Tyler to explain. When he didn't, they kept staring, until Tyler realized they were waiting, clinging to his every word. Tyler went on, "Six hundred and twelve years ago the peoples of the world came together in Havana, Cuba. The Singularity. Envoys from Asia, Europe, Africa, America agreed on the contact principle that has guided us ever since."

"And? And?" went Medea.

Tyler looked perplexed. He felt winded. Who were these people? At the same time, he was thinking of Sophie, and how they would get back, and things would settle down again. They had to get back! These people showed no recognition of the famous story. They wanted more, the story every child learned: "An Apache medicine man named Juh summed it up. This was soon after contact, when nations first started sojourning over the oceans." Still no sign of recognition. "There had been hostilities. Tough times. Famine. Plague. Brutal events. Juh said, 'Share everything'." Tyler shrugged.

"Who?" said Medea.

Tyler said, "Juh."

Aurore said, "Mother, I think that's j-u-h, a famous Indian war chief. I think."

The young woman who had served breakfast gruel that morning stepped from the sliding glass door near them. Tyler jumped when the glass door slid to the side to let her pass. She smiled and made copious greetings. She was dressed in red halter top and cut offs, bare legs, bare feet. Tyler averted his eyes.

"So what's going on?" said the young woman. "I'm getting vibes all through the place that the energy has shifted. Is something wrong? Is something right? Are there any problems?" She laughed.

Medea sighed, blessing the young woman with a bright smile. Finally, she murmured, "We're fine. Just talking."

The young woman said, "My name is Sheri. I probably told you that. Let me know if I can get you anything. I probably told you that." Her laugh whistled like a sniffle.

Medea said, "Tyler's folks—are they back? They took off this morning?"

The young woman, Sheri, did a little dance in place—ta-da! She said, "To tell you the truth I'm not sure. But it's a beautiful day, and when I get caught up on my chores I'm going down to the San Pedro."

"Castor! " went Tyler.

"Hmmm?" went Sheri. "Where'd you get those clothes? They look like the real thing."

"What's wrong with my clothes?"

Sheri sniffled, sauntered away from the three in lawn chairs. She walked around the patio, turned at the corner of the building and was out of sight.

Medea said, "What's 'Castor'?"

"The name of the river," said Tyler.

Aurore had it—she gave a whoosh with her mouth. "Beaver," she said. "'Castor' is beaver. Latin."

"Beaver," said Tyler. "The river is full of beaver. But Castor is the name from the old language. Latin, yes. The old name."

"I don't understand this, the Singularity. Can you elaborate?" said Medea.

Sheri came bounding back into view, her arm going up to point back behind her. "They're here! The blue SUV, right? It's coming up the road right now."

"What's 'S-U-V'?"

"Let's go!" said Medea.

Aurore and Medea flung themselves forward, pushed up with their arms, out of their lawn chairs, to their feet. Medea twisted around to get her backpack situated. She adjusted the camera. Tyler wasn't sure how to get to his feet. He leaned forward, kind of pulled up with his upper torso. Nothing. Aurore realized he didn't want to touch the lawn chair to push up. He was trying to get up without using his hands and arms. Medea lay a hand on his shoulder and he jumped to his feet.

Aurore took off, going first. Then a reluctant Tyler followed her. Aurore wondered if he were shaking. Aurore was shaking. She wondered if the world had been turned inside out. Analogy didn't work. Only fort: 'Everything that is, can't be.' 'And everything that isn't, will be.' But others were experiencing this, too. There was proof. Egress. Avenues of experience opened up like lifelines. Dare she think it? Dare she utter the words that so plagued the meme disease of Net glut? *Did her world have an alternate 'now'? Was there another 'now'?* She was the first person to know. She was shaking. Medea was behind her and didn't know, didn't realize yet.

The big blue SUV came off the dirt road from the county highway with a rooster tail of dust following it. The SUV pulled in to the parking area of the B and B. The backdoor facing the three burst open, the girl springing out. The other side's rear door opened. A foot, a leg, the small body adjusted as it left the vehicle: the little boy got out. The girl stood away from the SUV staring at the trio, her eyes on Tyler. Her face was hard to read. Finally, she guffawed, slapped her hands to her thighs, yelled, "You are in so much trouble! Mom! Dad! Tyler thinks he's Davy Crockett!"

Tyler's mouth moved as though he were trying to speak. He looked like he would cry. Aurore went to him, bent in close. She heard him whisper, "Lise," but didn't let on.

She whispered, "You know what you know. Don't lose that."

Aurore watched Medea come from behind Tyler and put her arm around his shoulders.

Tyler said, "I feel pekid." The blood drained from his face.

"Mom, Tyler's gonna puke!" roared Lise.

The small boy had come around the SUV to stand by his sister. His hand was in his mouth. Then he pulled it out to wave and point at Tyler. He screeched, "You look like a girl with long hair. You are busted!"

Tyler collapsed.

* * *

They met again at the dining room. They'd decided to share a special meal catered by the B and B, then they'd talk. Aurore and Medea got to the dining room's entrance the same time as the Gacks. Tyler gave a feeble wave. He was more than pale, almost yellow—

Jaundice? thought Aurore but didn't say a word, though she loved J's. He still wore leather leggings and moccasins, but now he was wearing a blue t-shirt. Thankfully, it bore no message. Medea was regal, motioning Aurore to let them go first. Lise hung back. Medea smiled to her but read the vibe so moved on, leaving her daughter with the girl.

Lise said to Aurore, "You're a kooky nerd. I like that." She extended her hand. When Aurore didn't respond, she grabbed Aurore's hand and shook it wildly.

Lise was pretty—but more than that—shapely. The type of girl who never bothered to acknowledge Aurore's existence. Aurore blushed. That was so unfair. Presupposition: lookism exemplified.

Aurore stammered, "We're in this together."

Lise crouched in close to Aurore, went, "All the way!" Then she flexed in a fast turning glide like a dancer, and headed for her family settling at their table.

Aurore thought, 'Poltergeist girls'. We are the Poltergeist Girls from here on. Sophie and her parents were already seated. She nodded to Sophie, then went over to take a place by her mother. She pulled out the chair. Sophie, too, had changed clothes. She seemed to be wearing a dress. Aurore blundered into her chair and wrinkled her nose for her glasses to adjust.

"What was that?" said Medea.

"What 'that'?"

"You know what I mean. That girl. Tyler's sister."

"She's kool," said Aurore. "You'd like her."

Sheri and the owners of the Rio Vista Bed and Breakfast, Daphne and Trip Whiting, served. The visitors ate baked chicken with raspberries and piñon nuts. They had little red potatoes and fresh asparagus. No habaneros. The meal was good, everything fresh, savory, and a welcome distraction from the issues at hand. Or, at least, that's what Aurore diagnosed. She didn't eat much. The raspberries were too sweet and looked like blood clots, the piñon nuts like rodent scat. How could she eat at a time like this? How could any of them? When one of the most important events of all time was taking place around them. Unless it was a joke? Some hoax? No! They had proof!

That word: hoe ax. Re-acts. Fake facts. Sub-tracts. The price of pajamas in Jersey City caused trouble for a mother in law in Greenland. People were always disappearing in plain view, never to be seen again. All over the world, inappropriate 'stuff' fell from the sky: blood, frogs, fish, yellow mists. Anomaly. Humans obsessed on anomalies, and freaks, because they made them feel better about themselves, imagined Aurore. When a person saw a child covered with fur or with extra flippers, they immediately had a gut slapping gasp of 'and I thought I was funny looking'. Hoaxes were different, with a different set of presuppositions. Great Moon Hoax. Cardiff Giant. Hans Pfall. Zimmerman Note. The Petrified Man. Hoaxes were different because humans insisted on believing any old thing. Thus: the hoaxster! The one who knows how to sculpt belief like butter. But who be the hoaxster here?

Princess Caraboo was like a dream come to life. A real live fairy tale. Reality could be difficult, painful...intrusive.

Further, it was exclusive. Yet, stories by their very nature were inclusive. So called civilization, Charles Fort was convinced, simply meant fancier and fancier delusions. People were worried about control, having it, losing it. Too prickly. Too predictable. Apply Occam. Ogham. Sorghum. What would Fort do? He reasoned that the only way to have power in any situation, or control, was to be more nearly real than it.

As everyone finished meals and had drinks replenished, Sheri and the Whitings busied themselves cleaning up. Sheri said to no one in particular but loud enough so everyone could hear: "I can start clearing people's places, if they want?"

Aurore rejoindered in her head: What 'people'?

Alan Rose stood up from his chair. "Thanks," he said, smiling and nodding to Sheri and the Whitings. "A scrumptious feast! I'm glad we had the chance to break bread together. Thank you, Medea, for the idea. We've had time to reflect on this situation perpetrated by our charming, overly bright, Indigo kids. And either Aurore's delightful story of habanero time warp is true; or, I guess we're left with the obvious. Someone shaved our daughter's hair. A very expensive hair cut. She said she did it herself. She said she's been doing it for years." He stopped, looked around the room. Aurore sensed that he was used to talking in public, holding grand meetings, when everyone waited with bated breath for his pronouncements. He said, "So?" Again, the dramatic pause. "We're leaving immediately. I'll settle our account with the Whitings." He nodded to them. "We're packing and leaving tonight. Right now."

Sophie sobbed in her seat. Her head bowed to her half filled plate not yet cleared. Her mom glared at her sternly. Sophie looked up slowly but would not meet her eyes. Sophie's face was drawn...so sad, thought Aurore. What could have made her so subdued? Obsequious? The truckling fool, mused Aurore, she had expected more of her.

Sophie said quietly, "'There are more things in heaven and earth than are dreamt of in your philosophy.'"

Aurore gaped. Hamlet!

Sophie's father tsked loudly and plonked down on his seat. He said, "Enough!"

Sophie whispered but they all heard, "I can't leave—"

Vincent Gack spoke without getting up. "Tyler doesn't want to leave either, Sophie. But he's not feeling well. How are you feeling?"

Sophie shook her head. Her father said, "Our doctor back home will straighten this out."

Slowly, Vincent Gack glanced around to the other adults. He cleared his throat slightly, swallowed, went, "Our daughter has suggested another possibility. Drugs."

Through a crying visage, Sophie managed, "What do you mean?"

Vincent Gack looked to Medea. He glanced away abruptly. His voice took on a tone, a very businesslike tone. "You're an artist. Perhaps your daughter made off with some substance...and she shared it with—"

Medea laughed cruelly. "That's absurd! I don't believe you said that. How can you think like that about your own kids? Don't you trust them? I've known them a little while, and I know they've never even thought about drugs. I'm going to pretend you didn't say that."

Aurore was staring at Lise who smirked at her prettily then a small nod.

Tyler said, "I've had plastique drugs for when I was little for the croup."

Susan Gack said, "'Croup'? Tyler, come on!" She screwed up her face, rubbed it with her hands, then kept her hands at her throat. "This is about trust? We know our kids. Yes, we do. Medea is right. Medea, you trust your daughter. Yes, I, too, am going to pretend you didn't say that, Vincent."

"Of course," went Medea.

Susan Gack said to the Roses, "You trust Sophie?"

Alan Rose said, "That's not the point. The realm of possibility—my god! Folks, our kids are perpetrating a hoax!"

Lise said, "Habaneros aren't poison or anything. I don't think. Maybe they can make you sick?"

Campbell Gack said, "What's a habanero?"

Tyler wailed, "Old Duckbill! He'll know what to do."

Susan Gack inhaled a second gasp. She was a tall, slim woman with a small face that easily showed concern. "Tyler, please. You okay? Please, try to relax."

"I can't leave," cried Tyler. "Either can Sophie. We have to stay close to where it happened. My intuition is strong on this. It may be our only way back. If it happened once, maybe it will happen again. I know that makes no sense but a certain logic nonetheless. I don't know what happened. I know I sound touched."

Alan Rose piped in with, "That's the first time I've heard a youngster use the expression 'nonetheless' in casual conversation."

Vincent Gack pushed back in his chair and the sound had Tyler pause. Vincent was tall and slim, too, but with a long horsey face given to smiles, now in an official frown. Vincent said, "Tyler?"

"This world you take for granted I do not know. It is not mine. Pas Sophie. It's fabrication like nothing I've seen. Your clothes. Your SUV's. Even your grass and plants are different. It makes sense to stay here, near where it happened, to figure this out. Aurore is right. Something happened. I don't know what it is. But you've all been very kind. For that, I thank you."

Lise crooned, "Dood! You are so wasted!"

Tyler snapped back, "What does that mean? Lise, why are you so febrile?"

Campbell yelled, "Umm! Said a bad word!"

Medea positively beamed when summing up: "It's not a joke. It's not a hoax. It's impossible but it is. I've talked to my daughter. I trust my daughter. We have to trust our kids. Even though it doesn't make sense right now."

Alan was agitated, drumming his fingers, fidgeting in his seat, as he responded, "What does that mean?"

Aurore didn't know it could feel like this. She inserted with her arms up, hands splayed, "It's not a hoax, it's an anomaly. I'd never seen these kids before this morning. How could we have concocted such an elaborate plan so quickly? Think of the details. Tyler told my mother and me a little about his life. It sounded real. But it was a different place. No B and B, right? But the river still, but with different vegetation." Aurore interrupted herself, embarrassed at her gushing. She gulped, finished, "Tyler and Sophie have incredible details about a life that's not here."

Alan Rose looked at his wife. He shook his head. He pounced, "That's not helping, young lady. That's not—"

Winona Rose interrupted, "We have to listen to our kids. Alan, we have to. I know my Sophie. This is Sophie. But it's not. I can't explain it."

Sophie seemed to be sliding downward in her chair. Alan hurried to her side, held her up. "What's wrong, darling?"

Sophie murmured, "Malade. Je suis malade. Je desire un medecin."

Aurore said, "She's sick! Call a doctor!"

Tyler said, "Call Old Duckbill! Whatever happened may happen again. We have to be ready. Peut-etre we should return to the spot on the river." He was almost panting. "We're going to need more than a regular bonesetter."

Aurore said, "The state physicist!"

Medea blurted, "States have no official physicist."

Tyler went, "The constabulary!"

Alan and Winona helped their daughter to her feet. He seemed to be trying to adjust. He said, "Insurance is my business. We're from St. Louis. In my work, we examine circumstances, try to figure what the risks are. And the most important thing right now is the health and safety of our kids. Sophie needs to rest. We'll get her to bed. Is there a doctor we can call in case of an emergency?" He looked to the Whiting's.

Winona Rose gasped.

Trip Whiting said, "Of course." Trip Whiting was in his 60s, a vet, a tinker, a hunter, a conservationist as they used to say, and he still had broad shoulders and a strong disposition. He went on, "Look, I'm an old Army man, Daphne was a school teacher, we been around the world, and this makes no sense. Maybe some kind of group hypnosis?"

Alan Rose snapped, "I don't know. Sure, why not? All ideas on the table tonight! So, okay, no one's leaving tonight now. What about that doctor?"

Daphne Whiting said, "I'll get the doctor's number for you"

The Roses made their way towards the exit, when Winona turned back to face the others. She said, "If these are not our kids, and something has happened like never before. Then where are our kids? Are they safe? Where are they?"

No one responded. The Roses left. Sheri cleared tables. She said, "Let me know if anyone needs anything. Maybe a good night's sleep will help."

Medea said, "I think we should all get some sleep. And we can see how things are in the morning." She sighed, flexed her shoulders. "See in the morning."

Vincent Gack looked worn out, embarrassed, sad, confused. "Sound okay to you, Tyler? You'll be okay?"

Tyler nodded.

"Should we call the sheriff?" asked Susan Gack,

pinched with anxiety.

Medea shrugged. "Missing persons?"

Lise Gack said, "Maybe habaneros have some kind of toxic brain chemistry."

Susan Gack said, "Lise, please!"

In the morning at dawn, before anyone was up, before the sheriff or doctor could be considered, or state physicist, some motion, or presence, in her bed woke Aurore. In the dim light of the curtained bedroom, without glasses, she peered next to her, looking at the girl next to her in her bed. She looked so familiar that Aurore wasn't frightened right away. Then when she realized who it was, she screamed in staccato machine gun bursts. Medea charged over in underwear from her nearby bed. With brilliant bright eyes, she studied the 2 girls in Aurore's bed. Aurore pulled away from the girl in her bed. Two girls in Aurore's bed. Two identical Aurores, one in flannel pj's grabbing for her red glasses, the other in a leather apron and leather halter top.

CHAPTER 4

Sophie and Tyler gripped opposite ends of the T of the 2 'wheeled' device driven by Graves. They had to huddle close to him to stay on. But they were getting better at keeping their balance, swaying and rolling with the movement by bending their knees and keeping their joints loose. The odd contraption moved at about 5 miles per hour, thought Tyler, hastily figuring by the way objects—a big tree or a pile of oddly colored rocks, were approached then receded behind them. No fumes...no exhaust at all produced by the machine he could see. They followed a wide trail along the west side of the river. It was flattened down enough to show it was commonly used. The river was even with the land here, hardly any bank. The river snaked through a marshy, muddy floodplain, seeming to merge with the land. Sophie had been visiting the area for the first time. Tyler had been coming to the river valley, border country with his family since he was small. Its unique vistas and historical ghost towns were what had gotten him interested in western history in the first place. So the dramatic difference between the overgrazed blast zone he was used to and this lush riparia here was blowing him away, which meant confusing him: where were they? How could this be? Horizons dominated by the very same mountains, making cutouts...range silhouettes Tyler'd learned to recognize years ago. To the west, the Huachucas...there they were! To the east, the Mules. The river valley was a wide, wide, flat bottomed bowl with this flashy, lifeblood artery running through its heart. Isn't that what he had assumed it was...once? Like when the Spanish had come? To the left of the trail and their route, to the west, a flat grassland of thick clumped grass sending out seed stems taller than a man. Now the grasslands they passed were punctuated with massive bodies Tyler first imagined were rock formations. But these rock formations moved! And they were purple! At least, 'purplish'. The beasts clumped through the clumps...munching them, cudding them up for supper. Small groups of aurochs grazed the grasslands. The auroch cows were massive with big heads, purple and brown hides, and thick shoulders. The animals barely noticed them going by. But their device was quiet. Tyler could detect no whir or wheeze or buzz from the transport. Tyler pointed out the aurochs to Sophie who looked and nodded abruptly. Tyler saw her eyes shone. She was as excited as he was. He couldn't believe it...he had to. It couldn't be real, obviously. Tyler closed his mouth. Graves noticed them eyeing the aurochs and snickered, mumbling something under his breath. But his smile and bright eyes kept them from thinking anything sinister. No bulls, anyway. Tyler wondered whether Jakes had managed to control that magnificent beast.

More aurochs ahead. Then, beyond them, white giraffes ambled by. Sophie was so surprised she burst out laughing. Tyler couldn't tell whether it was from joy or despair. Did his eyes shine like Sophie's? Tyler figured it was the clean, cool spring air for one thing. Isn't that what writers meant when they described the atmosphere as 'crisp'? He thought it was, but didn't know if he had ever experienced it. Tasted so fresh and alive? The sun, the wind felt better here...wherever that might be. He thought, I could drink the river. And the thought filled him with thirstiness and a vague displeasure that he sounded like a tree hugger. They passed the beasts, kept heading north on the trail. Black birds swarmed above them, making a racket. A V of ducks went over. A small doe stood in the brush watching them go by. Thrashers scolded in their rich music Tyler recognized from his backyard. The giraffes seemed to be following them. They must be coming to see what the humans were up to. To the west, the grassland dipped away, rolling and yawning, like the valley bowl was rumpled here. A few more trees, too. The only one Tyler could think of was hackberry but he wasn't sure if he remembered its distinguishing marks. Small leaves, small nuts?

They came on wooden structures like squat barns, some corrals, elevated water tanks, big barrels. The kids saw a few cabins to the west. They didn't see any people.

Graves said, "Jakes will be along shortly. We'll figure this out. Then we'll get you over to your folks'."

Tyler said too loudly, "Right now, I don't know what would be best. Or what we should do."

Sophie said, "We need to think. I mean, if this is some kind of hallucination. You can take us back to the spot you found us?"

Graves nodded. "Am I a hallucination?" Graves shrugged, nodded, his chin punching out to point ahead. "Yes, I can take you back to that spot."

A lovely group of blooming trees came down to the river ahead. Yellow flowers, buttery and reluctant. Not too flashy at all. Tyler thought they were some kind of legume maybe. Locust maybe? Here, the river had steep banks. The trees stood before a rocky cliff face, a finger of strata that thrust out in to the river. The river narrowed here, bubbling and babbling along fairly fierce. The marshyness was gone. To the far side of the finger, tucked into a nest of trees and boulders, a cabin. A log cabin with a broad stone chimney. Heavy duty corral in front.

Graves said, "Courage. We'll see. I still can't figure your witty witty ways." He pulled back on the T and the device slowed.

"Is this your cabin?" asked Sophie.

Graves humphed as he slowed the 2 wheeled device to a stop by the corral. He said, "After all the times you been here?" He shook his head. "Giraffes'll want in for now." He said, "Tyler, open the corral, will ya?"

Tyler said, as he jumped down, "The wheels of this thing are so weird. Are they made of some kind of gel? The way they slide and moosch—"

Graves went, "'Moosch'? Ha!"

Sophie said, "How many cabins on the river? I thought this land was all protected. How many people live here? Where's the town?" She stepped down.

Tyler worked the sturdy gate beam back, swinging open the corral.

Graves nodded, "You can feed them later." His eyes went to the telephone-pole sized feeding contraption in the corral, with what looked like a chicken wire cage on top. Tyler studied it too but didn't say a word. Graves nudged the T in front of him and took the thing up to the cabin to a niche on the side. Sophie and Tyler walked behind, trying to keep up, but also twisting and turning to take in the cabin and its busy yard full of interesting looking tools.

Sophie watched Graves park the device and she said, "Jakes has one, too. There's room for another one."

Graves said, "I can't tell what we're saying here. If this is a joke, I'm a fool. Hey, I accept that. If this is real, then what could have happened? The Sophie and Tyler I knew were replaced with a Sophie and Tyler I don't know." He stepped from the device, exhaled sharply. He slapped his hands together. Then he extended his arms and his hands touched the arms of Sophie and Tyler. "In the mean time, you are welcome to our humble abode. Come on in. I'll make tea. Jakes said he'd bring dinner."

Sophie and Tyler got in line behind Graves. Graves pulled back a latch on the door then pulled. No lock. They went in. Graves turned to close the door and fix the latch.

One large room, well lit, a rough square, with a network of lines (rope?) over the top. Below this pitched ceiling, about ten feet high, bunches of plants in neat rows tied to the ropes. The entire cabin, a plant drying room? So the smells were breathtaking, literally, making Tyler think of summer lawn mowing chores, while Sophie thought of the plant store her mom liked to visit in St. Louis every spring when she determined that year would be the year she got the garden in gear.

Graves said, "Come in. What you gawking?"

Below the heaven of plants, all tied by roots and stems, so hanging upside down, a large wooden table, wooden chairs and stools along its sides. The chairs looked blocky, with an odd proportion about them. The table was rectangular, thick, and its top surface had scoops in places. To hold bowls? Cups?

"Sit," said Graves. "I'll make tea." He moved around the table, to a floor to ceiling cabinet next to the corner sink with interesting looking faucets. Past the sink, opposite the table, the wall was almost all stove and fireplace. All in stone, the fireplace was big enough to stand in. Two chimneys for this cabin.

Tyler and Sophie lingered by the table, taking it all in. They put out hands to grasp chairs, tugged at them, found them amazingly light. They pulled them out listlessly. But didn't sit. Or had forgotten how. Or were just too worried and freaked by it all. The table bore a couple neat stacks of books and papers, then wooden bowls of fruit—mainly apples. A few ceramic cups and plates and bowls lay next to small metal implements. Many of them Sophie and

Tyler did not recognize—what could they be for?

Sophie said, "Where's the light come from?"

Tyler said, "No candles?"

Graves glanced back at her from the sink, his eyes taking in the bedazzled Tyler as well. The 2 young people looked stuck to Graves, as though something wasn't right for them. Graves said, "Sit! Me hearties! Please! Por favor! S'il vous plait!"

Tyler and Sophie dumped their bodies into the chairs they'd already pulled out. Tyler's arms fell to his sides. Sophie wiggled her chair in closer to the table, put her elbows up on the table.

Now Graves got busy at the fireplace. The kids could smell his success. He got a fire going. The stove was next, making a separate soft shushing sound as it heated up. Graves fussed with the stove, arranged a kettle on the right spot to heat. "Just a minute, now," he said.

Sophie said, "Nice place you got here." Her eyes were glued to Graves, as though staring would reveal something.

Tyler's eyes were taking in the rest of the cabin. He saw the wooden cabinet had shelving with utensils and pots and pans. Lower half of the cabinet with tall drawers. In between the upper and lower portions, an extension came out of the middle, about belly high, making a good surface that could be used as a cutting board perhaps. At the top, among the common utensils, ceramic and glass containers. Some were filled with colored liquids, while others had what looked like seeds or rice. The other half of the cabin had 2 cots arranged around a small table. There was a wooden chest. Square windows in every wall except for the fireplace wall. Just to the left when you came in through the door, a small desk with a chair in front of it. Every available wall had shelving going up nearly to the plants. This shelving held books, tools, boxes, skulls, mineral samples, funny shaped rocks or sticks or debris. Tyler yearned to investigate. But that would be rude. It was a museum of modern life on *this* San Pedro River. In the middle of one shelf, what looked like a broken telescope—

"Thanks, Graves, for helping us out," said Sophie. "But, seriously, where does the light come from? I don't see a single bulb." She still had her eyes foxed on him hard.

"Herbal inertial," said Graves without turning. "But I ain't no natural philosopher so don't ask me to explicate."

Sophie blurted, "What year is this, Graves?"

Quickly, Tyler went, "What country is this?"

Graves moved, checked his water, then brought the kettle over to the table with a green mitt in the shape of a clover. He used his lips to point out ceramic mugs. Sophie and Tyler reached for the mugs, positioned them for Graves. He poured, found his own mug and filled it.

Tyler was upset with his question. He wasn't even sure what it meant. He imagined in his head a picture of the continent. And he was way down at the bottom. Mexico was close. The border was always in the news. But suppose Mexico wasn't there?

Maybe it was a different country here?

Graves still didn't sit. He turned back to the fireplace, placing the kettle back on the stove. He dabbled with the fire. He took up a large pitcher by the sink and hefted it to top off the kettle. He put down the pitcher, murmured, "It'll be strong at first. Gunpowder."

Sophie and Tyler looked at each other. They each imagined the questions the other was thinking. They were running through the possibilities that might explain this mess. And none of them made sense. Tyler almost tried a half dozen approaches but shied away in time. Sophie now focused on her tea mug.

Kids in 'gifted programs' always can spot a fellow Brainiac a mile away. Sophie and Tyler recognized each other. The confidence of all A's made them plucky? But they were tense, too. They were scared. Should they drink the tea?

Now, Graves stood by his chair and looked like his well built form was suddenly making like a wooden soldier—he was at attention. He exhaled, slowly let his upper body droop, arms and hands loose at his sides. He was so loose! He straightened normally, sighed loudly, farted, and sat. "May the tea bring warmth," he said and took his mug and brought it to his lips.

Sophie whispered, "What is it?"

Tyler said, "I don't feel so well. No, I'm okay. Just my stomach or something. Maybe I should wait on the tea. Like Sophie said, thanks for your help."

"But?" went Graves. "You left a big fat 'but' hanging. Go on, finish it."

"We really don't know what's going on. I don't know you. I never met you before in my life. You seem to know us but we don't know you. At the spot you found us? We were taking a bite of habanero hot pepper. Just on a dare. There's a shimmer. I don't know what. And we're somewhere else. The river we were on was in the desert. It was different from this river. I can't explain it. It seems like the same place. I mean the river cutting through this valley, the same mountains. That's hard to miss. Same place, but different."

"Drink your tea," said Graves. "Perfectly safe." Steam wreathed his mouth and lips. He slurped. But the eyes above the mouth and nose were lively. Sophie and Tyler felt comfortable with this buckskin auroch driver, 2-wheeled device driver. Tyler and Sophie sipped their tea. It was quite strong, bitter. But it warmed them quickly, so they took a few more careful sips.

"It's good," said Sophie. "Thanks."

"What's for dessert?" asked Graves looking at Tyler.

"Desert?" went Tyler, his face shining with surprise at the joke.

Sophie said, "Tyler, you're the one who said you knew some of this place's history. It doesn't look like a desert around here now. I mean, no sand dunes or anything."

"Just giraffes," said Tyler.

"MeSop, BoRop, you named them," said Graves.

Sophie said, "But, see, Mr. Graves, there are no giraffes running around on ranches in Arizona. And no white ones for sure."

Graves looked hurt. "Sophie, I think it was your folks— you're from St. Louis, aren't you? Es verdad?"

"Yes, St. Louis."

"They're the one who helped design the giraffes. The albinism was some kind of plastique displacement. Moreover, you've been here visiting a while. Tyler brought you over. That's how we met."

"I don't remember that. Any of it. My parents don't work in plastics. But we are from St. Louis."

Then Graves smiled, said to Tyler, "What history do you know, Tyler? I knew you were a smart pup, but I thought it was in natural philosophy and the maths."

"That must be another me," said Tyler.

"Like we switched?" said Sophie.

Graves plonked his mug on the table. "Jakes should be in on this. Let's hold our horses for that discussion. In the mean, I'd like to hear Tyler's history story. Winter is over. It's the time of last stories. 'Winter all chewed up.'"

What did that mean? Tyler stared into Graves' inquisitive eyes. The man was so open, taking it all in without resistance. Tyler felt unsure of himself. He glanced around, away from the powerful eyes. Everything looked so homemade. Wood was cut and shaped for all sorts of uses. So who made the 2-wheeled device? It was as high tech as anything he'd ever seen. It had carefully machined metal seams and joints. What could he say? What should he say?

Tyler began, "I guess it starts ten thousand years ago

when people from Asia came over on the land bridge. They became the Indian tribes like 1000s of years later. Then the Europeans came and took over. Everything changed. You got the birth of Mexico and Mexicans. America had its revolution. Eventually, the US takes over out here. Another war. Border just down that way. What? Ten miles?

"Arizona used to be known for its 3 C's, 'cotton, cattle, copper'. The first atom bomb blew up in New Mexico. Not that far from here. The whole Southwest, Arizona and New Mexico, kinda used up country. Water tables shrinking. Abandoned mining sites toxic. Soil blown away after the cows ate all the grass. Then there's all the border stuff—"

Graves watched Tyler closely but could detect no hesitation as though Tyler were making anything up. The story came out: obviously he absolutely believed it.

Sophie said, "That's kinda what I was taught, too. But we never got real into western history besides the basics."

Graves' mouth made a straight line as he began to cry. Slowly the corners of his mouth curled down until he grimaced painfully. The tears gave way to a shaking sob, but then he sniffled and shook himself. "All that death to people and the land," he said. "That's a sad, sad story, maybe the saddest ever told me. I don't think I want to know want an 'atom bomb' is. Tyler, Sophie, I know another story...but Jakes is the story teller in this family."

On cue, they heard heavy thumps from outside, then a clatter. In the distance, animals bellowed. Aurochs? Giraffes? Did giraffes bellow? Sophie and Tyler twisted their heads around to glance at the door. A voice called. Jakes!

The latched door moved and in stepped jakes. He was shorter, stockier than Graves. He was also darker skinned with a rounder face. He grunted at them, taking in the tea party. "Am I invited? Room for one more? Una mas?" he asked.

Graves guffawed.

Jakes said, "Salutations, friends!"

"Trouble with the Crots?" went Graves.

Jakes closed the door, shaking his head, and mumbled, "Nah, Crots are good. MeSop and BoRop are up."

Graves nodded. "Tea?"

Jakes came over to the table and stood behind Tyler and Sophie, still twisted back to see him. He reached out to their clothes. He carefully took a little bit of fabric of their shirts between his fingers. He said, "Plastique?"

Tyler shrugged. "Cotton and rayon, I guess."

Sophie said, "Polyester?" and laughed.

"Polyphemus, I know," said Jakes and laughed, too.

Tyler knew he had heard that name before, but Sophie got it first: "The cyclops. The cyclops from the Odyssey."

Jakes eyed Graves. Graves went for the kettle. Jakes threw his arms up over his head. The hands came together slowly, palms meeting, looking like he was praying. Jakes sighed, exhaled, farted. Jakes shivered, then pulled up a chair. He said, "Tyler, I left dinner out in the trough. Would you fetch it?"

Tyler stared at him. Sophie started to say something but Jakes continued, "You guys always make supper when you come for a visit. Feed the giraffes, too."

Graves watched their silent looks of uncertainty. He said, "Reciprocity. How things work."

Sophie whispered, "I don't know what you mean."

Jakes said, "Go on, you two. Go get 'em, clean 'em. You make supper."

Tyler and Sophie left their seats at the table and went outside. Late afternoon, getting towards dusk, but they could see fine. They pulled the door closed behind them. They hesitated. Then Sophie said, "How do we get outta here? We got to get out of here!"

Tyler said, "How do you feel? I'm like dizzy or

something."

Sophie glanced around. "Look at the giraffes." The 2 elegant creatures were at the far corner of the corral, poking about the wire cage at the top of the pole...where their dinner should be. Their movements were so gentle and slow, like they were floating.

"White," went Tyler.

"Albinos? He said 'albinism', but why would you want white giraffes?"

Tyler shrugged. "Can you tell if they have pink eyes? Your parents 'made' them? Maybe they're good to eat?"

"Where are we? What happened? My parents took my phone. This was supposed to be a 'wireless' get away. You know the routine. I can't believe we can't call someone. I think we should go back to the spot where it happened."

"Yeah, you should have seen my sister freak when she had to turn in her phone. I doubt we'd get many bars here."

Sophie said, "Maybe we should go back to the spot, the exact spot we appeared here. Where it happened."

The white giraffes floated around the yard, tall heads all the way up, keeping their eyes on the kids. The kids entered their corral. The giraffes looked at them expectantly. Tyler said, "Oh my gosh—they recognize us!"

The kids couldn't tell if their eyes were pink. Sophie thought they looked blue. She found the 'fodder' in a wooden hutch at a corner of the corral. Close up, Tyler also saw the rungs going up the pole. Well, that's good, he thought. He sighed. He looked back to Sophie and said, "You think we'll go back if we return to the spot where it happened?" He snapped his fingers. "Just like that?"

Sophie snorted, darted her eyes up the pole.

It wasn't hard. Tyler concentrated, watched his footing. Fodder under one arm made it a bit awkward. The giraffes came over. They looked at him. He said hello. Stuffed the fodder into their wire basket. He held on so tight. He glanced around. A quiet distance with no wires or antennae or airplanes to see. From way up here, with the giraffes, he could see Sophie in a different way. He could feel how sour Sophie was. Just by watching her stomp around the corral, he could tell she was getting mad, building up a head of steam.

Tyler got down easily. Down below, he slapped his hands together, relieved to be done with that chore.

Sophie came up close. She spat, "Where's the fucking trough?"

Tyler felt better now. He knew she was upset. He knew they had to be friends to work this out: "What trough? Oh, for dinner."

She bounced into Tyler, coming right up against him. "The one with dinner *in* it." Her eyes bored in. She held his shoulders. She shook him. Then: "How do we get back?"

Tyler was sick of shrugging. He said, "Nothing makes sense. Our parents, what—"

Sophie interrupted, "They must be freaking!"

"But our parents are here! That's what Graves said."

"They can't be! It's gotta be different people. This can't be happening. What are we going to do? Okay, okay. No more freaking out. We have to figure this out." Sophie shook, sighed big, stopped panting. She stepped away from Tyler, took a deep breath. Then she pointed, "That must be the trough," she said and led the way.

The giraffes were happy, their thick tails with long stringy black streamers at the end twitching. Sophie and Tyler peeked into the trough.

Turtles. Three large, live turtles swam in the clear water of the trough.

After supper, Tyler helped Graves clear the table. The leftover vegetable stew with homemade bread had been delicious. Tyler carried his and Sophie's bowls to the sink. Graves was already there, filling one side of the sink with hot water. Soap suds blossomed, climbing to the top.

Tyler said, "You have hot water."

Graves gave him that look he was getting used to.

Jakes, still at the table, said, "I don't mind you let them turtles go, Sophie."

"You said we were finished talking about that," said Sophie. "This Sophie doesn't know how to kill and clean a turtle."

"Sophie," said Tyler fast. "They're just trying to help." He returned to the table, standing at the end near the seated Sophie.

Jakes raised his head, looked up. He said, "There's a knot here between us that we can't see right. You're not the same younglings. I mean you are, obviously, then, obviously, you're not."

Tyler said, "We have to get back."

Sophie said, "Maybe if we go back to the exact spot—"

Jakes said, "Where are the Tyler and Sophie we know? If you go back to wherever you're from, will they return here?"

Graves sang out a quick lyric about a kingfisher in a tree. Tyler tried to catch the words. It was like a poem.

Jakes said, "Only one thing to do."

Graves sputtered from song and offered, "I'll say."

"Old Duckbill," said Jakes. "It's not quite dark. We could go now. Or wait until morning."

Graves said, "Now should be better. Their parents—"

"Should we call their parents?" asked Jakes.

Sophie said, "You have phones?"

Jakes went to a shelf with books and bones. He extracted the long mechanical tube that Tyler had assumed was a broken telescope. Jakes returned to the table and set up the tube.

"What is it?" said Tyler.

Jakes said, "It's a commie. You know, a communicator."

"Where are we!" exclaimed Sophie.

Jakes smiled, then: "The Free State of Chichimeca, my dear." He stared at her, her anguish plain.

Grave said, "Jakes, let's just go. We can call later. Old Duckbill won't mind. When we get back we can call the parents. It's not late."

They hiked in single file along the river. It was so pleasantly cool and the air so refreshing no one minded the shadowy, narrow path. Insects bickered. Night settling birds sang in questioning tones.

Graves commented, "Animals come out at dusk."

"Why not?" Jakes answered.

Graves said, "Crack between worlds—best time of the day."

As they got away from the rocky narrows by the cabin the river opened again, got wider, slower. The banks were even with the ground again, so the going got muddy. They came to a wide stretch of river where the banks were lined with trees. No way to tell how deep the water was here.

"Castor," said Graves, nodding at the wide expanse, almost a lake. "Used to be able to get boats in here. Not so now. Now the river boats get in to about St. David."

Graves and Jakes sat at the bank, got comfortable. Pretty soon, Sophie and Tyler realized they might as well, too. "They sat.

Tyler said, "Who's Old Duckbill?"

Graves and Jakes wouldn't take their eyes off the water's rippling surface. They ignored the question and seemed to assume a deep concentration of faculties. Some kind of meditation came on, or maybe a trance? Sophie brushed her palms across her knees and settled, wondering if it was some kind of religious thing. The water line at their feet began to slap in small bipping waves. Farther out, a broil in the water began. Something was surfacing. A slicked down, brown body broke the surface. Couldn't see the head. Sophie thought, crocodile, but now, even in the dim light, she could tell it was fur, so a mammal. Like an otter? But so big! Tyler racked his memory to identify what they were seeing. It was way too big for a beaver. Obviously, a mammal so—a seal? A freshwater, desert seal?

The line from shoulders, across the spine, to the thick tail, had to be 6 feet. It wasn't a beaver's paddle tail, nor was it like a seal which had no tail. The head still had not shown itself. This broad tail slinked back and forth lazily. They could see the ripples. The animal had to be as tall as a man. Graves and Jakes did not alter their stance. They closed their eyes, hands resting in their laps. The head came out of the water—

A duckbill came out of the water and aimed skyward. Behind the bill, on the sides of a rounded head, small glittery eyes. Sophie and Tyler inhaled sharply, as the eyes took them in. Tyler leaned forward like he must get up, so Sophie touched a finger to his knee and he relaxed, settling again. The duckbill snapped, clapping water in a splash. Jakes giggled and raised his hand, his eyes wide now. Graves opened his eyes, lifted a hand in greeting, too. Old Duckbill kept his small eyes on Sophie and Tyler, but it was hard to tell for sure what he was looking at.

Finally, Old Duckbill said, "Ersatz." The voice was like nothing they'd ever heard. The voice went: "Gullery. Brummagem. Matter's more than measure. The river flows to the sea. For every day, there is a creation. These 2 are lopsided, not created here. Many rivers, many seas. These 2 from another many. They got in."

Tyler piped up: "We switched. I think."

"Entropy in all directions." The voice was bass, difficult, like an echo of a vibration. "Inertia in 1, now 2."

Jakes said with a peculiar lilt to his voice, "Tell us," extending his arms to include his companions.

Graves said, "Same, not the same."

Old Duckbill clapped his duckbill again. "How can this be? A tear? A tear! A rip. Rent! If it keeps tearing?" Old

Duckbill clapped his duckbill again. He said more clearly now, "If it exists, it is perfect. That's what we know. Big world comber. You're going to need a great one. Send for the nature philosopher in Santa Fe."

Jakes said, "Peggy Dreiser."

Old Duckbill blinked.

Graves said, "What's happening? How could this be?"

Jakes went, "Danger?"

Old Duckbill said, "Expect ready. She has the best mind in Chichimeca."

A kingfisher landed in a nearby tree. It was almost dark so the big bird looked gray and white. The bold head with crest and spearhead beak wagged at them. Its perch was a bare branch that jutted out into the sky. The duckbill clapped and water splashed. The kingfisher wheeled above its perch, wings kicking, and the bird laughed a harsh giggle, before returning to its perch.

"Halcyon," said Jakes.

Graves said, "Where are our Sophie and Tyler?"

The kingfisher laughed again, and both Sophie and Tyler swore the bird cried, "Here! Here! Right here! Right here!"

Sophie jumped to her feet. "No way!" she cried. "Talking animals? No way! We're hallucinating! You put something in the stew! Or the tea."

Tyler grabbed at her hand and shhh'ed her.

Graves and Jakes barely moved, watched Old Duckbill with all open eyes. Kingfisher preened.

Old Duckbill floated on his back and said, "Listen to your power. Happen danger. Happen result. Already happened. Tell Peggy to watch the leys. Going to take all of us. Even the Mexicans. And Crots."

Tyler blurted out, "Will we ever be able to go back?"

Old Duckbill blinked, murmured, "You must!" then sank down and disappeared.

Tyler realized that he had not heard Old Duckbill

actually utter words. No, the sounds or words or meaning had come right in to his head. Had Sophie experienced it the same way? He knew Graves and Jakes had.

Jakes got on the telescope looking thing when they got back to the cabin. He talked in one end and the response came out of the other end so the whole cabin could here. No wires Tyler could see. But Jakes didn't call Sophie and Tyler's families. Jakes was trying to track down Peggy Dreiser in Santa Fe. He managed to raise Dreiser's assistant. Dreiser was in Alburquerque, she said. The assistant, Katrice Bell, would relay the message. She understood the gravity of the situation when Jakes told her what Old Duckbill had said, and how it had been him who suggested the call to Dreiser.

Sophie and Tyler sat at the table, heads sunk low. They could hardly keep their eyes open.

Graves said, "We'll make up beds for you."

"What about our families? I'm worried about my brothers and sisters," said Tyler. "Should we call?"

"Wait until morning," said Sophie.

Tyler couldn't imagine why she wanted to wait now.

Jakes said, "You're afraid of what you might discover when we call. I don't blame you. This is complicated."

Sophie said, "Don't we stay for the night? I mean, sometimes? They won't worry?"

Graves grunted. Jakes said, "You 2 sleep."

"I feel like I'm asleep with my eyes open," said Tyler.

Sophie said, "We're just tired."

Graves and Jakes pulled out pads and fixed them near the cots. They piled up blankets and pillows on the pads. Sophie moved over to watch. Then she went back to Tyler at the table.

She bent in close to him. "I have to go to the bathroom," she said quietly.

Tyler nodded. He said aloud, "The outhouse?"

Graves looked up. Jakes went, "'Outhouse'?"

Sophie said, "I have to go to the bathroom."

"Bathroom'?" went Graves.

"Oh, oh," said Jakes. "Function shed is out back, around the back."

Sophie nodded and took off.

Tyler collapsed on a pad, moved to one side, pulling blankets over himself.

Graves said, "You oughta take off your fancy plastique shoes."

Tyler pulled himself up, contorting his frame, and slipped off his running shoes. No big duh—just sneaks. He fell back to his makeshift bed. Graves touched the shoes.

Sophie returned. Plants were dimmed. Jakes and Graves prepared for sleep, dropping their leathers to simple long john like under clothes. They snuggled into their cots. Sophie managed at the pad next to Tyler's. Then, before he fell asleep, he heard her roll over towards him. Her face was near his ear to whisper, "Wait till you get ahold of their bathroom!"

They slept.

At sunrise, Graves and Jakes began to stir. They were almost awake when a fierce knocking came to the cabin's door. Loud hooting and more banging sounded from outside. Sophie and Tyler sat up, gasping, rubbing the sleep from their eyes. They looked like wrecks. They looked sickly. They were pale with bags under their eyes.

Graves got to the door first and flung it open. Two men, one in a robe and the other in leathers, stood outside. The one in leathers squalled, "Katarina! Have you seen my Katarina? She's gone! And Simon here—his Terve is gone! Oh, the hurt, the fear and worry! Oh, damnation! Damned Crots! I know it was Crots!"

Graves pleaded, "Marvin Woker, easy, easy. Or you'll blow. You and Simon Quick are welcome. Come on."

Jakes had gotten up, came over to join them, said, "Crots? How do you mean?"

"We can't come in!" shouted Woker. "No time! Me and Simon are getting folks together for a search. You have to come."

Jakes said, "Of course we will help." He was glancing behind the men at their shaggy ponies. Then, he spotted another man come snaking up towards the cabin on a two wheeler. Jakes said, "More company."

Marvin Woker and Simon Quick turned to watch. Sophie and Tyler came up to the door to join the others, but kept back.

Woker said, "Maybe he's heard something."

Graves said quietly, almost to himself, "So here it is. We should alert Old Duckbill."

Jakes said, "Could your kids have gone off together? Taken a hike? Gone on an explore?"

Woker turned to Jakes, still shaking. "They're 9 and 10 years old. They don't leave without permission."

Jakes said, "Tell us what happened. You, too, Simon."

Simon Quick was slim in his cotton robes and he had a long pointed beard. His hair was cut short. He spoke with a thick accent, "We put to sleep last night. Cuddled in our beds. When this morning, and he's gone!"

The man on the two wheeler stopped the machine before the cabin, jumped off, came towards them. He announced between famished gasps, "Doris Skeels is gone! That's 3. Then all of the Gacks. Gone. Gone, man! That's more—that's too much. All from around here, in close proximity."

Tyler said, "I'm here."

The man said, "Ah, Tyler—right?"

The men looked over Tyler and Sophie with new interest, and Woker said, "What did you do to your hair?"

Jakes said, "Bruce Temblador, welcome!"

Graves said, "The Crots would not do this!"

Bruce Temblador said, "I never said they did. War is what I'm thinking. Mexicans!"

Woker cried, "First, Katarina's gone! Now these others! Stealing children! Our flesh and blood and soul. What kind of monster would do such a thing? It's too much to bear!"

Jakes said, "For Johnny's sakes, you know we will help. That's the way we do things. You know that. We'll find 'em."

CHAPTER 5

The new—to Medea and Aurore's eyes, Aurore interrupted their excitement: "Sacre blue! Pero I'm as startled as you: what we got here is a situation trepidation."

The other Aurore burst out laughing, as she hopped out of bed, keeping her eyes on the interloper. Her mother put her arm around her shoulder. "Who are you?" said Aurore. "What are you doing in my bed?"

"Votre lit? That's exactly what I was going to ask you. But this...is not my bed."

"I knew you were going to say that!"

Medea's eyes kept going back and forth, eyelids batting delightfully. Her Aurore had put her glasses on. The other Aurore did not have glasses. Finally, she managed, "I don't get it. I don't get any of this!"

The new Aurore said quickly, as though she recognized 'her' mother's flabbergastry, "This is not the domicile—abode, I fell asleep in. I am finding myself waking here. Bonjour." This Aurore's eyes flickered over the room beyond Medea and Aurore. She fixed on the lamp a moment. Then, she felt the sheets, rubbing the fabric between her fingers. Then, she rubbed at the pillow case. "Plastique?" she asked.

Before anyone could answer, or guffaw or groan, wild

cries came from beyond the door. They distinctly made out small boy sounds, hoots and hollers. But, also, they heard high pitched laughter and frantic sounds of concern.

Medea said, "Get dressed." She turned to grab her things and started pulling them on. "Both of you," she cried.

The new Aurore said, "I am dressed."

Medea said, "Loan her one of your t-shirts."

"She's smaller than me," said Aurore.

"What's a t-shirt?" asked the new Aurore.

"Move," ordered Medea.

The 2 girls simultaneously said, "Yes, ma'am," and got busy.

The 2 Aurores couldn't take their eyes off each other, so little busy got accomplished.

Medea said, "Come on!"

Aurore pushed up her glasses, nudging them into proper place. She said, "Medea, she doesn't wear glasses."

More commotion resounded from outside. They could hear doors slamming, people talking excitedly.

Medea said, "Who are you? How did you get here?"

The new Aurore swung her legs over to stand. This Aurore was lean, slim, her tight leathers fit her snugly. She said, "I am Aurore, your daughter. Why do...she calls you Medea? Who is Medea? As to how I got here—I don't know where 'here' is."

Medea opened the door of their room, glanced out. No one in sight. The room opposite theirs, the big family one, was the Gacks'. Medea strode across the patio to the Gacks' door. Voices and shouts! The source of the uproar. She knocked.

The voices calmed, quieted. Medea called, "It's me. Is everything okay? We heard yelling?"

Vincent Gack opened the door. He wore pajama bottoms and nothing else. He was so pale his skin was growing translucent Medea averted her eyes for a sec. He mumbled something, then he stepped aside, making a welcoming gesture with his hand to bring her in. Medea slid past him into their room. The Aurores held back. Medea found 2 Lise's at the table in the living room/kitchen area. They wore t-shirts and sweat pants. Identical Lise's except for the hair—the hair was different. The 2 girls eyed each other with smirking expressions as though they were carrying on a conversation of attitude. On the cot behind them sat 2 little boys. One was Campbell, the other was an identical Campbell but in leather shorts, white tunic, leather vest, and leather moccasins. Susan Gack stood between the cot and the table. She smiled at Medea but her eyes were too big. Her smile seemed panicky. She hadn't had a chance to comb her hair.

Medea said, "Look, 2 Aurore's." But they'd gone back to their room. "Well, that's new, a shy Aurore. Where's Tyler?"

Tyler's voice came from across the room. "I'm here." He was still in bed, on his cot, under blankets. He went up on an elbow. "Salutations, Medea. I hope you slept well. You could say we did exceedingly. Welcome to the family reunion. These are my siblings from my world."

* * *

Aurore sat on the bed next to Aurore. "You can wear some of my clothes," she said. She pushed up her glasses.

"What are those?"

"What?"

"The contraption on your face."

"Glasses. I'm near sighted. Aren't you?"

She shrugged. "I did the exercises."

"What should I call you?"

"Why not?"

"Why not Aurore?"

"We're doubles."

"Like twins."

"Or clones."

"I've never seen you before."

The new Aurore reached out and took Aurore's hand. "Oh," he said. "Do you feel that? Tingly. Where are we?"

"We're on planet Earth, United State of America, the state of Arizona."

"Anomalous!"

"You're into Fort?"

"'Into Fort'? I don't know...q'est ce que sais...what that means. I read Chapman. John Chapman? Swedenborg. Thoreau."

"Wunderbar," said Aurore. "I'll call you Neo."

"How would that make you feel? You know I don't like that. What is this place?"

"Do you know Sophie and Tyler from where you come from?"

"Sophie and Tyler? Castor. Of the river? Es verdad."

"What year is it where you live?"

"What year is it where you live?"

"2014."

"Ahhh. Not sure what that means."

"You look just like me. But you're skinny."

"You look just like me. But you're zaftig."

"Doppelgangers."

"Counterparts."

"Understudies."

"Stand-in's."

"Primavera 32, 612. My now. Your now?"

"There's another world where another me lives."

"How many are there?"

"What happened? Doubles? Then the kids who switched? It's gotta be related. I mean, suppose some kind of—" She pulled her hand away.

"It can't be good."

"Unless we're supposed to—"

"We are being directed? Mon Dieu."

"It started yesterday when Sophie and Tyler switched. I saw it happen. Old Sophie and Tyler disappeared, new Sophie and Tyler appeared. A flicker and it happened. And the new ones dressed like you."

"Impossible."

"We're the same but not. Maybe things don't happen exactly the same where we come from."

"Yesterday, the 'switch'? Today, doubling. Makes no sense."

"Like you all got sucked through. Why didn't we switch? Sophie and Tyler did."

"Two Medeas?"

"Can you imagine?"

"The cosmos?"

* * *

At the Gacks' rooms nervous astonishment made for the occasional gasp or outburst. Medea managed to squeak out that the doubles seemed to come from the same place the new Sophie and Tyler did. Tyler whined something about how they hadn't really been doubled, since that would imply they were identical. Which they weren't—each having his or her own memories, haircuts, scars, scabs. At which Susan Gack had wailed something like where's our Tyler?

No one answered. Medea didn't like the way the Lise's were eyeing each other. The Campbells looked at each other with delight, as if this was the best Christmas morning ever. Too many eyes, thought Medea. Too many of the same eyes! She wanted to get back to Aurore—both of them. They'd gone back to the room.

Behind Medea and Vincent Gack standing in the doorway, gentle knocking at the open door. Thinking it was Aurore, or both Aurores, Medea lurched around. Vincent Gack didn't move. He was stiff. He was tight. He was white as a ghost. It was Alan and Winona Rose.

"We heard noise. Can we come in?" said Alan.

"Twins!" exclaimed Winona, glancing in.

"We don't know," said Medea. "How's Sophie?"

"Sophie's fine," said Winona. Very slowly, she said, "She's resting in our room"

Susan Gack laughed strangely, but continued scanning the faces in the room. "Twins? Can you imagine? You'd think I'd remember something like that."

Winona rushed to her. "You okay?"

Susan nodded fast. Vincent announced, "What are we going to do?"

Daphne Whiting gently knocked at the open door. The adults turned to her. She smiled. Beside her stood Sheri and a man in desert brown uniform. He was a young, big fellow, wearing a cowboy hat. The name tag on his chest identified him as Sergeant Dan Vanir. He nodded to Medea but kept his no nonsense expression.

Quickly, Daphne inserted, "Hello. Good morning." She stepped into the room, taking in the doubles. She inhaled sharply. She found Vincent and Susan's eyes. "Hello, there," she murmured, continuing to be appalled. She nodded at the Rose's. Slowly, she said, "This is Deputy Vanir. He's going to all the ranches because of some—kids. Kids nearby. I mean he's asking around if anyone's noticed anything unusual." She gulped. The Lise's laughed raucously. Daphne continued, "So I told him about our situation."

The Lise's said together, "We have a situation?"

Medea gave the eagle eye to Vincent Gack, willing him to say something. Finally, he seemed to snap out of it. He came forward with extended hand to the deputy. "Vincent Gack," he said, shaking the deputy's hand. "Anything 'unusual'? What do you have in mind? Yesterday, our oldest got switched. Today, we wake up to the other kids doubled."

Alan said, "Glad to see you here, officer. I think we need help in this." He spoke very carefully.

Vincent said, "Let me get some clothes on."

"What's going on, Mr. Gack?" asked Deputy Vanir.

Medea announced, "Unless we're all hallucinating—"

Sheri tiptoed through the folks standing in the doorway and entered the room on bare feet. She stared at the Lise's and Campbells. She said, "Unless I'm seeing double—"

The Lise's leaned across the table and started slapping each other across the face, shrieking, "You bitch!"

* * *

The Whitings' bed and breakfast, Rio Vista, never had so many visitors. The deputy had called it in. Deputies started showing up shortly after. The sheriff was on his way. Who had notified the FBI. Who had called Homeland Security. The Department of Public Safety had 2 of their officers lending a hand. The state public health department had been notified. Notified of what? Daphne called a local physician who agreed to stop by because of the emergency which he didn't quite grasp. Daphne's urgency had convinced him to come.

By noon, Rio Vista had 5 law enforcement officers strategically placed. DPS managed traffic control. A couple deputies kept an informal perimeter around the place. The sheriff and his PIO (Public Information Officer) met with the FBI sector chief in the dining room, which rapidly was becoming a base of operations. They sat at the biggest table in the room. The table was crowded. The FBI had brought in 2 other agents from Tucson. Public health people included an epidemiologist and an emergency first responder. Meanwhile, the local doctor, Dr. Alvernon, was giving the kids a once over.

Sheriff John Wrigley was a small man with a flat top. His uniform made him look even smaller, as though he were a kid in grown up's clothes. His people had been in the county for 3 generations. Ranchers. Wrigley was well respected as a decent public servant whom people trusted. He said to the FBI's Special Agent in Charge, Alan Adler, "We sure don't have any record of these twins. You'd think we would have heard of it? Some of my deputies know the folks who been effected. They recall the people having one child. Course, we're checking. Double checking. But, anyway, why would people deny they had twins? Unless it was what? Some kind of mental thing? Some kind of breakdown?"

Adler had 20 years in the Tucson office. He'd originally

been a specialist in the hard sciences—toxins, NBC. In college he'd been a science nerd. But given his age and experience he'd

found himself guided to administration. Now he shook his head.

"What's the alternative? The Skeels' place is north of here. The Woker's south. Quicks' west of here. All about the same distance from here. See what I mean? It's just a thought. Like this is the center."

The sheriff said, "By God, what's going on?"

"One step at a time," went Special Agent Adler. "I want all the twins and their families brought here. We've arranged things with the Whitings. Then, the next group of homes further out, away from here, those families with kids, we'll evacuate. The first step is always containment. Then the public health people and our specialists go to all the houses. Do water and air sampling. So containment, find the source. Identify the vectors."

The sheriff humphed, then, "Source of what??"

Dr. Alvernon strode into the dining room. He nodded to the sheriff. "Sheriff."

The sheriff pointed to Adler. "FBI. Sorry, we don't seem to have any more chairs. Can someone please get the doc a chair!"

"I'm fine," said Dr. Alvernon.

Adler took his hand. "Special Agent Adler. How are the kids?"

"Fine. The kids are fine. They may look the same, but they're not identical."

"How do you mean?" said Special Agent Adler.

"Small things. Obviously, scars from old injuries are going to be different. They don't have the same marks. But it's more than that. Their accents, their language use in general. I'm no linguist but—"

"That means they're clones?" said the sheriff.

The others looked at him.

Special Agent Adler said, "Let's stick with the possible. At least for right now."

The doctor laughed. "Don't think we have many human clones yet. Well, something's going on. They don't move the same. Have you noticed? The way they carry themselves. I don't know, it's subtle. My concern right now: the parents don't know these kids. That really gets me. How can parents not know their kids? But the kids don't know them either. They recognize each other. Everyone looks the same. But—I don't know, where they from, who are they: they say everything is different here." He shrugged, made a face. "Mass hysteria? Possible? I don't know. In this day and age," he kept shrugging. "So if these are not their kids, then who the heck are they? Maybe they—I don't know. Pure speculation at this point."

Special Agent Adler said, "We're bringing over the other families. We'd like you to stay if you would. You're from around here. You may already know some of them. We have public health physicians on the way. But in the meantime—"

"What other families?" asked the doctor.

The sheriff said, "That's what got us on this in the first place. Got a 9-1-1 around dawn from a family on the other side of the river. The Quicks. Maybe you know them? Said it was an intruder. When our deputy got there, the family was hysterical. The intruder was an identical twin of their little girl Catherine. Catherine, I believe her name was. Anyway, 2 more calls then, all nearby, the Wokers and the Skeels, and for the exact same thing. All calling about kids. Same exact deal. All three families had only the one child, who woke up with a 'double'. They woke up and found their child...twinned? My deputy, Dan Vanir, happened to stop by here at the B and B to see if anyone had heard anything, and, well, you know the rest."

Special Agent Adler said, "These other families had the one child. Here at the B and B, the Gack family had 3 kids. Two were doubled. The older kids, Tyler Gack and Sophie—Sophie's from the Rose family visiting here, tourists, they're not doubled at all. They claim to have been switched. Switched from someplace else. The same place the doubles say they're from. Sophie and Tyler made their claims yesterday after hiking on the river. And the 'doubling', whatever it is, happened in the early morning hours today. It all seems connected. We'll need to check out where Sophie and Tyler went on the river. See what's there." Adler paused, shook his head, glancing at the others. He felt compelled by the story. That is, he was fascinated at its oddness, but also felt something else. Like this was beyond his training, education, or pay grade. Is this what he had been waiting for?

He went on: "First, we contain this. Also, for right now, we contain information. No leaks. We don't want this getting out causing a panic. We need to have a grasp of what we're dealing with."

Dr. Alvernon said, "Sure, I'll stay."

Sheriff Wrigley said, "We better get on top of that 'grasping', cause if we got a dangerous situation, containment or no, we'll want to let folks know in the valley. In case they need to evacuate."

* * *

Now there were 6 families at Rio Vista besides the Whitings and Sheri: the Gacks with their 5 kids; the Rose's with their one switched child; the 2 Catherine Wokers and their family; 2 Thor Quicks and their family; 2 Doris Skeels and their family; and 2 Aurores and her mom. The FBI had brought in supplies, including a ton of communications equipment and a makeshift, portable lab. Homeland Security delivered a truck load of cots, blankets, food, and bottled water (just in case). The isolated B and B made for a perfect contained position. The Whitings supervised logistics, where to store supplies. Sheri helped. Medea organized teams and soon had the rooms set up for each family. The men from Homeland Security gave her a cheer. She bowed graciously. She seemed to be everywhere at once helping out.

The main dining room, the biggest room at the Rio Vista, had its tables pushed to the side, against the windows, and loaded with communications gear. Two special agents from Tucson manned the equipment. They had a direct line to the DC office in no time. They were working on a direct line to Atlanta—for the CDC. On the opposite side of the room the largest table, surrounded with chairs, was left as a meeting place. The 14 kids were examined by Dr. Alvernon, then interviewed by the FBI. Afterwards, a confab between authorities led them to decide to put all the doubled kids together. They were guided to the largest room where the Gacks had been lodged. The room had been cleared of Gack belongings, plus excess tables or lamps or dressers were removed. Fourteen cots were set up side by side like a barracks. A tight fit. But containment was achieved.

When the Lise's were led to the cabin by Susan Gack, the Lise from here quickly caught on to what was happening. She shouted, "You can't keep me in here like a prisoner! I don't want to hang out with these kids! At least give me back my phone!"

The other Lise cried, "Mother, I know what you're doing! Sacre blue! I'm the oldest so you're making me in charge of this chaos of curs!"

The Campbells came over and grabbed for their sisters' hands, but the sisters pulled away, so the little ones took hold of their sisters' arms above the wrists. The boys were determined, and they tugged their sisters towards the cots.

Susan Gack said, "It's just for now. For a little until we can figure what's going on. In case it's contagious."

Her Lise said, "Like we have some disease?"

The new Lise said, "Impossible! C'est reve!"

Two little girls, both with long brown hair, big brown eyes, sobbed, "We want our nana!"

Susan Gack said, "Patience, sweeties. You're the Catherines, right? Your mama is right here. Your mom and dad are talking with the police officers. Then all us parents are going to meet with these people who've come to help, and we're gonna figure what we should do next."

The little girl in the plain white night shirt cried, "My name is Katerina!"

One of the Lise's snarled, "Let go of me!" to Campbell at the same moment the other one screeched, "Unhand me!" and yanked away from her Campbell.

Sophie who had been stretched out in the back, walked through the cots, and called, "Sagesse! Langsam! We are here. We must get along. Everyone is trying to help." She stepped up to the Lise's. She put her arms out, hands on the boys' clasping hands and said, "Easy there, young'uns. Sisters aren't made of taffy."

A Lise snapped back, "Oh, that's a lot of help. Thank you very much."

The Campbells ran off into the cots, began burrowing under the cots, crawling across the floor on hands and knees, following each other, whooping the whole time. The Catherines cried and clasped each other tightly. A pair of young girls came in to the room with their father, Teddy Skeels. Teddy Skeels was a short, healthy fellow, but he looked scared. He said, "This is Doris." He paused. "This is Doris."

Tyler sat on his cot in the corner near the cots of 2 little identical boys, one named Terve, the other Thor.

The Aurores were being interviewed by Adler and another agent. Her name was Special Agent Karen Connely. She was an expert on children. Child psych, Aurore figured. She was a middle-aged woman with big hair. Special Agent Connely said, "Aurore, you're the one who saw the 'switch' with Sophie and Tyler. You saw it from the beginning. When things changed."

Both Aurores answered, "Is that a question?" They looked at each other aghast.

Aurore blasted, "Neo, you have to let me talk! She's always doing that."

"Progress zed," said Neo humphing. "Why shouldn't you interview us separately?"

Special Agent Adler nodded. "Good plan. We've already talked to everyone else. You're our last. We saved the best for last. Because you're witnesses too? But that makes sense: we do you both separate. Okay?"

Neo sprang from her chair and walked out of the dining room. She ran into Sheri immediately who said, "Nice duds!"

"'Nice duds', qu'est-ce que?" went Neo. "What is that?" Neo and Sheri continued gabbing as they wandered off .

Special Agent Adler grunted, spread his hands on his knees. He straightened, looked hard and serious at Aurore. "What's going on here, Aurore?"

Special Agent Connely's eyebrows knitted. She touched

her hair.

"Quarantine," said Aurore. "You'll want to control the affects. Until we know how big the area is."

"What affects?" said Special Agent Adler. "What do you know about all this?"

Aurore read his face. Like all adults, he seemed worn out and confused. But he was genuinely interested she could tell. Adler could tell she was enjoying this. She was thrilled. Two intelligent, articulate people thrust together. They had to trust each other.

Aurore said, "I think the time-space continuum has ripped." No response. "I think."

Special Agent Connely went, "Ah, like a science fiction story. You read a lot, don't you?"

Adler smiled. "Too much TV, kiddo. But I appreciate your insight. Hmmmm. So how would this have happened? This 'ripping'?"

"Don't make fun. I don't watch too much TV. You're gonna need a physicist."

"A physicist?" said Special Agent Connely.

"You have to test all frequencies. Not just air and water. But like background radiation. UV. IR. MW. Especially right at that spot where it started with Sophie and Tyler. We left some rocks at the spot. The exact spot. I can show you. Neo won't know where it is. And you'll want to test the habaneros."

Special Agent Adler scratched at his nose. "See that's the thing. Habaneros? Sure, makes sense as anything else. You're enjoying this, aren't you?"

That afternoon when the parents met with the sheriff, the FBI, Homeland Security, State Public Health, and the CDC on Skype, there was some commotion so that the meeting did not go well. Adler tried to run the show, keep it simple and straight. Parents were scared, exasperated. They were upset they'd been given separate rooms from their kids. Everyone wanted cell phones back, which had all been confiscated—parents too. Nothing was clear. Nothing was decided. The experts would do their job. It was a waiting game now to see what turned up.

A group of birdwatchers showed up at Rio Vista for their package deal, only to find their accommodations under emergency quarantine. The Whitings had spaced on calling them to cancel. Then a bus load of hippies who'd been camping at the river stopped by to see what all the commotion was about. If you were anywhere near the river, it'd be hard not to notice all the cherry topped vehicles and uniformed officers at the isolated bed and breakfast. All were sent on their way.

The Whitings and Medea got everyone fed and calmed by dusk. Special Agent Adler tried to smooth things over from the earlier discussion. He gave a little speech to the kids and parents, but they seemed preoccupied with their dinners' packaging. He said for right now everyone was safe and healthy. He joked about electronic devices and it would make more sense to communicate after we knew what was going on. So logical! No one was happy, but a desperate exhaustion crept through. He asked for patience. Tomorrow, the agency's top scientists and medical people would arrive. Including a physicist. The parents were too stunned to say much, which was probably just as well. No one really understood the depth or extent of events. The kids were sequestered to the big room, under guard. The parents made do in the other cabins and rooms, women in one, men in the other.

Eventually, the kids' room settled to sleep sounds. Sighs. Final gurgles of tears choked back. The 2 Aurores lay side by side in the dark on neighboring cots.

"I don't like 'Neo'. You could be the 'new' one. From my vantage."

"You know what I'm going to say before I say it."

"But we're not magic."

"No, I don't think so."

"So what we do—"

"—is switch clothes!"

"No one will be able to tell."

"Except I'm fatter."

"No one will notice."

"And you get to call me 'Neo' now!"

They didn't hear the Campbells, the 2 little boys, sneak to the window, snap out the screen and climb through. The 2 little boys dropped to the ground outside. They held their hands over their mouths to keep from laughing out loud. They kept low and scurried away from the patios towards the river.

CHAPTER 6

Old Duckbill clapped his bill splashing Tyler with river water. Tyler, sitting on the bank of the river, smiled and patted drops from his hair. "Thanks," he said, "I needed that. I'm kidding." Tyler didn't know what he needed. Then he remembered Old Duckbill didn't understand 'kidding'. Quickly, he added: "That was for my headache?" He tried to chuckle. "I didn't mean to gush. But now you know everything."

"You're failing," whispered Old Duckbill. But Tyler couldn't see his bill move when the words came out. How was he doing it? Old Duckbill floated lazily, waved a forelimb. Then: "I am glad you came."

"I don't know why I came. With these kids missing now? Including my brother and sister? I don't know what I'm doing." He sighed, he shook, he shrugged. "I felt like a walk after all the commotion. Graves and Jakes went out with the other men to search for the kids." Tyler pulled his knees up to his chin. His hands on his ankles. He spoke fast: "I remembered where we went last night, even though it was getting dark. It was easy to find your pool." He breathed in deeply, noticed flitting birds with yellow patches along the opposite shore. They were coming down to drink. He murmured slowly, "I am weak. Sophie and I both feel weird. We just—we're so worried about our parents. They must be sick looking for us, wondering what happened."

"Your parents here?"

Tyler shook his head. "Both sets? Doesn't sound real or possible. We don't dare contact the ones here yet. Not yet."

Old Duckbill replied, "You mean your parents there."

The beautiful morning warmed delicately, though the big sun promised more. This was Arizona sun, thought Tyler, and in a few months it would be unbearable, penetrating. Tyler could hear quail calling. The one sharp inquisitive note went on and on. The breeze cooled the drops clinging to his skin. Tyler could smell water, herbs, then a sweetness he couldn't put his finger on. Though he'd only been up a couple hours, he felt like he needed a nap. But after Woker and the others had shown up, an exhausting chaos of frantic speculation had hit them all. Plus, Woker and Quick knew the Gacks. Tyler didn't recognize them, and had said nothing. The men had noticed their clothes, their haircuts, but were too preoccupied to pay much attention. When they did get too inquisitive, Graves and Jakes encouraged a change of subject. Graves and Jakes'd promised to join the men in the search that was being organized. They would meet up at the Woker place. They had the men promise not to do anything rash about Crots. The Crots were their friends and neighbors, so they wouldn't let old prejudices sway their worries.

As soon as the men left, Jakes and Graves had gotten busy on the communication device—the commie. They wanted to contact Peggy Dreiser to give her an update. They couldn't even find her assistant.

Sophie had commented, "You must have some sort of central computer that keeps track of people, so you can call them."

Jakes had smiled as usual. "Does not compute. Como se dice—"

Graves and Jakes had pulled together some supplies, readying to join the search. Jakes had said, "Stay here. With any luck, this will be a short excursion. There and back again."

Graves'd said, "You know we don't believe in luck."

Tyler'd asked, "Should we call our parents?"

Jakes had responded, "Just as well to wait. Until we know more. Woker will have gotten word to the Gack family here. So—"

Something happened to people when children went missing. Tyler had seen enough 'amber alerts' on TV to know how panicked people became. The men he'd just met were close to panic. He was worried that his parents would be freaking. But if the Sophie and Tyler from here, were there...then his parents would not just be freaking. He and Sophie had agreed to wait and they would contact the parents here later. After Jakes and Graves left, Tyler said he was going out to take a walk.

Old Duckbill said, "How does the world work, Tyler?"

"In your world?"

"Mustn't it be the same?"

"Things are so different."

"Breath, Tyler. You breathe. I breathe. This world breathes. Here, hear your breath. Hear your breathe. Air here is not your air. Can you tell? Though you seem a breather? You are not of this place. I am not sure what that means. I don't think you are going to die. I mean right away. I'm 'kidding'."

"I don't want to be rude: how do you talk? I don't see your bill moving. Where I come from duckbilled platypuses do not talk. Or get so big. Or have vocal cords. I realized you had to be a platypus when I was walking over."

"Don't you want to know about the breath?"

"Sure. I mean, I'm sorry. Go ahead. I was just wondering."

"You talk," said Old Duckbill, "so you must be breathing. I breathe, so I must be talking?" He splashed water again, floated forward on his back then backward over the deep pool. "Where's that bird?"

Tyler didn't answer, thinking the platypus was asking about the kingfisher. Did animals talk here? What did the platypus and kingfisher discuss?

Old Duckbill continued, "Breath. Yes? Air. Yes? So many types of air. The air in this space, here, the Chichimeca. Layers upon layers of air, of breath...then of time, memory, experience, events. Where you from, there, the same there air? Here air."

"How's it set up? How does work that way?"

"You keep interrupting when I'm waxing grandiloquent." He turned his body so that he was facing the bank where Tyler sat. "This is Chichimeca, bounded to the north and the west by the Rio Colorado, to the east by the Rio Grande. South by the Rio Sonora and the Rio Yaqui. South of Chichimeca is the Aztlan Republic—Mexico. Our capital is Santa Fe, then to the south Ciudad de Chihuahua. Two capitals then. East of Chichimeca is America. I know of the United States of Africa but no United States of America."

"Ah," went Tyler. "It's like the world—what the world would have been if—"

"What happened if—"

They quieted. Tyler rearranged his hands on his knees. What should he do? Why had he come to see Old Duckbill? Nothing made sense. It made him dizzy.

Old Duckbill went, "Ahh, you want answers, solace, treats." He floated backwards away from the bank. "You think I have...you think I explain. Make you better."

"I don't know what to do. How can this be happening? We have to go back to where we came from. What if we are stuck here forever?"

"Breath of our life, breath of our minds and souls, breath of this space, intermingled now with your breath."

Tyler slapped his hands to his knees. "I don't know what you're talking about."

Old Duckbill was silent.

Tyler replied, "I don't fit. My breath is bad here. Is that what you're saying? Me and Sophie stick out like sore thumbs. Our air is different from your air? When we switched, we dragged some of our air over here? And that's bad?"

"What's wrong with your thumbs? Primates take those things so seriously. Tyler, yes, affirmative, you're from a different air. And the switch more so happened because it was possible. That's what's worrisome. A bubble is a break, an uprising, an unannounced opening, unexpected...a leak occurred. But why a switch? Why didn't the missing children switch? Where are our Tyler and Sophie?"

"A switch? An exchange? Crisscross? They have to be in my world. With my parents. I think."

"'Something is rotten in Denmark.'"

"Denmark?"

"Bad because? Because I fear that if you don't go back, there will be continued leakage. Perhaps more children will go missing. Because if this is a switch and it was not perfect, then there might be a slight drag from here to there."

"Sophie and I leaked here?"

"Peggy Dreiser—she's an aerologist. A natural philosopher. She'll know what to do."

"She's held up. Unavailable, anyway."

Old Duckbill floated forward until his big curving bill was touching the bank beneath Tyler. "I'm old, Tyler. People come to confide in me. Suppose the universe was an egg, an infinite egg, and right next to it, another egg, another infinity, another universe, where you come from."

"I should go find this Peggy Dreiser. I'll find her. I have to before it's too late." Tyler rubbed his hand over his face and mouth. "Maybe it's not eggs but balloons. And if one leaks into another—well we know what can happen. Bang! The whole thing kerplow!"

Old Duckbill thought on this, clapped his beak.

Tyler said, "Is this telepathy? How you're talking to me? Are you talking to me in my head? Like a dream?"

"I may not know what to do, but I am good at listening. Humans are always on the verge. Are you on the verge, Tyler?"

"Verge of what?"

"Telepathy impossible. Peggy found that out. No, I'm an anomaly. A plastique sport. A freak of nature. You know how humans favor freaks."

"What's plastique? I keep hearing that term."

"Plastique like changeable. Mutable? Plastique is what the modern world is all about. Change. Plastique, our substance, our very essence is a code. Language we decipher. We'd be fools if we did not learn this, then how to activate. Yes? Our world. Plastique and inertia, it's what keeps the human on the verge, the way they like."

"Inertia? Like physics?"

"Over a hundred years ago, natural philosophers were all agog on electromagnetics. Then a man named Tesla, a human, changed the world. He developed a cheap power source that everyone accessed based on inertia."

"So no electric lights or—"

The bill clapped and Tyler pulled back to miss the spray.

Tyler said, "Plastique is like what we call genes and stuff?"

"When the Europeans came to the Americas 500 years ago, they found native cultures thriving on husbandry. Crossing, re-crossing, wild plants mainly. New plants under the sun! The rest is—"

"Your history."

"Not mine."

"I'm worried for my parents—both sets. I'm worried about the missing kids. Maybe we started it. This leaking? From the habaneros? I have to find Peggy Dreiser."

"Leakage, in general, worrisome. Odd metaphor. After all, what happens when a carefully balanced system leaks?"

"It deflates. It collapses. Right?"

Old Duckbill backed from the bank, floated.

"I better get back," said Tyler. "Everyone is so upset. Will they call the sheriff or army about the Crots?"

"No army," said Old Duckbill. "You have no reasons not to trust the Crots. Nothing is as it seems during leakage. You are weak, you are strong. Breathe, live. More to worry about Aztlan, the Mexicans. They have interests in the southern border. For some time. All along here, we find their accoutrements. Be fierce, my human friend. On the verge means opportunities. Come back and see me." Old Duckbill submerged and was gone.

Tyler headed south, back towards the cabin. The trail was easy to follow. Not much brush. A silvery gray hawk circled overhead. A crash through some reeds must have been a large furry mammal. He followed the river, and the river changed faces, from wide pools by Old Duckbill's place to a flat, shallow stream with no banks. Then it wrapped around gravel bars and rocky ledges, past stands of hackberry and ash.

Out from behind a gray boulder on the other side of the river stepped a centaur. The same black hair with red headband, then the familiar features, identified the Crot as the leader Graves had spoken to yesterday. What was his name? Tyler considered high tailing it out of there. Turning and running. But where would he go? Back to Old Duckbill? How could he outrun a horse-man? The platypus didn't seem worried about Crots. Tyler found himself shaking, but he raised a hand in a feeble wave. The centaur did the same. They weren't centaurs! They were Crots.

Tyler managed, "What's going on?"

The man's face was stern, almost grimacing with pressed lips. He pushed at his braids, then lowered his hands to the weapon belt at his waist. He said, "We want for you to come with us. Important. C'est vrai. Es verdad. You savvy?"

Two other centaurs—Crots, clattered forward from behind the boulder. Both were males, shirtless, long dark hair in braids, but younger looking. Tyler couldn't remember their faces. Had they been with this older one earlier? None of them had drawn weapons but Tyler figured to go along for now.

One of the younger ones, the bigger of the 2, smiled, went, "Okla, you found the man. How did you know?"

Okla? motioned to the big one and said, "He'll ride with you, Bish."

Bish splashed into the shallow river. He came forward, positioning his wide back to Tyler. "Hop on," he said, "I won't bite."

Tyler swung over the Crot's back, grabbing on the tufts of hair that conveniently ran down the middle. He leaned forward, braced his thighs and legs. Tyler said, "Where we going?"

But Bish launched into a bumpy canter following the other 2, straight back into the river to turn around, and Tyler had all he could handle hanging on. They came out of the river, birds spraying away in all directions, the tails of the other centaurs disappearing fast. Tyler saw a vibrant red bird sally over the river. They clambered up the short bank, around the boulder, heading east. Soon they were on a trail that branched away due east.

* * *

Sophie said, "Where's Tyler?" It had been hours. Graves and Jakes were back from the search. Sophie had stayed at the cabin feeling morose, so made notes on paper Graves had given her before he left. She had a pen in her pocket. She'd made a list of everything she had in her pockets: pen, lip balm, tissue, cough drop, habanero plastic bag. Then she'd made a list of everything she could think of that might be relevant: dates, times, weather, questions, answers, possibilities. This took about an hour. She'd tried to nap.

Graves managed to dim the lights so the cabin had a particularly dreary feel. The 3 of them sat around the table looking miserable. The search had turned up nothing. The Gack family wanted Tyler back. Immediately. Sophie's family here also wanted her back. In front of them lurked the commie.

"He's out walking," inserted Graves. "Clear his head. Think better—"

"He's a city boy—" said Sophie, "like me. He could have had an accident."

Jakes sighed, rubbed his nose. "We wait a little, then we go get him. He headed north." He shrugged. "Old Duckbill will show him home. He knows everything going on at the river. In the meantime, well, still no contact with Miss Dreiser."

Graves nodded convincingly

Sophie said, "He didn't know what happened to us."

Jakes shook his head. "It's important we contact Peggy. The families in the valley want to know what she thinks. Aussi, we have to come clean about you and Tyler. We still haven't told them the whole story. We have to contact your families. Your parents, aussi, are concerned. We have to, Sophie. It's only fair."

Sophie jumped to her feet. "How do you know this

Peggy person can help us? Maybe the universe has gone crazy. Maybe we're stuck here forever."

Graves grunted. Jakes smiled broadly, nodded.

"You two make me crazy!" shouted Sophie.

Jakes said, "Mayhap there's a bad situation in Alburquerque and Peggy can't leave."

Graves said, "No, Sophie means—"

"I know what she means," said Jakes. Jakes eyed Sophie, and Sophie calmed and nodded. "She's our greatest natural philosopher. You two here, the disappearing children, she'll know. She'll be most likely."

"Oh, Peggy, for sure," went Graves. "She's an air-seer."

"Maybe time's running out," said Sophie, "for us to get back." She fell into her chair, slumped, an idea forming in her head. She sighed, said, "What's with the white giraffes, anyway? What are you doing with giraffes out here?"

Graves smiled but Jakes spoke: "Giraffe milk? Ever tried it?"

Graves added, "Makes you tall so you can see—"

* * *

The Crots galloped to their village. But it was a stiff gallop as though they wouldn't run full out, as though they were being formal. Tyler hung on, hands twisted in hair tufts. Bish jolted him along with every step. Tyler had his left hand safely secured, but his right needed a stronger grip. He released his right hand and lurched to grab farther up along the horse body...to a deep fold in its mass where the horse flesh met man flesh. What was this? It felt odd—

Tyler took a quick look behind him. He could see in the glance that the green ribbon of the river was still a handy marker, cutting through the bowl of grassland. He saw they were gaining elevation, along the bowl of the valley's curvature. Here, the grasslands mounded in easy rises…hillocks. Tyler figured if he got away and headed back to the river he'd be able to find his way. The village wasn't far. It was on a flat topped rise wider than the others, with a good view in all directions. The path widened as they approached in single file, now led by Okla. The brown-yellow village seemed to be laid out in a circle around the hill. Small and large, brown-yellow buildings, none more than a single story, and many homemade constructions of grass and sticks, clustered around the hill's perimeter. Some buildings had smooth, 'synthetic'(?), perhaps manufactured, materials included in them.

As they cantered into the village, more centaurs appeared and ran up to them, all with the same short brown horse parts. Lots of non-centaur people too. They didn't appear eager to dismember him. They seemed curious, excited. Tyler noticed right away they were regular humans—kids, women and men, in simple, white cloth clothing. They did have similar features, with long black hair, in both men and women. Tyler went by a man standing at the path's edge. He looked normal…from the top…Tyler, close by now, saw that his legs seemed short. Tyler averted his eyes. All of the so called regular human men were short. Maybe they were just a short people. Then Tyler learned why—

Okla led them to a long building with fabric (canvas?) sides. Like all of the structures, it was pale, brown-yellow like the grasslands. Open-sided ramadas were on either side of the long building. This long building had a metallic, shiny material for a roof which Tyler couldn't identify. A broad door in the front of the building swung up then over to Oka's heave and shove, like a garage door opening back home—just bigger.

Okla motioned for them to enter. Tyler slipped off Bish's back. Tyler went right over to Okla, blurted, "I have to get back."

Okla looked startled at him.

"Will I get back?" asked Tyler.

Okla said, "Don't say it like that." He held out his hand and took Tyler's hand. He squeezed Tyler's hand. "Patience." He released Tyler's hand and moved into the structure.

Villagers gathered behind them watching, talking quietly. A short, fat dog with brown spots on a white body with a big head ran up and sniffed Tyler. The dog announced with a serious voice, "He's human!"

Tyler saw some of the villagers laugh. One of the women shushed the dog away.

But the dog hung around, watching Tyler. "I'm Fido," said the dog between slurps of a big tongue. "You know how I can tell?"

"I'm Tyler. How can you tell what?"

"That you're human!"

"How?"

"You smell!" The dog chortled in gasps and slurps which must have meant humor. "You smell like human come out of chemistry. Like only a human can smell. Bien sur!"

Now the interior of the structure Okla had led them to was very odd to Tyler who followed the 3 'centaurs' in. At first Tyler thought it was a barn or stable because of the stalls all along the back. Then, on the other side, up front, his eyes went over a heavy table the length of that wall. Glowing bulbs occurred every few feet over the table. On the table, scientific equipment, including what Tyler immediately recognized as a microscope. But this mad scientist microscope had shoulder pads and some kind of neck brace. The other equipment looked equally forbidding but Tyler couldn't identify it. Complicated glass tubes came out of heavy boxes with gauges and valves.

He was now ogling what was happening in the stalls at the back of the building, where the 3 centaurs casually split in two. What? Tyler gasped at the site. The men stepped from their horsy bodies, their short legs coming out of the horses' legs. The horse bodies had no head so were easily secreted into stalls. The headless bodies were slung with ropes that hung from the stall walls. Tubes with needles descended from top panels, and the needles found their way to the same spots on the 3 horse bodies. Nutrients? Water?

Okla strolled over to Tyler. All he wore was a white cloth around his waist, tied up between his legs, secured with his weapons belt. He was bare foot. He nodded to Tyler.

Tyler said, "The horses are just for—"

Okla inserted carefully, "We don't call them horses. They're our steeds. They're faster, stronger, get us places." He paused. Then: "I'm going to wash up, get some clothes on, then we will talk."

Tyler managed to utter, "Do you know where the missing children are?"

Okla smirked.

Tyler said, "Old Duckbill said you were not the problem. Old Duckbill said—"

Okla said, "That animal can't talk."

Tyler babbled, "Old Duckbill said it had to do with the air—"

Okla puffed to Bish, "Old Duckbill can get in your head. Be careful always about who you allow in your head." He turned to some nearby comrades: "Take this sorry sight and get him cleaned up. He does stink. We'll talk then." He turned to new people who had come in to talk to him.

Now Bish was about the same height as Tyler, though his broad shoulders were double Tyler's. He put his arm around Tyler's shoulders. Bish said, "Coyote's got your tongue, boyo! One thing at a time, n'est-ce pas?"

Tyler steadied himself. He was so nervous, tired, confused that he blurted, "How do you—those are like horse's bodies, but not really?"

Bish hiccupped with laughter, "Huckle, boyo! Plastique!"

Tyler saw Okla, still standing nearby, glance at them and smile. Tyler managed, "I know but—"

Okla interrupted this time: "Tyler."

Tyler calmed, looked into Okla's eyes. Okla said, "It's our conglomerate." Okla could tell that Tyler still didn't get it. Okla went on, "We are Plastique."

* * *

Tyler suffered an old lady Crot to scrub down his hands and arms in what he assumed was some kind of public bathroom. Along the walls long tinny sinks. No commodes. The floor was cement (?) with drains down the middle. There was no front door either, just an opening. Tyler leaned over a wide, tinny sink as the old lady hummed and scrubbed. She avoided his eyes. Finally, she motioned for him to take off his clothes, also pointing to his sneakers.

"Why am I here?" asked Tyler.

"Because you stink," said the old lady. "No time to waste. Take off your ropas."

Tyler took off his t-shirt. She fingered it quickly before laying it aside. Then she applied the soothing oily soap to his shoulders and neck. Tyler felt invigorated. The soap smelled of herbs. Now he smelled of herbs, and he realized he had been smelling this sweet, slightly medicinal smell since entering the village.

"I'll finish myself," said Tyler. He bent to undo his sneakers, pulled them off, then his socks.

The old lady stepped back. "Good," she said. "Bueno. Tres bien."

"What's your name?"

"Lozen."

"I'm Tyler."

"You are not from here," she said.

"How do you know? How can you tell?" Tyler had paused in his disrobing, hands at his belt.

"We saw you come in. When it was happening. Two days ago, on the river."

"You saw it? You mean when I first met Okla? I thought that was about aurochs."

"Always about aurochs. No, we had to see."

"What did you see?"

The old lady stared into his eyes and nodded. Clearly, she'd been determining how much she could tell him. "Crots believe life has an inertia in itself. That we can sense, monitor. At that spot you came in and the others left there was an irruption. Peggy Dreiser noticed this as well. Oh, yes! She did. That's why she's in Alburquerque for the Great Machine. Yes, it has been seen. You are seen."

"Isn't Peggy Dreiser coming here then?"

"No. Now she is deep in the machine. Feeling the leys. She understands life's inertia though she is not a Crot. She needs to see you. Both of you. It will allow her to understand the irruption. What happened. She has to taste you. You taste terrible. Finish your cleaning."

Tyler pulled off his jeans and underwear. And continued his stink removal on his own. When he was finished, the old lady, who'd turned around, walked to a shelf, came back to offer him a towel. He took it, dried himself. Rough cotton? At least he assumed it was cotton.

Tyler thanked the old lady who seemed to take it for granted that she would wash a grown boy, a young man in his prime. Tyler swallowed his pride as she handed back his shirt. Her eyes met his for a second and he felt it. He gasped, took the t shirt and pulled it over his head. By the time his head was through the hole, she was gone. She was a small woman and her legs seemed normal. The one room building must have been some kind of communal water supply.

A head peeked into the opening. It was Bish. "Ahora. Maintenant. Everyone's gathering."

Tyler went, "What?" Then Tyler joined Bish outside. He felt good, almost refreshed. "What's gathering?" he asked.

"To hear the talk, to make the time, this moment."

"What talk?"

"You talk?"

"Me talk?"

"What must be done."

"What must be done?"

"Come. Okla and the others are waiting."

Tyler followed Bish the short distance to the village's center, an open area at the crest of the hillock. The fire pit at the center was cold. Thirty or forty people had come together, standing in a circle. Tyler quit trying to count them. He didn't want to talk. He had no idea what he'd say. A few centaurs joined them. Oh, the proper term was 'steed'? Women and kids. Bish pushed Tyler ahead, through the Crots, to the fire pit. Tyler looked around and quickly found Okla. He felt better right away. Okla was dressed in a white shirt and white pants. He was bare foot still, and now flanked by 2 older women in loose fitting robes. One in off white and the other in pale yellow robes. Some kind of simple wrap.

Okla began: "Coyote!"

Fido howled.

Everyone nodded and glanced around. Some had smiles. Some watched Okla intently. Tyler tried to relax.

Fido quipped, "Tell it!"

Okla got started: "Coyote, transcripterase of worlds. Coyote, messenger whose path leaves open doors! Coyote has been with us since the beginning. When we emerged from the Earth, Coyote was there. Through all the levels below, all the levels above, Coyote was there. Running back and forth between worlds. You know how dogs are."

Fido had worked his way to the fire pit, and he laughed and looked around for support. No one was joining in. His laughter muffled, only a small wisp of chuckles came out of the side of his snout. The Crots near the dog, Tyler could see, were all smiling.

"Coyote was there in every emergence. And every time we came to a new world, Coyote ran back to the old one. Then he'd run back to the new one. Coyote kept the worlds open. Kept the doors open. A delicate balance. Symmetry. Between all worlds, past and present, present and future. All of time. All histories. Harmony. From another world, this boy has arrived. But where is Coyote?" Okla opened a hand and pointed to Tyler.

Fido commented, "He ain't Coyote!"

Okla said, "It doesn't take a Natural Philosopher to know that boy is not from here. He glows different. He feels different. Peggy Dreiser must make an assessment. We are Plastique, our raison d'etre is dealing with change, promoting change. Yes? Our entire harmony, the balance between worlds is at stake. Peggy Dreiser must see these children from another world. Jeopardy! For if there is congress between worlds with no Coyote, or guide or portal, then no world is complete—or safe."

Tyler knew what he meant! He'd heard it all before. He grunted out loud, "Leakage!"

Fido hooted to the general laughing response.

Okla went on, "I suggest our apprentice take him to her. Peggy's in Alburquerque. We can be him there now time, real time...in hours. Slings. I have spoken."

The 2 old ladies next to Okla nodded and stared at Tyler. One spat into the fire pit. The other chuckled, said, "Make sense, makes sense."

Everyone was watching Tyler. Everyone was staring at him. Tyler gasped, "What about Sophie? I thought Peggy Dreiser was coming here? I think I should stay here with Sophie. She and I can get some habaneros and do it over again. We'll sit in the exact spot and we bite down simultaneously."

The old lady who had spat grunted. She wiped her nose, said, "What the hell you talking?"

Okla said, "We speak the same language. Even from different worlds. The worlds communicate...as possibilities—"

"Huh?" Tyler felt so stupid. Tyler wanted to run. He wanted to get back to the river and navigate from there. He and Sophie would stick close to Graves and Jakes, and they would figure this out. Air? Coyote and world hopping? Sure! That made sense like centaur horse bodies made sense? Steeds! Tyler wanted to head back to the river, stretch out near that wide open pool, and take a nap.

Tyler managed to squeak, "What about Sophie?"

A young woman stepped into view by Okla. She had long black hair like the others and was dressed in loose fitting, white shirt and pants. She spoke, "We have you. Sophie is with Graves and Jakes. They'll know what to do."

Tyler turned to Bish, who was smiling broadly at him, so Tyler's urge to bolt did not come true. He shook his head. Bish shook his head then nodded.

Tyler wondered how everyone seemed so...certain? How could they know? But, clearly, as the old woman, Lozen, had explained, they had detected something when the 'switch' had occurred.

The young woman spoke again, "We should meet up in Coltrane. Then you and Sophie can get to Alburquerque. That's what the leys indicate. We have to be careful. South of here is all stirred up. Aztlan."

The old woman who had spat said, "Like a hornet's

nest!"

The young woman went on, "We saw this happen. We knew what to do. Okla found you. Not Sophie. Graves and Jakes will take care of her. We have you. We meet up in Coltrane, then to Peggy. We go now."

Tyler said, "But Peggy Dreiser is coming here!"

Okla said, "We speak the same language but we have trouble with your causation. Peggy can't come because of the machine. The Great Machine has been touched. Since your appearance. Since the switch. Which we don't know exactly is a switch, because we don't know where our Sophie and Tyler went. For sure. Or where those kids disappeared to. All over our world, perturbation."

The young woman said, "Peggy can't get away. The Great Machine."

Bish said, "Could it be the Mexicans?"

The young woman shook her head. "We don't think so. No tech we know of can do something like this." She shrugged. "I guess it's possible?"

Tyler thought, Aslan, Narnia? "Aslan? Like from the Narnia books?"

At this last utterance the faces in the circle exchanged their first nervous glances.

Okla shook his head. The old women looked away. The young woman hushed Tyler.

Tyler insisted, "But I should stay! In case we go back. In case we have to go back together. Me and Sophie should go to the exact spot on the river we appeared and chomp down on a habanero."

Fido barked and barked.

Okla looked sternly at the dog and the dog quieted. Okla said, "Tyler, this is here do. Now action. Hush now. Tyler, this is Lu, our apprentice. Lu, this is Tyler from another world. Tyler, she will be your guide."

From beside Tyler, Bish spoke up: "I should go too. We'll ride to Coltrane for the buckets. Slings'll get them to

Alburquerque in no time."

A centaur clattered in place, attracting attention, and its young man said, "Lu can ride me."

Bish said, "I'll take Tyler. Then Tom here can return with my steed."

CHAPTER 7

It wasn't exactly a sleep over, or a slumber party, at the Rio Vista Bed and Breakfast. Everyone was too frazzled by the impossible to have much fun. The visitors at Rio Vista slept as best they could. It was a sleep of fear, the fear that smells sweaty because of all the popping taunts and worst case scenarios, plus the tossing and turning. A couple FBI agents stayed awake near their equipment in the converted dining room. A couple law enforcement types nodded off in strategic spots around the place in lawn chairs. You might say that Special Agent in Charge Alan Adler stayed awake on the cot set up in the corner of the dining room, but it would be more accurate to say he had entered a mental space beyond sleeplessness, or sleepfullness...a zone of scrutiny. He was stretched out on the cot, down to his under shirt and pants, socks on. His black brogues nestled neatly on the floor beside him. He had a small notebook on his chest, but he wasn't writing in it. It was just in case. He was trying to break it down...the components of events? Then, potentially, he could come up with tests, trials, leading to a chain of causation. Like a flow chart? He was trying to conjure up possibilities. His eyes flickered with the flickering communication equipment displays nearby. The 2 agents kept channels open. They regularly checked with the feds, then Wrigley's people, then the state police. The entire area was tight—

After the chaos yesterday, Special Agent Adler knew they would have to close the road. Too many visitors. Sheriff had to turn back a circus act for goodness sakes yesterday! Word was bound to get out. Stringers from Tucson...camera crews from Tempe...the media circus would descend on this peaceful bit of nowhere, where somewhere else had barged in. What did that mean? He couldn't figure the connection between Sophie and Tyler and the doubles...but he knew there had to be. The sheriff and his deputies were going to each house in the area to warn residents of a possible 'spill' or 'leak'. They would make a widening circle of visits until all the nearby homes were called on. Most of the families would high tail it out of there without a fuss. They'd have the area sealed before noon. It wasn't even dawn. Special Agent Adler was getting ahead of himself. Science fiction, physics, alternate worlds—now he wished he'd read some of that stuff. He knew how popular it was. And so odd how these girls, the Aurores, were so well versed in it. What a strange pair of smarties they were. As though events corresponded to their interests? Well, he smiled to himself, perhaps that silvery lining to the blue-black sky outside the dining room window meant a possibility had inserted itself.

Simultaneous to the 'putting-a-lid-on-it' protocol, everyone had had to turn in their phones and electric devices. This went over exceedingly. But how else to keep the proverbial lid intact? Now everyone was obsessively extrapolating...everyone was speculating on what exactly had happened here. All these minds gathered together to take apart an unlikely situation, that seemed more allusion and illusion than fact. Then: who had done this? What force was behind it? What was the technology involved? And of course: why? This morning all the possibilities seemed absurd, doing Adler little good. Yes, there was a silver lining to the loops that posed as consciousness for him: dawn beckoned. Adler rallied to the jabbing bolt that flared in his head, words on a flyby banner: time to get up! Put it on hold, and take on the day as though you knew what was going down. Nothing made sense. Duplication? Clones? Mass psychosis? Hysteria from a chemical agent? Biopsychoterrorist assault? When available options are impossible, what was left?

Tomorrow—today, the big shots...ha! today, the big shots would show up. CDC people. FBI physics department on full alert, with direct feeds to Cal Tech and Michigan State. This morning their reps'd be there. The chitter of the radios, their lights, the quick and precise movements of the operators made Special Agent Adler slow his breath. He prepared to stand up and move—

* * *

The two Aurores lay inches apart in adjacent cots. They'd barely slept, in and out of consciousness, waking to find the other's eyes boring into her. Everyone around them seemed to be out at last. They were in the kids' room. They thought it precious. Here they were, perhaps the only 2 people in the world who really had an idea of what was going on, and they were relegated to the kids' room. Of course the Aurore from here had had to brief the Aurore from there about contemporary physics—black holes, worm holes, alternate universes. The Aurore from there knew the basics of Atomic Theory—the nucleus and the electrons, the protons giving the atom its identity. But in her world there had been no atomic bomb. No Hiroshima. No Nagasaki. No Chernobyl. No super collider outside of Geneva. No Fukushima. But there was a Geneve there, world famous for its instrumentation. They prepared themselves for a dawn experiment.

The Aurore from here had several secrets she pretended to hide from herself. She considered whether she should share them with the new Aurore. Or would she already know them? She was not the Star Child her mother wanted. If her mom found out! Aurore's secret reading methodology for one thing. Did the new girl know? No one must know! She was so embarrassed. There was another secret, too. This one, too, she was not allowed to admit out loud. There were areas in her heart she only teased and touched lightly. Too scary! She missed Da so much it hurt. She was so embarrassed, as though this were a weakness. She could feel his absence.

Was new Aurore embarrassed much of the time? She didn't get that impression. Medea could 'sense' her insecurities, so what did she feel with the new Aurore? What was it like with the same mom not named Medea? Aurore wondered if it meant, Medea saw the new Aurore as better than she was.

Not all secrets were mistakes or mysteries. Some secrets were delightful: Aurore had learned to embrace her isolation. Her loneliness and distance from others was antipodean...she was hyperborean. That is, she moved away from entropy. She embraced the Fortean moment. (She disliked romantic chick flick stuff.) She found it unnatural in the contemporary world to find delight in anything. Just using the word, 'delight', could be damning. How did this relate to the new girl's world view? Neither was afraid of curiosity. Did that count as bravery? They were both ready for the experiment.

All Aurore's life she had been waiting for an adventure with interesting people. She'd never imagined that would include herself as instigator!

They'd already switched clothes and glasses. They looked forward to their first social encounter...whether they could pull it off—

The new Aurore from the leather gear wearing world

asked Aurore again, "Pourquoi? You assume if we re-enact particulars, exactement, it will happen same?"

"An experiment," whispered Aurore, adjusting the leathers she now wore.

"You think if Sophie and Tyler return to the exact spot—"

"Don't hex it! We have to try."

"You are capricious, bold, silly." She sighed and smiled, pushed up on the red glasses. "Just like me. We will get caught, yes? At least now I get to call you Neo—"

The Aurore from there felt smothered in the layers of clothes she wore to give her a chunky appearance. She kept touching the red glasses on her nose...but that was the way the other Aurore did it. She said, "Spectacles."

"We say glasses. Only, I would say 'spectacles'."

"C'est vrai."

They'd cut their hair the same. With a flashlight and a Swiss Army Knife's tiny scissors. They'd hid the hair. It was a rough cut. The new Aurore was delighted with the Swiss Army Knife. So many experiments...so much entropy.

They'd get the new Sophie and Tyler and go to the exact spot where it had started. The only drawback, habaneros. They'd have to rely on the Rio Vista kitchen. Every Southwest kitchen kept assorted chiles.

The Aurore in leathers, the new Neo, now whispered, "What do your parents do in Chichimeca?"

"Artists," Aurore answered. "They're here working on a project with Plastique. We're from New Amsterdam. We're Americans. Plastique is here."

"They aren't divorced?"

"What's 'divorce'? To cut a horse in two?"

"Separation? Irreconcilable differences? You see Da?"

"Of course. I see Da every day."

It welled up inside her. She fought back embarrassment. Embarrassment was entropy...was giving in. "Divorce is legal, marriage contract kaput. Irreconcilable differences."

"People separate. D'accord. Why not? But why would the authorities be involved? Why did Mother change her name?"

"She's an artist. Just remember to call her Medea. And act...antsy." She paused, swallowed. She said, "You get to see Da."

The plumped up Aurore started to say something but realized it wasn't a question. The girl seemed troubled, saddened about not seeing her father. The new Neo slipped from her cot. She bent into Aurore's face and whispered urgently, "Come on."

Aurore sat up and swung her legs over the edge of the cot. "What's 'antsy'?"

Sophie and Tyler liked the plan right away. While everyone slept, they would experiment. Sophie and Tyler, Aurore and Aurore tiptoed through the kids' room without waking anyone. And without noticing the Campbells, the little boys, were gone. A smudge of light came in the windows. But it was silver filigree, thought the Aurores. Each moment could be perfect, they both thought simultaneously. A deputy sheriff in a chair outside the kids' room was fast asleep, stretched out, his boots pointed in opposite directions. He was drooling, his chin low and pressed to his chest.

Sophie, Tyler and the Aurores kept going around the building to the big patio. They huddled together at the wall, still in shadow, while Aurore went for chiles. Aurore in leathers (new Neo!) hurried to the kitchen. She passed the dining room. A quick peek through its windows, and she saw Agent Adler standing and stretching, facing away from her. She slid past to the kitchen. The leathers chafed at her skin and made rustling noises as she moved. But she felt tough, slinky in a way she never had. She could do this!

The kitchen refrigerator cracked open a gusher of light which startled Aurore who quickly slammed the door. She came to her senses. Opened it a crack, did a scan. The door had produce bins. The chile drawer held: anaheims, serranos, jalapenos, with a single pumpkin orange habanero sitting off by itself. Ostracized by the other peppers? What if there had been no habanero? Would serranos work as well? Aurore snatched it up, closed the refrigerator door gently and got out of there on tiptoe.

When she got to the patio, she didn't see anyone. Then the 3 kids came out of the shadows by some stacked lawn furniture. Aurore held out her hand, palm out. In the dim dawn light, the habanero orange was a soft glow.

Sophie said, "It looks like a little organ—"

Tyler said, "Like a miniature green pepper. What could a pepper do—"

Sophie, huskily, half whispering, half groaning as though she would burst into tears, went, "Verde! Verde! Verde!"

Aurore in layers said, "Alors, let's do this."

Sophie stood next to her. She looked her over. Then back to the other Aurore in leathers. She said, "You switched."

Neo closed her hand around the habanero and exhaled sharply. "We have to go." But she paused, staring at Sophie. "How did you know?"

"You smell...viva la difference! I think it's the ...sneakers? You call them 'sneakers'? They smell of chemistry, and pestilence."

Both Aurores responded: "Beau."

Neo added, "Great."

They moved in single file from the patio to the trail that cut through the grass. A casual glance from various windows at the B and B would have betrayed them. But no one was looking. They moved fast. Neo knew the way and her heart was beating fast as it ever had. When they got to the break in the trail, they slowed, knowing they were out of visual range. They kept in single file and Neo led them to the spot.

Aurore said, "You sure it was here?"

Neo was on hands and knees looking, feeling around, not worrying about Monerans, or Arthropods, at all. She was grabbing around on the ground trying to find the rock pile. Finally, "Here! You have to stand here! No, squat!"

Sophie and Tyler came forward, saw the rocks, squatted on either side, facing east and west, just like before.

Aurore used her thumb to pry open the top of the habanero then pull it in two. She handed the slightly sticky, juicy fragments to Sophie and Tyler.

"All at once, you have to do it at the exact same moment," said Neo. "You have to bite into the chile and hold it in your mouth without spitting. No matter what."

They held the pieces of habanero between thumb and index finger.

Tyler said, "D'accord." He nodded.

Sophie said, "This is going to be fire? Burn? Feu!"

They bit down.

Sophie spat out hers first, then danced around fanning at her mouth with her hand. Tyler spat his out. His face was flushed bright red. Tears ran from his eyes. He gasped. They both danced around and spat.

Tyler managed to squeal: "Are we back? Let's go visit Old Duckbill! I have to feed the aurochs!"

Sophie, whirling around, cried, "Merde! Did we switch back? No!"

Aurore said, "We need more habaneros. We should get back."

Neo said, "That was the only one. Maybe the other chiles work. Now, we have to have a story, for when we get back. That makes sense."

Tyler shrugged, said, "We'll tell them about the chile. We'll tell them the truth."

Sophie said, "It was an experiment, yes?"

Aurore said, "We went to the spot. I wanted to show it to you."

Neo said, "You wanted to show it to us."

They moved back to the trail slowly. Tyler hesitated. He said, "I think I'm wanting to stay at the river a time. I'll be shortly. I'm fine. Tell them I'll be right back. Tell my family not to worry. Just a moment to meditate."

Sophie said, "You know Castor like you know your heart."

Tyler said, "Do you feel it? Aurore. Aurore? Do you two feel it?"

Aurore nodded glumly. "Of course." She said, "I'm going ahead." She hurried along the path. Sophie followed after her.

Neo scratched at her plump cheek, slapped at her bare knee. "Let her get ahead. It's the way it would be. Tyler, they'll be freaking. So don't dally. You know dally?"

He nodded.

"Agent Adler said the physicist was coming today." She shrugged. "I don't feel it. Tyler, not sure—at least not yet. Don't give up—"

"What is 'freaking'? Freak show? Freak storm? Freaks of nature?"

Neo looked at him sternly, meeting his eyes directly, as she'd seldom done with a boy. She rolled her eyes. Tyler got the message and he turned and looked back at the site. The little stone pile. Had he built that pile? After he'd...come through? He thought he might cry. He needed to lie down.

Neo took off.

Into the giant trees along the river, Tyler headed. Marshy there. He picked his way to a steep bank. He skipped over to the other side, sat on that bank. The sun was rising mightily. He heard birds, insects. He wanted to bend down to the river and take a big gulp to rinse his traumatized mouth, but Aurore had warned the water was not safe. Don't drink it! How could people live in a world they fouled?

He heard a voice nearby go, "Hey, amigo."

Tyler watched as a long haired, fully bearded older man in colorful garb came out of a patch of tangled willows. "Hi," he said. "I'm Homer. Hey, what's going on up there at that bed and breakfast? All those cops?"

"What's a 'cop'?"

The man was close, looking over Tyler. "You're not from around here, huh?"

Tyler fumbled to say something and at last croaked, "Sweden."

"Sweden. Inter-resting. Inter-resting. Well, no pun intended, but you feel like the proverbial fish out of water. Something about your aura—"

Tyler went, "Yes." He smiled. He carefully went on: "Something happened a few days ago." He shrugged. "A couple days ago. We find ourselves here. Your world."

"Hmm," went Homer. He reached behind himself and pulled out a plastic water bottle from his back pocket. "Here," he offered gesturing, then tossing the bottle to Tyler, who promptly missed it, not realizing at all what the gesture of 'tossing' was about.

The bottle bounced and Tyler retrieved it. He examined the bottle. "How do you get it out?" he asked.

Homer took the bottle, pulled out the inner cap that allowed squeezing out in a stream. He showed Tyler how to angle the bottle to his mouth, when to squeeze so it didn't go up his nose.

Homer smiled through the whole instruction. He said, "Something happened here for sure. I don't know where you are from but I know what will happen with all the law enforcement around. Whoever you are, wherever you are from, you are welcome to join us. We're camping down here little ways on the river. Come over and meet the circus? You know what a circus is?"

"Circus?" Tyler nodded. "I love the circus."

"Sure. We're Crotalus! That's what we call our group. No electronics, no computers, no cell phones. Ha! We drive around seeking adventure. We do puppets. We have great puppets—giant puppets. That's what we're known for. But we also travel the ley lines. We knew something was happening here. You're part of it. We're on our way to Duke City. You ever been there?"

Tyler shook his head, gave the water bottle back.

"Well, Duke City is having a psychic fair. We're performing. There will be hundreds of people there. You should come. One of the biggest psychics around, Pamela Dreiser, will be there. You could talk to her. Figure it out. Why not? You'll like it. We'll watch out for you..."

Tyler gasped. "Dreiser? I know that name."

* * *

Special Agent Adler sat at the table in the dining room they used for briefings. It was past dawn and the day was already exciting. He studied his coworker, Special Agent Connelly, next to him. She looked barely awake. Or, maybe, she hadn't slept yet. Her face was puffy. Now the morning light from the windows was generous. It was going to be a beautiful day. Her face began to beam as she must have come around to realize the significance of this dawn, at least its complexity, especially after he'd briefed her on what was going on. Adler'd told her what happened. Sophie and Tyler and the Aurore doubles had snuck out to the river. They'd returned just as Aurore's mother was sounding the alarm. That woman was all over the place, trying to help, giving orders, calming kids. The other kids were all accounted for. They'd found a popped out corner of the back window in the kids' room. So they knew how they'd done it. Everyone was shocked at how easy it had been for them to get away. They could not afford such a thing happening again. Adler said he'd told the kids, "You realize how glad we are you're okay? We have no clue what might happen next." The Aurore from here, Adler told Connelly, had answered in French. She was smart, clever, ready for adventure—that girl! Then, Adler had explained to Connelly, Tyler was still at the river. He hadn't come back with the others. The Aurores had been enlisted to take law enforcement to the spot. Sophie had implored, "Tyler knows the Castor. He'll be fine." Adler said he had asked, "Castor?"

Special Agent Connelly came around some more, pulled herself together, said softly, "Still no sign of the boy? He's still missing?"

Adler nodded. Adler knew letting the kids get through security would look bad to the folks coming today. They had to find Tyler ASAP. Get him back here before they arrived. The entire scene was endangered, slippery, crumbling. How could you control that which was unclear? Unclear mean uncontrollable? Adler looked at Connelly's sleep deprived face and said, "The boy can't have gone far. We'll find him. They'll bring him back. Reinforcements on the way." He shrugged and sighed. "For now, we bring back in here every kid. We go through it again like we did yesterday. We get them to talk, make them feel comfortable, safe. See if they saw something. Maybe they overheard the older kids last night. Do they know anything about Tyler."

Connelly managed a grim grin and nodded, "Makes sense." Her mind had a hard time getting around more interviews, doing the whole process over again, but she knew Adler was right. Should they interview the doubles together? They hadn't tried that. Should they interview the doubles separately? Could they have some kind of influence on each other? Could the kids...know things about each other? Connelly said, "The kids went to the spot...where they came in?"

"Exactly. They even managed to find a habanero."

"I take it, then, it didn't work."

Adler shook his head. He said, "Aurore, both of them, figured it was because they didn't have enough chile."

"Chile."

* * *

The 2 Campbell boys were escorted in to the dining room after Adler gave his nod to the agent at the door. Across from the 2 FBI agents, sitting there quietly, calmly, the 2 Campbell boys. Two little boys—their heads stuck up above the table, and they had their hands nicely folded in front of them on the table.

Connelly said, "How are you two?"

"Fine," they said in unison.

"Slept okay?"

"Fine."

Connelly said, "Feeling fine, huh? Good. I guess we had a little excitement this morning. Do you know anything about that?"

The 2 little boys nodded. Then they both slumped over and giggled in to their hands.

Connelly glanced at Adler who grimaced and went, "Did you see the others leave?"

The 2 little boys wouldn't look up.

"Did you hear them going out the window?"

They started giggling again, harder this time.

The 2 FBIs pressed their lips and shook their heads.

"You have to tell us, or your parents, if you know anything. It could be very important. We want to keep everyone safe," prompted Connelly.

Adler grumped, "You 2 sitting here, giggling. What's so

funny? You know this isn't a joke. We're worried about a teenage boy, maybe lost out there in the desert. Okay? You got it?"

The 2 heads tilted to the side and said, "Got what?"

Connelly sighed. "I need an aspirin. And coffee." She rubbed her temples. She said to the boys, "You understand how important this is? We're in this together. We're trying to figure out what's what. In the meantime, we all must follow the rules. No leaving the bed and breakfast. Stay with your parents or in your room."

The boys said, "'What's what'?"

Adler said, "You're the 'new' boy, right? Where are you from?" He paused and the boy looked puzzled. Adler went on, "Where you from?"

"Chichimeca," said the Campbell from there.

The other boy spoke up, "I'm from Glendale, which is by Phoenix."

Connelly smoothed back her hair. How could a little boy make up such a story? How could parents not know they had twins? Connelly said, "What do your parents do in Chichimeca?"

"Furs," said the boy.

The other Campbell said, "We already told you. We already talked about this."

Sheri burst through the dining room doors. She panted. "Bunch of black SUVs coming down the road!"

Adler nodded. He scratched at his upper lip. It was a gesture that put people at their ease. He imagined it made him seem more human? The boys watched him. He looked back: 2 identical little boys, but dressed differently, as though from different eras.... Cute kids! He said to the boys, "You guys are acting funny. You okay?"

They shrugged, said, "Twice is nice. Twice as fun. Well, we can't make ice cream appear."

Connelly said, "You can do things you couldn't before?"

They stared at her.

Connelly said, "I'm going for coffee." She got up, smiled at the boys.

Adler said, "Okay, you guys. If you think of anything, anything at all that might be important, that you think we should know, come find me or Agent Connelly right away."

* * *

SUVs are made for power and space. You can pack an SUV with a ton of equipment. Literally. The lead SUV deposited the most important addition to the scene: Paul Button, a 45 year old career NSC troubleshooter. He shook Agents Adler and Connelly's hands and smiled broadly. "Kids got away from ya, huh?" It was his only greeting. Then he started giving commands to the passengers and drivers of the flotilla he seemed to command.

Adler pondered. Adler went over it again to make sure he had it right. It was all in the brief he'd emailed to Button. He wanted to make sure he'd followed protocols. He wanted to have a true timeline as well. Trip Whiting had made 2 initial calls that had gotten things rolling. He'd called Sheriff Wrigley and Dr. Alvernon. Sheriff Wrigley had notified the state police for back up right away. When Sheriff Wrigley had visited Rio Vista and seen what was going on, he had immediately thought, 'kidnapping', so had called the Tucson FBI office. Then, as the weird story unfolded, he'd contacted public health officials. The local public health guy had stopped in at Rio Vista yesterday, freaked out, crossing himself repeatedly, and vacated the premises. He must have notified the state public health department. Those state folks were coming in today. Who must have contacted the CDC. So who had notified the NSC? It must have been someone from his office.

Each SUV that arrived represented a different approach. All under Button's command. The state public health officials' SUV held medical equipment, lab stuff for carrying out an array of tests. They were basically epidemiologists with a set of fixed steps to evaluate a scene. They were short handed now, as most of their people were at the Navajo Nation working up a Hanta virus outbreak. Physicist Adam Budge came in the FBI's special unit SUV with seismographs, radiometers, various full spectrum collectors, an oscilloscope, and a magnetometer. He wanted to set up right away. His 3 assistants went at it. The CDC had flown in a specialist as an observer. Her name was Dr. Jeri Downs. CDC needed a formal invitation to get involved.

Funny, thought Adler, how important it was to follow correct protocols about inviting in the experts. Isn't that what you had to do when a vampire was at your door? Invite them in? What an odd thought. Like something Aurore would have come up with.

Too much coffee, not enough sleep: worry—no, impossible worry was causing him to adapt, adjust, shift.

Eventually Paul Button took over the dining room command center, giving it his own flair by having the cots removed and more work tables set up for his own communication gear and specialty equipment which he did not explain to Adler. His assumption of command was implicit. Adler kept out of the way. He'd gotten the email memo: full cooperation with Mr. Button was ordained. Button then pulled together Sheriff Wrigley, First Officer Mendoza of the State Police, Special Agents Adler and Connelly, Dr. Downs, Dr. Budge, Joe Garcia—the leader of the state public health team, and the local doctor, Dr. Alvernon for a meeting in which no one could sit because work was going on all around them and there were not enough chairs.

Button was brief, terse, piquant: "Containment

correction! Got it? Containment besmirched. Containment's not just removing civilians' cell phones, but egress. We have the personnel now. No one's going out for a walk on the river period. We need that boy found and brought back pronto."

Sheriff Wrigley said, "My men are on it."

Button continued, "Adler's evacuation plan is on schedule—hmmm."

Button was a thin man, not overly so, but no excess. The khakis didn't help: all he needed was a pith helmet to complete the image. When he grunted, it came out higher pitched than he would have wanted. More of a sickly hiccough.

Special Agent Adler avoided scratching his lip and looked into Paul Button's eyes. "I assume you read my preliminary report—"

"Your notes? I saw your notes."

"In that report I said there were certain anomalies that demanded—"

Button interrupted abruptly: "Anomalies like visitors yesterday? Yes, I saw that."

Sheriff Wrigley managed to insert: "Yes, sir, we stopped them, turned them back."

"So close though," said Button sadly.

"For sure," went Sheriff Wrigley, laughing limply.

"Too close," finished Button. "The circus coming to town, hey?"

Sheriff Wrigley said, "Bunch of hippy kids. No big deal. On their way to the Duke City. They left before the boy took off if that's what you're thinking."

Special Agent Adler said, "I was referring to the anomalies: 1) switched kids, or at least kids who suddenly have a new identity; 2) doubled kids, twins really, in families that have no knowledge of twins; 3) all kids concerned assert a recollection of a place they claim to have come from that is not here."

Button went, "Why—why—why this word 'switched'? Why are you using it? I thought you were alerted because of a kidnapping?"

"Actually," said Adler, "I think it was the kids themselves that started using the word, 'switched'."

Dr. Adam Budge burst from his corner of the discussion with a loud, "Just what do we have here? I need to know why I am here. What am I here for? I can check fault lines, magnetic fields, even radiation. Sunspots? Sure. But those natural processes influencing human behavior? Don't think so. What's going on?"

Adler said, "The kids' stories are convincing. They didn't know each other before a couple days ago. Yet the stories describe the same place, this other place in great detail."

Joe Garcia said, "Similar things happen all the time, all around the country. Bunch of kids at the same school all get a rash. Or start laughing. Uncontrollable laughter." He shrugged.

Budge said, "A rash? Hmm? The past 20 years has seen a lot of public discussion of physics' fascination with the concept of the multiverse. Yes? By the time this speculation got into pop culture, everyone has his or her own alternate reality."

Dr. Downs blurted, "Please call me, Jeri. I realize I am just an observer, so I assure you I will stay out of your way, but at this juncture I believe it opportune to mention: the biology is sacrosanct: they have the same DNA. The doubles? They have to be twins. So the question is why would the parents deny this?"

"Otherwise, what?" said Button. "Some secret cloning project when the children were born? Possible? Highly improbable." Button seized control: "Cope. Adjust. Shift. All possibilities must be considered. A contagion? We check on that. Something in the air, in the water. Same. Same with sunspots. Earthquakes. Mass psychosis? Fine:

we diagnose, we treat. There must have been a trigger.

"We need to rule out any international involvement. Not even sure what that means. But I'm sure you follow me. Follow me? We need an assessment in 24 hours. I need to know whether this—these incidents pose a threat to national security. By tomorrow.

"Public health folks, science people get to it. We establish our evaluation. Containment is assured. The rest of us know what we have to do. Twenty-four hours, then."

Dr. Downs said, "What does 'switched' mean? Switched from a place? Change of location? Or switched with someone else? Exchanged. The kids from here went to their place. And the kids from there came here. But also the kids from there came from the same place the twins came from. So why did the twins, or doubles, come here? Why were only the two switched? How are the twins different from the singletonians who switched?"

Paul Button nodded too broadly, unable to hide the grimace, interrupting with, "This is what I like to see. We're popping. Let's do this."

Dr. Downs said, "I'd like to interview the kids. Interview the parents."

Button said, "We'll set up a schedule."

Special Agent Adler ahhed and ohed in embarrassment, then, finally, every eye on him, said, "The kids are tired and scared. Whatever happened to these kids, whatever these kids are, whatever is going on with them, we have to protect them. Which is damn difficult if someone or something we don't know about is doing this *to* them. See what I mean? We need to be ready to provide protection, no matter what form that might take."

Special Agent Connelly said, "We have to ask, what if what the kids are saying is true?"

Button stared straight ahead, then muttered, "I'm not following." Then, in a professional roar: "We're growing donkey ears here, people! But I'm glad we got this out in the open. Cat's out of the bag. Okay? Now—bang! time to get serious."

* * *

That afternoon when Sophie realized that Tyler had not returned, she began to worry. Everyone around her, including this world's family, was worried about everything. Sophie had never experienced such isolated, or separate, people. She thought that made it worse: worry on top of separation made people downright scared. They had all sorts of devices and inventions for long distance communication, yet had such a hard time being clear to each other. No one seemed to trust anyone else. When she tried to explain about how Tyler knew the river, they just looked at her as though she spoke a foreign language. Sheriff deputies and state police and FBI agents scoured the river looking for Tyler. Sophie could tell by the way they moved that they'd never be able to find him. Sophie didn't think they had a clue about understanding what knowing a place was...what that meant.

Now there were more people coming in to the Rio Vista travel lodge. That's what Sophie assumed the place was. And these people were identified as agents and specialists, scientists and doctors. This science was not steeped in Natural Philosophy; instead, it seemed to focus on technique, lists of instructions to follow. Like a manual. Sophie knew she was in for more probing and questions. She also expected more tenseness. She didn't doubt their science; but she didn't see how it would explain their predicament.

Sophie believed this the best of possible worlds. She believed in the perfection of life as taught by Jonathan Chapman & Emmanuel Swedenborg. Nature was perfect because that's all there is. One worked to be part then: to embrace, to enhance, to further that which was already in effect. In St. Louis she had never had the opportunity to become so close to nature. Big city life in America, in her world, offered the human experience. Of course, there were parks and nature trails, but— Chichimeca and the river had been a life changing experience. The words of Chapman had been lovely poetries before. Now she felt she understood. St. Louis, with its hustle and bustle and industry, seemed connected to a big world. But distinct from nature. Chichimeca was quaint, a nation living by its own interpretation of human traditions adapted to nature. She and Tyler became friends on the river. They both were interested in each other's point of view. They were both fascinated by Natural Philosophy. Awareness of nature brings understanding, they assumed. This understanding should be behind all actions. But Tyler had never been out of Chichimeca. Certainly, never to St. Louis. Sophie didn't have many male friends in St. Louis. They were becoming close, and now—

Sophie had spent time with these parents. They were her parents...the same. But these parents were rich. Extravagant. They didn't seem to know anything beyond the emergency *right now*. She couldn't tell if they listened, or simply waited for their turn to talk. They were so rushed, busy, fast. She hated the idea of hurting them, adding to their worries. She knew they must be worrying where 'their' daughter, their real daughter was. What if things didn't go back to the way it was? Would she be able to learn their ways and be their real daughter? It hurt to imagine that. Felt so wrong!

Sophie thought of her real parents. Their devotion to art and science—Natural Philosophy. The fascination they had with plastique, which had brought them to Chichimeca. They had traveled the world, studied with leading intellectual figures of the time. It wasn't that they were smarter or better than these other parents, Sophie missed their understanding: when she talked to them, they listened, and changed, and gave something back to her right away.

Sophie yearned for it: for everything to be back the way it should be. She had assumed that art and science were her true calling. Now? Sophie felt embarrassed now at how she had begged her parents to send her to Paris to study, instead of visiting Chichimeca. She thought, it's good to shake up one's expectations. Then she had fallen in love with the Castor and—

The insights she'd garnered were worthy, the ongoing meditative connection would guide her. Did the people here contemplate? She and Tyler must show them how? She dreamed for a moment: she and Tyler woke at the river, visited Old Duckbill, returned to their parents, and families, and familiarity.

She felt sad she knew what she had to do. She owed it to Tyler. She would find him. Yes, new guards, new sentries, but she could move now. Tyler had taught her. She thought like him, knew the river like he did. Well, not as good as he did. She was as surprised as he at how the river had changed here. But maybe that was good. Maybe that would enable her to follow his steps.

* * *

Before dinner, before dusk, Special Agent Adler gathered everyone on the back patio. It was cool but not unpleasant. Lights did the trick. Quite a crowd now: all the families, the doubles, the Whitings, techs, scientists, law enforcement people. Button wanted to keep Adler as the face of the operation. Adler thought it was the right move. You don't want to confuse civilians. Too many new people constantly being introduced brought trepidation, as Button might say. Besides, people cringed at the acronym NSC, thinking it stood for nefarious activities that 'Big

Brother' was foisting on an unsuspecting public. The word 'conspiracy' was avoided at all costs. and Adler and Connelly had had a little time now with the people. There was some trust. Adler hoped.

Adler began, "Well, you can see we have a lot of new people with us. Security and specialists for sure. Lots of interviews and testing going on. Thanks so much at this difficult time for your cooperation. We want to make sure everyone is healthy. We want to make sure everyone is safe.

"You can also see these folks have been busy putting up tents out here in the back. Most are for their fancy equipment. One over there will be food service. We've got tables and chairs set up. So bear with me, we're going to be doing a lot of picnicking over the next few days. This will take just a minute more now, then you can go see how government chow is. I'm kidding. We'll be bringing in fresh produce—fruits and veggies, every day. I'm sure it will be fine.

"A final point: we all know the rule now. No one leaves the B and B without authorization. But there should be no need to leave anyway. And no electronics. Right? Everything turned in? Good. If anything comes up, ask Special Agent Connelly or me. We'll do our best to make sure you know what we know."

Medea stepped forward from her place by the building and strode closer to Adler. She announced, "You've been very kind, Agent Adler. Considering the circumstances, we have nothing but praise for all who've come to help. For that, we thank you. I was thinking if I had my cameras back, I could be chronicling these unusual events. Eventually, people will want to know what happened here."

Adler said, "I don't see why not. Let me talk to my people and get back to you about that."

Lise called out, "What about TV?"

Adler smiled and shook his head. "We're working on it. We'll get some tablets or something fixed up so the kids can watch movies. We're working on it."

Lise said, "I don't see why we can't have our phones. Like once a day. You know, just to check in."

Adler nodded and smiled. "Let's get a handle on things first, before we start announcing to the world what's happening here."

Winona Rose inserted, "What is happening here?"

Special Agent Connelly answered with, "We don't know yet. But right now there appears to be no danger. We're doing our best to figure this out. Right now, we seem safe."

Winona Rose said, "Was my—" she paused a beat, then: "daughter kidnapped?" She started to cry.

Sophie put her arms around her mother saying, "I'm here, I'm here."

"I know, I know," said Winona Rose softly.

A man and his wife with 2 little girls grew agitated. The man was Marvin Woker and he said, "My wife and I been talking about this bit with our kids separated at night. Seems to us, it might work better, if families stayed together. We parents could take responsibility to make sure we knew where our kids were all the time. I bet we could re-arrange our sleeping quarters, or I bet you guys have more tents and cots."

Alan Rose said, "Alan Rose here. What Marvin says makes sense. Not quite sure why we had to separate from our kids in the first place."

Connelly said, "Mr. Rose, if you will remember, we were not clear about the nature of events, so to be on the safe side we thought it best to keep the children together."

Winona Rose said, "Are we in danger?"

Adler interrupted: "One thing at a time, folks! We don't think anyone is in danger right now. It's getting dark." He glanced around, got the sign from the cooks in the mess tent, went on, "For right now, let's have some dinner. We're going to have to be patient here. Right now, we keep things as they are. Now let's eat."

Trip Whiting said, "So we're under house arrest?"

"Of course not!" said Adler.

Whiting said, "I mean, what if we want to go? This whole deal is pretty kooky but in the meantime life does go on. How long do you think this will take? Are we talking days? Weeks? I got a business to run."

Teddy Skeels said, "What if we want to go?"

Connelly said, "With both Dorises?"

Adler said, "Let's eat! I know it's been frustrating. Hang in there, folks. By tomorrow we should have a better idea what we are facing. I do want to extend a special thanks to the Whitings for their patience with all of us showing up like this. I assure you the Whitings will be fairly compensated for all they have done for us."

Connelly said, "We all have a lot of questions. And now we have a team of experts. We're on top of things, folks. We appreciate your cooperation. Agent Adler and I promise to give you all a briefing every day, so you know what we know."

Alan Rose said, "How long are you going to keep us here?"

Adler said, "I don't know if that's the right way to look at this, Mr. Rose."

Marvin Woker said, "Well, I still don't like it about the kids."

Medea said, "I think we should eat. Talk more later. Right, guys?"

After dinner, and hearing way too many complaints about the food, then supervising kids and families, Adler tried to get everyone's attention before they broke up. He wanted to talk about Tyler. After Adler assured everyone they'd find Tyler, Mr. and Mrs. Gack thanked him. Adler gently wove his way back to the admonition that everyone must stay at the B and B. He hoped it was getting through to the kids. Then Mr. Gack wanted to go on one of the patrols with the security people to find Tyler. Adler said he didn't think that was a good idea. He could do more good here with his kids. Tyler had to be close—they'd find him. He couldn't have gone far. They had to hold tight, bear with the inconvenience.

Dr. Alvernon spoke up then to say everyone appeared healthy, all the kids, including the doubles. He shrugged. For right now, he agreed with Adler, that they should continue with the interviews and testing.

A man, whose little boys had doubled, Simon Quick, raised his hand, said, "What's with the headaches? Notice how everyone who hangs around the doubles gets headaches?"

Connelly said, "But the kids are okay. They're not getting headaches."

Susan Gack batted at a moth fluttering by her face as she stepped forward to say, "Tyler said he felt weak. Very tired. I don't know?" Now, she shrugged, and her tall slim frame seemed to quake as an emotional tidal wave passed through her.

Connelly said, "Thanks for bringing that up, Mrs. Gack. Maybe Mr. Garcia—I hope you all have had a chance to meet Mr. Garcia of the state public health team, can help us here."

Joe Garcia moved under a patio light so that he had something of his own spotlight. He said, "This is an incredibly odd situation we find ourselves in. And we all know what happens when something unusual occurs: stress. Yeah, you parents know what I'm talking about. We all know how we can react to stress with things like headaches, stomach aches. Even sleeping problems."

Connelly said, "We've got plenty of aspirin."

Garcia said, "We should know more very soon. Then we can make recommendations. And if tomorrow we still do have questions, we can get help from the CDC. They've already sent an observer to us by our request."

Lise glanced at her double then spluttered out loud, "We're causing the headaches, aren't we? We've got like powers."

Several people started talking at once. Sophie wiped her mouth delicately with the paper napkin she'd held on to from dinner, giving it an extra rub because of the napkin's unusual texture she was not used to. Sophie meant 'wisdom' in both worlds. She had to trust herself, her own sense of necessity. She whispered to her mom, "I'm going to the loo."

Her parents glanced at her, nodded. Their furrowed features spoke of worry and concern and confusion. Sophie knew her dad was getting frustrated. His voice was rising. He was getting angry. People here talked, then acted. In her world, people watched, listened, then acted. As the saying goes, 'Look first, then see." Sophie pushed through the crowd, went into the main building.

She immediately turned left, away from the bathroom, and saw the deputy framing the far door, lit up by the outside lights. She came around with grace and speed, proceeding to the right. She went into the bathroom, shut the door. The window above the sink was small and dark. She left the door unlocked and squeezed through the window. No guards. She went along the bed and breakfast buildings, on the opposite side from the patio and yard area. She kept close to the walls, until she came to the end. No guards. Where were the guards? Les flics? They were all down at the river hunting for Tyler. She hurried to the fence line which was thick with brush and brambles. Keeping low, she moved along the fence line as far as it went, picking up a number of stickers. No one spotted her. Or gave the alarm. It was past dusk so difficult to see perhaps. But, now, at the end of the fence and its limited cover, she would have to make her dash to the river across open fields. It was a long run. She would be exposed. She was brazen, outré. She must allow for novelty, 'new things under the sun': she had to attend to her intuition. She didn't have any time to think about it. Her parents would sound the alarm in minutes.

Sophie kept low, bent over, and scurried for the river. When she made it, her heart was pounding. She'd picked up a thorn in the soft part of her arm. She paused to pry it out. Tyler never got pricked. She wended her way into the brush and trees along the river and headed north...where Tyler would go...in the direction of Old Duckbill.

It was a good plan. Well, she didn't really know if it was a good plan. But it was a plan.

Why would he go without telling her? They were amis. Unless he'd taken ill—

What if Tyler was sick? Peut etre he slipped into quicksand? Or a miasma? She calmed enough from her scramble to catch her breath. She wasn't feeling great but like the man had said, it was stress...distress. Malade. Misericordia. She hadn't yet felt the weakness and tiredness that Tyler complained of. But why would he go without telling her? They had to stick together. Maybe Aurore's experiment had failed because they didn't have enough hot peppers?

Night came in a complex blackness before the stars could come on. She kept up her pace, fast, certain. She hadn't known how to move like this in St. Louis. Tyler had shown her. She fell into the ease of movement, when intention and awareness merged with muscle. Her senses primed to instantly adjust her gait as necessary. It was a dance! She moved in, with, on the river. She knew the law enforcement people did not know how to move like this. They seemed thick and clumsy. So far, no lights or people on the river. She would sense them. This world so unhealthy and unhappy? These people, their talk, their lists of questions, seemed based around either/or, like tracking a billiard ball. Everything had to be this way or that. She covered a couple miles before slowing. Brush and greenery seemed to melt and flush and merge around her. Her eyes adapted. She rubbed at the sore spot on her arm. She heard goatsuckers but couldn't see them. Coming down to drink? Or chasing insects? Were the animals here the same as there? They'd already noted how the plants were different. Here, the rich rot smell of the riverbank made her squinch her face, wrinkle her nose. Stinky. Merde. Not the rich smell of natural decomposition at all. This was not the Castor, this was the San Pedro.

Her boots got muddy. These were the hiking boots of the other Sophie so fit fine. Sophie was determined to give them back in good condition. Now her feet were soaked but she pushed on. The rush of cold on her feet was exhilarating.

Her real parents must be worried to death. What would they think of the other Sophie? If that Sophie had ended up in her place? They would have calmly listened, watched, considered. Then, when they'd heard about the missing kids in the river valley, they would have ciphered the news, following the new parameters to some understanding. Or they would have called for help like the people here did.

Sophie thought, what if they were right here? Beside her right now? In this exact moment with her...but in another angle—another place? Was everything she did mirrored exactly by the Sophie in her world? She reached out a hand. Could she reach out right now and make contact? Was the other Sophie doing the exact same thing? Could she pull her across? Swap places? Switch? Her hand felt the cold teasing air and that was all.

She followed the river but stayed under cover. They had to have men up and down the river searching for Tyler. She'd seen no one. They'd never see her. They'd never find Tyler. She'd find Tyler. They should stay together. They should stay near the place it happened...where they came...in? through? In case it happened again? Then they would switch back? Aurore's experiment must have left out some crucial component.

Animals!

She could smell them. Now she could hear them. She stopped, folded into herself and around a cottonwood, making herself invisible. The horses could smell her, maybe that's why they were making noise. One sounded hurt. She moved into a crouch, went to hands and knees, pushed her head around—

Darkness changed again, because of the revelatory skies. Maybe it was her relief at seeing familiar infinitude. She could make out the Milky Way. The blanket of night sky glared over an open area before her. Perhaps an arroyo had collapsed here, then eroded to a flat branching spot on the San Pedro. Two horses in the middle—saddled. Two men stood near the horses.

Sophie burst from cover with: "Graves! Jakes!"

The two men jumped. One went, "Whoa!" The other yelped, "Who's there?"

Sophie hurried to them. They stepped back. She was so excited but their defensive posturing made her slow. The wild thought they'd been sent to find her was quickly put to rest. They were dressed—

Graves said, "Hey, kid, you scared us to death. We thought it was a chupacabra. Jakes' horse seems to have gone lame. We're just standing here with our fingers up our ...noses...wondering what to do."

Sophie laughed nervously, put her hands to her mouth. Slowly she said, "Ca va? Mes amis—," she stopped, sighed, then: "You don't know me? You don't recognize me?"

The man called Jakes said, "You okay?"

Graves went, "Easy."

"Je suis Sophie. Sophie. My parents came from St. Louis

to work in plastique. You've been showing me around with Tyler?"

Jakes went over to his horse. He patted its neck. He rifled through the saddle bags and pulled out a flashlight. "Here it is," he said. He shook it a second then snapped it on and turned around. The yellow light hit Sophie's chest and shoulders. It was enough light for the 2 men to know they did not know the young girl and they said so.

Sophie said, "Tyler—have you seen Tyler?"

Graves shook his head. "Nope. Don't know any Tyler."

"He's missing. I was looking for him."

Graves and Jakes said no, they'd seen hardly anyone on the river for a couple days. That's when the horse had gone lame. They'd been camping since then on the river, thinking the horse might improve with rest. No luck. They'd figured they'd take off in the morning, but the horse's pain seemed to indicate it was getting worse. They were hiking out now, going for help for their horse, when Sophie appeared. They couldn't figure what the girl was up to, why she insisted she knew them. But she'd known their names.

Finally, Jakes said, "Well, shoot, we're not getting it done standing here in the dark with a flashlight. This draw cuts through fields that are being used for pasture. You can tell. At least you can in the daylight. So we walk our animals out from here until we find the ranch house. There's got to be one not too far. Maybe we can leave our horses in the rancher's corral until we figure how to get a vet over here. Then Sophie can call her folks, see if this Tyler showed up. You don't have your phone with you?"

Graves said, "Sounds like a plan."

Sophie said no, shook with it, but vaguely agreed to follow them. She suddenly realized the futility of her quest for Tyler. Things were too different here. All her certainty and exuberance crashed. She wasn't thinking straight. What was she thinking? Was it the stress? Tyler's absence had upset her. She couldn't stop wondering where he was, then she could imagine where he was. No! She'd go at least as far as the ranch. She could get her bearings then. Decide whether she should go back to the bed and breakfast place or hide until morning when she could go on with her search for Tyler.

It was slow going with the injured horse that grunted and moaned when its bad rear right hoof came down wrong. But it was easy going, open fields as they got away from the river. And, sure enough, as the lay of the land sloped up, they could see a light from a ranch house. The lonely dim light offered a slight halo over the wooden house. The county road beyond the house ran in its parallel course to the river.

Sophie knew where Tyler was—he was on the river. Maybe in trouble. She said, "I think I'll wait here. See what happens. You go on. Vite." He had to be back at the spot where it happened. She knew it.

Graves said, "Oh, come on. At least to the house. Your folks'll be worried. Tyler will be okay."

Jakes said, "It's getting chilly. With those wet boots," he shook his head, then continued, "a long dark night out here alone without a blanket. This boy you're looking for. I bet he's settled down for the night."

Sophie said, "I thought of that."

They trudged to the ranch house with the slow plodding horses, and came on an empty corral. They went ahead and released the horses in the corral after removing their bridles and saddles, slinging those over the top rail of the corral. Tithe owners wouldn't mind: this was ranch country after all. They shined their lights at the house but couldn't see anything.

Jakes shrugged, waved her along with them. "Come on. You may as well. You don't want to sleep out here without a drop cloth."

"Qu'est ce que sais? 'Drop cloth'? What is 'drop

cloth'?"

The men gulped, waved their flashlights. Graves said, "You're not from around here?"

The two men, maybe in their thirties, seemed healthy, clear, connected. Sophie liked them. They were chuckling over her French. They got to the front of the house before the county road, just as a vehicle's lights far to the south crashed into view at the speed of light. The lights shrieked to say 'hello, here we are', long before raucous engine noise alerted them to the intensity of the oncoming engine. Roaring up the road, closer and closer, a big, growling machine.

Sophie cried, "So loud! Mon dieu!"

Graves said, "Someone's in a hurry. Gotta be law enforcement, huh?"

Jakes said, "No red lights. Maybe somebody looking for someone? Maybe looking for this Tyler, huh? Could be."

Grave said, "Could be. Hey, I don't think anyone's home here."

The barely lit house betrayed no movement. The three exchanged glances, and Jakes pounded on the front door. Nothing. They trotted in place, mini-pacing together on the wooden porch, watching...waiting for the oncoming vehicle.

It was close now. Suddenly its lights went out. It came to an abrupt stop with a screech, its tail end wagging about. The engine roared as it was revved some more. The vehicle buckled and bucked, moved ahead again slowly. No lights. It crept down the middle of the empty road towards them, now standing in front of the ranch house.

Jakes said, "Goof balls! Must have seen our flashlights."

Graves said, "Better see what's up."

Jakes said, "Friends of yours, Sophie? People looking for you?"

"No," said Sophie. "No one's looking for me. Pourquoi?"

The vehicle, a big blue SUV, stopped in front of them.

Jakes called, "Hey, the driver of the SUV—check it out!"

Sure enough, the big blue SUV's driver's window levitated downward and Lise stuck her head out. She giggled, then: "Sophie! I knew we'd find you! Come on! I know where Tyler is. Promise!"

Jakes watched the girl in the SUV with a certain amount of disbelief. What the heck was going on, he wondered. She was so animated, loud as an explosion. She was babbling on to Sophie ...something about 'doubles'...then about a 'circus' that was going to the Duke City, but first they'd have to go through the next town, Coltrane. That's where Tyler had to be. Jakes could see that there was someone else up front, on the passenger side. Finally, another girl leaned over so they could see her in the SUV's interior lighting.

Graves said, "Wow—identical twins."

"Je suis ici, aussi, Sophie. Don't be afraid of this bitch!"

Driver Lise squealed with laughter. "Come on, Sophie. I'll tell you everything. Us doubles, we can do anything. Guess what? Before it was discovered you'd taken off, some deputy got bit on the river by a bear!"

The other Lise said, "Oso? No, oso. Taxidea. Monsieur Badger."

The girls laughed like it was the funniest thing in the world. Then the driver said, "So everyone went over there to help the guy. Boom! Your parents discover you're gone. They go ballistic. I lift my parents' keys! Boom!"

"Voila!" cried the other girl.

The driver said, "Me and Lise knew what we had to do. We knew we would find you. ESPN, man!" She burst into a squall of laughter.

Graves said, "Young lady, are you old enough to be driving?"

Lise yelled, "Lose the goons, Sophie! We're outta here!" She and the Lise on the passenger side went into hysterics.

The driver managed to lisp: "If we'd stayed, Sophie, they would've cut us up like frogs. We had to get out, Sophie. Come on!"

* * *

In the children's room, Neo in buckskin read to the kids from a story book. Aurore sat closely. The little ones quieted. Parents all complained of headaches so they were busy getting prone elsewhere. The kids didn't get headaches. Neo didn't mind the job. She felt compelled to be with the little ones. They were so familiar to her by now. She should have asked the other Aurore if she'd known these kids before. Now they all acted as though they'd known each other for so long. Neo felt undercover. Subterfuge. Fine tuning...she was honing her skills as a girl from another world. Clandestine. She rolled her eyes at the silliness.

Speaking of which: the kids of both worlds loved 'George and Martha'. Adventurous hippos! It got their minds off the other stuff. Neo didn't get headaches. Neither did the other Aurore. They felt charged, taking charge. Well, no one else knew what to do. Is this how adventures worked? Is this what made people interesting and heroic, rising to the occasion of entropy gone wild? They were good with the kids, watching over them eagerly, for signs of—did the kids have powers? Then wouldn't they—the two Aurores, as well? She'd tried to move a hair brush with her mind in the bathroom. No go. She wondered if Tyler and Sophie could. She knew Tyler hadn't been feeling well. She liked this Tyler more than the other Tyler. This Sophie, too, was different but in a good way. She didn't seem as sickly. The thing was this Tyler and Sophie didn't seem to have any sense of school hierarchy. They seemed just like people, not just kids.

She couldn't tell much from the other Aurore. She wasn't sure if she liked the other Aurore. Well, of course she did: it was like looking—living in a mirror. Suppose a person walked around all day holding a mirror up to herself? But then it didn't work: the mirror cracked. This was because they had separate, different assumptions. And the new Aurore was toned, fit, supple. Buff. Neo had never been buff. She didn't even know how to play sports. She was learning the assumptions. Actually, she was getting more familiar with her own assumptions, trying to fathom her double's. She would do her part at this time of entropy. Relations were so subtle, or nuanced, now. No, that wasn't it at all, not a silly make believe: nothing subtle here, it was all in your face action, change, breaks. Ah, the basic assumption was she'd screw it up. Rhapsody of self loathing. If the other Aurore knew this? She would say something about having an open mind, sensitized to the little hints and biases of this other world. Thus, they could navigate. The Aurores were each other, guided by the necessity of the moment. In so being, they moved against the rush of events...sheer, unadulterated entropy. And if the other Aurore found out about her secrets, then navigation would collapse?

She could tell the little guys were tiring. Twins sat together around her on their cots. Some of them had their arms around each other. All the little double faces with subtle differences stared at her with big eyes. Mirror, mirror! The Campbell boys sat closest, their eyes on Neo deepest. Neo paused at the end of the hippo resolution...denouement...and looked back at the Campbells.

They said together, "You drift. We can tell, Aurore."

They pronounced her name perfectly. "You have other things on your mind?"

Aurore smiled. "Bien sur! Besides river horses, you mean? Please call me Neo."

They said quietly so as not to disturb the others, "You know who you are."

"Can you read minds?" asked Aurore.

The Campbells shrugged, "Twins."

They didn't go on to explain. Aurore looked away. Neo, the book down, started to rise. Aurore and Neo knew what they meant.

The Campbells said, "We might should have to sit apart." Suddenly, they looked sad. "Soon, we mean."

"What do you mean?" Aurore crouched down in front of them, close.

The Campbells held out their right hands. The little fists extended index fingers. The index fingers slowly moved together. When they were an inch apart or less, a blue spark snapped between finger tips.

Some of the girls cried out. Had they seen the spark? Had they experienced something this? Neo went to their cots and sat beside them. She snuggled with them. Aurore went to the little boys. She thought it was Thor, who said, "You're brave."

The Campbells got into their cots.

"Sleepy time," said Neo, addressing everyone. "I bet Sophie and Tyler are on their way back right now. And when you wake up, voila! We'll know for sure."

One of the boys, Torve or Thor, a few cots away said, "Leave on a light. I like these lights. They're brighter." They all knew which one he was.

* * *

Aurore and Medea sat outside in the back porch on lawn chairs. They could see twinkling lights from flashlights, far away little blurts of light, rising, falling, twisting, disappearing by the river.

"Look like lightning bugs," mused Medea.

Aurore said, "Fireflies. Flutter byes."

Medea said, "Are you scared?"

Aurore said, "Why am I scared? No. Je suis—I was thinking what's the worst thing I know. The scar-de-ist? The divorce. Yes? Where's my father? That's terrible. This? This is an adventure. C'est exotique!"

Medea grunted out a non-ladylike 'huh'. "The divorce? You're trying to hurt me? Come on! Frenchy, yes, what do you think is happening? Your double is certainly good with kids. You were never that crazy for kids."

"Pretty soon the whole world will look at this place."

"Isn't that bigger than the divorce? I'm surprised you bringing up the divorce. You never want to talk about it."

They were silent, as they both knew that was not true. The flashlight white lights continued to dance. It got cool. No breeze. Very quiet kind of adventure night. Vehicles must have been coming up the drive to the bed and breakfast, for new sounds and lights flashes banged about. The building, or where they were sitting, flattened or filtered the incoming data. The world was a sensory show now. Everything suspect. Everything unusual.

Medea said, "This is our first chance to talk and you bring up the divorce."

Aurore kept still. She might have broken cover. She was glad Medea couldn't see her squirm in the dark. She had to do fast. Switch the subject, convince this mother. She said, "Medea." She said it lazily, as though the three syllables were steps to their closeness, their intimacy. Then: "Pleach."

"'Pleach'?" Medea laughed, said, "Orpiment."

"What's that?" said Aurore, suddenly curious. Then she took back her surprise with a gasp, as she realized it would be out of character for her double.

Medea gasped.

Did she know?

Aurore shivered. She liked this Medea. She wondered if she loved swimming in freshwater springs as much as her mother did.

Medea said, "Can you read my mind? Do you guys have powers? Anything noticed? Would you tell me if you could?"

Aurore said, "Comme ci, comme ca."

Medea blurted, "What if this is some weird government experiment gone horribly wrong? I won't let them separate us. I'm not having headaches." She sniffed, wiped her nose, then rubbed at her eyes.

Aurore said, "I know you will."

Medea said, "Do you want to call your father?"

"They won't allow...communications."

"They'll have to eventually. Too many people are involved. We're not prisoners. They won't be able to cover it up."

A skunk ambled onto the porch about 20 feet from them. It grumbled as it sauntered by, sniffing, fretting with its front feet, that stomped out a slight tom-tom beat. It moved along, checking out every pebble or stick in its path.

Medea said, "Ha! Pretty! Like Flower, right? What's 'pleach'?"

Aurore said, "Polecat! They are no flower, Mama!"

"No, from the movie, silly goose! Now what's 'pleach'?"

Aurore thought about the expression 'movie', like Kino she thought.

CHAPTER 8

All hell broke out when Sophie pulled out the habaneros' plastic bag from her pocket and showed it to Graves and Jakes. It was all bunched up from her pocket so she had to shake it out. They couldn't believe it. It was impossible! Sophie had not seen them too upset before. They did it differently from what she was used to. They said it was too small a weave. Sophie explained it was not woven. Grown more. Like in chemical vats. A petroleum product, she thought. People were always trying to ban them. Graves pulled the bag over his head.

Sophie, pre-med, straight A, debate team captain, student council rep, high school student grew flustered and it came out like this: "Oh, that's real smart. I wouldn't do that if I were you." They acted like children, thought Sophie. She controlled it, got logical: where was Tyler?

Jakes yanked the bag off Graves' head and tossed the flimsy thing on the table before them in the cabin.

Graves popped, "Proof it! You are from an impossible world!"

Jakes made the pronouncement: "People willing bags out of complex chemicals that won't break down."

"Petrol? That's not reasonable," said Graves. It seemed to upset him. His protest voice came out: ."The

Commonweal!"

"This is the bag I held the habaneros in," explained Sophie for the tenth time. Then: "The chiles?"

"I could smell them!" went Graves.

"Habanero from Havana, yes? Well, splendid," said Jakes. "But I never heard of Havana being famous for its chiles."

Graves said, "Chiles from another world. Oh, Sophie, if what you say is true, and now with the kids disappeared, then what? What can it be? What am I gonna do if Jakes switches with another Jakes from the impossible world?"

"It can't work like that," said Sophie, firmly shaking her head. "I really don't think it can."

Graves and Jakes waited for her to explain. They put their hands together in front of themselves, achieving a quiet intent.

Sophie said, "It's not impossible to me. My world, I mean. What is impossible to me is your two wheeled...things, whatever you call them, and your white giraffes, and talking platypus." She waited, watching them. "No? Nothing?"

Graves said, "Pods. They're called pods."

Jakes said, "We have to get you to Peggy. We have to! Graves said, "You know why we call them pods? You know, from pseudo-pods?"

Sophie shook her head.

Graves said, "They're from single celled organisms?"

"The weird tires on those things are single cells?"

Jakes said, "Why do you say it can't work like that? Are there laws we don't know?"

Sophie shook herself, trying to focus, trying to be clear: "I'm tired. Sorry. Okay, see, it's not logical. It's reasonable to assume that whatever has happened follows the same basic laws of physics, cause and effect. Whatever conditions existed that sent us here, aren't going to suddenly pop up on you guys. I don' think?"

"Laws of nature?" said Jakes.

Sophie nodded.

Jakes said, "The laws of nature are not random. They are fixed."

"That's what I'm trying to say."

Jakes said, "Nature is not capricious?"

"What do we do now?" asked Graves.

"What people always do," said Jakes. "Ask questions."

Graves said, "We have to talk to Peggy."

Sophie answered, "Peggy Dreiser, right?"

Jakes said, "It's not too late. I'm going over to Old Duckbill's. See what's up. The whole valley's stirred up. But Old Duckbill will let me know if he's heard anything about your Tyler."

"Maybe where Tyler went?" suggested Graves.

"We have to find him," said Sophie.

"We will." Graves nodded, smiled at her. His bushy eyebrows went up giving him a comical look. Sophie smiled back weakly.

"Yes! Perfect, then, back in a flash!" said Jakes and stood away from the table to make his exit.

"More tea?" asked Graves after Jakes had gone.

"I'm fine, just tired," said Sophie.

They sipped in silence, sitting at the table for several minutes. Sophie wondered if Tyler was ill. Asleep somewhere on the river, curled in a painful ball. She knew they had to stay together. He was her link, her proof that she wasn't crazy. He would be needed to go back when they returned. It just made sense. It was logical. She would not give up. He was from her world. They would do this together. And the Sophie and Tyler from here? Where were they now? They were in their world with their parents?

"You're worried about Tyler?"

"I'm tired." Sophie swallowed. "Sorry."

"Are you sick? Been a trauma, these few days."

Sophie said, "The families on the river must be so worried about their kids. And my parents here, Tyler's, too."

Graves slurped at his tea, nodding. "They know you're here. Safe. We didn't exactly explain the details. But we'll wait until tomorrow to tell them. As for the little ones missing? We'll find them. They can't be far."

"Suppose they aren't far at all? Maybe they're right here. But in the other world we're from? Maybe the other Sophie is right here right now at this exact moment but in my world?" She held up a hand. She opened it, extended her fingers.

Graves was quiet. Slowly, he said, "Sophie, the whole valley is looking, Crots too."

"Why are people afraid of the Crots?"

Graves watched Sophie with a somber expression. She looked away.

Fast, Sophie said, "Do you have police? Law enforcement?"

"When you don't know things like this, it makes me wonder. The Crots? It's a long ago story. But every citizen is in the militia. We are law enforcement."

"What's the nearest town?"

"Coltrane?"

"I remember it! We went through Coltrane to get here. How far is it?"

"Fifty kilometers? You've been there? Waterfall City! Folks come from all over to see the Butterfly Lords."

Sophie couldn't take it anymore. She bowed her head. But Graves was sweet. She wouldn't insult him. She muttered, "What are you talking about? Coltrane I saw was a burned out old mining town. Almost a ghost town."

Graves shook his head. "You're scaring me."

Sophie craned her head up. "How many people live along the river?"

"The Castor? I don't know. Hundreds? Maybe a

thousand. The river is almost 200 kilometers long."

"But there's no villages? Or towns? Or shopping centers?"

"'Shopping centers'?" Graves put both hands on the table in front of him. Palms up, like a supplication. "Sophie, everyone takes of his or her own needs. 'Shopping'?" He shrugged.

Sophie said, "So no consumerism?"

"Don't even know what that means. Like builders? The Crots have assemblies every few kilometers. They're 'centers' for monitoring plus some testing for plastique. But consuming? Not sure—most of the real lab work is done in cities like Prescott and Tubac or Ciudad de Chihuahua."

Sophie was inconsolable. "I never believed in centaurs."

"They don't like that name. They're not centaurs. They're men on steeds. Their heritage is Athabascan. They've gone by many names. Indeh. Dine. Apache. Navajo."

"Indians? Those are Indian names."

"'Indians'? What an odd, old name? I believe that was a name from before the Singularity."

"The Crots are testing, doing all this lab work?"

"Plastique."

"Whom my parents work for here?"

"Everyone works for plastique or leases from them."

Sophie began to shake. "I can't think. I can't take any more."

They were silent, and Sophie settled.

Jakes came bursting through the door with the news: 'Old Duckbill knew! Crots got Tyler. They're taking him to Coltrane to catch the sling. We gotta move fast. First light, we take our pods to Coltrane. We should be able to catch up to them."

Sophie burst, "Why? Why would they do that?"

Jakes was panting, but managed: "To get him to Peggy

Dreiser as soon as possible, which means you have to go too. It would have to be that way. Peggy must be very worried about your presence here."

"Uh-ho," went Graves. "And she can't get away?"

"Why did they take him? Why didn't they ask me to go? Why would Tyler go without me? Why wouldn't he tell me?"

Graves said, "I'd better get some supplies together." Then, he got up from the table and busied himself at the shelves pulling down items.

Jakes caught his breath, went for a drink of water. He drank. He said, "We'll need money."

Graves grunted.

Jakes could tell Sophie was having a hard time accepting the news. He said, "The Crots have a whole other level of information from the animals. Communication. Commies. You know? The Crots must have figured there was no time. They heard something from the animals maybe. Or Peggy. They did it."

Sophie said in a tiny voice, "What does that mean? What kinds of information from the animals? You mean about me and Tyler? How did Duckbill know?"

Graves made a whistling noise, then: "Old Duckbill knows all. Ha, that sounds funny. But he's a watcher, keeping eyes on things. Any of the families find their kids?"

"My parents—they okay?"

"Yes," said Jakes, "they're fine. They know you're here. And, no, none of the kids has been found. But only Your parents expect you tomorrow so." He nodded to Sophie.

She knew what that look meant. They were off to chase down Tyler tomorrow. The parents here—

Jakes said, "Looks like they're putting together the militia. They'll meet with Okla, beef up the borders."

"What are we going to do when we get to Coltrane? Bring Tyler back?"

Graves said, "Young lady, you're going to go with him to see Peggy. She can't get away. You have to. Right, Jakes?"

"Of course."

Graves said, "Only one more question from me, Jakes. Are folks taking bangers?"

"Of course, they'll take bangers," said Jakes.

"What's a 'banger'?" asked Sophie, not liking the sound of that one bit.

* * *

Lu on Tom was explaining to Tyler on Bish that they would head south, take him to Coltrane and put him on a sling for Alburquerque. Not that difficult to catch her words, as she and Tom were ahead of them (they were moving in single file into the desert) and the dry morning breeze blew her words to his ears. He could hear her. He understood her. It was very clear. Lu's words went right on in because he...trusted her? Tyler thought of calling out a question, like 'what's a sling', but had to keep his attention on staying on Bish. He was sore already, his inner thighs red and raw. He found his attention wandering to Lu's slim legs and ankles clasping the sides of Tom's steed. The white tunic or gown she had worn was put aside now. Now she wore a white top of cotton, Tyler assumed, with white cotton pants, moccasins.

Tyler knew they were heading away from the river. This was the fastest way to Coltrane? Tyler didn't think so. Coltrane was to the north and east. Why were they heading south? The high desert grasslands gave way to an alkali plain that held the occasional creosote or agave. Other cactus, too. Some grasses and low weedy vines. Tyler knew *Opuntia*, with the big beaver tail pads. He suddenly felt weak, forcing his hold on the ropes lashed around his mount. He held tightly. Tied to the ropes were stuffed cloth bags and leather pouches, also stuffed. Other equipment was tied on as well: metal rods, a bow, a quiver of arrows, a small shovel. They weren't moving that fast. But Tyler was not used to horseback riding at all. If it wasn't for Lu's occasional word or sound, he wouldn't have held on. He would have given up. The way he felt he didn't know if he could go on, he knew he would go on, and he wanted to spend more time with Lu. He'd never get used to riding. He called to Lu: "What's a 'sling'?"

Bish interrupted the exchange: "Right now, focus on where we're going. We head south because the Mexicans will think we've gone east. They'll assume we head straight to Coltrane. This way we'll circle Whitewater, reconnoiter with jaegers, and you'll get to Coltrane faster than anyone. The sling doesn't leave until tomorrow."

Tyler tried to focus. What was necessary right now besides holding on? "I'd feel better if Sophie was with us. I don't know what I'm supposed to do with Peggy."

Bish said, "It's what she's to do with you."

Lu called, "Sophie will be fine. You'll see. Old Duckbill has set things in motion. Graves and Jakes—you know them?"

Tyler sputtered, "Yes, we met them when we got here. When we first got here."

Bish said, "Enough talk. Focus."

Tyler wondered if Bish was some kind of leader. He seemed older than the others. They treated him with respect. But either way conversation with Lu was cut short.

The steeds were wide but short. Bigger than ponies, smaller than horses, the hindlegs were massive, muscular. The front legs merged with the rider's. The rider's moved with the steed's legs. Tyler's eyes went back to Lu's legs in leggings, the moccasins on her small feet. But Bish went, "Giddy up!" and they launched into a canter, with Bish moving up and around Lu and Tom, taking the lead.

Tyler couldn't tell if they were on a road or simply some animal path. What could live out here away from the river? This time of year was not too hot, the sun not too killer bright. Yet. And his question was eventually answered as they saw south of them a smudge of green. Where there was green, there must be water.

"An oasis. We must be near the border," commented Tyler.

Lu guffawed from behind. That's all Tyler could think to call the sound she made. He didn't dare turn around. He held on. He imagined her strong legs neatly curled around her mount. She was a natural rider. Tyler was sore. She called up, "No border near here!" He watched the green smudge get bigger—

"The border's 400 kilometers that way," said Bish. "No time for a geography lesson right now. You and Peggy can talk all you want later when we get you there. The first seep is coming up. We're almost to Whitewater."

Tom added, "No one would expect us to come this way." He snickered.

Bish tsked him. Still, he went on to explain: "This is where we have a lot of Mexican incursions. So it was a toss-up. Take a chance, get there early. That's what we're doing."

Tom said, "They think the wide open, the alkali, the flats, is empty, they figure they can penetrate. But we know. We keep an eye on things. They will not be expecting us to come this way."

Tyler concentrated on staying on his mount. He could hold onto the ropes. He could hold onto the steed's scruffy mane. He could lock his legs. That was awkward and ended up hurting. He couldn't do it any of those things for long.

The oddest thing happened to Tyler's eyes when they approached the green smudge, which turned out to be brush and small trees. The visual translation transitioned to vegetation made him think he could see in farther, deeper. It had him hopeful. His eyes were acute, so he couldn't be that sick. This was a small oasis? But the probe of his eyes seemed to fasten on then highlight a big brown blur standing in the green, standing up to a tree, big heavy front paws pulling down branches, to a massive, melon head with a tongue that could be a boa constrictor it was so thick. Yes, he could focus better. He had to see it clearly through the blur. What was he seeing? His eyes took it in: a thick heavy tail from the creature's bottom, no doubt aiding its balance. Suddenly, into sharp focus: and Tyler knew what it was. It was a giant ground sloth.

Too large to be a man. No, he wasn't mistaken. It was way too hairy to be a man. Not a bear. Didn't feel right for a bear. Didn't focus right: the proportions of this blur were nothing but megafauna muscle symmetry. More marvels, thought Tyler. More monsters! Not a bear's at all—what was happening to his eyes? Sun stroke? The sun wasn't that bright yet. It was a giant ground sloth. Was he seeing things? Had he been seeing things all along? Would that take in account why he was riding across the desert on a centaur? No, on a steed!

When they were close enough, Tyler knew it was a giant ground sloth standing up on its tremendous back legs to have at the green branches of the trees. Tyler couldn't hold back: "Ground sloth!" he whickered. The beast continued to stuff its maw with leaves and twigs. It didn't bother to glance at them, so consumed by its feeding.

"A beauty. We'll go around it," said Bish. "This is the first seep of Whitewater. And him here, it's a good sign. No intruders lately, that's for sure. We'll get to the bigger ponds where the jaegers gather. Make a camp. It's going to get plastic now. From here on."

"It's a giant ground sloth," whispered Tyler. All the picture books he had ever studied as a kid of the Age of

Mammals in ancient America came to mind. Megafauna! Then all the web pages and Internet sites which included films of the giant creatures as they must have looked. He'd seen them CGI style. Now real life, right in front of him...style. They'd been extinct—what? Eight thousand years? Ten? Unless they didn't go extinct here. Or else plastique brought them back? Is that what they do?

It was so big and strange looking. Its limbs, its head, its neck were...thick.

Tom added, "Fast change, yeah. Watch for quicksand."

Tyler implored out loud, "But what is a giant ground sloth doing here?"

"Well, they like to forage at the seeps. Not many of them left," said Bish.

Tom said, "The plan was to re-introduce the ancient predators and prey, but not all of the species wanted to come back."

Tyler couldn't turn back to look at Tom, to wonder what the heck he was talking about.

Lu said, "Project Lazarus."

Quickly, Tyler went, "You have Jesus?'

Bish said, "Of course we have Jesus. Come."

They made a wide arc around the small oasis with the giant ground sloth. Tyler couldn't tell what else was beyond the brush, back in there. Was there a pond back there? Must have been! Then south of them the horizon seemed dotted with green. They moved on, Tyler reeling. The green dots became green oasis with bigger trees. It was easy to see the oasis islands of green were getting bigger.

Pretty soon a Crot appeared from one of the nearest green islands. He stepped out of the green and waved, then galloped to them. Bish and Tom waited for him to approach.

"Gomps," panted the Crot.

"How many?" said Bish.

The Crot was bare-chested as the others, with thick black hair held in by a headband. He was out of breath, slipping his bow over his shoulder as he had held it to the side running over. The Crot said, "Family of four."

Bish grunted.

Tom said, "Well, hello to you, too, Moss!"

Bish said, "La chasse?"

The Crot whose name was Moss said, "Hey, Tom. Hey, Lu. Yeah, there are hunters around."

Bish said, "You know why we're here."

Moss nodded. "This is the boy?"

Tyler puffed out his breath. "I'm Tyler."

Moss went on, "Well, the good news I told you. The bad?"

Bish said, "We knew it was perfect."

Moss continued, "We got sign. Scouts to the south say Mexicans."

"Tanks?" went Bish.

Moss nodded. "Zest! We know how to handle this. No batty fang here, brother. They want an anointing, we know how to bang it."

Tom sighed, nodding. "Perfect."

Moss explained, "This is the corridor they come up. Testing us. They think they're testing us. They send in spies. They don't seem to put two plus two together, that this is where we want them to come in. Some folks just can't see a hole in a ladder. They want plastique of course. Blood samples. Everyone wants plastique. Something for nothing. No, not through here they won't. Bottom face now: we figure they're real curious about him." He pointed to Tyler.

Bish said, "Don't be shinning for a fight. Scoot when you can. Scoop when you can't. You know what they say. You got word back?"

"Of course," said Moss.

"How many scouts out here now?" asked Bish.

"Maybe 20. It's a cat and mouse game. They come up. We appear. They fall back. But they ain't meaters. So far. So far we've had few problems. Well, I mean, nothing we can't deal with."

"So far," said Bish.

Tyler said, "How could they know about me?"

The Crots stared at Tyler.

Bish said, "We're camping out this way for the night. See who shows up. We'll find a spot. Then out of here first light. Tank traps set?"

"Perfect," went Moss. "You'll get 'im to Coltrane. Don't worry that." Moss stepped backward, turned sideways. "Back on patrol!" He waved a hand to them. "Good to see you out at Whitewater, Lu!" Moss grinned broadly at her. Lu smiled and waved. He galloped back to the green island he had come from.

Bish said, sighing, "Another hour. We have plenty light. We'll get out among the jaegers, set up camp."

They road on another hour, until Tyler was so sore he'd turned in to a bright smear of mute pain. Tyler watched as the Crots 'dismounted' from their steeds. There was enough light to see it clearly. They strung elaborate ropes and harnesses to hold their steeds up by trees. Tom and Bish completed the odd task. Lu had dismounted and was pulling away bags and pouches of supplies. Soon she had a fire going.

Their camp was by a large pond surrounded by trees and reeds. The reeds indicated where the mushy ground started. They avoided the reeds and kept to the high ground. The shoreline, almost a beach, sandy not mushy, already had other campers. Crots were camped nearby. As the last of the dusk light gave way, Tyler saw tarps strung from trees, unfurled bedding. The Crots greeted Tyler's group with friendly calls and gestures.

Tyler said to Tom and Bish as they came to the fire: "Do you have to feed them?"

Tom said, "The steeds?" He explained, "They're born complete. But we water and feed them as needed."

Bish said, "Plastique grows them."

"I know, I mean I see. I guess," said Tyler. "And you're plastique?"

Tom and Bish looked at each other and smiled. Tom said, "We're Crot. Let's eat!"

Bish looked at Tyler quizzically: "What? Did you think we were landlords? Or splicers?"

Lu had managed to get the fire under control and ready for a grill to be placed over it. She had a couple metal pans on the grill already, their contents bubbling cheerily.

Tyler nodded slowly. It hurt to move. He was sore all over, but especially his chafed thighs. Gingerly, he found a spot near the fire but out of the way of the others. Tom and Bish had a comical, somewhat duckish, style of sauntering around. Were they sore, too? Tyler was too tired to laugh or feel embarrassed. Bish finally noticed Tyler's obvious anguish.

Bish said, "Not used to riding?"

"I never rode before in my life," said Tyler.

Tom went, "Ow!"

Bish said, "You have to get to Peggy Dreiser. Sorry, but that's clear. We'll find a jaeger. So no more riding for you."

"We hope," went Tom.

Bish snorted. He said, "Signs. Aren't. Good."

"What do you mean?" asked Tyler. "Why do you say this? Shouldn't Sophie be with me?"

Bish said, "We know your parents. Everyone agrees."

Tyler exhaled harshly. He found he was shaking. "My parents agree? My parent here, you mean?"

Bish grunted, nodding.

Tyler went on: "I thought people didn't like Crots? I'm sorry, I don't know what I'm saying. It's just that I thought...the Anglos...were suspicious of you."

"What an amazing thing to say," said Lu.

Tom laughed. "There ain't no English 'round here. Well,

not that we know of—"

Bish said, "Ahh, you thought we were landlords of the people along the river. No, no. There is some resentment, fear based on old stories." He shook his head. "No, something happened couple days ago that does not happen. We're all in this now. It affects all of us. So. Maybe what happened was not supposed to happen. This is—it brought you here. We think the Tyler and Sophie from here are wherever you were."

"How do you know? How could that be?"

Tom said, "Can't you feel it? The tension in the air? Prickles in the way the world moves now?" He gasped. "It feels complicated and sticky. It feels abrupt. Can't you hear it? The whooshing in your ears, slightly off from before? Not right. Not perfect at all. The animals know."

Lu pulled the pans from the grill awkwardly with a cloth but didn't spill much. She dished up in small bowls, handed them out. The 3 Crots pulled out small wooden spoons from pockets or belt bags. Tom and Bish had their spoons in their side pouches, while Lu's came from her shirt. Tyler could see she had a leather pouch hanging under the front of her shirt. They started eating. Tyler watched. Everything they did fascinated him. He felt like a little kid just waking up to the world. It was exhilarating and scary and new.

He said, "You mean like the way animals know before an earthquake?"

Bish and Tom and Lu seemed to ignore him. But maybe it was the light? Maybe they didn't see him clearly, or he didn't see their body language response? Maybe his tired eyes had seen too much? They kept eating, the food still hot, so lots of blowing and stirring. Tyler bet that each one of them carved his or her own spoon.

"Did I say something stupid?" asked Tyler.

Still no response. Then, Lu said softly, "When we eat, we eat. When we talk, we talk."

Tyler said, "At Graves and Jakes' place they had some kind of communication device to call for Peggy Dreiser. I think they called it a 'commie'? That's how they knew she was in Albuquerque."

Bish lowered his spoon. "That's Alburquerque."

Tyler continued, "So you have communication to send word, to keep in touch, so everyone knows what's going on? Like telegraph?"

Lu said, "I don't understand where you are going or where you're from when you talk this way. What are you doing?"

Tyler said, "Don't you have some kind of electronic communication? Can't we...call Sophie? Or Graves and Jakes?"

Tom shook his head, said, "Those are inertial."

Lu said, shaking her head, "Doesn't work that way."

Tyler said, "Inertia?" He swallowed, reached for his food again. It was still warm. He didn't feel like eating. He shook his head, almost said something, thought better of it. He tried his soup or stew and found it tasty. Suddenly, he was hungry.

Bish said, "Mexico, Aztlan, they trust electronics."

"So do Americans," said Tom, slurping.

Tyler paused from eating and said, "What about radio? Do you have radio? Or walkie-talkies?"

Lu and Tom giggled, liking the latter's name.

"Radio," said Bish. "We have radio."

Tom said, "Radio is everywhere. Invisible force. The field how inertia works."

Bish said, "Mexico has electronics, wires everywhere."

Lu said, "They move away from inertia, so away from the lessons of the Singularity."

Tom said, "Americans love electronics. And the

French? They are feu feu over electronic gizmos."

Tyler said, "What about computers?" They didn't respond so he added, "How do you handle information?"

Lu said, "Oh, I know what you mean! Difference engines. Information devices. And you are asking how do we move information around and store it?"

"Right!" cried Tyler.

"Plastique," said Bish. "We turned on the animal net work a long time ago. So we could send and receive information."

"Old Duckbill stores it for us," added Lu.

"The animals are your computers?" said Tyler.

Lu giggled and Tom followed suit. They were like kids terribly embarrassed at some impossibly naïve kid.

Bish came on strong: "Enough for now. Eat. Rest. We'll be up before light. Lu, do you have anything for his soreness?"

Tom said, "Lu's our herbalist."

Lu got up from her place by the fire and went to the saddle bags. It was dark now but she had enough light to find what she was looking for. She came over to Tyler, sat beside him. He saw by the fire light she had a button...no, a disc of wood it looked like. A small round container like people in his world used for lip balm.

"Yes," she said, "let me help. Pantaloons."

"What?" went Tyler.

Tom said, "Take off your pants so she can put on the salve."

Tyler scooted away from his place by the fire. "I can do it

myself," he said. He said it too fast so they knew he was scared.

He was scared of Lu's straight forwardness. He reached out his arm to Lu who handed him the button. Tyler took it, fussed with it to see how it opened, saw the top unscrewed. He managed to get to his feet, stood wobbly, and limped a few paces into the dark to apply it to his aching thighs.

The stuff smelled funny and was a bit greasy but it did seem to help right away. The burning cooled. His raw skin felt better, but he still ached deep in screaming muscles. He thought he could stretch now, extend his legs. He might be able to sleep.

Tom was cleaning the dishes, putting away supplies. Lu sat by the fire smoking a pipe. Bish had already settled down, stretching out on his blankets.

Tyler found the pads and blankets that Lu had indicated were for him. He fell to a prone position, then he fell into darkness, a deep darkness that promised rest. He was too tired. For a second, he did flash on Sophie. But he knew she was safe with Graves and Jakes. She must be wondering what the heck happened to him. Then he flashed, what the heck was he going to say to this Peggy Dreiser? He had no idea what was going on, what had caused this, whatever it was. But no more thoughts were permitted in the soothing dark. He felt himself go away.

Lu's face was in his ear. She smelled of girl and herbs and something sweet. He felt her breath. She said, "We move! Now! No sound or bother. Come with me now."

Tyler thrust himself up on his arms. The pain in his legs shot right back. "What's going on?" Still dark, Tyler barely could make out Lu before him, her hand extended to him. The fire had died down. Motion all around! Crots saddling up or whatever they called it. Vague shapes, horse bodies with men, moved in and out of the dark.

Lu helped him to his feet. "Can you ride?" asked Lu.

"We have to," said Tyler. "What's happening?"

"Mexicans!" hushed Lu. Then: "Close. Too close. The scouts got traps around here, but still—Bish wants us out of here. We have to find the hunters. We get out now. Before there's trouble. Put some of the salve on."

Tyler heard steeds clattering off in various directions.

The dark and cool pre-dawn made the sounds grow then dissolve. Lu's tone made him realize it might be dangerous.

Lu was pulling together supplies, bagging it all up. She said, "Bish and Tom are mounting. We pack supplies, we're with them."

Tyler tried to help with the pads and blankets. She had her own way of rolling things to compact them. They thrust the supplies into satchels and saddle bags. They hauled them in the dark to Bish and Tom ready to go. Lu tied on the bags in the proper fashion. Tyler and Lu got astride their mounts. No flashlights. No lights of any kind. Just activity, certain and sure doing what it must.

Bish said, "We're off!" He trotted from the camp. Tyler held on. Tom kept alongside, Lu atop him. They moved on a trail away from the water and brush. Pretty soon they were into the open desert.

Tom said, "They may need our help."

Bish may have been about to say something. Tyler wanted to ask what was going on.

A Crot clambered up to them. The man said, "Bish, they're close. Closer than expected."

Bish said, "You can lead us out of here, Mantel? You know where the jaegers are?"

"Follow me!" cried Mantel.

Bish and Tom and the new Crot trotted off in single file. The sky was a black dome broken up by fierce stars. Tyler held on, trotting harsh to his thighs. He assumed they were crossing the open lands between seeps to get to the next seep. They kept up their trot. The black sky lightened. Tyler couldn't tell for sure.

Ahead, light? Hard to tell. Artificial light? He wasn't sure. Maybe they were moving east? Faint shapes ahead too. Couldn't make them out. Maybe it was dawn? Maybe his eyes were adjusting. After the vision of the giant ground sloth, his eyes might have...enhanced? That's just crazy! He had to keep it here—

They pulled up to a rocky outcropping. It was a ridge of earth and sand and gravel, maybe 30 or 40 feet long. In spots nearby, creosote had accumulated enough debris to make tussocks. A couple Crots were already there. They had the light. But it was not a flash light, but the odd misty glow device like Graves and Jakes had had in their cabin. The Crots exchanged greetings. They all knew each other. The Crots had other devices: metal rods fit together to form tongs. Of course, bows in their hands, quivers with arrows across their backs. Everyone huddled close without talking. Lu stood up on Tom's back to peer over the ridge.

Bish whispered to Tyler, "We rode right into them. We didn't foresee this. Sorry. I should have led. I should have suspected."

Lu said, "Tank's coming!"

One of the new Crots mumbled, "Too late."

Bish said, "Come on, Elve, not that bleak. Trap around here?"

The Crot Elve replied, "Over that way."

"And the hunters?" asked Bish.

Both of the Crots nodded, pointing to the east.

Bish moved up close enough to the outcropping so that Tyler, too, could stretch and see over the ridge. He saw that the land beyond fell away in a sweeping, slightly down curve like a shallow bowl. He couldn't see much detail. Rocks, gravel, dead brush. And coming straight up this course, a white light. Definitely a light. Not one of the fuzzy glow lights of the Crots, but what looked like a genuine incandescent light to Tyler.

Tom and Bish reached behind themselves for their own metal rods. Tom lay his bow nearby with a couple arrows. The other Crots all held their tong-like metal rods ready. The metal rods pinched at the end around blue discs about 8 inches across. One of the Crots from the outcropping sped off to the right, to the west into the dark. It was the one Bish had addressed as Elve.

They watched the incandescent light advance. The tank? The tank crept closer. Tyler realized it must be a small tank. Maybe the size of a mid-sized car. Now Tyler could make out the underpinning of the vehicle, what it rode on. It was a large rubbery, flowing mass, no wheels or treads at all. It was similar to what the 2 wheeled devices of Graves and Jakes used for wheels. Now, too, he could see that the front end, illuminated by the incandescent light, held 2 long rods pincered around a blue gray disc, but this disc was three or four times the size of the Crots'. Where a normal tank would have its cannon mounted, tongs.

A shriek sounded and the Crot who had sped off came out of the dark from the west of the tank and galloped right in front of it. The Crot held one of the long tong like affairs. The Crot swung his arm back then whipped it forward hard. There was a loud 'bang!' and the turret of the tank glistened momentarily. The Crot was past the tank now and hightailing it up a rising dune of sand and gravel to the east.

Crots cheered, yelling, "Schnell!" and, "Vite!"

"Well done, Elve!" called Bish.

The tank's turret scrolled around, stopped. Rods whipped back and forth then a huge 'bang' sounded. A sandy patch near Elve's hindlegs blew up in glittering light. He kept going. The Crot was over the dune and out of sight.

The tank's turret swung back and forth, first aimed at the dune then at the outcropping. The tank edged toward the dune. It moved slowly, carefully. Tyler realized the bulgy material the tank rode on may not have been good in sand. The tank hesitated. Growling, it made metallic whirring sounds. It continued. Slid. Maybe it couldn't navigate sand?

Bish yelled, jerking forward. Tyler clung to the ropes. Tom and Bish and the other Crots all trotted out from the outcropping and charged the tank, swinging back their tongs. Bangs followed, then all around or on the tank, glittering patches burst.

The tank came to a stop. Now it was at an odd angle on the dune, but it had to turn its turret to respond to the barrage coming from behind. The tank moved sideways, the turret swinging over. And the more sideways it moved, the faster it seemed to slip. It was slipping! Sliding? The tank rolled over on its side in the sand. The trap worked! They always do. The ballooning underpinning boiled in heaving waves trying for a grip.

The Crots yelled and whooped. One word was clear in Tyler's ears: "Enfilade."

Bish backed away, called for Tom. More Crots were galloping up. One called out, "Perfect, Bish!"

Bish grunted, then to the Crots: "We have to go. We were lucky. We have to get this boy out of here."

A Crot scout from the south joined the group, panting miserably. He pointed to the south. "Another tank coming, heading this way. And a truck."

Bish said, "They'll pull this one out of the sand. Then they'll crawl out of here with their tails between their legs."

The Crots laughed and jeered. Bish said, "We're off at dawn, just like I said we would. We can't put this boy in any more danger."

Bish and Tom rode away, moving east. Tyler hung on, not knowing what to expect. But morning light now. He began to see his surroundings more clearly. He could see they were approaching another green area. Another oasis? A seep? When all at once hippos (it looked like) came charging from that green area towards them.

Tom yelled, "Gomps!"

Tyler realized they were not hippos at all. Three of

them! Hippo sized—well, not as fat, the 3 animals, 1 large, 2 smaller, squealed in rage or fear when they saw the Crots. They did a wide swing around, u-turning back to the green seep. Tyler saw they looked more like tapirs maybe, but not as tall. Big, brown, with little hair, and elongated heads. Mini-trunks?

Gomps!

Now, just as the gomps made it back to the green, a big boxy container on real wheels with tires exploded out of the brush and trees nearby. The larger gomp and one of the smaller ones zigzagged away, disappearing in the green. The third one, a smaller one, made the mistake of reversing itself and tearing away almost as fast as a horse to the Crots and the open desert. Tyler finally understood that the big container was the back part of a truck that was continuing to back up, chasing after the gomp in reverse.

The truck and gomp passed the Crots and appeared to be heading right back to the outcropping.

Bish said to Tyler, "Your ride."

Lu said, "The botany that infernal device obliterated!"

Bish said, "You can botanize later. We'll follow to the kill site." They trotted after the hunters' truck and gomp, back the way they had come.

The gomp had slowed down and so had the truck. The truck stopped when the gomp did. The gomp stumbled, almost fell. It was exhausted, terrified. A man swathed in gear appeared from the back of the truck. Tyler couldn't see from where he looked how the man had gotten out of the truck. He held a large set of tongs, whipped them back and hurled them forward so that a loud bang cracked the morning as the gomp's head exploded.

"Chasseur," said Tom. The man waved to the Crots. Tom whispered, "Now, that's a banger!"

Bish said, "No trouble. Go."

Tom and Bish sauntered to the downed gomp. The

hunter was inspecting his kill. The Crots were cautious, suspicious, auspicious. When they were close enough, the man said, "Well, ruined the head, so there's that. But a few hundred pounds of meat for sure. This the boy?"

Tyler could appreciate now that the truck looked like an RV, like with a camper on its bed. It took him another moment to comprehend that this RV was set up backwards. Instead of the engine and cab up front, the tall camper was up front and the cab was in the back. So the engine was in back too? The truck hadn't been backing up the whole time at all.

Bish said, "Yes. You're good for Coltrane?"

The hunter said, "Clean and bag: we're done."

The 'camper's' front was as big as a garage door and like a garage door it had rolled up. Tyler could feel frigid air puffing out of the back. Condensation made little clouds. The hunter went up to the 'camper' and hopped in. He disappeared for a moment, then came back holding a hook on some kind of rail hanging from the top. He pulled the hook attached to a heavy chain down, then jumped from the truck, the chain dragging behind him. He set about hooking the massive beast, then fussed with a control pad dangling from wires in the corner of the trailer. The chain pulled taut then slowly raised the creature.

Tyler must have looked puzzled by the whole thing, gomp, vehicle—

Bish said, "Culling."

The hunter said, "How does it look?"

Bish said, "Mexicans already today. You'll have to be careful."

The hunter nodded, watching his prey. "We know that," he said.

When the gomp was raised by its back legs off the ground, the hunter pulled from his side a long thin blade. He eviscerated the beast and the guts plunged forth. He cut off the remains of the head.

The Crots sighed, puffed.

The hunter said, busy with his blade, "You gotta get the scent glands right away."

Bish seemed irritated and made a downward motion with his hand.

The hunter said, "We got our quota. We're done here. I'm satisfied. We got 4 tons of meat. It's back to Coltrane for us." He watched Bish's face and realized the Crot was tense. He watched the Crots staring at him. "We're done here. No problem. We're on our way."

He touched the control pad and the carcass moved up and was pulled in the back of the trailer. Then he walked away from the hanging, bleeding carcass and to the side of the refrigerated shell. He banged on its wall, shouting, "Back! Back!" They were still watching him with what could only be called suspicion. "I had to let my driver know. She's set. No worry."

The ponderous, backwards, RV/truck on big real tires backed up, carcass swinging. The hunter followed. The truck swung around, now its trailer faced to the east. The hunter turned back to the Crots, came back to them, and said, "Bish, right? We've met. I'm Kai. Kai Schubert, American hunter. We'll get your boy loaded."

Bish looked to Tom, their eyes locked. Then Bish glanced his eyes over to Lu. Lu said, "They'll be in Coltrane long before. I have to go."

Bish grunted. Tom said, "Lu, I'll come along behind you, to pick you up in Coltrane for the ride home. I won't be long. You can count on me."

Bish said, "Tyler, you go with the hunters."

Tyler was a mess. His legs ached. He was trembling with excitement and fear and disgust. The smell of blood overflowed everything. He had never been in a war. He no longer could think straight. His mind was at war with his senses. He had seen far too much that was impossible. He slid, fell, slobbed off the side of Bish's mount. Lu was at his side, kneeling by him quickly.

Lu said, "He's going into shock."

Kai Schubert said, "Ahh, neither fish nor fowl."

Bish said to Lu, "Take care of him. We'll talk to the hunters."

Tyler was underwater with hippos all around him. No, they were tanks. No, they were gomps. So blue, it seemed the sky and water had traded places. This is death, then, he imagined briefly. Terrified, he tiptoed back to consciousness: not even in my own world? Not even knowing what was happening? What was going on? He had to know what was happening before he died. It made perfect sense. Lu had some leaves out, which she'd pulled from a bag at her waist. She rolled the leaves with the palms of her leaves.

"Quid," she said, "chew these."

Tyler had no clue, but did what he was told.

Bish and Tom stood by the hunter, but their eyes were on the outcropping. Several Crots had taken up positions behind the rock outcropping where Tyler and the others had stood. But, too, they crouched behind tussocks and really any protuberance that might be used for cover. Their eyes were to the south: another tank approached. The blue shaded south quickly lighting up. Same front light, same size, same rods on turret. Small tanks. On blubber bottoms. Maybe like a hovercraft? When it got close enough, its metal rods went whipping back and forth, lobbing off blue lit explosions on the rock outcroppings, or any sandy bump that hid a Crot. The Crots returned fire. A couple arrows banged into the tank and bounced off. The tank slowed its assault as it neared the stuck tank. Care in the sand! The Crots, too, quit banging out their meaningless explosions on the tank, but they continued their screeches and war cries. From its side a grappling hook on a chain shot out. The hook jammed right into a seam of the floundered tank. The chain got taut and the tank started pulling it out.

Bish said, "Kai Schubert, you catch us at a turning point. We have to stay to help the others. But we have that boy. The one on the ground there, who needs to get to Coltrane as fast as possible to get today's sling. He must be kept safe, free of the Mexicans."

Kai Schubert seemed satisfied, nodding to Bish. He said, "Our license's been extended? This isn't our war." He smiled. He started to remove some of his outer garments, tossing them in to the trailer. The tong like device had been laid to the side. He turned to Bish. "He's sick?"

"No," said Bish. He paused a few seconds. "He's having an adjustment."

Tom had his eyes on the hunter's tong. "Is that a Bozko Banger? One of the new ones?"

"In America, they're perfectly legal," said Kai Schubert fast.

"Legal enough to pulverize that gomp's head," said Tom.

Bish said, "You'll get him to Coltrane so he can catch the sling. Lu will go, too, and be responsible for him."

"I'll talk to my driver," said Kai. "We'll be out of here before that other tank is out of its trap."

Bish nodded. Tom thanked him. They trotted away to the outcropping.

Tyler sat up. Lu helped him, then kept her hand on his. Lu's other hand stroked his head.

He said, "That feels good. I'm sorry. I think I panicked." He shuddered, went on, "That animal had a lot of guts."

She said, "A Gomphothere. A gomp."

"What else do you have here?"

"Dog faced bear? Camels? Giraffes?"

Tyler shook his head, forcing a smile. "Thanks, Lu."

She said, "Can you walk?"

"Yes."

"We're going for a ride. But no horses."

They stood. Tyler released her hand from his. They heard cries from the Crots. They turned—

Now a truck drove into view from the south. It had no lights on, though it had headlights on a front end that looked like every other truck Tyler had seen. Behind the cab with driver at the steering wheel was a large cargo bed covered by earth-colored canvas. It looked like canvas. The truck looked pretty much like every Army truck Tyler'd ever seen. Army trucks like this carried soldiers—

Tyler looked at Lu. Lu looked back. Neither had ever seen such a thing unfold.

Lu moved with Tyler, trying to help him, but he shook her off. He shuffled, limped his way to the hunter's trailer.

The Crots held their fire, jeering all the while. They would allow the tank to pull up its comrade, then they would be set on their way. But the truck was different. Back up? Reinforcements? They hadn't seen a truck like this up here at Whitewater before.

Soldiers came out of the back of the stopped truck. In two groups of seven each, soldiers hustled single file down both sides of the truck to the front. They made a line there, where they stood between the truck and the outcropping and the tanks. Their heavy tan uniforms smudged them blurry in the dawn desert light. They looked thick and cumbersome. Tyler couldn't make out their faces. They cradled weapons in their arms, not rods or tongs with blue discs. To Tyler, they looked like rifles.

Bish hollered loud as he could: "Projectiles!"

Kai Schubert came around the truck to Lu and Tyler. Lu had her pack and bags of supplies. Tyler had no idea when she'd managed to get them.

Kai Schubert went, "Greetings! You're coming with us now. I want you both to jump up here with me. It's cold but we've got coats if we need 'em. We'll move up front soon as we can. Right now, we have to go."

Kai, Tyler, and Lu climbed into the refrigerated hold as the Mexican soldiers opened fire. Immediately there were screams, then bangers let loose. More gunshots. Kai pounded on the wall of the cold compartment, until the truck lurched forward. Kai yelled to Tyler and Lu: "Don't look! Don't look!"

In the dawn light that changed from blue to gold, Crots were dying, lethally punctured with high tech ballistics that went right through rocky outcroppings. So the Crots were not fools, and they fled their positions to gallop in all directions, knowing that to survive must mean confuse the shooters with too many moving targets. A Crot named Moss led 2 other Crots in a mad dash to break up the soldiers' line. They charged in firing arrows and blue bangs. A couple soldiers fell. The Crots wouldn't let up with banger and bow. Gunfire wiped them out.

* * *

Sophie clung to Graves' leather belt, on the pod smoothly racing up the gravel/dirt road east of the river. It was a main thoroughfare for the area, following the landscape rising with the contour of the river valley. It was high desert grassland now, sacaton grasses Tyler had taught her. They were heading east, to the mountains, Puertos de los Mulas, where Coltrane lived. They'd left the river, passed the Crot assembly. Sophie learned they were not centaurs, when she saw the women. And when she saw the...unattached men.

Because the pods made little noise, they could talk. At least try to. It's not quite accurate to say the pods made *no* noise. Sophie finally learned that the faint buzz she'd assumed was a vibration from the pod's movement of the cellular 'wheels' was actually some kind of static from it. That's what Graves explained to her. She was feeling inertial system reticence. She was feeling inertia. Of course all life forms could feel inertia. Graves was shocked to hear she had no clue what he was talking about. They talked about both of their worlds. What Sophie told them, upset them. What Graves and Jakes told Sophie, confused her as it seemed impossible.

Sophie wondered when she'd wake up. She'd pledged to herself, control. She wasn't going to lose it. She wasn't kidnapped for goodness sakes. She was waylaid. She was lost. But she, also, was a smart and diligent student. She was trained: she had to see the situation clearly. Analyze! That's the way to understand, isn't it? Observation? Assessment? This desert world—

Now it was bleak, white, hellish desert. Away from the river and green belt, everything seemed white, or gray. What did she see? What could she learn? She thought of her mother's fondness for white gold jewelry, how the desert color matched this white gold luster. She saw how the air moved over the desert in little puffs, tiny outbursts of dust in white and gray. It happened all around her, tussles of desert rose up in gusts, spun, settled back to the ground. Dust devils! Like mini-tornadoes. They had those in St. Louis but not so mini. She watched the desert breathe, she thought. She saw that the view, its alienness, pulled at her—

In America, in St. Louis, the green, the forests, the streams and lakes, were up close. Right in her face. Intimate. The presence of green life so near and familiar. Comfortable. Even though it did seem to push at her.

The opposite here. Nothing pushed close. And it better not—Sophie thought, 'thorns'. No water, little humidity. Green, now, a dream in the distance, of back at the river. So her senses reached out. She observed thick bunches of sacaton. Then patches of brush—thorny bushes, green, gray, black. Mesquite, she recognized. Some had yellow catkins, like fuzzy caterpillars hanging from the branches. The mesquite emerged from the cracked earth in 2 or 3 twisty trunks. There was agave. She knew agave because her father had mentioned how it was used in the making of tequila. Bunny ears she recognized, then barrel cactus.

The valley was wide. They were heaving up, inertially ascending the eastern half of the wide bowl. In all directions, mountains. This wasn't just a view, it was an awareness of space: the mountains did not make walls, they made open invitations to understand the land changed. Must have been volcanoes? Up thrusts from down deep. Geology! The grand sweep was familiar to Sophie because it was pretty much identical to what she'd seen in her world...at the bed and breakfast.

She heard birds. She was clinging to anything recognizable. She knew the crow and the quail. Graves had identified quail calls for her. So this place was familiar. This place was not another planet. It was a dream? It was a vision? She thought of that boy, Tyler. She thought of school and her parents back at the bed and breakfast. Kept coming back to her. She couldn't keep the thought away. Now she'd wrecked it, her concentration. She'd been feeling almost regular, close to the landscape, but now she was back to worry.

Now, Graves said to her, "Ever hear a paisano cry?"

Sophie thought 'paisano' meant like peasant. She wondered if he was making a joke at the expense of the poor? She asked, "This isn't some racist joke is it?"

"'Racist'?" went Graves.

Sophie wondered if these people were primitive. But that couldn't be it. Look at the pod—very advanced technology it seemed. Plus, primitive sounded mean. Graves and Jakes had been kind. She observed, she learned. She said, "You don't know the word 'racist'?"

Graves said, "No. 'Race'? I know 'racy', like a story that is, you know, about men and women, and them's getting frisky."

Sophie gasped. She said, "Don't you have Jesus?"

Graves answered, "How do you mean 'have'? Christers are common, it's a noble path to the perfect man." He hesitated. Sophie felt his body sigh. "Paisano is the big bird that does not fly. It is not a racist."

"Oh," went Sophie, "the roadrunner. Beep, beep!"

Jakes even turned about to glance her way. Jakes and Graves had no clue about her sound effects. Graves tried it: "Beep! Beep!"

Jakes laughed. "Paisano don't sound like that."

Graves said, "I was trying it out."

Jakes continued: "People believe what they want to, so the key is to want what is best, what is real."

"That's the dilemma Rimbaud solved," said Graves.

Sophie said, "Sorry." She shrugged her shoulders but knew neither of them could see. Communicating on the pods was possible but—

Jakes said, "Humans believe in anything. So it's not the believing that's important, but the selection of what to believe."

"That's true," said Sophie.

Jakes said, "Two hundred years ago there was tremendous violence. War. Savagery."

Graves said, "The War of Necessity, when the nations all went mad."

"What about the Revolutionary War?"

Jakes said, "The war was an opportunity. Consolidation, make the peace. Choose wisely."

Graves added, "That's when Chichimeca comes."

Sophie persisted, "During the Revolutionary War?"

Jakes said, "A war to end war. A war of necessity to make sure it wouldn't happen again. Here, too! Mexicans fighting Califia and Tejas. Californians fighting about anybody. Back east, Americans fighting Europe.

"Chichimeca was...different. Separate. A watershed system, watershed government."

Graves said, "We have been since Havana. We had

little in the way of an organized military. But we had something they did not. Leverage?"

Jakes said, "At the peace of Havana, we became clear. How we depend on each other."

Graves said, "The Crots."

Jakes nodded so that Sophie could see. He was being very dramatic. He looked serious. This was important to them. He said, "We'd opened up pathways. Communication with the ecos...the Ley lines."

"The Free State of Chichimeca," said Graves proudly.

"I don't understand how this war ended?" asked Sophie.

Graves said, "The last war."

Jakes called over from his pod, pointing out some horses passing by, then some camels. "Take a look! What a ride! Ships of the desert!" The animals went by and a couple young women on pods followed, waving. Were they herding the animals? Jakes and the others waved back.

Jakes said, "The last war ended war. The great Napoleon did it. Rimbaud explained it."

"How?" asked Sophie. Sophie knew who Napoleon was. The other person sounded French?

Jakes drove alongside them, looking closely at Sophie as though he couldn't believe her but must. "Napoleon forced an end to hostilities. Borders were set. Coalitions formed, alliances. Rimbaud was a philologist. He had the two most important things to say in all the languages of the planet: 'take care of each other, take care of the Earth.'"

Graves repeated it: "'Take care of each other, take care of the Earth.'"

"What's that?" asked Sophie, pointing to an animal that was looking out of a thick stand of mesquite near the side of the road. The head was big, the size of a big dog's, with what might have been a beak? The head looked armored?

A cylindrical head, then a massive shelled body waddled forward a tiny bit more, out of the brush. "It looks like a VW," said Sophie.

"Glyptodont," said Graves, slowing by the thing. He lowered his eyes, gave it a little bow. Sophie saw Jakes do the same. "They usually stay closer to the river. This old timer must be on a mission. Huh?"

Jakes said, "Sophie, see how the acacia make an island of plant life. They make a canopy like a shade umbrella for the plants and animals underneath. Glyptodont must be visiting, checking his charges, watching, learning. He'll share later, when he's back at the river."

Now the armored head had found them, the small eyes looked and learned. The glyptodont kept its head down. The plates across the top of its head extended behind the head and thick neck, across the creature's body, like a giant turtle. The shell billowed rotund in bumpy gray and brown grandeur, giving it an almost militaristic look—not a turtle at all, more like a mini-tank. Sophie decided, it definitely had a homemade look.

"They're friends," said Graves.

Sophie said, "It's huge!"

Graves said, "Like an armadillo?"

Sophie said, "That's a mammal?"

Jakes said, "The Crots are famous the world over for their work. Resurrection Biology. No? You know of it not?"

Graves said, "Leverage." Then he blinked his eye at Sophie. He must think the single word explained—

Sophie said, "Why were those men yesterday morning so concerned about the Crots? They didn't seem to like them."

Graves said, "Long ago—"

Jakes said, "Old stories, folk lore now, about Crots stealing children?"

Sophie turned back to watch the creature disappear

behind them. She said, "So you have prejudice?"

Jakes said, "Everyone has a right to be as big an ass as everyone else."

They straightened, got going going again at their regular pace.

Sophie said, "So you trust the Crots to be take care of Tyler?"

Graves smiled and nodded.

Where was she going? What was she doing? Was this right? She and Tyler would meet up in Coltrane? Why—how... there were too many impossible questions. The trick was survival. Don't go crazy. That's what she held on to. She knew how to think. She knew how to analyze? Was that what was required right now? Glyptodonts were fine—wonderful, but this world was not her world! Extinct megafauna, Tyler had called them. Well, that was those aurochs; he hadn't seen the glyptodont. Still—she should stay near the spot they...came in? She'd get Tyler and they'd come right back to the river with Graves and Jakes. They had to stay together from now on. It just made sense. But all these people wanted them to go see this Peggy character.

The road got steep. The overpowering white glaze of desert light gave in to color now. Now they were definitely ascending. More brush, green too. And trees. Rocky outcroppings were common, and these red and orange. The mountains were coming in close. The view changed: dominated, now, by rough mountain skyscrapers that could glitter. Quartz, thought Sophie. She seemed to remember a Jeopardy answer about the most common material on Earth's surface being quartz—silicon. The same planet then: same geology, same topography.

Jakes had told Sophie they could make 15 kilometers an hour, so the trip to Coltrane would take maybe 2 or 3 houses, depending on how many stops they made. She wondered if having a passenger and going uphill slowed them. Did the pods need to recharge? Refuel? Did they need to excrete waste? She didn't understand the faint feeling of something like a charge, maybe electrical, what they said was static, that emanated from the pod. She held on, watched the landscape, waved at the occasional passersby on pod or horse. A few rode by on odd wooden bicycles that seemed to have too many gears. A car and a truck went by, that might have been from her Earth. They looked similar and had real tires on metal wheels.

She missed Tyler. It was strangely lonesome being here without him, as though she were even more isolated. Graves and Jakes were nice, but they didn't see how important it was sometimes to have someone back you up, that you weren't crazy. Someone who could appreciate your wonder at the constant onslaught of impossible sights. When they were together, she could glance at him, feel his nearby presence, find some familiarity.

Jakes was talking now. He was close but far enough that Sophie had to concentrate on hearing him. "What?" she called.

He repeated, "We have to act fast. Get you with Tyler in Coltrane, the sling to Peggy's, then right back here to your folks."

"We have to bring Tyler back to the river" said Sophie.

Jakes stuttered a moment, then called: "Tyler's parents, your parents are worried. That adds to the soup. All of this at once. So we move carefully. Every step, a choice."

Sophie didn't like the sound of any of this. The plans made without asking her. She didn't know what to say.

Graves and Jakes concentrated on their 'driving'. Finally, Graves said, "Coltrane's a wonderful place. Chichimeca's best artists live there. It's a town of waterfalls and festivals. Beauty demands a city like Coltrane."

Jakes said, "Greater than the sum of its parts."

Sophie said, "What's a sling?"

They made a couple stops to stretch and relieve themselves. The road got steep. They entered a canyon they had to crisscross to ascend, back and forth on the switchbacks to make their way up, climbing the mountain. The road cut through forest now, cabins here and there, some corrals. A few more substantial home made of stone with tall stone chimneys. It was a mixed forest that included pines Sophie saw. She wished Tyler was here. He would know the names of the trees. She didn't. She could name the blood vessels of the heart, but couldn't remember the difference between deciduous and coniferous. Little run off creeks were common along the road. Rocky overhangs, interspersed up the side of the mountain dripped, joined, plunged: would be waterfalls.

They stopped by some smooth red trees that looked like they had muscles flowing through them. Sophie stretched, drank some water. Graves gave her a delicious biscuit. Sophie spotted squirrels chipping in the rocks and pointed at them to Graves.

Graves said, "Yeah, lots of squirrels. Ground squirrels, tree squirrels. They carry news of the mast. And you wouldn't believe the quail up here. Yummy! Three different types. Do you like bar-b-q'ed quail?"

They got going again. The occasional truck or pod or herd being hustled down were all tended by people who waved and called to them. The road was very steep now. The second stop was in oak trees because Sophie noticed all the acorns.

Graves commented, "Pigs go for acorns."

Sophie was beginning to realize the lay of the land: the mountains above the valley made like islands. Above the desert, rocky red behemoths rose straight up. At the tops, Eden? Sophie thought that some of the pinnacles looked like ships tossed in an angry sea. Not many cabins up here. Rough cliff faces had dark angular birds diving, spinning by them. Smooth, pink upheavals of stone melted to pastels in front of her.

Jakes said, "We're almost to the tunnel."

"Pretty up here," said Graves. "Rough. Lush. Those are the sentinels. Oh, oh, in the madrone about eye level, to our right, to our right!"

Graves slowed the pod. Sophie searched the area. She saw an intent face staring back at her. Small bear body? Maybe more like a monkey? No, no. Beautiful face really. Foxy? Smart looking? But also a little bear in that face? Like a bear cat? Fur a cinnamon rich brown. Bright eyes, long snout, small rounded ears.

Graves said, "Chulo monkey."

Jakes said, "Sophie, do you know what a ley line is?"

Sophie shook her head, tearing her eyes from the chulo who decided to vacate the premises anyway.

Graves said, "Wonder what's playing at the Rialto?"

"Please," said Jakes.

Graves chuckled. "They always have the latest Ronald Reagan film."

Jakes said, "Ley lines crisscross the Earth." Sophie waited for more.

Jakes explained: "They're the natural seams or stress points where energy accumulates. And if you build a tall enough tower there of inertial material, you can whip a cable kilometers to the next ley tower."

Graves said, "The sling."

They came to the tunnel at the range's divide. On the other side here, everything flowed down the other way. A different down on this side. They stopped before the tunnel. Sophie tried to read the incised inscription in bold, big letters that was over the tunnel. It was in a language she did not recognize.

Graves saw her staring and said, "Dine."

Sophie still looked confused.

He said, "The language it's in."

Jakes said, "'Here, beauty soars.' The Crots already

have Tyler here or we're early. Beat them to it."

Graves said, "No sign of 'em along the road. They must be going around the mountains, the southern route."

"Which takes longer."

Sophie said, "When does the sling...go?"

Jakes said, "It leaves in the afternoon. Usually. We'll have

to check. Plenty of time. If we keep moving."

"What's at the Rialto?" sang out Graves.

"Let's go," said Jakes

They proceeded ahead slowly on their pods, entering the tunnel. The tunnel was wide and tall, and Sophie could see light at the far end. They had the tunnel to themselves and quickly got through it. As soon as they left the tunnel they were greeted by a large welcome sign. It was the first thing Sophie's eyes fell on. The large wooden sign was carved with vines and flowers. The full grandeur of the blond wood came through suggesting the sign was writhing, about to blossom forth.

"Welcome to Coltrane!"

Sophie said, "Is that wood? No, it's too light colored. Is it plastic?"

Graves shook his head. "No, no, acacia. Right, Jakes?"

Jakes called back as he moved ahead: "Locust!"

The second thing Sophie's eyes took in was the expanse, the way the tunnel opened above a canyon valley that swept out like an expanding green sleeve, bound by 2 long, steep and rocky walls. Expanse in green: green and stone sang merrily with waterfalls: in every direction close by and farther, water cascading down. Sounds of water dominated, then light breeze ruffling leave sounds from the trees, then kids calling out maybe even singing. She had a clear view. Her eyes quit gasping. She pulled in her vision and focused on the houses and structures nearby. Up against the canyon walls, on either side, wonderful adobe apartment complexes, then some wooden structures, stone ones. Sophie assumed they were 'cliff dwellings', because that's what the brochures at Mesa Verde had called them, when she had visited with her parents just a week ago. But these buildings were not ancient. They seemed sparkling new. Some were painted. Some glittered with quartz. The houses on the canyon floor were mainly wood, but built in odd patterns or styles she did not recognize. Eccentricity seemed the key here. Instead of rectangular box models, these were triangles and hexagons. Some were painted extravagantly. The nearest was striped in gray and pink. Another was painted turquoise. Wow, a hippy town, thought Sophie.

Green and waterfalls and painted houses! The canyon which was Coltrane welcomed them. Sophie felt she was witnessing something special. She'd never imagined a city that thrived on natural refinement. This city seemed part of the terrain. It did not interrupt natural growth, it augmented it. The attractiveness was inflammatory. It was compelling. Sophie wanted to go in, get acquainted, not just witness. She hadn't felt this good or clear since their 'arrival'. She wanted to do something...to do anything that would express her excitement at such beauty. She would settle for a quick explore of its roads and gardens and waterfalls.

For there were gardens in most of the homes' yards she could now see, as they began their descent. Her mother would—no, she couldn't right now. Not now. Go with it right now! Gardens often overlapped, forming green zones around a pair or three houses set near each other. The road was paved now. They passed wonderful fences made from natural objects, including bones, shells, antlers and oddly shaped branches. People stood in their yards or by their houses and watched them go by. A diversity of faces, too: brown faces, black faces, white faces. Sophie couldn't help but wave. Her eyes followed the gardens, the flowers, the vegetables, the meandering fences of bones and antlers. The texture to the place was fiercely organic, natural, sensual and alluring. She could smell food...cooking fires. Then earthy herb smells dominated. Then flower nectars—honey suckle. She couldn't tell. It was so sweet—

Jakes said, "First thing we do, we check the sling schedule."

"Holy soul," went Graves. "Let's go, lumpies!"

Some Crots trotted by, nodding to them. The road widened with sidewalks and more houses lining it. Houses now were 2 and 3 deep along the sides, then they climbed up the canyon walls. And there were side canyons that had their own arrangement of homes. With all the green, plants and trees and flowering bushes, it was easy to think the top house was simply hanging there, jutting out, preposterous, levitating in green. Dirt walkways and stairways connected houses up the sides of the canyon.

Not far from them, they heard the sound of a big truck spasming with metallic clamor—the universal cry of a dying vehicle. It could only be a truck, and one with the good ol' internal combustion engine in it, thought Sophie.

They were descending now through larger homes and building, and even more marvelous gardens. Small waterfalls tinkled down rough rock faces to catch basins. Kids played in the water. Pods went by. A woman on a horse. A man in a chariot being pulled by llamas. Then a vehicle that looked like a mini-car but no exhaust, no tailpipe Sophie could see. Lovely rock gardens, too, with cactus and succulents in effortless sprays. Wooden houses, stone houses, Sophie was beginning to realize that a lot of people must live here. This was a city. A small cabin held large metal objects in its front yard. Sophie realized they were sculptures. Abstract designs that might have been metal waterfalls caught in the act of tumbling. The homes went up even higher now, new levels in the canyon walls.

Next to the road now, a drainage ditch that guided a

small stream. Wild flowers and brush plied its banks. Yards held swings and bird baths and more sculptures Sophie assumed. Some of the sculptures were stones piled in formations, some were wood. More people now, too. Of all ethnicities and ages, dressed in a range of colors and fabrics. Most, however, dressed simply and wore sandals. A boy on a pony went by. No saddle. He stared at them on their pods. Bicycles, too, clattered by, wooden and metal. They were entering the main business part of town. A few shops had already been passed. Sophie could tell because of the large glass windows in the front that displayed various items. They went by too fast to figure exactly what the items were. Now the buildings passed seemed larger. Long narrow buildings made Sophie think of business offices. They came to a large circular area surrounded by giant trees. Small groups of people, young and old, sat about the park. Some ate from baskets, drank from bottles. The grass was green and clean. Not a speck of trash. Benches held people reading. Picnic tables held folks talking animatedly.

Jakes said, "We could stop for lunch."

"A pretty spot," said Graves.

Jakes sighed. "We better find out about the sling."

They followed the road farther, into the center of town with larger buildings still, some 4 and even 5 stories high, lining the street. Large front windows displayed clothes, books. Machine parts? That's what Sophie assumed they were. They were down town. People crossed back and forth across the road. People hustled along the sidewalks alone and in groups. Moms pulled kids by their hands. Men looked serious and conducted discussions as they walked. Young couples walked along hand in hand.

Jakes said, "We'll stop by the post office."

Sophie said, "Don't you have to recharge them?"

Graves said, "'Recharge'? What? You want to charge lunch? Attack it?"

Another group of Crots trotted by taking up most of the road. Graves and Jakes pulled over to let them pass. Other people on pods glared at the Crots. At least Sophie took it to be a glare. Graves and Jakes waited for them to go by.

Coltrane was built in the heart of the Puertos las Mulas around a high central valley drainage that was L-shaped. The long arm of the L ran west to east, so Graves and Jakes and Sophie had come in from the western edge of town through the tunnel. Downtown by the post office was the L's elbow, then the valley plunged north, up the Gulch, the shorter arm where much of the industry was located.

Graves and Jakes came to the post office. They left their pods in special slots along the back wall of the post office for that purpose. Then they walked. This was the heart of town, indeed, with crowds and busyness sweeping them up. They hopped along, stepping through people, smiling, saying 'excuse me' and 'con permiso'.

Sophie had to ask over the noisy street, "You don't chain them? Your pods? They don't need a key?"

Graves said, "What for?"

"Well, in case someone wanted to steal one."

Graves said, "Why would someone do that?"

Sophie said, "I smell smoke."

They walked from the post office into the Gulch where a parade took over the street, bearing a long painted banner that showed what Sophie thought were math symbols. The people with the banner wore brown robes, men and women. Some people called to them, making fun. Others called back to leave them alone. There seemed to be another park here, where the Gulch began. Food vendors had little booths set up, wooden stalls open at the top to let the smoke out. Grills sizzled with frying meat. In the Gulch, immediately, the traffic got crazy, bumper to bumper vehicles of all sizes clamoring to get through.

The Gulch was a broad side canyon, Sophie saw. Before they were all the way in, she looked to the east where the mountains opened up. That must be the other entry to Coltrane. Where Tyler would come in? A truck honked at her. She moved quickly. Graves and Jakes nodded to her, motioning her forward.

The trucks had odd designs painted on them: big circles with slashes and lightning bolts. Were those Greek letters? A circle with a maze inside it was not. Some big trucks had the trailer part in front with the cabin behind, as though they were backwards.

Sophie realized this was just like a busy city anywhere, then wondered where the telephone poles were? Where were the wires? Up the Gulch, the city stink of exhaust and sewage dominated just like any city in the USA. But no sirens at all. It was a hippy town of course, peace and love. Is that what this world really was, the hippy world?

They came on a 2 story stone building on the Gulch that had a spire coming out of its roof, but aimed straight out over the road. Sophie said, "It's the unicorn building." Her friends did not laugh. The sign over the entrance to the building simply read 'IT'.

Graves saw her studying the initials. He said, "IT: Inertial Transport."

Jakes said, "Sling offices."

"Shouldn't we see if Tyler's here?" asked Sophie.

"We can ask inside," said Jakes and opened the building's main door and went in.

Graves held back a second, then said to Sophie, "What are you thinking? If the Crots took the southern route, which apparently they did, there's no way they're here yet. See what I'm thinking? What are you thinking? We need to align our thoughts."

"Thanks, Graves," said Sophie. She followed him in to the building.

The inside was big and roomy and reminded Sophie

right away of a bank. The far wall was a silvery surface with colored numbers and letters blinking off and on. But it wasn't digital. Or electric. A long wooden counter stretched across the front of the room. It was punctuated with wooden dividers, 5 of them, much like an old fashioned bank would have for its tellers.

Graves saw her staring at the large 'board'. He said, "Itineraries. Sophie, the important thing is for you and Tyler to be together and get to Peggy. Right now, that's what Jakes and I suggest. Duckbill backs us up. So we'll find Tyler, talk to the Crots, see what they suggest. We'll try to call Peggy again. Why not? Slight modicum she's finished in Alburquerque. Maybe she can come here." He shrugged dramatically. "If not, you'll have to go there. We'll see."

Jakes had gone to an open spot at the ticket counter. Sophie and Graves watched him at the counter talking to the agent. They talked a lot.

When Jakes got back to Graves and Sophie, they both could tell he was puzzled. He hesitated speaking; his hands kept opening and closing. Finally, he grasped his hands together, held them in front of his belly. He said, "Tyler's here. Crots already got his ticket."

Graves inhaled sharply. Sophie shook her head. Graves said, "We meet up at the sling then?"

"Two hours. Maybe a fraction more."

"We have to find Tyler," said Sophie.

"The Crots will get him to the sling. He'll be there," said Jakes. "Actually, the agent didn't say 'Tyler'. The agent said a young Crot woman bought 2 tickets not too ago."

Graves shook his head slow, then his eyes brightened, and said, "We ask the Butterfly Lords."

Sophie thought she was being ironic about the hippies here. Now what? "You're kidding?" went Sophie.

"Come on," said Jakes. "We'll get some lunch, think it

through. We'll go to the Crots, see what they know. Plenty of time!"

Graves said, "Tickets for today?"

Jakes went for his shirt pocket and pulled out a thin wooden square with a spire stamped on it.

They went down the street to a Dine place known for its excellent lamb stew. Graves and Jakes had metal discs for money. Sophie said they looked like play money. Graves and Jakes could not grasp the concept of 'play', as in games and pretend. Of course they knew *play* as in imagination and joyousness. They settled in to their meal, hearty, meaty, complex spices. Thus fortified, they continued up the Gulch, passing oddly shaped cars, more animals, then trucks that barely moved. Ah, Sophie realized: they were taking turns, pulling into various warehouses and fenced in industrial yards. At the end of the Gulch where it began to narrow and climb back into the rocky canyon, there was a tall red barn. A corral next to that had a few Crots trotting in circles. No waterfalls back here. The area was dry and rocky.

Jakes walked over to the entrance to the barn where a big Crot stood, the steed body much heavier, rounder than the ones Sophie had seen. Sophie and Graves held back, let Jakes make his inquiry.

Jakes returned to them and motioned them to follow. They headed back the way they'd come, down the Gulch. Jakes walked slowly. Trouble! Graves and Sophie both felt it.

Jakes explained: "Mexican incursion near Whitewater had twelve Crots dead."

Graves groaned. He had to stop to absorb the awful news, hand pressed to the top of his head.

"There's more," said Jakes. "I asked if Okla or any of his people were here." Jakes shook his head.

"What does that mean?" asked Graves.

Jakes said, "Which part? Either Okla had to send Tyler

here with Crots this man did not know; or, something triggered the Mexican attack that made them change plans. Lethal!"

Graves said, "But they bought a ticket? He's here. We find him, we get to the sling."

Jakes said, "We know what triggered this. No wonder Peggy Dreiser is so busy!"

War?" said Sophie. "You think it's because of us? Because we showed up here?"

Graves, fast, went, "No, Sophie—"

But Jakes interrupted: "Crots are organizing defenses. Militia's called out. It hasn't sunk in yet in Coltrane. Santa Fe and Chihuahua know. This complicates things for Peggy prismatic."

"I don't understand?" implored Sophie. They were all used to each other's confusion now—and questions, so knew right away what she didn't know. But there was no time—

"We have to get back," said Graves. "They'll need every man."

Sophie said, "But if Okla's not here, then who bought the ticket?"

Jakes said, "There's a lot of Crots in Coltrane."

They slowly shuffled back up the Gulch, towards the L's elbow and the post office. They used the sidewalk. Sophie felt delight; she felt pain; she felt lost. Every little thing suddenly seemed complicated. She gulped, tasted stew. She stayed near her friends. Large buildings, which she assumed were warehouses, were perhaps more: the nearest building opened massive front doors to let a truck emerge. It was one of those odd backwards trucks, with the trailer part up front. The 3 caught the smell immediately. Sophie saw a sign over the entrance that read 'Abattoir'. She couldn't remember what that meant. The big truck waited for its chance, waddled on to the road, then pulled out and around to a side area for parking. The truck shut down.

Sophie said, "Stinky."

Graves said, "La Chasse."

Jakes said, "Those hunters just returned...from where?"

Jakes took the plunge across the street towards the parked truck. The cab was in the back with its door opened, swinging wide. Jakes went to see.

Sophie and Graves waited watching. Graves explained, "The Lazarus Project. Hunters from neighboring areas cull the wild herds. See, the Crots didn't want to bring back any ancient predator."

"Saber-toothed tigers?" went Sophie.

Graves said, "Exactly. Smilodon. Oh, there's a few of them. But—so the animals are butchered here. Fresh game sent all over the world."

"Butterfly Town is a butcher's shop?"

"Well, I don't think of it that way. That way makes it sound nasty."

"What's Jakes doing?"

Graves said, "Jakes wants to see if they saw something."

Sophie said, "Looks like it. Jakes's bringing the truck driver over. It's a girl."

The young woman was in a get up of gaudy scarves tied around her top and neck, over her head. Her baggy heavy pants were black. Tools and leather bags hung from her belt. She wore big work boots. The young woman nodded to Sophie and Graves.

Jakes said, "Tell them what you told me."

She smiled broadly. "Un heur—one...hour. Hour a go hunter truck came in with...its big...big quota?"

"That's right," said Jakes. "Quota. She parles Francais."

"Oui, c'est vrai. So, so, so, maybe four tons, cinq?"

Jakes looked at her hard.

"So, so, so, the hunters had passengers. A boy and a girl."

"Where are these hunters?" asked Graves.

The young woman shrugged. "I knew the driver tiny bit. They unloaded, cleaned up, left. Must have parked their rig uptown by the highway?"

"They took the boy and girl with them?" asked Jakes.

"Yes?" replied the young woman. "Kino? Cinema? The driver said they were going to a film? Perhaps they went to a film?"

They were in the center of town, up from the elbow, having walked out of the Gulch to the heart of Coltrane, and Jakes was talking, "It's not who are the Butterfly Lords, it's what are the Butterfly Lords?"

Graves said, "You'll see."

Jakes said, "Sophie, the Butterfly Lords have different ways of knowing." He paused. Sophie looked away. Jakes and Graves could tell she was exhausted. "You've handled all of this...whatever it is...well."

"For someone like me?" Sophie completed his thought, or she thought she did. She saw that Graves was unsure or bothered by her response. She added, "You seem to imply your world is 'better'."

Jakes smirked. "All we can know is what we know."

Sophie said, "All these hippy slogans—what can they actually do? I mean it sounds like you're going to war?"

"Ha!" went Graves, then to Jakes he asked: "Why are so many truck drivers for the hunters French girls? Tres joli!"

Sophie said, "Don't change the subject!"

Jakes said, "I don't know anything about 'hippy towns'. But I understand you must defend your world. After all, it is your way of knowing."

They traversed the narrow streets at a good walking clip. They were all anxious with the news. Sophie knew that whatever else happened, Graves and Jakes would soon leave her. The maze of small streets got remarkably steep. They zigzagged up and over the streets, some paved, some dirt. Odd little houses that couldn't have been more than 2-3 rooms with carved trim and stained glass windows were common. Their path evened out, opened a bit. Sophie saw trees ahead, their tops waving above the houses and greenery. They came to a small circular park surrounded by these trees, with the sweetest little waterfall tinkling down the cliff side in its center. Flowers of all sorts and swarms of butterflies gorged the park with color.

There were large white butterflies whose wings flared like tissues. Small ones were colored yellow, orange and blue. Some had dots. Some had elaborate eyes. Some had epaulets of red and orange. A number of people were already at the park, but they hung back near the wide, gated entrance, so Sophie and the others did too. A young woman sat alone on a bench in the park. She had long dark hair and Sophie could see twinkling butterflies in her hair. She wasn't sure whether they were real or jewels. The young woman wore a simple white dress, with bare legs and feet.

Though Sophie stood towards the back of the band of park visitors, it was clear who the cloud of butterflies made for. Small and large butterflies of all colors formed a halo over Sophie's head. Graves gasped with delight, smiling at Sophie.

Jakes immediately went, "Make way, make way!"

Graves whispered huskily to her, "It's right, Sophie. We knew you were special."

The young woman from the bench inside the small park had come out to see what the butterflies were doing. She went over to Sophie and took her hand and led her through the people into the park. She sat Sophie at the bench and held a finger to her lips.

Sophie nodded but had no idea what was expected of her. The cloud of butterflies around her was growing. They did not alarm her. They did not touch her. Actually, it was almost pleasant being in their midst. She had a slight tickling sensation, like the pod's static feel, that seemed to grow across her skin. But maybe she was imagining that. She felt herself calm. She closed her eyes naturally, not worrying about the butterflies, slings, or aurochs. She thought of her parents, their home, St. Louis, then high school. She thought of everything that happened since the bite of habanero.

There was that static again, like white noise in her ears that translated to ticklish trembling hairs on her arms and wrists. Like she was sensing electric activity of…the butterflies? Of her own brain? Maybe it was just the normal electric activity of her nerves. Maybe some other source. She saw how she went back and forth, calm and meditative, then rational, certain and explanatory. She thought, Peggy Dreiser? All at once, the static faded away or lifted and there were words in her head: "After Mela, you must go back to where it started."

Sophie said aloud without opening her eyes, "'After Mela, I must go back to where it started.'"

She opened her eyes. The young woman with butterfly hair held her hand still. Jakes stood nearby smiling at her. Graves kneeled near her, and he was nodding.

Jakes said, "Tyler was here. An hour ago. And the Butterfly Lords said the same thing to him."

Sophie murmured, "Where's Tyler?"

Grave said, abruptly, "Guess what? Surprise! Ha! The folks with Tyler went to check out the Rialto before they go to the sling. See what they're thinking?"

"There should be enough time if we hurry," said Jakes.

"They want to go to the movies. We're going to the movies?" asked Sophie.

Graves chuckled. He stood up, extended a hand towards Sophie. He helped her to her feet. She sighed deeply. The butterfly halo had dispersed. The young woman released Sophie's hand and clasped her shoulder instead. She said, "You are fine?"

Sophie said, "I think so."

The young woman said, "Sometimes there is dizziness."

"Yes," said Sophie. "I am fine. Merci."

The young woman smiled, dropped her hand to her side.

Sophie left with Graves and Jakes. People still hung by the entrance of the park watching the butterflies, watching Sophie depart.

The Rialto was close. Down from the butterfly park but still above main street. The Rialto was a large, ornate, stone building. Sophie was thinking the style was referred to as 'Victorian'. Wide stone steps led up to the glass enclosed ticket booth behind which the main doors opened. The ticket booth was lit up brightly. They took the steps fast, and Sophie read the big stone letters above them, 'R-I-A-L-T-O'. To the sides of the ticket booth tall inset displays showed posters of the latest feature. *Bonzo Goes to Mars* with Ronald Reagan! The poster's pictures made Sophie wonder if it was some take off of *Planet of the Apes* to poke fun of the ex-president. In the poster he seemed to be surrounded by chimps in astronaut suits. She couldn't figure why the ex-president would be made of fun here and now Then Sophie remembered the ex-president had been in films back in the day. Black and white movies. Besides, wasn't he dead now?

The Rialto must have been between shows because there was no one around. No ticket taker sat in the bright aquarium of the ticket booth. They had the front of the theater to themselves.

Graves pointed to the poster Sophie was staring at. "He is the most popular, most beloved actor in the world. And he's old now. He's gotta be what, Jakes? One hundred years old?"

Jakes said, "I don't know. Come on, Graves. We're looking for Tyler."

Grave said, "Maybe they went in to the feature?"

Jakes said, "Look at the times. No matinee today." He said this very dramatically, spinning around from the booth to Graves.

"No," said Sophie. She wasn't dizzy as much as light headed, as though she had just awakened from a nap. And she never took naps. She realized she was exhausted. She could faint. She never fainted! She would not faint.

Graves read from the ticket booth announcements. Graves grunted. "We're early," he said. He looked at Sophie, noticed her discomfort or unease.

"There's no time," said Jakes. "We must have missed them. We have to get to the sling now. No choice. That's what they'll do when they realize there's no matinee. We'll take our pods."

Sophie and Graves facing Jakes had a view away from the theater, so they saw them first.

Four people approached from the west. Tyler was with them.

Graves slapped his hands to his thighs, gave out a big 'yip'. Then: "Tyler!"

Jakes saw him. They all cantered down the steps to the foursome. Two women, 2 men. The older woman wore scarves over the top portion of her body and over her head. Her heavy black pants looked familiar. Her belt hung with packets and tools. The younger woman had thick dark hair and wore a simple white shirt and pants with moccasins. The man with Tyler was in leathers. The older woman called to them, "Too early for the Kino? C'est vrai?"

Sophie recognized her accent and wondered why truck drivers here were French women.

Graves called out, "C'est vrai."

Jakes called, "Es verdad."

Sophie and Tyler ran to each other. The other man said, "Kai Schubert here, and this is Lantine Bouche, my driver. This is Lu, one of Okla's people".

Sophie and Tyler embraced just as the earthquake hit.

CHAPTER 9

No, Aurore from here did not think it could feel like this. The excitement brought a startling clarity. A certainty that was a form of happiness? She did not feel trapped, because she was not alone. The Poltergeist Girls, Aurore and Neo, who really were Neo and Aurore, would punch through this conundrum. Panjandrum. Fandango. Anomalies and delight! Carnivale! Laissez les bons temps roulez!

They didn't have enough habaneros. That was the problem. Why it hadn't worked when they'd tried their re-enactment. To duplicate 'the incident' they would need the exact amount of chile. Maybe the time of day was important? All things were inter-related. The Fortean matrix against entropy. What came next? The exact duplication of events!

Aurore wished she had her pad or laptop. Because the 'specialists' were all talking mass hysteria and Aurore knew some tasty sites that detailed the history of famous mass hysteria episodes. She was dying to tell the story of the Mystery of Little Miss Nobody, July 4, 1944.

* * *

Graves and Jakes met in grad school at the University of Arizona. They both studied American History, though of different eras. Graves favored the West before the Mexican War of 1845, the so called Colonial Era. Jakes did after the war, American expansion and the 'conquering' of the West. They graduated, made a promise, went their separate ways. Jakes took a teaching job in Colorado. Graves ended up as a Colonial Archaeology consultant for the southwestern National Forests. The promise was that before they got 'shackled down' by jobs, family, kids...before they got old, they would ride the Coronado Trail. It was to be an historical re-enactment. And a heck of a lot of fun. Bringing one cell phone in case of an emergency was their only contingency plan. Then, it was discovered that the cell phone was faulty—it didn't work!

To adventure!

Now Graves and Jakes sat in the backseat of a fancy, new SUV and felt very uncomfortable, knowing they had not done the 'right thing'. They were barreling down the narrow county road, leaving behind the San Pedro River and their horses; and they were heading east to the old mining town of Coltrane. They had to make them stop. Or at least they had to get out? How had the twin girls been able to convince them to come? The twin with the accent had pointed out that if they were concerned for the kids' safety, they should accompany them as 'interested bystanders'. The very second they had, still protesting, gotten into the back of the SUV, the other twin, who drove, had hit the gas.

They said people were after them. Their parents of course. But the story blurted out by the twins and the girl, Sophie, involved more than parents and sheriff and FBI. There was talk of 'doubles' and 'switching', and something big no one understood. Something big was happening. And it started right here on the river. The planet itself might be in danger. No one knew. Graves and

Jakes listened with open mouths and didn't ask questions.

The story's drama unfolded with an awful impossibility that suggested it had *not* been made up just to placate them. Then, again, Graves and Jakes were not used to dealing with teenagers. 'Doubles'? 'Switching'? The twin with the accent, named Lise, and Sophie were from another place. This other place was the very same river valley, but different.

Evidently, the kids were high on science fiction. But they claimed they didn't know how they had gotten there. Now they were on a perilous rescue mission to find Lise's brother, Tyler, who was a switched kid. Sophie was a switched kid, too. The other twin was named Lise, too. The Lise's were doubles. Apparently, the switching had occurred first, then the next day the doubling. Grave and Jakes stared at each other across the dark back seat and imagined that each was wondering how to talk to these kids without getting killed in the SUV.

Cyberelectronic kids of today, coaxed through endless CGI games, had concocted a drama to dumbfound the old people?

Just as a joke? They had to get control of the vehicle. Graves suggested to Lise she should slow down. After all, she didn't want to draw attention to the SUV—

Lise, the driver, went, "Oh my God, they'll have road blocks! I mean after Tyler, they went kinda chronic. Which is why it was so easy to sneak off in the SUV. I mean, by then, Sophie had vanished too. Parental units on overload. Total panic! FBI on freak out. Everybody freaking! No idea what was going on."

Sophie's head swam. All this 'freaking'! She felt dizzy when she looked out the window at the fiercely lit up desert that went shooting by. Tyler's sister, who she knew slightly, had pointed out the speedometer. Sophie couldn't believe the numbers the red needle pointed to—even in miles.

Suddenly, Sophie understood, and she exclaimed, "Internal combustion! This is an internal combustion machine!"

Her Lise replied, "C'est vrai!"

Lise, the driver, said, "Don't get all alternate worldy on us, Sophie. You are here now and we want to get Tyler, too. He's bound to head to Coltrane. It's the only town nearby. There was something they were talking about. I heard something about a circus?"

Sophie shook her head hard. "Circus?" She was holding on to the door next to her. The two Lise's were sitting close. She managed, "He was on foot. Could the circus have given him a ride?"

Jakes said from the back, "Sophie, what do you mean 'internal combustion'? What else would it be? You say it like it's a surprise?"

Sophie said, "We have internal combustion."

Jakes shut up, unclear with her response.

Graves said slowly, "These road blocks: I see what you're thinking. We could be driving in to a trap? They're bound to be out looking for you. It's not too late to turn around."

Sophie had turned her head to the back, but she couldn't make out Jakes and Graves' faces from the weird dashboard glow. They had been kind to her. She turned her head back to the front. Lise, driving, moved her right hand over the other Lise's left hand. Tiny blue lightning bolts crackled between them. Sophie saw blue sparks flashing between the Lise's. She gasped.

Graves and Jakes gasped as well, calling out questions.

Lise, driving, interrupted in a loud voice: "Pretty neat, huh? Maybe, we got super powers now. We give the adults headaches."

"Tout les temps!" cried the other Lise, and they both laughed.

Sophie, quickly, inserted, "Mauvais! Peut-etre, don't do

that. You shouldn't do that. It doesn't feel right."

The Lise from her world scooted over towards Sophie, nodding.

Jakes was now saying: "This is too much, you guys. What's going on? "

Graves added, "Like static?"

Jakes said, "How could that happen? You guys are charged?"

Lise next to Sophie said, "Prickly? Makes the goose bumps."

Driver Lise called out, "No way! We got special powers now, we doubles. What about you, Sophie? What do switchers feel?"

Sophie said, "Weak. Malade."

Graves said, "Maybe we should get off the paved road? I bet they won't have road blocks on the old ranch roads. And those old roads go right up to Coltrane. We studied the map for our trip, that's how I know about them. You have to get back on the highway at the end. But these unpaved back roads are the one we were going to follow. It'll be slower, but if Tyler is walking, it shouldn't matter."

Jakes said, "What are you—you're encouraging them! We're taking a big chance here."

Graves whispered, "At least she'll have to slow down."

Staring into Graves' face, Jakes mumbled, "I guess. Keeping them out of trouble."

Lise looked into the driver's rear view mirror, finding Jakes' eyes. "It is taking a chance, but now you know we're telling the truth. Right? These are unusual circumstances, right? Special circumstances require special actions? I mean, how many girls you know can make lightning?"

The other Lise said, "We better not touch, soeur. You gentlemen, you better not get out. Stay with us. In case. D'accord? So stay. Think the right thoughts."

Sophie said, "I think I am going to throw up."

Lise hit the brakes, swinging over to the shoulder. "My parents will be madder at puke on the upholstery, then me borrowing the SUV."

Sophie managed, "So fast. Makes me dizzy."

Graves said, "Okay, Sophie? You going to be okay? There's a turn off pretty close actually. Should be just ahead. It should have a sign."

Sophie swallowed, nodded slowly. "I'm better."

Lise guided the SUV ahead and the headlights sprayed across the mesquite tangles on either side of the road. Didn't seem to be a turn off anywhere. Not a break in the brush. She kept the speed down, while Graves told her they were close. A marker with a triangle and a number came up on the side of the road opposite them. Graves pointed it out. Lise slowed, then reversed to head back to it.

Graves said, "This is it."

Lise stopped. Past the marker, the mesquite tangle climbed right over and through a barbed wire fence. But along the fence, a space. A narrow dirt road ran along the fence. It seemed 'open'. Lise turned in, cut around the mesquite, hoping not to scrape the SUV's sides. She knew all about mesquite thorns, having experienced their piercing stealth many times before in Glendale. She made it onto the narrow strip of road. She said, "You're sure this will take us to Coltrane?"

Graves said, "There'll be a few more turns, then it should connect back to the road that goes right in. These aren't used much anymore."

Lise hit the gas, braked, started up again, held back, followed along the barbed wire until it ended. Graves told her to go right. She did. She couldn't tell exactly whether she was always on a road. But she knew this landscape had been ranch country for a long time, so it made sense there would be ranch roads crossing it every which way. Soon the headlights seemed to be gobbled up by brush on all sides. Had she lost the road? She proceeded down the path of least resistance. A few mesquite limbs did swing and smack along the SUV. Lise kept driving, picking her away along. Mesquite thinned. Their path opened to a blasted looking, over grazed bare spot. Looked like the aftermath of war. White, almost bleached looking. Not too hard for the SUV. A clearer road defined itself, at least since the last turn. Mesquite and creosote, some yucca, dotted the area shown by the headlights.

Ahead, but to the side, Sophie could see where a big tangle of brush was coming up. Light couldn't penetrate it. Sophie thought, I will not be sick. I do not feel helpless because I am not alone. When we find Tyler, I think we'll be able to figure this out. Sophie spotted little side trails that made a labyrinth atop a maze in the brush. Animal paths. She and Tyler would have investigated! She and Tyler were explorers, eager to discover, anxious to understand animal inhabitants. Where was Tyler right now? Where was her 'double' right now? In her world?

Tall brush was on all sides now. They were driving down a mesquite tunnel. Sophie caught the glint of animal eyes ahead, just for a second, reflected from the headlights. A murmur of movement? She didn't say anything.

The Lise she knew pointed excitedly at where Sophie had noticed movement, saying: "Voila!"

The SUV slowed. The other Lise said, "What? What?"

A shadow returned, went solid, stood by the side of their meager road. Lise called out, "Taxidea! I've seen them at the Castor."

Sophie knew Taxidea too. She felt some odd relief at the sight of the animal.

Lise, driving, said, "What are you talking about? What's a taxi doing out here?" The SUV barely crawled. "Aha! An aminal!"

Graves and Jakes leaned over from the back to look and

Lise stopped the SUV.

Graves said, "It's a badger."

Not 10 feet from them a large desert badger was leaning up against the thick trunk of a mesquite. The tangled crown of the mesquite made an umbrella over him. The badger twisted its head back and forth. Its body tensed in this twisting, like it was about to attack or dance.

Lise, the driver, push buttoned her window down and called out, "What's it doing? Is it sick?"

Jakes said, "Rabies?"

Sophie said, "He wants us to follow him."

The other Lise, her Lise, said, "Bien sur! Follow! S'il vous plait!"

The brown and yellow creature with black marks along its sides and head looked like a little bear. Or a wolverine, thought Graves. Its movements and demeanor did not appear sickly. No foaming at the mouth, anyway. The animal seemed clean and groomed, solid and hearty.

The badger grunted out a sound like 'Fah!' and fell on to its forelegs and ran down the middle of the dirt road in a galloping gait, which seemed a tad comical because of its short limbs, and grunting emissions. That is to say: Graves, Jakes, and Lise from here heard a grunting.

"Vite! Vite!" cried Lise.

Sophie responded, "Schnell! Schnell!"

Their driver frowned, letting out her own grunt, then got the SUV headed after the badger. They moved slowly. The badger stopped, waited for them. The badger took off on a side trail. Lise said, "It's so narrow!" But she turned, followed, adding, "Where did the beastie go?"

Graves said, "Don't lose him!"

Jakes said, "You're encouraging them."

Lise called, "Encourage away!"

A short side trail the SUV barely squeezed through and the brushy opened to a cattle pond. The badger waited for them by the tank. Ranchers bulldozed make shift ponds in low spots to hold the monsoon rains. They called them tanks. Water meant a halo of green around the tank. This time of year, there couldn't have been more than a couple inches of water. The badger tiptoed up to the water line, avoiding the puddles along the muddy bank. The SUV was close enough now, its lights on the tank and badger. The mud was all chopped up. They didn't dare get any closer.

Lise called, "Should I stop? Turn off the engine?"

"Leave the lights on," said Jakes.

Lise turned off the engine. The silence came on. Everyone watched the badger as it entered the water. Just enough to cover its feet. The badger looked back at them.

"I'm turning off the lights. I don't want to run down the battery and be stuck out here with Mr. Badger." She hit the lights.

An explosion of darkness mated with silence to play their senses like musical instruments. A separate, distinct song to this desert night! Their eyes adjusted to star light. Everything turned deep blue-black. Their ears adjusted to clicks and snaps of vehicular settling sounds. Now they couldn't see if the badger was still there?

Sophie said, "We have to go see."

Jakes said fast, "Why? What do you mean? What does a weird acting badger mean in your world?"

Lise nodded, staring at her hands. She said, "In our world we all communicate."

"What does that mean?" cried Jakes.

Sophie pulled at the door she hugged. She had no clue how to open it. Lise tried to help but couldn't do it either. Lise, the driver, leaned over the other Lise to show how, but a blue flash between Lise's pushed her back.

"That was a big one," she said. "I felt that." She nervously giggled.

Graves straddled the front seat, leaning over to work the door for Sophie. It opened. A rush of night air and night sounds, insects, birds, breeze poured in.

Jakes lay a hand on Graves' arm. "This can't be good," he whispered. "It's foolish! What are we doing!"

Graves said, "We'll see."

Sophie swung her legs around to step out of the SUV but paused. She said, "Regardez!" She pointed.

The badger leaned up against the open door, looking in. Its wet and muddy paws were leaving a mark on the upholstery. Its alert, bright eyes reflected stars. The badger seemed smart and urgent.

The badger said, "Come, please. To talk with you."

That's what Sophie and Lise heard. So Sophie and Lise followed behind the badger to the cattle pond. The others stood by the SUV watching them, then turned to each other.

Lise, their driver, said, "Did you hear what I heard?"

Graves said, "It can't hurt to watch."

Jakes said, "What did you hear?"

They walked closer to the tank, slowing to pick their way through the mud. They found a dry spot.

Time worked for Sophie and Lise. They stood before the cattle tank that was also a diamond of attention or view. The night percolated perception and the water was a focusing selector. They settled on Old Duckbill rising from the water on his back, long tail paddling lazily. The forelimbs rested on the furry belly. Old Duckbill's head was angled back such that the duckbill was aimed straight up. The duckbill twitched, splashed. Old Duckbill said to them, "Sophie and Tyler must go on to Alburquerque to see Mela Dreiser. After Mela, they must go back to where it started. The doubles must go back to where it started, too. They should not touch. Overlap is possible."

Graves, Jakes and Lise started from their sitting positions. They were cross legged on the dry spot before the tank. Now they shivered and shifted, looked around with confused expressions.

Lise's head cleared enough to say, "Did we fall asleep?"

Graves whispered, "Dawn," and pointed to the east.

The other Lise and Sophie picked their way through the mud to join them. They were smiling, big smiles, excited, making a game of jumping between dry spots.

Jakes said, "What happened?"

Lise and Sophie giggled.

Jakes repeated, "Did we—"

Sophie blurted, "Beau! We have a plan. We go to Coltrane, then Tyler et moi to Alburquerque. Tyler and moi!"

Jakes said, "Albuquerque? What are you talking about?"

Lise, from there, said, "Old Duckbill. He said there was 'overlap'. I am not sure what that means." She looked at their faces and read the fear and confusion. "Old Duckbill? He communicated with us."

Sophie shook her head, said, "No commie."

The other Lise got to her feet. "Hermana," she said, "all I know is we were walking over to see what's up, what you guys were doing with the badger—"

Jakes interrupted with: "We came to this dry spot."

Lise finished, "And next thing: boom! It's dawn!"

Sophie and Lise kept their big grins.

Driver Lisa groaned, stretched, then, "Hey, where's the badger? Where did he go?"

Sophie said, "He had to get back to work."

Graves huffed: "The badger hypnotized us?"

Jakes said to the driver Lise, "Can you drive? I'll drive! I'll drive us back. This has gone on long enough."

Lise looked at him with disbelief. "I got the keys, jefe. You guys are welcome to take off. Go for it! We don't care. I said I was driving to Coltrane to find our brother, and I am. No buts about it."

Sophie and the other Lise went, "Beau!"

Jakes stared at Graves. Finally, Graves replied: "Well,

unless you want to wrestle these girls to the ground and take their keys, I say we go with them to Coltrane, then we can figure what's next. See what I'm thinking? How to get back to our horses, etc."

Jakes said, "This is freaking me out."

Graves said, "These are 'special' circumstances. We have no choice. We go along with them for now. Something. Is. Happening."

Lise, the driver, said, "Let's get out of here. You still know the way on these back roads?"

The other Lise said, "What's hap?"

Lise giggled, groaning, "I've created a monster!"

The drive to Coltrane was uneventful following the ranch roads, that started to climb as they got into the foothills of the mountains. Lise and Sophie were exhausted by whatever had happened to them. Whatever they had experienced. They slept most of the way. They were not bothered by the bumps along the rough ranch road, nor by the newly invented daylight. Driver Lise, and Graves and Jakes, felt oddly rested but unclear. They tried to go along with it. The road to Coltrane wasn't long. Graves and Jakes worried about police. They were worrying about what the authorities in general would think of their aiding runaway kids. But what exactly had happened with these kids? Were the FBI really involved? 'Switchers' and 'doubles'—it all seemed a bit much. So how to explain the crazy blue light sparks? They gave up speculating. Coltrane was a certainty. They were quiet into town, while the two up front slept.

They had to get back on the paved road to enter Coltrane. Graves guided Lise to the necessary turn onto the state highway. She shifted her driving stance, picking up speed. The two men in back had come to see that she was a pretty good driver. Morning light fell on empty highway cutting through the mountains. These mountains jutted up like excited reefs around an island rising from the desert floor. Rock formations could be famished galleons thrusting above petrified seas. A tumble of mountains, bare at the top, in different colors and textures. They were ascending, so changes in vegetation. Piñon and juniper covered the mounding slopes on either side of the highway. They passed a few houses. A car went by going the other way. It was so strange to see the other car, as though it intruded and shouldn't be there. Or, *it* was alien, disturbing their reality. The tunnel into town came up. They passed through it and were in Coltrane.

Coltrane, or what was left of it, was plopped in the Apache Mountains along an L shaped canyon. The tunnel delivered them to the start of the ragged long arm on the west side. They were heading downwards now, to the center of town. There was some traffic. A couple joggers ran along the main road. Wooden houses came to the curb, then, behind these houses, more houses went up the sides of the canyon, in some places as many as five levels. Many of the houses were in disrepair. Broken down trucks and clunkers hibernated at the side of the road. Trash was plentiful. Knotted sneakers hung from telephone wires, their poles excavated by greedy woodpeckers needing hidey holes for their acorns. The whole place looked like it could use a coat of paint. At least a good scrubbing. Maybe it was the woodpeckers fault.

The canyon slopes were mostly bare from overcutting and erosion, with only a few trees dotting the rocky surfaces. The trees had been cut for fuel for the smelters a hundred years ago. Lise and Sophie woke up to stare around them sleepily. Sophie clung to her door. They were taking in this Coltrane. They both started to shake.

Sophie cried, "We have to get back!"

Lise next to her said, "Old Duckbill said—you know what he said."

Driver Lise said, "We're here. It's okay. We'll find Tyler."

Graves said, "Sophie, what is it? Why are you upset? What's wrong?"

Sophie managed to sigh herself still from her burgeoning tears in order to say, "Waterfall town. The city of waterfalls. The Butterfly Lords! No waterfalls here." She shook with it, sighed, then quietly, like a murmur, "What have you done?"

Lise said, "Mi familia...we visit Coltrane. For fests, events. City of waterfalls. This is not the city of waterfalls!"

Graves said, "Alternate worlds? The multiverse? I don't get it. Two versions of the exact same place? This is science fiction, a popular trope. I don't understand. I don't get it. You guys came through... from there? To here? But that can't be right, can it? It's not possible."

Jakes said, "Maybe *too much* science fiction? And it preps or prompts the imagination? Seriously, what are we talking about here? What, or how, does this suggest a way out? A resolution?"

Graves said, "Listen, we were re-creating Coronado's trip. Right? We wanted to be as accurate as possible. With the same tech Coronado had in 1530. Right? We were trying to imagine another world, weren't we? Another time is another culture is another world. See what I'm thinking?"

"These kids are re-enacting another...time?" Jakes said.

"Sure, it's a re-enactment," said Graves.

Lise said, "We'll go downtown and park."

Sophie said, "How will we find Tyler in this place?"

The Lise's both shrugged. Together, they said, "We'll find him." They glanced at each other and cleared their throats in a funny way.

Jakes said, "You guys, you know we have to call the police. Let them know what's going on. Your parents must be sick with worry."

Sophie and Lise nodded at each other.

Jakes continued, "I think you need to think about what you're doing. You have to get back to your parents. None of you is eighteen. You have to realize that if there is something weird going on, that your running away with the family SUV could make it worse."

Lise slowed as they got downtown. Now the street was cracked and narrow, lined with battered shops, cafes, official looking buildings, then a bunch of hollowed out empty shambles of buildings. A few cars crawled by. People sauntered down the sidewalks, going on with lives that never entailed following a badger into the desert.

The center of town, the crook of the L, had the post office and convention center. A parking lot stretched behind those main buildings. More traffic now, more people, but Lise slid through the congestion into the parking lot and found a place. They came to a stop.

A long haired young man ran up to Lise's driver's side window. She made it go down. He said, "You can't park here."

Lise went, "We're not the droids you want."

The man ambled off.

Sophie turned to face the backseat travelers. "You both have been kind in a difficult situation. Your counterparts, from where I come from, would be pleased. And I thank ye for this. We will find Tyler here, then he and I must go to Alburquerque. The Lise's must return to the river. This is what our parents would want. We know this. You must follow your own hearts about what you must do."

Graves said, "Sophie, I'm just remembering something about the way you say Albuquerque. You keep adding that extra R: 'Alburquerque'. Don't you see, Jakes? That's the old, original, colonial name!"

"At least in our world," said Jakes.

"Jakes, don't be like that!" went Graves. "Sophie, I wouldn't have missed this adventure for the world. Thanks to you guys!"

Jakes moved in place, stirring, stretching, then grabbing for the door handle. "Do you see how this whole situation puts us in a very delicate position? As the adults here, we could be charged with, I don't know, aiding and abetting? Kidnapping?"

Graves said, "You're overdoing it. Obviously, the blue lights and badger talk mean something. We're not going crazy."

Lise belt out: "Short trip!"

Graves continued, "Let's see if they find Tyler. Then we can call. The horses are okay. We'll be back in no time."

Jakes shook his head but he knew it did no good. He hadn't yet opened his door, so did now. "If we find this Tyler, and they go on to Albuquerque, with or without the extra R, before we alert authorities, we'll get blamed."

The Lises said in unison, "No! You won't!" They looked at each other but kept their distance. Again, together, they said, "This is a unique situation."

The other Lise added, "Unique. Un bon mot."

The Lise who'd driven said, "This is special, and we're special. O, so special! How many girls can shoot lightning bolts out of their finger tips?" She turned off the car. She opened her door and got out. She leaned back in to glance over her passengers. She said, "Come on, let's go find Tyler."

The small group, proceeding past the post office, got their bearings, crossed the main street to a park. The two men held back. They argued but quietly, following along. In the park they came together in a close circle. Down main street, a rainbow parade marched: people with banners and in wacky clothes danced along the street.

Jakes was nervous. He blurted, "What now? Where to?"

Sophie said, "This way! The Butterfly Lords!"

"Oui, oui!" cried Lise.

The two girls led the others into the heart of Coltrane.

They went up and down some steps. They followed along in single file on narrow stairs that climbed bizarre zigzags. Dead cars, garbage, animal poo was everywhere. They passed a big hotel, a church, and a school. The people they encountered were friendly, smiling, nodding to them. The girls were lost. They couldn't find the Butterfly Lords. By an old Victorian monstrosity, now all boarded up, they paused, looked around. Lise and Sophie went up the steps to have a better vantage. Sophie reached the top of the steps and looked around.

* * *

Tyler Gack of Chichimeca knew not to go, but the small man was so earnest, Tyler went along the river with him to the gaily painted circus wagon...just to see what he meant about this 'psychic' (?). He felt weak, his lower back hurt. But the going had been easy along the river. A path had been carved by many feet. This was not the Castor he knew, with its low banks and marshy lowlands. This was the much feebler, steep banked San Pedro, lined with giant, tangled cottonwoods. No aurochs here. There would be no graze for them. No albino giraffes or megatherium either.

But the small man he followed was so pleasant, so certain that Tyler found himself curious. Up until then, no one had seemed open to such possibility. The people here seemed always rushing to their expectations. An impossible situation may require an impossible possibility? What would Johnny Appleseed say? What would Old Duckbill advise?

Quickly, he saw the vehicle was like no circus wagon he had ever seen. No horses, or oxen, for one thing. And it wasn't made out of wood. It certainly was adorned with the colors and banners of a circus wagon. Across its side in an arc was painted in tall letters, *Crotalus.* The vehicle's internal combustion engine must be up front. It was backwards! Drivers sat up front in a cab. Windows up front, but none on the sides. It was some kind of truck, Tyler decided.

People by the truck: a young man and a young woman. The man was hanging out of the back of the truck. Loading or unloading, Tyler couldn't tell. The young woman startled Tyler with the color of her hair. It was like nothing he'd ever seen. A strange, unnatural red? She was busy around the area behind the truck. Maybe they had had a camp, though there was no evidence of a campfire. Maybe they were breaking camp?

The young woman with dazzlingly metallic red hair paused in her work, her arms Tyler now could see were burdened with rolled up pads. She surveyed the 2 approaching and called out, "Bishop's picked up a stray!" She continued to the back of the truck where she handed off the stuff in her arms to the young man.

The young man in the back of the truck had long hair and short legs. He was busy throwing in the stuff from the young woman, then he finished and jumped out. He was short and well built. He wore a bright pink button down shirt and bring pink trousers. His feet, like the young woman's, were bare. Tyler had never seen so many tattoos on people before, on this young man and young woman.

"Bishop," he said, "I thought we were leaving? Kai's finished with the tune. He says the engine's groovin', just purring."

"Like a caravan?" went Tyler weakly.

"Good to know," said the man Tyler knew as Homer, who now opened wide his arms and turned to Tyler. "Welcome to Crotalus!"

The young man said, "And this pup has dreamed his whole life of running away to join the circus, Bishop?"

"He looks underage," said the young woman with the startlingly bright hair.

"Tyler, come! Please! This is Tommy, our juggler. And this is Luanna, my assistant. A psychic herself, good with all forms of magic."

She said, "I eat fire."

Tyler was bustled over to meet the two. Tommy's tattoos peaked out of his shirt sleeves. He must have tattoos all across his chest and shoulders. He shook Tommy's hand. Tyler turned to Luanna. He stared at Luanna's face as she took his hand and held it. Her face had a number of metal points and what might be jewels sticking out of it.

Luanna smiled, released Tyler's hand, and said, "He's cute."

Tommy said, "Love your get up."

"What do you mean?" asked Tyler, who had been dressed by his mom here. At least, she'd tried to—

Tommy said, "Your clothes? Your very cool moccasins."

"My family here borrowed me a shirt."

"You live around here, Tyler?"

Tyler nodded. "Not far from here, but far the same."

Another man came from around the truck wiping his blackened hands on a cloth. "We're good to go, Bishop."

Tyler said, "I thought your name was Homer."

Luanna said, "That's his Crotalus name. His show name. Because he's a story teller. Basically."

The new man was big and older than Luanna and Tommy. He looked Tyler up and down. "Who's this?"

Bishop said, "Tyler. Kai, this is Tyler. Tyler, Kai."

Kai nodded to Tyler, then asked, "Are we getting going? Heck with the sheriff, we can still make Coltrane. Do a show tonight?"

Bishop nodded. He looked very thoughtful, serious but clear too. He said, "Listen, everybody, this young man is imperiled. Take a second. Come close. Gather round. No worry, Tyler. Let them come close to you. Yes, good. Feel it. See? See what I mean? I figure—"

Luanna finished for him, "Mela Dreiser?"

Kai said, "Where is she now?"

Tommy said, "Last we heard, she was in the Duke City."

Luanna murmured, "Not that far."

Tyler shook his head and raised his hands and stepped away from them. "You sense things?" he stammered.

"Easy," said Luanna. "Sure, yes, we do."

Bishop said, "You do too, Tyler. We can tell you're not from here."

Tyler backed up into a stump that perhaps had been used as a seat, but now was a tripping obstacle. Tyler went over on his back. He lay there, trying to concentrate.

Luanna knelt by him. "Tyler. Tyler, look at me. Okay? Okay. How do you feel?"

Tyler whispered, "Confused."

"I'll make tea," she said. She offered him a hand and he took it, and she helped him to his feet. "Here. Sit here on the stump by me where I can take care of you. And we got a pot of beans and fresh tortillas. Super yummy! You hungry?"

"Thanks," said Tyler, arranging himself on the stump. He sighed. He looked at the men who stood nearby. Luanna returned to the back of the truck and pulled herself aboard. "Beans," said Tyler.

"Don't worry," said Tommy, "we're Vegan."

"Chichimeca," said Tyler. "I'm from Chichimeca."

Tommy laughed. "Super! Whatever, dood! We're all Americans."

"You're Papists?" asked Tyler.

Bishop interrupted, "Luanna will get you some tea and something to eat. She can throw your Tarot if you want. She's got the sight."

Tyler had heard of the Tarot. He said, "So far, no one here seems to know Swedenborg? That one girl, Aurore, at the 'bed and breakfast', she'd heard of him."

Kai laughed. "Swedenborg? Bet Bishop knows about Swedenborg. Right, Bishop?" He leaned into Tyler as though to share a secret, whispering, "His parents were old hippies. They were into all that stuff."

"Let him breathe," said Bishop. "Take your time, Tyler. We may be able to help."

Tyler said, "I know a Dreiser. Everyone does. Pamela Dreiser?"

Luanna jumped from the back of the van and said, "Pamela. Mela. Pa-me-la. See?" She handed Tyler a rough clay cup with steam rising from it. He took it, eyed it carefully, held it close to his face and blew on it.

Then it came to him and he got it. "Oh, yes," said Tyler. "I see! Pamela. Mela."

"Good," went Luanna. "Do you like the tea? It's herbal. Here's a burrito. I didn't know if you liked it hot."

Tyler took the burrito with his other hand, looked it over.

Bishop intoned, "Dreiser has access. She's the one right now. All like that. We trust her for the really good time."

Tyler sipped the fragrant tea. It was good. He sipped some more. He could feel it coursing through his body. He sipped, had a bite. It was delicious. He ate and sipped until the burrito was gone.

Kai and Tommy sat cross legged on the ground in front of Tyler. Luanna stood next to him, at his side, close. Bishop was directly in front, standing there, but not looking at him or the others. His eyes closed. Bishop became a humming sound, as he conspired the moment into a story. This is what he said:

"I was fat, now am lean. I was bat, now am shrew. I was blind, now can see. I was fast, now am slow. Once upon a time, I had a teacher by the name of Oklahoma Zen. He showed me how I pick my concentration. What I decide to focus on or emphasize is my story. Oklahoma Zen could take a man's measure. He passed along this personality impress express suppress. He taught me to be a story teller.

"He passed along peace. Stories and peace, we are soft treaders: once upon a time, there were Beats and Diggers and Trogs, all the way to hippies. And we were there. We've always been around. We go around making things a little more right. Why not? Someone has to do it. And we stumbled right into you, Tyler. It can't be an accident. An anomaly? Of course! Life delight! We will do you right. We can help, Tyler."

He bowed his head to Tyler.

Tyler had gone along with the story, with Bishop. He comprehended this is how Bishop felt and thought. He was an intense, good man. But how could he help him find his way back to his own world? Shouldn't he go back to the bed and breakfast for Sophie? They should stick together! But if he went back now the folks there'd never let him out of their sight again. He couldn't stop worrying about Sophie. It made him sick. He felt wretched. He couldn't abandon her. But that's exactly what he had done when he wandered off after their re-enactment attempt.

Yes, this was a story. This was his mad story that had no plot he'd ever imagined. For example, apparently, they had a Pamela Dreiser here, too. What could she do to help? If she was like them, Tyler pondered, she might not be able to do a thing?

Tyler sighed, straightened his back. He liked these people. This place, these people: overworked and intense. But he didn't have a choice: he had to trust them?

Tyler knew he was expected to respond...to say something. Tyler said, "Thank you. You remind me of Old Duckbill."

"I'll take that as a compliment," said Bishop. "Feeling better?""

Tyler nodded and Luanna put her hand on his head and tousled his hair. She asked, "Who are you, Tyler?"

"Tu ami, j'espere."

"I'll take that as a compliment. What's your story, Tyler?"

Bishop said, "Don't push."

Tyler said, "My family has been in Chichimeca since the beginning. Though our people lived up north. My parents came to the Castor to start their fur business. Hides? Tanning? You know? I help with the aurochs. I help with my parents' work. Sophie was visiting with her family from St. Louis. They're Americans. Her parents were working with plastique. Came out to work with them. Sophie's the other person—the other person who came here with me. Well, we came here...from our world together. She came with me. We don't how. Or why.

"Sophie and I had become friends right away, when they first got here from St. Louis. Her family were educated, not papists. Scientists. We liked to explore the river, meet its inhabitants. Nature is perfect. So much to see and learn. In our explore. So, we were on the river, exploring, talking. Something happened. There were lights. And Sophie and I were here. This river you call the San Pedro. There was a girl there. Her name was Aurore. She welcomed us. She said she'd seen the whole thing. We had switched with the Tyler and Sophie from here. My parents here are not the same. Sophie's parents here are not the same either. This whole world is not the same. I believe the parents here think we are mad. The parents called law enforcement. At the bed and breakfast, all these people, all very upset, but no one knows what's happening or what to do. I wandered off. That's what I know. That's how I got here. I write poems."

Tommy said, "Albuquerque isn't in our plan."

Kai nodded. "It's a side trip. Excursion al dente. A detour?" He shrugged. "We could do it. One step at a time."

Luanna said, "We are all poets," which made Tommy

squeak with laughter.

Bishop said, "Right now, we go to Coltrane. See about things from there. See what turns up? Sound good? One step at a time, indeed."

Tyler said, "Waterfall City?"

Luanna knocked on his head, said, "Coltrane's a dump. No one has any money."

Bishop said, "Listen to you!"

Kai said, "When do we leave?"

Bishop said, "'When the hurly burly's done—'"

Tyler finished, "'—when the battle's lost and won.'"

Bishop smiled. "Dusk. We move out at dusk, in the crack between worlds. It'll be perfect. We'll be invisible."

They sat awhile. All of them sat. And Tyler stretched out his legs and bowed his head. He closed his eyes. When he jolted upright, he was scooting off the stump. They were looking at him. Not staring at him so much as seeing him. Then, they closed their eyes. And Tyler closed his eyes again, after getting comfortable on the stump. Could he rest, or sleep, sitting up?

Tyler wasn't sure how long they rested, but when Crotalus got to their feet, he did too. The light had changed. It was late afternoon. Kai and Bishop went around to the front of the truck to get in. Kai was also the driver. Tommy and Luanna guided Tyler to the back of the van. Tyler smelled sage. He smelled herbs and cooking oil and dirty clothes. Tyler stepped up, pulled himself in. Luanna came next. Tommy had to push Tyler forward so he could get in. Tommy swung the back doors around and pulled them tight, locking them. Luanna had scooted ahead of him, calling, "Come on in. Get comfortable."

To Tyler's right were 2 bunks, one on top of the other, loaded with sleeping bags, pillows, clothes. To his right, a wall of shelves packed with jars and old coffee cans that must have held herbs. They sure smelled like it. Under the shelves, on the floor were boxes and a trunk. These were bulging with masks, musical instruments, and costumes. In the front on one side was a sink and small built in stove. Five gallon tubs of water were stuck under the stove. The other side had a cooler which made a seat for Luanna. She pointed to the area next to her and patted it with her hand. It was a niche of pillows and pads where a person might curl up and read or just sit. Tyler folded himself into the niche. Tommy came up and leaned over Luanna to pound on the window that opened into the cab. Bishop turned to push open the window.

Bishop, or Homer, had an easy, sweet, open face and Tyler liked him. Now he said, "Everyone ready?"

Tommy said, "Good to go."

Kai started the van, gassed it a little. "She's fine, fine, superfine!" he said. "Ready as she'll ever be. Let's get this road on the show!"

He put the truck into gear and started pulling away from the turn off they'd parked in. He guided the truck back to the county road and turned right.

Tommy called, "This isn't the way to Coltrane!"

Bishop said, "We know."

Kai explained, "We're taking the long way around to avoid you know who."

Bishop said, "Road blocks."

Kai drove carefully, keeping the speed down. Dusk came on and the pale white desert terrain went silvery. Kai turned on the headlights.

Tommy moved back to the bunks, ducking in to the lower. Luanna stretched out her legs and bare feet. She rolled her shoulders. Tyler watched her.

Then, Tyler said, "Bishop knows his way around here."

Luanna smiled, said, "Bishop knows everything."

Bishop called back, "I can hear you."

Luanna laughed and said, "It's his Indian blood. We all have a little Apache blood, don't we? We are all Apaches now?"

Tyler shook his head. "I'm sorry."

Luanna went, "Apache?"

"Maybe I heard the term in school. From history class?" said Tyler.

Luanna looked at him oddly. She shrugged, then, "One thing at a time."

They made it to the state highway that ran along the border. From there, Kai turned left. East. The highway would go around the mountains, so enter Coltrane from the east side. Maybe 30 miles.

They drove into the darkness and everyone was quiet. Tyler wanted to talk. What would happen in Coltrane? What about Sophie? He wondered about Sophie, his friend. Again, the overwhelming impossibility of it all struck him full force. No, he did not want to talk: he wanted to rest. But how could he rest? This Pamela Dreiser, the one here, what could she do? What could anyone do? It was beyond comprehension. Switching, doubles—how could it be explained?

The back of the truck went dark and Tyler seemed to have to concentrate on the glow from Luanna's shoulders and neck. She had her head pressed back onto the wall behind her, exposing the curve of her neck. Her eyes were closed. All Tyler could do was watch her. Two metal points stuck out above her lip. Her cheeks held jewels. He watched her glitter and sparkle. Until, finally, she opened her eyes into his and said, "Take a picture, it'll last longer."

Tyler was startled, had no idea what she meant, so twisted in place like he was trying to get comfortable.

Bishop called out, "There!"

Kai took his foot off the gas pedal, and the van's throbbing speed let up.

Bishop cried, "Back there! Not far."

No other lights coming or going that Kai could see, so

he came to a stop on the highway, put it in reverse and headed backwards.

Bishop said, "That little turn off, on the side, here, in the yucca and brush. Turn in! Turn in! Cut the lights!"

Kai did as he was told, guiding the truck into the small turn off in as far as he could. He cut the lights.

Tommy huskily whispered from the back, "What's going on?"

Luanna said, "Bishop saw something."

Tommy called, "Are we off the highway enough?"

"Among these yucca gentlemen," said Kai, "I don't think anyone can see us."

Luanna asked, "What did you see, Bishop?"

Bishop was staring out his window. He rolled it down, stuck his head out. He opened the door by his side and hopped out. Kai got out from his side after him, then walked around the front of the truck to join him. Because the window was down, the people in the back could hear Kai whistle softly and go, "Wow!" They could let themselves out, but it was easier to wait for Kai who opened the doors, pulling them wide.

Tommy got out first, then Luanna, then Tyler. In the sudden immersion into dark and quiet, Tyler made out the forms of many people, mainly it looked like men, standing among the cactus, huddling with Bishop.

Luanna said, "Buenas tardes."

A few voices softly returned the greeting.

Bishop called, "Tommy, bring some water. Luanna, we got any of those beans left?"

Everyone got busy but Tyler, who mainly stood around trying to keep out of Crotalus' way. In the dark this ended up meaning bumping into sharp tongued yucca as well as stumbling over rocky ground. The people whom Bishop had spotted turned out to be Mexicans, he learned. How had Bishop seen them hiding in the yucca? Tyler found a safe spot to the side and realized he could understand their Spanish though it sounded different. The accents were different. Bishop seemed able to converse with them, too. Kai and Tommy made sure everyone got a drink. Luanna, in the back of the truck which showed some light, called for Tyler to come help. He walked over to the rear of the truck. She stood at the stove warming tortillas in a frying pan. A big black pot bubbled softly next to the frying pan. She watched Tyler climb in, find his way back to her, then she turned off the light. She said, "Don't want to let our light out, you know. I'll dish 'em, you roll 'em. Okay?"

"Los burritos," went Tyler.

"For sure," said Luanna and started moving fast. Splat of

beans to the warmed tortilla, then she spatulaed it over to a plate in front of Tyler. Tyler rolled it up as best he could. Luanna already had another tortilla going.

She said, "Tuck in the ends first, then roll it up. They won't be so messy. That's fine." She spooned another glop of vegan beans to a tortilla, and leveraged it to Tyler.

When Tyler had five burritos, each rolled better than the previous one, Luanna told him to take them and give them out. She said he should find out how many more were needed.

Kai helped Tyler give out the burritos. Kai gave one to a young Mexican woman, not much older than Tyler. Tyler saw how exhausted she looked. Her clothes were torn and filthy. Lots of 'gracias' were uttered.

Tyler called out to no one in particular: "How many more should we make?"

Bishop said, "Keep 'em coming!"

Kai said, "We're doing fine!"

Bishop said, "This one boy has a thorn in his leg. He's hurting. Tell Lu."

Tyler returned with the plate and Luanna slid a warm tortilla with beans on to it. She asked, "How many?"

"Alles. Es todo."

Luanna glanced into his eyes, nodded. "All we can make."

Tyler said, "Bishop said one of them is hurt. He said to tell you."

Luanna tsked, "Needs doctoring? First we feed them."

"Who are they?" asked Tyler. "What are they doing here on the side of the road?"

"Illegals," said Luanna.

"What do you mean?" said Tyler in a hush. "Illegal people? How can that be? Oh, war then."

Luanna smiled, shimmered, shook with it. "No, no."

Tyler said, "Some say Mexico will invade, and we'll have a war. But America said it would support our sovereignty."

Luanna moved another loaded tortilla over to Tyler. She said, "Wow. You guys are Chichimeca? Mexico is too poor to have a war. These are the poor. Deadly poverty. The desperate. They risk their lives to come here. We have to help."

Tyler finished tucking and rolling, shook his head but didn't know whether Luanna had seen the motion. "I don't understand. Yes, we are Chichimeca. It's an old name. But Mexico is rich with technology. They use petrochemicals. People say they use projectile weapons. But that's a rumor. Gossip. We don't know for sure."

Now Luanna shook her head with what Tyler could see was frustration. "Not sure we're talking the same things here, Tyler. It's like one conversation about two different places at once. All I know is these folks are hungry and thirsty. So we help out. It's not much. But what else could we do? Maybe we can help whoever is sick."

They ran out of beans. Burritos were eaten up. More thanks and sighs. Bishop sat on the ground next to a young man who leaned back on his arms with his legs stretched out in front of him. Only a couple cars and one truck had passed, not slowing or swerving by them at all. They tried to think themselves invisible. All you had to do was think the right thoughts, or at least that's what Bishop seemed to suggest.

Bishop had Kai get a flashlight. Luanna and Tyler stood near them. A few of the Mexican men and the woman watched close by. The others sat or stretched out as best they could in the brush. Kai brought the flashlight. Bishop took it and talked with the man quietly for a moment. The man nodded and put his left hand on the side of his trousers of his left leg. Bishop had a pocket knife out. He unfolded it. He couldn't hold both, so he had to hand the flashlight back to Kai. Bishop cut the trousers about 3 inches near the man's hand. When Bishop touched the tear to open it more, the man shuddered, gulping in pain.

Bishop said, "Sorry," then, "con permiso," and motioned to Kai to bring the flashlight to the tear. They both saw it. Kai sucked his breath. A swollen red knot made a mound about the size of half a lemon.

Bishop went, "Thorn's still in there and it's deep."

Luanna said, "I'll make a drawing poultice."

Bishop said, "We'll have to draw it out carefully so it doesn't break up. It could take a while."

Tommy said, "We're here for the rest of the night for sure."

Kai said, "Get used to it."

Luanna got back in the truck and Tyler followed after her. She turned on the ceiling light. She put on the stove a clean pot, added water to it, and set it to boil. She turned off the light. The light from the fire on the stove was all they were left with again. She sidled away from the stove and over to the wall of shelves. Tyler made himself flat against the bunk side.

Luanna said, "I need herbs."

Tyler kept himself flattened as she set about her search. She described the herbs she would need. She worked in the faint glow so she had to sniff each container carefully. She went through jars and old coffee cans.

"Golden seal to cleanse and stop infection. Hyssop is good for inflammation. Then burdock and comfrey to draw it out."

She found what she needed and took the materials to the stove, put them in the pot. Next, she found a clean hand towel.

"It's near boil, it's ready fast," she said. She put the folded towel into the pot. "We'll add water as needed, keep it going. We can add more herbs as we need, too." She waited for the first bubbles. She reached in to the pot and pulled out the small drenched towel. She squeezed it out lightly.

"Tyler, add more water to the pot when it boils down. Make sure it doesn't boil over. I'll give this to Bishop and we can start the process."

She left Tyler and he carefully moved over to the stove. The pot was barely boiling. He added a little water.

This went on all night. Luanna went back and forth refreshing the towel. Tyler stayed at the boiling pot. Finally, Tyler collapsed at the niche and may have dreamed. He may have thought of the last couple days. He couldn't remember. He felt weak and cloudy. He remembered watching Luanna move back and forth. He felt guilty. He should keep up on the water. He tried and then he slept.

It must have been dawn when Luanna woke him. Light came in from the front window above him. The interior reeked of herbs. Tyler got to his feet. He stood near a smiling, but sleepy looking Luanna.

She said, "We got it. He's good! They took off before light. The thorn came all the way out. Every speck of it. We're going to get going. Bishop wants to catch 40 winks back here. He was wondering whether you'd want to sit up front with Kai."

"Where will you be?"

Luanna reached out a hand and took his arm. "Right here, silly. I need some shut eye, too."

"'Shut eye?'"

Tyler scooted past Luanna and out the back of the truck. Bishop and Tommy were there, scanning the yucca and brush.

Tommy said, "No one will ever know what happened here."

Bishop said, "Leave only footprints. And magic." He smiled to Tyler. "Ready to go?"

Tyler said, "Yes."

Tommy said, "We're getting in back for a little shut eye."

Tyler said, "Later you'll have to explain to me this 'shut eye'."

Coltrane was an old mining town that had peaked in about 1915 with over 30,000 inhabitants or stragglers, then miners and gamblers and entrepreneurs. Small settlements built up around various digs where a mine sent down a shaft, then erected an elevator to it. Now, Coltrane was a slightly living ghost town of around 5,000, including a bunch of hippies and artists, and a lot of Mexican-Americans. When you entered from the east, you went past the open pit in pastel chemical colors, like oranges and odd blue-grays. Then you came into town, got off the state road to the main drag. Right away, you're facing the old brick Victorian edifices of the town center, a big old hotel, the post office and convention center. The intersection and park by the post office and convention center made a traffic hub.

Kai had to calm Tyler when they went by the open pit. Tyler was so shocked at the monstrous sight he'd had to close his eyes until Kai said they were by it. Kai murmured to him that he was okay. It was all going to work out. It had to. What other choice was there? Then in town, when Kai was looking for a parking space, Tyler, eyes open now, started gasping. Kai guided the truck through the traffic. People on the sidewalks and jaywalkers were pointing out their vehicle, waving, hooting at them. Kai was satisfied, saying that was the best way to get the word out, the grand entrance into town. It was a circus tradition.

Tyler managed another, "What happened?" But then was sorry he'd asked, as there could be no explanation in this world. Kai couldn't imagine Coltrane any other way. This was what he expected.

Kai shrugged and said, "I'll have to park in the back. Over there. Hey, maybe we can set up back there in the overflow parking lot. It'll depend on the cops." He swung the truck to the left behind the convention center. A tall long haired fellow got out of their way, offering a little wave as he passed. Kai said, "We're not the one he wants."

Kai parked in an open area, without many vehicles. He motioned to Tyler to tell the others. Kai called, "Home again, Flanagan!"

Tyler turned and leaned into the window behind him. "We're here. Somewhere. C'est tres tres...strange."

Tyler could hear Tommy snicker.

Kai called out, "What?"

Tommy called back, "Let's get outta here!"

Kai and Tyler got out of the van and went around to open the back. Pretty soon Tommy, Bishop, and Luanna were with them. They still looked pretty groggy. And Tommy and Luanna were still dressed as before, and barefoot.

Bishop said, "Did you tell Tyler about your friend?"

Kai nodded. "No, but I should give her a call. Make sure it's cool. Should we walk?"

Bishop said, "Time to see what happens next. How this will work. You okay Tyler?"

Tyler nodded. "What was Kai to tell me?"

Kai said, "Check this out: my friend Lantine here—she lives in Coltrane, is a pilot. She has her own plane. See where I'm going with this? She's one of us. And she knows Mela. She can fly you to Albuquerque."

Tyler nodded. "I am to fly to Alburquerque? You mean the slings?"

"If we can arrange it," said Kai.

"We can do a show right here where we parked," said Tommy.

Luanna went up to Tyler. "You're a bit pekid, lad...as me gram used to say." She pushed close to his ear: "What's a sling?"

Tyler smiled weakly at her.

Kai was walking away from them. "I think there's a pay phone by the post office."

They followed behind him. Tyler said to Luanna and Tommy, "Don't you have shoes?"

They grinned. Tommy said, "These are our inner outer feet."

"'Otter'?" said Tyler.

Bishop said, "Come on. Into the future."

Kai stood at a pay phone, pressing buttons, phone pressed in his neck.

People went in and out of the post office. Old raggedy men sat on a bench by the phone, wheezing and staring. Kai talked into the phone.

Tyler listened, watched. "It's like a commie?"

Tommy said, "We ain't commies."

Bishop said, "Hush. He means another mean. Why don't we walk? Kai'll catch up with us."

Luanna took Tyler's hand and led him past the post office, then across the main street to the maze of small side streets behind it.

"Where are the waterfalls?" asked Tyler.

Luanna squeezed his hand. "No waterfalls here I know of," she said. "Maybe if it rains?"

Bishop and Tommy were behind them. Kai came hurrying up fast to join them. Luanna and Tyler paused, turned, heard the words, "It's set!" and Bishop's giggle of joy.

They walked into the heart of Coltrane. Old buildings were boarded up or their roofs were collapsing. Trash littered the way. Broken down vehicles and trucks collected in weed filled lots. They went up stairs. They climbed down stairs. They moved through alleys. The people they passed were friendly. No one seemed too surprised at Crotalus' clothes or colors or bare feet. In fact, many of the locals seemed to be dressed similarly with bare feet, too.

Bishop guided them down a narrow road. There was no traffic, so they walked down the middle of the road. Ahead was a large Victorian structure that was boarded up, but it was clear it must have been a grand building at one time. It had steps up to its entrance. On the steps, some young women. Some men stood below them, looking up to them.

Tyler's eyes went over the young women on the steps. Finally, one of the young women, a black woman, met his eye and immediately yelled, "Tyler!"

Tyler felt his knees turn to jelly. He would not faint. He had to hold on now. It was Sophie!

They came together, Sophie rushing to him first, and at the moment they embraced, the earthquake hit.

* * *

Lise said, "This was the moving picture house, oui?"

Sophie nodded, kept looking.

Coming up a narrow street towards them, another small group of people, young and old, male and female.

Sophie cried, "Tyler!"

Lise followed her gaze and spotted him with the

approaching group. "C'est vrai!" She said, "Mon frère!"

Tyler heard the cries and his dull features brightened. His eyes flashed with happiness. He moved to them.

They ran to each other. When Sophie and Tyler clasped, the earthquake struck.

CHAPTER 10

Special Agent Alan Adler, team leader of the FBI at the Rio Vista Bed and Breakfast, blurted unkindly, "Then why weren't we turned to jelly?" No response. "It wasn't an earthquake."

He was fed up with the unimaginative handling of a series of anomalies, the like of which the world had never seen, by specialists brought in by the feds. Especially irritating were Dr. Jeri Downs of the CDC, and an NSC troubleshooter, Paul Button. Now these people, with their allies, sat across from Adler at a table in the bed and breakfast's dining room which had been turned into a command center. Since yesterday's event, the techs had gotten the generators going so the dining room's bristling communications equipment, computers and sensory devices were back online. Adler knew how to read a suspect's body language, and he could read volumes in the squirming tics of the two specialists. The scientists, medical personnel and law enforcement people sat at the table avoiding Adler's eyes.

Adler continued, "A shock wave's a shock wave. Right? I mean, it acts in certain predictable ways, regardless of what triggered it?"

A scientist at the table, Don Virnig, a short man with

big eyes and balding pate, said in a surprising bass voice, "It was unlike any explosion we've encountered. Certainly, not an earthquake. Our instruments were knocked out fairly quickly, so all we can do is surmise. We didn't get enough readings."

"Nuclear?" asked Sheriff Wrigley.

Button said, "No, we told you that. There's no sign of radiation. Just for practical purposes we call the earthquake which was not an earthquake an earthquake."

The scientist with the deep voice looked away, looked down, looked back up. He seemed to be directing his voice skyward. "Not nuclear. Some kind of annihilation. Maybe what we'd expect when matter and anti-matter obliterate each other. I don't know. I'm just throwing that out since this seems to be a science fiction story. We just don't know. The shock wave went out in a spherical manner as all shock waves will do, but, yes, then something happened. It seems to have had some kind of...delay? A jump? We don't even know how to describe it. Like a sonic boom skipped the booming but had a beginning and end? But the shock wave jumped? I don't even know what that means."

Special Agent Karen Connelly nodded, raised a hand above the table, said, "Not much destruction right around the site where we think it originated. I mean, trees knocked down. But it's as if the shock wave hadn't built up yet?"

The scientist shook his head, shrugged. "We're speculating."

Since this latest incident, they were mad with doubt and confusion. When too many impossible things happen at once, and the so called people in charge are just as susceptible to the shock of the never before experienced as the next guy, control gets fidgety. They'd called in for more experts, who'd be there pronto. Fast, the sequence of events was becoming a national emergency. The casualties and the property damage in Coltrane had insured that. Actually, the entire circumference at a radius of thirty miles from ground zero had been impacted by the 'shock wave'. Minor damage at the point of origin, then this thirty mile jump.

Paul Button and Dr. Downs were restrained in their self confidence. They both got up from their folding chairs at the table. They only had eyes for each other as they slowly walked over to the window across the room. Adler followed their every move. Next to him, Connelly sat worrying about her boss, his anger, then the imminent danger that seemed to be crowding their charges, a set of kids that had somehow doubled and switched, though the switched kids were no longer around..

Sheriff Wrigley inserted, "Now that the governor has called out the National Guard we won't have no worries about security. We got the doubles back. We've got good leads on the switched kids. I don't see anyone getting away from here again. In the mean time, I gotta get over to Coltrane to help out. Things are a bit rough there."

Special Agent Connelly felt compelled to add, "And we think the switched kids went to Albuquerque. Why is unclear. The circus people and this Graves and Jakes presented irrational stories about what happened and why. They believed these stories."

No one blinked or nodded or responded in any way. They had all been through this too many times by now.

Connelly continued, "To sum up, somehow Sophie and Tyler were reunited in Coltrane just when the explosion, or whatever it was, occurred. Did they cause it? We don't know. It seems unlikely? Then they seem to have been whisked away by other parties to Albuquerque. The clear implication: there are people out there who know something about what's going on. Or at least more than we know. Moreover, the circus people, and Graves and Jakes seemed willing to talk, but turn out not to have much information. Of value I mean."

Downs and Button, by the window, were nodding. Adler was looking down at the yellow pad in front of him. Connelly went on, "Graves and Jakes do seem to have been simply passersby. They check out. They have been released. They are apparently coming back here to get their horses to continue their re-enactment journey."

Outside the window where Downs and Button stood, and hunkered down out of sight, the two Aurore's listened to every word. They kept some distance between themselves. They knew the two scientists were at the window above them, looking out. They'd never look down. It was not allowed. The Aurore's had it timed perfectly: they had four minutes before one of the children's matrons would be after them. Together, they mouthed and whispered, "I say we stay."

Adler lifted his head and said, "We have no choice. With the kids back, with the uncertainty of events, we have to evacuate everyone from here within the thirty mile radius."

Button, still looking out of the window, muttered, "We don't have the switchers back. We have to get them back here. I say we stay. Why Albuquerque? What's in Albuquerque?"

Dr. Downs also stared out the window and said, "Apparently, there's someone in Albuquerque who can help. We're checking that out. For now, we focus on the most likely scenario. Talking badgers are outside our jurisdiction. The hippy circus seems to...sense something. But they are awash in metaphors we are unfamiliar with. Mucho marijuana smokers. They call it a breakdown of space and time, which is probably as good a metaphor as anyone can come up with."

Button turned around to face the table. He said, "Okay. Fine. We know it was not an earthquake. I agree. Seismic data was clear. At least it was until the equipment shut down. Some kind of explosion occurred down there, less than a half a mile from here. At the exact spot where the switching, for lack of a better word, took place. See the logic? Origin? Start? The question now is will it happen again? Maybe a bigger explosion and from right down there?" He pointed out the window with an outstretched arm. It was a very dramatic gesture.

Dr. Downs said, "That seems unlikely. Unless we're dealing with phenomena that's never been imagined." She snorted, shrugged. "Well, one thing at a time. Seriously, how do we know it's time to evacuate? Maybe it's better to keep the kids here. Near the site. It is logical. I say we stay. The Lise's seem to think it's imperative. They seem to think the switchers will return after Albuquerque."

Button said, "Agree. However, since the blue light manifestations, we have presumed to separate the doubles, supposing the proximity of the doubles to be dangerous. Could their proximity to each other have caused the explosion?"

Adler could read they were near collapsing. How long since they'd slept? All of them had too many questions and not enough sleep.

Button lowered his arm, jerked about nervously. "For now, we hang on for now. Two corpuscles." His arm came back up, his hand out with two fingers standing up.

Adler pushed back from the table, glaring back at the faces around the table. Sheriff Wrigley looked pale. The other scientists and doctors and technicians glared with faces clouded with barely contained, bug eyed shock. Adler said, "So some kind of explosion less than half a mile from here, and the shock wave kinda makes a hiccough over us only to blast a town 30 miles away? But you think it's safe to stay?"

The sheriff shrugged, shook his head, and sighed. "Listen, I need to get to Coltrane. The governor's called out the National Guard." He pushed away from the table, stood. "I'm off." Then: "Now, I kinda wish it the mass hysteria, like what Dr. Downs here first brought up. At least that would be something we'd know how to handle."

Dr. Downs giggled. "Mass hysteria handled? Ha! Yes, that would be good. You know the Aurore double from here knew all about mass hysteria. She gave me a very nice lecture on the history of mass psychogenic illness. That young lady was able to summarize everything from the dancing plague of 1518 through the Tanganyika laughter epidemic of 1962. She even knew of the penis panic of Singapore in 1967. She told me a story about something called the Mad Masser of Gattoon. I believe it was in Illinois in the 1930s. I had never heard of that one. A veritable polymath of odd information." She shook her head. "Continue with your 'corpuscles'."

Connelly asked, "Were the children 'chosen' because of their abilities?"

Dr. Downs shook her head. "The Woker, Quick, Skeels, and Gack children all seem fairly normal."

Button approached the table, arm up, 2 fingers tall. "Two corpuscles. One: we need more data on the explosion. What did it do in the EM sphere? If we reverse engineer its characteristics we may we be able to trace back its origin. What is the likelihood of another explosion occurring? Two: human terrain—who knows about this? How could they know? Communication; specialization. There are people out there who know more than I do about this. Find them. We find answers. Homeland Security is chomping at the bit to get involved."

The girls made their dash for it, always keeping a space between themselves. The new rule was doubles were kept separate. This was difficult for all. The Lise, Campbell, Thor, Doris, and Catherine from here were confined to their own room under the watchful eyes of 2 law enforcement women, so called matrons. The Lise, Campbell, Terve, Doris, Katerina from there had their own room and monitors. As a safety precaution the parents, the Gack's, the Quick's and the Woker's and the Skeels, were limited in how much time they could spend with the children. No one knew how dangerous the situation actually was.

Respective Aurore's were supposed to be in their respective rooms. But they had had to go to the common bathroom...instead of their room's because the kids were always using it...*at the same time.* They were very curious about this meeting. It had been going on all night. The discussion confirmed their fears. The adults were pointless—full of entropy. Going in all directions. The Aurore's were worried about the switchers, Sophie and Tyler, whose parents were freaking out. They were worried about the world blowing up, and it being their fault...doubling...switching...basic laws of physics tossed in the basura. The blue sparks might mean—had they caused the explosion? Besides, here, there, the Aurore's had switched.

Finally, at the bathroom, they ducked in, pulled the door closed. The Aurore from here flipped the light on. They stared at their two faces in the mirror. Practically identical except for their clothes, but everyone now was sharing clothes so that wasn't as vivid a difference as at first. The Aurore from here had started to call the Aurore from there Neo who didn't like the name. But now things had reversed. The Aurore from here insisted on now being called Noe.

Noe said, "'The mad gasser of Mattoon?'"

Aurore said, "You had a plethora of notes. I related the information to the authorities as you suggested."

Noe said, "Understood. But really 'mad masser of Gattoon'? Medea is already suspicious."

"How is—"

"Medea," they both said, then both nodded.

Noe said, "She's not handling...annihilation well."

"I'll take care of her," said Aurore.

"Yes, you will. And when things shift back as they are bound to, I will be with my parents again. Both of them. Right now, we stay here. Close to the spot. We have to get more habaneros."

"C'est vrai! Es verdad! That's the plan. If the shifting back is fooled by our charade, then we take turns. Moi y ma doppelganger. We don't know for sure it will work. Suppose I got stuck in your world forever? Will it work?"

Noe nodded. "Tres difficile?"

"Bien sur! We're committed. I mean you're an explorer, I'm an explorer. We're the Poltergeist Girls now. That's what you named us. We turn entropy around, make it negentropic. We—you know what I'm going to say before I say. You know all the arguments why this must be done."

"I do," went Noe.

They were quiet, knowing their time was up, watching each other in the mirror. Then each raised an arm and turned their hands to face each other's. They began to move their hands in, together. Closer and closer, their open hands came together. At about 6 inches apart, a blue light glowed from between their hands. They hesitated, stopped, held their hands there.

Together, they said, "Always knew you were there."

Then: "The mirror goes on forever, infinite regression. There are other people with us here at this moment through the thin air."

A knock came to the bathroom door behind them. The two Aurore's pulled their hands apart.

Noe said, "I'll go first." She exhaled, then: "Coming! C'est vrai!"

"Come on Neo or Noe or whatever you call yourself!" It was the lady deputy from the sheriff's department who had been assigned to the doubles from there.

The two Aurore's looked at each other, said silently,

"Sew it back together at the chile spot!"

Noe opened the door, hit the light, and came out quickly, pulling the door shut behind her before the deputy could see inside.

Noe said, "Ici! Je suis la!"

"Sorry," said the deputy, whose name was Susan Few, "but you know the rules. We have to get back."

Another woman, a monitor from the here contingent, an FBI woman named Natalie Espinoza, walked into sight and Noe and Few could tell she was nervous. Special Agent Espinoza went, "Aurora?"

Few said, "No, this is my Noe." She fastened her eyes on to Noe's eyes. "Where's your double? What are you two up to now? I swear. Come on, this is no time for monkey business."

Noe was tempted to reply smartly about Anthropoids and monkeys. "'Monkey business'? Que? What is that? "

Few rolled her eyes. "Come on."

Espinoza said, "If you see that girl, you tell her to get back PDQ!"

Few nodded to Noe, saying, "She'll know what 'PDQ' means."

Noe and Few returned to their room. Deputy Few got back to her chair by the door to sit with the other monitor. The kids were seated at their table while one stretched out on a cot. No parents around. New rules! Were they dangerous to their parents from here? But if so, couldn't they control that danger? Emanations? Effusement? Leakage? Noe smiled to her comrades at the table and went to join them. Excruciation egress? Katerina and Doris sipped juice through straws in juice boxes. The kids at the table were happy to see Noe.

Katerina blurted, "They're wax. These boxes are made of wax." Her big eyes made a question.

Noe gave a 'huh' sound and sat. Terve and Campbell were playing a game with cards and paper and pencils. In the game each card play meant a different drawing had to be made. Noe saw elaborate suns and moons and monsters had been completed. Noe thought, little boys always draw the same things. Overlap?

Katerina said, "I miss my double."

Doris added, "Me too. I won't touch her!"

Noe said, "The blue light scares everyone, including us. We're going to have to wait and see what happens. No one understands how we got here. So no one is sure what to do. Lise said Old Duckbill meant for us to stay close to where it started. Es verdad, Lise?"

Lise was the one on the cot. She did not answer.

Noe patted and tickled each of the kids at the table. No blue light. It only happened between actual doubles. And the kids squirmed in delighted agony with her attention.

Campbell said, "I want my double." He shook his head and stared into Noe's eyes. His face was stiff, his lips making a thing, tight line. "We say we won't stay. Not forever. We know this. So do you. So I have to see him now."

Noe said, "For now?"

Campbell said, "To play. It's important we play. We know how."

"I know you do," said Noe. "The parents here think they know what's best, just like they do in Chichimeca."

Noe went over to the cot where Lise lay. She dropped down to the cot next to Lise. "Hey," said Noe.

Lise leaned up a second, eyed her, let her head drop. "Grass is cheaper. Hay's expensive this time of year. Or did you mean 'hey' as our doubles are always saying? You want to be careful, because when we get back Chichimeca everyone will know who we are."

Noe smiled. "Funny how idioms latch on like burrs. Like 'lumpies'—how the folks here don't know that one."

Lise grumbled, "Language is the problem. We all speak English, but we can't communicate what happened. What we saw or what we know is not their see and know. I had to tell my story over and over again. To the FB's, then to the science people. Then to the parents here—it's agony for them. But I could tell: they think we're making it up!"

"Tante pis," went Noe. "In loco parentis! We have no choice but to trust them. Especially now after the explosion. They'll come around. They want what's best for us."

Lise turned on to her side and faced Noe more directly. "Suppose they don't know what's best?" She shook with it. "I miss the other Lise. I never knew anyone like her. I know I sound like a little kid. Savez-vous? Do you feel it? Like something missing that makes you unease...uncomfortable, but you can't put your finger on it?"

"Tell the science people?" said Noe.

"C'est vrai. They don't even know about inertia."

"Or not?"

"Don't twins have a very close...essence?"

"Hubris?"

"Is that a word? No. Sympatico?"

"We're not twins."

"Maybe it's a word I learned from your double. Do you like your double?"

"Oui."

"Do *we* know what's best? I mean, if they don't, the parents. Old Duckbill said overlap was possible. He did not say it was good. Not exactly a strategy for what to do—"

"Overlap."

"We do know what's best. We have to. That's what being human means. That's the way things work. We have to go back to where we came from. The switchers have to switch back. If anyone can figure this out, Peggy Dreiser can. In the mean time, what should we do?"

"We have to keep them calm. So they won't do

anything rash. All of us kids have to work at this."

"You know they have no clear understanding of inertia? They know nothing of plastique minds. They don't communicate with the land at all. They can't talk to animals.

"Look at me talking so much! I guess because of my sister. On account of how much she talks here. She always has something to say and says it."

"Your double?"

"Don't you think of yours as a sister, too? She likes to talk and talk—"

"I don't know. All this talk. I guess it's what they do here. We don't have to talk." She shrugged tiredly, shaking her head, wondering what she was getting at. "I mean, we are not forced to talk. We can be there, the way we are there, here. Can't we? I guess we can do this. Keep 'em calm. Like you say. So the adults won't interfere with Sophie and Tyler in Alburquerque."

"They pronounce it Albuquerque."

"Different history?"

"They don't know the Singularity at all. They have war all the time."

"All the time?"

"I don't know. Overlap makes me think there's hope. You know how Old Duckbill can be. He said the switched kids had to go to Alburquerque. Then what? They'll come back here, and we'll all go to the spot where it happened."

"Peut etre...maintenant...with plenty of habaneros. Ground zero. The umbo. The epicenter. We are neither here nor there. For now we wait."

"In between?"

"Intercalary?"

Lise purred, "I'm tired and scared. And I want to see my sister."

Noe said, "Interstices."

"You two really like to play with words."

* * *

Aurore settled in with Campbell and Thor and Catherine playing Crazy Eights. She was able to catch on to the game fairly quickly. And losing the first few hands made the kids laugh and appreciate her clowning around with them. Doris was on her cot napping, holding her yellow monkey, or just feeling sad. Lise sat near the door with her parents and Sophie's mom. The monitors huddled close by to listen...to monitor. They seemed so serious!

Aurore patted Campbell and Thor and Catherine and smiled at each. Campbell said, "I miss my brother!"

Thor said, "He's not your brother."

Doris waved her hand and popped, "He's a double!"

Campbell said, "We know."

Aurore saw the adults' heads turn to them to see what was up. Natalie Espinoza went over to Doris' cot. She sat on the cot next to her and comforted her.

Catherine whispered, "She's a baby."

"Ahh," went Aurore. "No mean. No mean."

Campbell said, "You mean, 'don't be mean'," and laughed.

Aurore shook her head. "We don't want to upset the parents. Yes? Tell them we are beau, yes? So they won't worry."

Thor said, "You talk like the kids from there."

Campbell giggled and called out, "Beau!"

Aurore thought, entropy. She shrugged and left the table, wandering over to the door where the parents and Lise were seated. Lise's parents were very upset with Lise, but also they were trying to understand. They wanted any information that she might have forgotten about Sophie. Sophie's mom craved it.

The door to their room opened and Medea came in. She

saw Aurore and said, "There you are."

Aurore said, "Mama?"

Medea wrapped her arms around Aurore and drew her over to the cots. She sat and had Aurore sit next to her. "Now," she began, then she shifted, sighed, and gasped: "Are you okay? Did you get any sleep?"

Aurore stared at her mother. Medea was disheveled. She hadn't combed her hair, she needed a bath. The strain and worry were clear in her face. "Mama," she said. "It's going to be okay. We are to wait here."

"But the explosion! It's terrifying. Whatever it was—"

"Something's happening. We will switch back? I mean the doubles have to go back. That just makes sense. It's logical. Everyone back to where they belong?"

"No one knows for sure." Then, staring at the floor, she whispered, "The other Aurore, I asked her about your father."

"Oui."

"She said we were still married there. She said we were traveling artists, making a living in villages and towns we visited. Like gypsies?"

"'Gypsies'?"

"Okay—Roma. Better?"

Aurore nodded, smiling.

Lise gave a loud groan and Aurore and Medea turned to look. Susan and Vincent Gack nodded to them. Sophie's mom, Winona Rose, looked away in the opposite direction. Was she weeping?

Aurore stood awkwardly. "Entropy. I have to go help," she said. She smiled at her mother. "No tumult. No obfuscation."

Medea tried a smile. "Trepidation. Palpitation. You're so confident, my little tortilla chip. You never cease to amaze me."

Aurore opened her mouth to say something but changed her mind. Her mom caught her holding back and said, "Think before you speak? Nice!"

Aurore went up to the group by the door. Medea was right beside her. Aurore said, "Okay?"

Winona Rose said, "Why Albuquerque? Why did Sophie and Tyler have to go to Albuquerque?"

Aurore answered, "They pronounce it differently. Al*bur*querque."

"That means what?" asked Winona Rose.

Aurore said, "They include the extra 'r'."

Vincent Gack said, "Like an old name?"

Susan Gack said, "Aurore, we're upset. And Lise's had enough questions. Enough of the third degree. Right, sweety?"

"I'm no sweety, don't call me that!" said Lise. "When do I get my phone back?" She was exhausted, angry, fed up. Everyone seemed to assume she was in on this and had more info. She didn't know anything about the people who had taken Sophie and Tyler. She didn't know anything about their motives or what they were up to. Besides, she missed her double. She had never imagined a Lise like that: quiet, smart, demure, motivated, disciplined. She could tell the adults were also exhausted and fed up, so she added: "I'm done." But she said it quietly, almost a whisper, as she really didn't want to spark more 'debate'.

Vincent Gack did his fatherly duty: "Young lady, taking the car was one thing, but there's a lot of other things going on too. So, yes, it was a kind of emergency. There were mitigating factors. We understand this, but do you understand in an emergency we have to be able to count on you?"

Lise said, "You talk down to me like I'm a dog. Am I grounded for life?"

Aurore inhaled, not sure at all what that meant.

Susan Gack shuddered. "Lise, this stunt you pulled is nothing compared to what's happened."

Winona Rose said, "Lise, I appreciate your patience. I

lost my Sophie, then I lost the new Sophie. Can you understand my worry? You were one of the last ones to see the new Sophie. I hope I haven't been too obnoxious."

"Sorry, Ms Rose," said Lise. She didn't know if that was enough so: "Like I told you, and the FBI, and the science people, and that weird Dr. Downs, I don't know why they have to go to Albuquerque. But with everybody looking for them now, it shouldn't be hard to find them. All I know is that Sophie and the other Lise got some kind of message. How many times do I have to say it? Maybe the circus people know."

Vincent Gack said, "A message from an animal?"

Susan Gack said, "The circus people aren't talking."

Lise said, "It's not polite to make fun. You're making fun. I have responsibilities too: I need my phone!"

Vincent and Susan Gack sighed and swallowed and gasped at once.

Aurore wondered about the circus called Crotalus. She wondered about the word. Then 'Crots'? She knew all about the Crots. She knew her double did not. So there was some kind of correspondence (?) between worlds? She'd have to talk to her double about it. Likely, then impossible, then she wondered about the other Lise. What did these Lise's know? What could doubles do? How did she feel about her double? How did Lise feel about hers? Sisters? Twins? Did she like her? Their thoughts...these people were so different. She had to take care with Medea so much.

Lise stood, stepped away from her chair, then scooted past Aurore and Medea.

Medea said, "Aurore, why don't you play some cards with Lise?"

Aurore said, "Yes, why."

Winona Rose said, "I better go find my husband. He's pretty upset."

Medea said, "We all are. What more can we do?"

Aurore said, "We're here for right now."

Vincent Gack stared at her, then said, "We're trying our best."

Susan Gack nodded, bowed her head and cried. Medea went to her side immediately, put an arm around her. "Let's go make some tea. Nice cup of tea."

Aurore and Lise at the table. The little kids eyed them with grins, welcoming and teasing. Campbell said, "Wanna play?"

Lise grumbled, "Drop dead."

Aurore inhaled.

Campbell went, "Ummm! Gonna tell!"

"I'll put all your Star Wars figures in the microwave when we get home!"

Campbell laughed. "You will not! Besides, we aren't going home. Me and Campbell are going to his house."

Aurore said, "Don't. You'll trouble your parents."

Campbell said, "Maybe there'll be another 'splosion."

Thor picked up on their talk, huddled closer, said, "What do you mean?"

Campbell blurted, "I have no mean. Right, Aurore?"

Lise said, "You're talking like the kids from there. Stop it!"

Campbell's lip quivered.

Lise gasped. "Okay, okay, I'm sorry."

Campbell whined, "I want my double. We won't get too close."

Lise said, "They have to go back."

"Why?" asked Aurore.

Campbell said, "I want to go with him!"

Lise said, "I don't know why. But they have to. Doesn't it make sense? Doesn't it feel right?"

Campbell said, "I don't know what feels right."

Aurore smiled, said to the table, shrugging, "Why be afraid? So far, it's strange, but we're okay. I don't want to be afraid or worry. This is an adventure. We need to consider. We can be still, like meditating, think about our doubles, to figure this."

"Why?" asked Lise.

Doris came over to the table. "What are you doing?"

Campbell had his eyes closed now and said in a mutter, "We're mediating."

Lise breathed out in a hiss: "Meditating," and closed her eyes, too.

Doris took a chair, studying the others with slow breathing and closed eyes. She said, "I'm gonna tell!"

Aurore closed her eyes. She thought of the Poltergeist Girls. What did that mean? Things were so different here! How were here and there connected? Were they? She imagined the other Aurore. They *were* connected. She could see her. Her face was thinning. She enjoyed herself so much, even though she knew it was the descent into entropy. Ahh, everything was a game to her? Her double? Her sister? From here, wondering and wandering thoughts, same things, then different, then ghostly manifestations of the Poltergeist Girls, then moving between worlds. Everyone was quiet at the table. Doris closed her eyes and thought about the other Doris.

* * *

In the other room Deputy Few watched the children sitting together around the table with even breathing and closed eyes. Her eyes moved from child to child. She stood up and walked over to the table. "You guys?" she said weakly.

No response.

Deputy Few went to the other woman assigned to their room. The woman, with the FBI and named Brina Dalky, watched Few approach. She asked Few, "What are they doing?"

"I don't know," said Few, "but I don't like it."

"Go get Dr. Downs. Let them know what's going on. We were to report anything unusual, and this seems unusual."

"You go," said Few.

Dalky hurried from the room. Few returned to the table and sat nearby on a cot, keeping an eye on her charges.

* * *

The two Aurore's were thinking, is this overlap?

The Aurore from here could see how her double's thoughts and words arranged. She built in an inevitability to her reasoning. She assumed everything would be resolved. She knew everything *could* be resolved. Aurore from here saw how her self interest guided or filtered her assumptions. This was because she was separate, a monad, and trust for her, between people, was difficult.

She understood what Poltergeist Girls meant. They were like ghosts to each other. Everyone imagined who she was. Everyone wanted to be a hero. So the doubles were meeting their ghosts? Ghosts quite different from what was imagined? Still, Poltergeist Girls could...touch? embrace? between worlds? Tangible tact! Attraction! Repulsion! Magnetic ghosts! Then she panicked: the other Aurore will know my secrets!

The Aurore from there could see how her double's thoughts and words were piled up in disarray. Bourbeux. There were these complications, spider webs of memories and inferences, she couldn't follow. Random and scatter. The main thing: they were going to do this right now reaching, a moment together for good. This Aurore had total trust in others, in nature, in the Real. Individuality, she saw, meant a way in to be with others. Her double thought individuality was a way in to be unique, distinct, separate.

Both Aurore's, in the two rooms, eyes still closed,

blurted at once, "Poltergeist Girls!"

Few and Espinosa, in respective rooms, wrote it down, thinking it was important.

Then the Campbell in Espinosa's room came out of it for a second to say, "They had juice boxes! No fair!" Then he went back to his closed eye stare.

Espinosa wrote it down.

* * *

Dr. Downs and Special Agent Connelly rushed into the room with Dalkey. Few waved them over and put a finger to her lips. Doris giggled. Dr. Downs whispered to Special Agent Connelly who promptly turned and walked out of the room. Downs

wanted her to see what was going on in the other room. Connelly had worked with children in extreme situations much of her professional career. She had no children of her own, but she had a sharp intuition with children and seeing the group's behavior now scared her. And she already was pretty shaken up! She tended to agree with Special Agent Adler that the area had to be evacuated for the good of all. But the kids didn't like the idea. The Lise's on their return had both insisted that they should stay by the spot where the switching had first occurred. Their reasoning was unclear but it seemed to imply or assume that some kind of switching back might happen, so it was important to be close to the spot if/when that occurred.

Connelly knocked at the door of the other room. Special Agent Fiona Sims opened it. "Karen," she said. "Something's happening. Oh, you know? I was just coming to get you guys."

Connelly and Sims moved from the door and approached the table with the children all sitting quietly. What were they doing? What had brought this on?

Special Agent Espinoza sat near the table watching the children, listening, striving to hear and interpret the little cries and occasional word, so she could write it down.

Connelly waved Espinoza over by her and Sims. She said, "The same thing's going on in the other room. Dr. Downs had me come over here to check. Just leave them alone for now, write down everything they say. I'm going back to the other room, let Dr. Downs know."

Espinoza said, "No blue light. You think they're safe?"

Connelly shrugged. "I don't know. This is new to all of us."

Sims said, "Spooky. Like if all the kids are doing it, are they in some kind of contact? Or communication?"

Connelly said, "Stay here. I'll be right back." She hurried from the room and returned to the other one, where various FBI and NSC personnel were setting up cameras to film the event. Dr. Downs stood to the side. She looked pale. Connelly wondered how she had been so confident about mass psychosis, but now?

Connelly went up to Dr. Downs. She leaned into the doctor's ear: "They're doing the same exact thing in the other room."

Dr. Downs clicked her tongue, shook her head, whispered, "Correspondence!" Then she clicked her fingers at the NSC tech. He scurried over, leaving his camera on its tripod. She said to him, "Get a camera over to the other room. Same thing's going on over there. Film them. Timing has to be perfect. It's all in the timing. Now. Go."

"Got it," said the tech.

The other cameraman was already filming.

Dr. Downs said, "I want to see the others."

Connelly and Downs left the room, trailing the tech with equipment. She said to Connelly, "Security corpuscles on the river are reporting animals. They seem to be massing. Not sure if that's the right word. Animals are suffering hysteria? Mass psychosis? Why not? How could that not be? Cows and horses even. Animals are coming together, massing, amassing—is that the right word? At the exact spot. Is that a word? 'Amassing'? Is that the right word?"

Connelly didn't respond as they got to the other room. Espinoza and Sims huddled near the table with the kids. The tech set up his tripod, made adjustments, got filming.

"It's the oddest thing," said Downs to Connelly softly. "Certainly twins have a special closeness that allows for coincidental overlap of emotions or thoughts."

Connelly said, "I thought telepathy was impossible."

"It is," said Downs.

* * *

At the Crot Assembly east of the river, on a swell of desert that provided a great view of the valley, Crots, with and without steeds, and a group of emergency specialists and militia from all over Chichimeca, gathered in the square. Graves and Jakes joined them. As did families from up and down the river, including the families with the missing kids. Peggy Dreiser had authorized the militia to muster. She had called out her experts even before the Battle of Whitewater. Okla and his wife, Era, officiated but it was a free form meeting, and everyone had a chance to talk.

Most of the talk so far concerned the missing children and the earthquake. Were the two events related? What kind of earthquake was that? No one had ever felt anything like that. Were they at war? Was Mexico invading even now as they talked? People were worried about Coltrane. Lives had been lost. The militia was stretched from the southern borderlands to Coltrane.

Graves commented, "New waterfalls?"

Jakes countered with, "The quake seems to have originated near here, by the river, where we first saw the kids. That's what the specialists are saying. So why was Coltrane affected but the Assembly here was not?"

Theories and explanations had been tossed about. At least the Crots had succeeded in convincing the parents that it had been the best thing to do, getting Sophie and Tyler to Coltrane, where they'd been able to make connections, slinging their way to Peggy Dreiser in Alburquerque. Impossible for Peggy to leave Alburquerque yet, but when she actually experienced the kids, she'd have a better idea about what was going on. They were needed in Alburquerque. This is what Peggy said. She would be able to advise what their next steps should be after their visit. This is what they all knew to be true.

The Aranas, the Roses, the Wokers, and Quicks, and Skeels, and Gacks were little pacified. They had children missing. They were more than distraught. They stood around, near the front of the square, with their arms around each other. Parents holding each other close, panicking about their kids.

Johan Wrig, the region's chief constable, introduced the newcomers, "Ali Adler is chief investigator with Peggy's Circle. He happened to be in Prescott when Peggy contacted him."

The tall man was dressed as a city dweller would think country clothes should be. He wore big boots. He was thin, but he also had a commanding presence of intelligence and clarity.

The constable continued, "Adler, here, brought his own team with him. Plus a lot of equipment. Then, this here, is Theresa Downs and Paolo Button from the national militia. They've been instructed to call out our local militia for border duty. No one knows what the Mexicans are playing. No one knows if they are behind these latest shenanigans. Ciudad de Chihuahua is on full alert. No one is sneaking through Whitewater."

Ali Adler thanked Okla and Wrig and raised his arms over his head. He called, "We, in the Circle, know what you're thinking. Ahora! This is new, we all know that. And this is horror—missing kids, earthquakes. Seems impossible. And we know what we know when things get impossible, because it is real. Together, it is real, we are real. We are here to understand. We are here because this is the place it started. Ahora!" He lowered his arms.

A voice called out from the crowd, "Science works!"

Ali Adler smiled. "Peggy will be here as soon as she can get away, so for now we establish our team here."

The woman, Theresa Downs, was dressed in leathers with a formidable knife attached to her belt at the side. She was well built, big, strong. She motioned to her assistant, Button, and he nodded to her. She said, "Friends, how bad is it? The Battle of Whitewater will not be soon forgotten. The children are close—we sense this. All of us do. We know this. But where? The ley lines are not talking. The ley lines seem to be buckling, at least changing. Life lines are chaotic. The animals say so! The animals want to understand. But there's no worry: the switched kids will get to Alburquerque. Peggy will see them. She'll know then.

"Peggy's working on the Great Machine at Alburquerque even as we speak. She can't leave until that situation is stabilized. She'll be able to make a determination when she sees the kids. In the meantime, militia from all over Chichimeca are moving south. We secure the border. Ciudad de Chihuahua at this time is in no danger."

Whoops and hollers resounded from the crowd. A few questions were shouted out.

Downs said, "One at a time, por favor!"

Jakes asked, "Graves and I should return to the spot? We might want to?"

Downs said, "Agreed. Old Duckbill said, 'overlap is

possible'. We are not sure if that is a good thing. Certainly overlap can go—diverge ways."

The Gack woman, Susan, said, "Overlap—so we can get our kids back? And our Tyler? Not this other Tyler?"

"And our children," added a chorus of Woken, Quick, and Skeels' cries. They recited their names, the names of the disappeared kids.

One parent asked, "Does it mean they will be switched back?"

Theresa Downs shrugged, saying, "We have no reason not to think so. It should go back? I mean, if it switched here in the first place. Doesn't that make sense?"

Graves choked on it: he grunted, then: "Nothing may make sense ever again."

Susan Gack went, "Don't say that!"

Graves said, "Overlap? It's a metaphor? Metaphors can lead to treachery."

Era said, "Humans lead to treachery. Metaphor is just a tool. No, what I am concerned about is if it spreads. Will Crot children be next?"

"What if there are more earthquakes?" someone shouted from the back.

The talking dog, Fido, low to the ground and a bit tubular, made his way to the front and even jumped up on to a female elder's lap who was sitting in a chair. The dog was panting hard and had a wide smile across its foxy face.

Fido the dog said, "Animals getting thinks from Old Duckbill. Overlap is the best zone. We go for overlap."

Downs said, "What does that mean?"

Graves said, "How do we 'go' for overlap?"

Era said, "Overlap means go back?"

Fido shook himself, panting. Then: "Overlap means overlap. What is always here is always there. Ways to overlap."

A couple Crots on mounts came galloping into the

Assembly and made their way through the crowd. The scout in front, a young male named Tom, announced, "Animals are arriving at the spot. They are coming to the place the new Sophie and Tyler arrived."

Susan Gack gasped. Marvin Woker called, "What now?" The Roses began to cry. The Arana woman stepped away from her husband, who reluctantly let her go, and moved towards the dog and said, "Is that good?"

Fido raised up on the elder's lap and everyone could see the tail going strong. He began to bark, "Woof! Woof!"

The Skeels and Quicks wanted to go to the spot at once to see.

Okla said, "Let's have Graves and Jakes down there. One step at a time. Fido's a good boy!"

CHAPTER 11

Pamela Dreiser thought to herself, 'the cathode ray tube is the retina of the mind's eye', that line from that old movie. Then another Pamela Dreiser thought to herself, 'platypus'. Each second could be a different person. How many Pamela Dreiser's were there? She preferred Mela actually. And the one sitting here was equipped with tiny suction cups across her head and upper chest, sitting before a rack of cathode ray tubes. She loved to play with read outs. She reset the numbers of her instruments and tried again. The numbers had been drunk lately, getting worse the last few days, then today staggering about lopsided, then no response at all. The experiments at Sandia Labs, on Kirkland Air Force Base, in Albuquerque, depended on her ability to predict the past. That's how she saw it; that's what she told the professors. The psychologists and physicists running the experiments had some predilection that she should be able to predict the future. She told them expectations created 'quantum wave fronts'. You mention 'quantum wave fronts' to a bunch of scientists and they about wet themselves in anticipation.

Pamela could read the oscilloscope in front of her well enough to see that her readings, when they did come through, made no sense. Other devices had numbers all over the place. Readings seemed chaotic, panicky random. Things were not going well. Prediction was about repeatability, was about control. The machines were not responding. Who was in control? Nothing had made any sense over the past few days. She forgot why she was here. Then remembered the wrong reasons.

Then...the phone call...then the earthquake. This was her second week at the lab and things had been going well, at least blandly at first. She hadn't wrecked their instrumentation. The phone call implied, pointed to, said straight out: it wasn't her. Everyone seemed to know this, but they still needed to tell her. What could she do? Then the earthquake wasn't her either. Now what? She knew this term 'earthquake' was simply a label slapped onto something momentous. Had she known this was going or coming? Animals can predict earthquakes. What if it was not an earthquake? That's what the indications were. What if something happened to be going on about the same time after she got here? That made a kind of sense but...no coincidences!

Pamela had heard of the studies at Sandia Labs and volunteered to be tested. She needed the do re mi for one thing. And the timing was perfect, as she would be able to pay her fees at the psychic fair afterwards. She saw the testing as an opportunity. Maybe she would 'come out' after the tests, at the fair, with some kind of proof and explanation of her abilities...her gifts? This period of her life right now seemed critical. But you don't have to be psychic to believe that. She assumed she'd been led here. Blah blah. She always thought that. Then got mad at herself for having a big head. It never made any sense. Fantasy novels' stereotypes of egress, or ways to explain 'magic', were not explanations. They were metaphors. She was not living in a novel or a poem. It was difficult to articulate like to like. Then, it was not. But you couldn't eat a metaphor. The choice, the selection of which word to take, was a road to take. So, for sure, total start of the tests went brilliant, first week without a hitch, without much interesting data but still—

'A future dinner might be mice', said a Pamela to a self, and the Pamela at Sandia buckled with entropy: yes, some joy gulf limitation or border or boundary had ruptured, or trembled. Gone fluid? Rogue? What! People's guilt kept multiple world theories ripe—since folks were terribly eager to figure what would have happened if they'd gone that route, instead of this one. Humans question selection. Humans love to play 'guilt', because that means they get to focus on themselves alone. We live in our minds' talky talk, wondering if we made the right decision. Pamela, these last few days, had experienced a reluctance...a bifurcation, without knowing what was called 'actually going on'. She'd been a scat doofus bystander these past few days. What should she have done? What could she have done? She was terribly auspicious: the membranes' interstices fail and too many worlds at once. Overlap? Pamela was bound to it. Then not. Selection dreamt couldn't. Then she dreamt shouldn't. It was so difficult to know the value of a sensation.

A lab tech, complete with white coat and a pocket protector, named Mark Pease, came in from the observation room to the human subjects' room lined with cubicles. "Mela," he said, moving up behind her at her cubicle, "you're tense." He reached out to her, his hand coming towards her shoulders, but then at the last second he pulled back. Instead, he wiped his mouth, and went on: "Your vitals are all over the place. Machines acting up. What are we getting today? So easy, now this. Clean data, now what? These last few days—maybe mice climbed in the console and made a nest in the wires? We're checking. Sensor array disarray! Ha! You've been great, Mela. Maybe today—considering the earthquake, nah, but it started getting weird before the quake. Ragged, just ragged data raging direction. I don't know! I don't know, what do you think?"

She mimicked an earthquake. Read outs clattered. Mark went, "See! See here! See that? Now! Boy, I could feel that one." He pointed to her displays. "You? How do you do that?"

Mela pushed away from the computer screens and the surrounding electronic apparatus. She sighed, blew out, then turned to look into Mark's eyes. "Perhaps. Ragged, raging glitch, Mark? No, no, glitch with duh bitch!" She placed her hands in her lap and smiled at him. Her peasant blouse, blue jeans, and sandals, her typical outfit, had had Mark saying she looked like a 'hippy princess'. She didn't feel like a princess. Or a hippy. He looked away fast. She felt a stain of conscious jumble, as though too many dreams had happened, then suddenly 'come back', then suddenly never were, as though he'd been away and didn't know how females lived. She felt like she'd spilled a glass of red or pink consequences across her white silk field. She'd thought she was going clear, but she saw now it was a case of day dim day dreams. Scribbles taking over—

Mark said, "Don't say that." He said it softly.

"Could I have done something to the equipment? Then with the earthquake, the machines got even more upset? Are they fighting back? Feeling a little pekid? The news said it was an unusual event. I mean for an earthquake."

Mark said, "That's on the 4th floor. Here, on the 5th floor, we focus remote viewing."

The Department of Defense and the Department of Energy had spent millions of dollars since the 80's trying to figure an effective, rational assessment of the phenomenon known as 'remote viewing'. Intelligence suggested the Soviet Union was deep in research on this and related concepts. Was it real? Could it be used as a weapon? An intelligence gathering system?

"What's on the 4th floor?"

"Women's interaction with electronics. Question: does a woman's menstrual cycle affect electronics, or do electronics affect the menstrual cycle?"

"You're smart, Mark. You've been kind and helpful. I appreciate it."

"You're doing fine, Mela," said Mark. "Even bad data is still data. Definite anomalies here. Dr. Reder and Dr. Milgram are excited. Data makes them giddy."

Pamela, or Mela, smiled. "Knowledge does that," she said. "And they are knowledge workers. Right now, they're in their offices talking it up. How they will present the data. Who will receive the awards. I see this picture they have of me."

"Yeah? You can tell? Can you really see it? Like a picture? We assumed remote viewing was more about the future. Limited, shadowy, time's arrow stuff. More timely guess, than prediction. But it's not, huh? One thing for sure, Mela, it's an interesting way to live."

Mela chuckled, "True, Mark. I'm just timely talking—"

"Let's focus. Try again? Keep it pure."

"I like that," said Mela. "Shall we play again? Shall we play a game?"

"Of course. I'll reboot. Don't think we need to recalibrate. We'll start in a sec. Watch for the red light. You sure you're up for this? You want to? We could take a break?"

"No, data is still data, right? We will give the good doc's something to behold and beguile, that will warm the cockles of their hearts."

Mela slid her chair back into place with the toes of her sandals. She felt comfortable...

...all her life Pamela Dreiser had felt comfortable...with the pictures, the cascades of pictures that clattered through her head. Imagery! Ceaseless atoms, drops from the river, rebelling, demanding. Imagery set free? No, it was more! Well, not at first. At first she thought she was crazy. Her parents complained she daydreamed too much. She and her parents would be out on errands or going to a movie, Pamela held in hand, dragged along; then she would suddenly jerk awake, or catch up, or wake up, and they were somewhere else completely. Like she'd been gone for a while, even though her parents had noticed nothing, even though she had continued walking along and being with her parents.

The problem was most people thought daydreams were silly, crazy, a waste of time. Self-indulgence was a sin in America. After all, what are dreams? Hallucinations? And what kind of people had visions? Prophets and Pamela! They were head trips, mind games, so self-indulgent selfishness preached her folks. The doctor visits began: her parents and doctors thought she had epilepsy, a brain tumor, or ideational collapse. She learned to remember what they needed to hear. In remote viewing, or whatever the heck it was, the key was knowing what people wanted to hear. She had come to see that this background noise, whatever it was, what was different about her, was also what made her clear, as though her awareness was tied to it.

As a kid, these image insertions with lost time, or day dreams extreme, were bubbles. Everyone likes bubbles, even kids. Bubbles seem light and airy, but also playful, and present in their stark short life. In comix, the bubble hangs above the character's head signaling secret thoughts or emotional states...or simply the characters' dialogue. The bubbles in comix were invisible but necessary visible. Bubbles had a translucent texture that felt like fancy air. Bubbles were silly but never trite. As long as she could remember, she had been going away to bubbles of place, of image, of thought. Bubbles abounded. She entered a bubble. Is that how it worked, or just how it began? Quickly, she learned they were not daydreams but outbursts. Pretty pictures in bubbles didn't quite do the experience justice. Maybe there were secret captions talking to other Bubbles? Bubbles pushed their way in to her head whenever they wanted—early on it was dizzying. Each bubble had integrity, a gravity of propensity. She learned that because other people did not have this going on, that her assertion of her experience irritated them. The bubbles burst....

When she was very young her parents had taken her to the beach, and lolling on the sands, in perfect ease, the little girl had a pristine view of a bubble with an older self here at the very same beach, with a young man with a mustache. And the young man had kissed her, her first kiss. The bubble burst. Her parents didn't know what she was talking about. They insisted she was playing out something she'd seen on TV. Another time, at the same beach, still very young, she'd seen a bubble of the very same beach with a large reptilian beast crawling ashore. At least she thought it was a reptile. Not a gator for sure. Maybe a giant beaver with a long, broad beak for a mouth? She didn't know if the creature was wicked and mean, or nice. Young Pamela had been scared.

Her parents worried over her. The worry led to tests and counselors which offered no help. She had learned to say what they wanted to hear so that they would leave her alone. She felt bad for her parents, whom she did love. But it was too much for them. She felt she was a liability to their contentment.

Bubbles proliferated, all themes, all textures: from people she knew and did not know; from animals prehistoric and current; from skies that mirrored her present sky, to skies bleak and dark and totally alien. She lived these bubbles. She could concentrate on them and know if they held lessons she needed to learn. This was handy and impressed people. But she had to be careful. Too much lesson, too much fear from the folks. And the bubbles burst, and she knew that visual metaphor was just a way a kid could maintain. She had to maintain, right? It sure didn't seem to be a worthwhile power; rather, it was a glitch in her personality. That's all.

She kept a notebook, started her own code of bubble taxonomy. As a teenager, she started correlating bubbles to things that happened, or how they actually had happened, or what would happen after. Correlate did not mean control however. The bubbles served their purpose person, their hard, real time lapse. Then she changed tools. Or metaphors. Or times.

She knew a boy in high school who was 2 years older than she was, and he had a mustache and his name was Aaron. He took her to the beach and kissed her.

When would the giant reptile crawl onto the beach?

People tended to be nervous around her, her peers, her teachers, even her parents. She grew to understand that she had a unique sensation of life. It was not limited to a specific time and space reference either. Her experience was expansive: bubbles as possibilities? Or bubbles as other times? She learned she didn't know what that meant. That was words to stand for something, like 'bubbles' did. She understood she sought some kind of control of her experience. The bubbles burst.

She left home as soon as she could. But not for college. Her parents were struck with how mature and confident she was. They were glad to see her go. Pamela worked odd jobs, usually as a waitress or dish washer. She was a maid at a Days Inn. She ran an all night gas station's cash register for a while. She traveled. All the places, all the towns and cities, barely kept up with her other travel. She'd only stay long enough to make a roll to pay her way to the next town. Bus trips, bus stations, bus station creepy bathrooms across the nation. She always had the local library card and read and studied as she could. She held a question to the fire of her fervor: of what value was this? Was it an ability or simply an excess? A liability? Surely, she was not the only one like this?

All through history, stories of odd ducks, who may not have had bubbles, but did have their own brand of *beak*? Everyone takes advantage of his or her talents. It's what we humans do. At first, bubbles seemed mainly chaos and contradictions, so to *use* them meant trying to use their lessons here in her face-to-face day-to-day gambit. There were options but none worked or helped much. She tried gambling, she tried mind melds, she tried flipping the die. She met people who may not have been exactly like her but did grasp what she was...at least in an intuitive way. This led her to recognize sorts—tribes of people: it was as though she knew everyone she met. That could be incredibly yucky.

So ways of knowing, what was her way, the way only she knew? Bubbles were not an explanation. Daydreaming meant nothing, so of little help. She started calling herself, Mela.

The red light came on but nothing happened. The machine stopped! Machines confused! Beguiled! Wretched! More than upset, the machines claimed clamor and sought succor. She studied the cathode ray tubes, heard the sputter of the speakers coming on, and she said just as Mark said, "You have an emergency phone call."

Mark said, "What did you say?"

Mela pushed back and came to her feet. "I should take it," she said, going through the motions to protect Mark. She removed suction cups. Was this it? Was this the convergence—the overlap? She exited the room with cubicles. She entered a room with a wall of electronics where Mark sat monitoring and recording. He held out Mela's cell phone. He said, "It was ringing in your bag," nodding to a side desk where her purse lay.

Mela took the phone and held it to her ear. She went, "Yes?"

"Lantine Bouche here," said the woman's voice. "The game is afoot! You've been expecting us, so I will forego the pleasantries. I've just flown in from Coltrane with a couple young pups. My arms are tired!"

Mela smiled, said, "Where are you?" Right away a bubble popped in her head of a white boy, a black girl.

"We're at the main gate of Kirkland. They wouldn't let us in."

"I'll be there in a minute." She flipped the phone closed.

Mark Pease said, "Look!" He pointed at a screen. "It just came back on. Wow, wow, wow, this is impossible!"

"What is it?" asked Mela.

"Flummox! You fixed it?"

"Me? Are you recording?"

"Of course."

"Everything came on when I took the phone?"

"Pretty much. Like it all came together? But you weren't even connected."

Mela grabbed her purse, nodding, smiling to Mark, thinking 'attenuation', but saying, "Something's come up."

Mark pleaded, "Now? Right now? This is the point we been waiting for."

Mela quivered, smiled, left. She tingled with potential energy. She didn't know if it was appropriate to feel like this. Hadn't there been casualties in Arizona? But did this have to do with the earthquake? Why did she assume it did? The phone call from before had been vaguely alarming and persuasive. Now she felt strong, ready. Bubbles dissipated. Ready for what? She couldn't tell. What did overlap mean? Yes, the game was afoot! She would need all her faces. She hurried to her van, which she sometimes lived in.

Clarity, calm now. To be of use, she had to be on. That was her code word. It was as though her skills, gifts, abilities held her hostage: she paid the ransom in day to day accommodation. She got behind the steering wheel.

Could she drive? The van started up. She saw it happen. She felt charged. She saw how things had been disrupted, so now? It was now, if she wanted to deal. On. The past few days: an opening—?

Coltrane was the town in Arizona that had suffered the earthquake. Could the 2 young people have been involved? How could that be? Maybe it wasn't an earthquake?

She let the van drive itself slowly from the parking area into the traffic of the Air Force base. The gate wasn't far. And when she actually eyed the gate coming up, the vision was not. It had nothing to do with rods and cones, the color palette. Baffling! To see, to view, to look was re-routed here. She almost had to pull over and stop the car to catch her focus. For from the other side of the gate, she could make out, off to the side with the parked cars, waves of blue light, emanating, blasting the sky with pulses of energy.

She waved to the guards, smiling at their consciousnesses to make it through without a hiccough. Turned into the parking area. She'd never seen anything like it. Energy pulses could come in all colors, or combine to white light. What was happening here? Extreme auras? Invisible explosions? Crossed phases? Radioactive light show? She parked.

Lantine Bouche appeared in her driver's side window. Mela rolled down the window. Lantine was a beautiful woman, a pilot, an explorer, a seeker friend. Lantine said, "I borrowed a car from the airport. We don't have much time."

Mela turned off the van. She swiveled to the left to open her door and stepped out. Lantine gave her a big hug. Mela couldn't say a thing.

Lantine said, "We knew you were the person to see. Come and meet them."

Lantine took Mela's hand and led her over a few spaces

in the parking lot to her borrowed car. Standing in front of the car were three young people. Two girls, a boy. One of the girls was not making the blue. Mela recognized her. Their eyes met.

The young woman, her name was Luanna, said, "We knew you'd know. This is Sophie and Tyler."

The young black woman and the young white boy looked sickly. Blue light continued to stream from them, or pulse from them, or move out of their bodies in shock waves of intensity.

Mela managed, "Is it safe to touch them?"

The two looked sad at her words. They avoided her eyes. Luanna placed an arm over each of their shoulders. She said, "Sophie, Tyler, this is Mela."

Mela stepped forward and held out a hand. She shook both their hands, and right away knew the story. She said, "You're not here."

Tyler murmured, "That can't be it."

Sophie said, "Mela? Pa-mela Dreiser?"

Mela smiled, shook her head.

Sophie persisted: "Do you know Old Duckbill here?"

Mela said, "All at once. Let me consider—"

Lantine inserted, "We left Coltrane right after the earthquake. Basically, we flew out of there in the nick 'o. Word was you were here. Contact, right? You got a call? We knew you would know what to do."

"You—yes. Perfect. I fixed things here. Done, it's set. So yes forever." She paused, losing track of what she was saying. Then her mind cleared: "They have to go back. To the spot...the exact spot where they first...entered."

Sophie said, "Old Duckbill said 'overlap'. Do you know what that means?"

Mela was struck by the power. It made her see something. Not a thought bubble exactly, but actual, real bubbles in water, with an animal floating under the water, then at the surface: above water, under water. Overlap?

With a big beak like thing at its front?

Lantine said, "Is that your cell? In the van?" When Mela did not answer, Lantine went over to the van to retrieve it. Mela was too busy watching the two kids, allowing the energies to come, to go, to blast, to sizzle, to congeal, to point, to guide.

Lantine said, "You better get this? Guy sounds pretty freaked." She held out the phone to Mela.

Mela went through the motions of answering her phone. Right away, Mark's voice came on: "Mela, you have to come back. Looks like over the last couple days, you changed the equipment. I mean, just now it's caught up, or I guess at least it's now able to function. Like you re-programmed everything? This is more than proof: this is a major breakthrough."

Mela said, "Mark, I have an emergency. I'll let you know soon as I can," then she hung up.

Mela said, "We have to leave right away. They're after us. Yes?"

Luanna came over to give Mela a hug. She whispered in her ear, "They are after us, yes."

Lantine said, "I'm getting refueled right now. We can be in Coltrane in a few hours. Then we'll see about getting back to the spot. We knew we had to find you."

Luanna said, "I knew this was no wild goose chase."

Tyler said, "'Goose'?"

Sophie said, "There are no waterfalls in this Coltrane."

Lantine said, "We knew you could help, Mela."

Mela nodded. "It has begun. I assume the blue light from these two?" Sophie and Tyler looked scared, their eyes too wide and pleading. "What happens if they touch?" No one spoke. Mela made a 'hmm' sound, then continued, "Their presence here: correlation, compilation. The experiments I been conducting here, then today it matches. Their presence has made it—well, me I guess, balance? Is that the right word? Like a teeter totter between here and Arizona, and there coming here re-set symmetry. C'est vrai? Odd, huh? Here, now was necessary. No wild goose chase. Our presence at this spot was necessary."

Sophie and Tyler didn't look comforted. Luanna and Lantine did, smiling encouragingly.

Mela said, "But now—I have to take my van back. You can follow me to my house to drop it off, then I'll go with you."

Lantine shook her head. "No time. Lock your van. What? They might tow it? Right now we gotta go. We fly back. With you."

Tyler gushed, "Do you know what's going on?"

Mela said, "How so? Yes. No. Go. No go. There are all types of knowing."

Sophie said, "I know you. You are familiar in our place."

Tyler said, "In our place, we say Natural Philosophy? Negentropy? The punctum? We have a seer you know?"

"Ahh," went Mela. Then: "One or many? Or only one force, action, experience, expectation. Or one collision? Perhaps overlap means this? The coming together? Maybe thoughts, dreams come together at one point. I don't know. Like a punctum?"

* * *

Outside of Coltrane, just a few miles to the east out of the mountains, a flat topped swell of land perfect for launch. Or catch. Sophie and Tyler had no idea what they were looking at. Beacons? Antenna? Spires? Tyler kept thinking, 'Sling?' But Sophie avoided looking any more, and saw only dirty, yellowish sky washed out by wind and dust, the unhappy haze of the dry landscape. That made her pull back, and she thought of St. Louis and home, and her parents. Well, she and Tyler had found each other, so now the promised trip to this Dreiser person. She slowly came around to the sky again, stared up past the spires, saw that the yellow wasn't dirty at all. Rather, a kind of white-gold glaze?

The sling outside of Coltrane was a small one, so the white needles were only about 1000 feet high. Two white needles, one coming, one going, stood erect in a fenced in couple acres of land. A small block building was just inside the fence's gate. The slinger teams were men and women, and they were nervous. They had finished loading cargo before the earthquake. Actually, they hadn't felt much up here, away from town. But it had been enough for them to go over their calibrations and reference points with the required eye of perfection. Slings could abide no perturbation The teams had been able to confirm the needles were affable. So far, so good. They tried to show confidence to the four who would be passengers.

Finally, Tyler said, "I don't get it. What's a sling?"

Lu said, "We get into the gondola, then the needle slings us."

Sophie said, "You gotta be kidding."

Lantine said, "It works. It'll be fine. Es todos!"

Sophie cried, "But where's the engine? The motors?"

Tyler said, "You know a person's got to believe in something, for that something to work. Well, I don't believe in this."

Lantine nodded, said, "I don't blame you. That was scary back in town, what with the tremors. Now we are called to Peggy Dreiser. We must."

Lu said, "Trust us."

Lantine and Lu showed Sophie and Tyler how to climb in, then how to strap themselves in to the gondola. A tight space without windows so it was dark and stuffy. The seats were extra fancy, Sophie and Tyler thought, half chair, half bed. Plush. Lantine and Lu got themselves strapped in. They were the only passengers this day. The sling would whip the gondola on its spider web, superstrong filament through the air toward Alburquerque. They would have 3 change offs on their route.

Sophie and Tyler were terrified, especially when they realized they would be travelling upside down some of the time. But they were securely strapped in, and Lu and Lantine asserted the laws of inertia and spin. They could all be comforted that it made total sense and was safe. Accidents unheard of. The men at the sling had assured them that stability was key, on, unruffled, unperturbed. The slings were happy, they'd said.

Launch pressed them into their seats. There was no fancy countdown: Lu just said they were gone. Then they felt lifted, then they felt tremendous pressure. They cringed, they cried out in little gasps. Lantine whooped! Finally, exhaustion won over fright, besides Tyler and Sophie had their eyes clamped shut. They slept through most of the journey. The change offs when the gondola's filament met the next needle's filament were just as well not observed, as they looked impossible. The filaments whipped the gondola around the subsequent needles, releasing them to the next needle. The passengers did feel surges of pressure, thrusts of gravity change, but they kept their eyes closed.

Lantine and Lu got out of their harnesses quickly in Alburquerque. The slingers there already were unloading cargo, then opening the passenger compartment of the gondola. Lantine helped Sophie. Lu helped Tyler. Tyler was having a hard time coming awake. At first he thought he would puke, but Lu touched his cheek and he felt better. Sophie asked if they were there. Was it over? She had a headache. Lantine gave her a hug and said they were, and she was fine. Lu helped Tyler to his unsteady feet. He clung to her hand.

Tyler said, "Dizzy."

Lu said, "Sit. Slow. We're here."

"We have to do this," said Tyler. He shook his head, stumbled a bit towards the gondola's door.

Lantine stepped over to Lu and Tyler in the small compartment. Lantine said, "First sling ride is always like that. Like you left part of your soul back there in Coltrane. It'll catch up. You might have to reel it back in. But you'll be fine." She smiled.

Sophie said, "Tyler and I are sick. We've been getting worse."

Tyler tried to be cheerful: "I don't know if we're sick. Maybe. I hope I didn't leave any of my soul back in Coltrane."

Lantine said, "Come!"

Lu looked worried.

Sophie made a face, a look of determination. "Whatever is happening is weakening us. It wasn't just the sling. Maybe we're dying."

Tyler stared at her. "Sophie," he said. But he didn't know what to say. His mouth hung open. After all, he hardly knew her.

She looked at him, smirked. "I know," she said, "we hardly know each other, and now I'm talking about dying and stuff." She exhaled sharply. "Well, I don't know whether we are dying or not. I do know that we been through an awful lot these past few days. We have to get back to our own world. We have to. That's all I know. Doesn't that seem to make sense to you, Tyler? Can you think of anything else we should be doing?"

Lantine said, "Peggy will know."

Lu said, "Peggy Dreiser will know. That's why we are here."

Tyler shook his head. "We're not following." They looked concerned, but also confused. He said, "Why did we have to come here? What will she know?"

Sophie went, "What exactly will she know? How?

Suppose that wasn't an earthquake?"

Tyler said, "Suppose there's a war?"

Lantine said, "Let's find out." She showed them how to exit from of the gondola.

They stood in the sling field, four tall white needles towering above them, and could see over the valley to the river, the Rio Grande, and beyond where even larger needles, three of them, towered over the city of Alburquerque. These were silvery and shiny. These gigantic needles poked into the sky just the way they poked into their eyes: unbelievable, audacious. Tyler figured they were twice the height of the sling needles. The needles were the center of the city. Large squat structures with silvery cones or spires at the tops were arranged in concentric circles out from the silver needles. Green areas surrounded each structure. Boulevards, too, lined with smaller buildings ran out from the center. Two large buildings at the east and west appeared to be stepped pyramids, silvery along the sides, reflective, catching sun light, casting it in all directions. They had the largest green areas surrounding them.

Above the city, balloons, zeppelins, floated, strayed, sauntered in the sky.

Lantine said, "We need to get an assist to the Great Machine." She raised her voice to the men and women slingers working around them. "Anyone going to the Great Machine?"

A slinger came up to her. "Elephant People wandering that way. I think they're going to the zoo. I seen 'em coming up this way. Go see if you can catch them. They'll give you a ride if you don't mind the tiswin."

"Gracias!" said Lantine. "Merci beaucoup!"

Lu, Sophie, and Tyler hurried along behind Lantine, who seemed to know her way about. Lu called to Lantine, "These two need water. We can't let them dehydrate."

Lantine grunted, left the sling area behind to check out

the main road, clearly busy with machine and animal transport. Sure enough, coming up the road from the west, so heading east, a couple elephants pulling tall sided wagons. Lantine easily caught up to them. The driver, who sat in the front of the tall wagon so she could see over the elephant, held the 'reins'. The woman was dressed in white.

Lantine called to her, "We need a ride."

The wagons were wood with tall painted sides. The side nearest Lantine showed elephants grazing across a great valley with a river in its center. Looked a lot like the Castor Valley, thought Lantine. But it could have been the Rio Grande Valley and probably was. Below the valley portrait, in tall, pink letters was 'Loxodont'."

"Bein sur!" cried the driver, who leaned over and nodded to Lantine. "Por favor! Jump in back. Not this wagon, the other one, behind us. The second one. Just knock. She'll let you in."

The elephants moved steadily, slowly, staying to the side of the road so that faster vehicles could get by them. Lantine waited for the first to pass, calling out to the others to catch up. Each elephant had a woman in white holding the reins from her wagon top. Each elephant had bright pink circles painted on the sides of their heads and on their thighs. Lantine waved at the woman on the second wagon. The second elephant had a big head with stubby tusks, but it was bigger than elephants Sophie and Tyler had seen at their zoos. The elephant in front with the first wagon looked smaller, had smaller tusks.

Lantine double stepped to the back of the second wagon where there was a door. She stayed up close to it, walking fast, and knocked at the door. The door opened and Lantine called, "We need a ride."

The door opened all the way. The woman behind the door glanced at them, nodded. She was small with long dark hair in a simple white dress like the others. She had pink dots on her cheeks. Lantine jumped and pulled herself up and in. Lu and Sophie and Tyler managed to follow suit. Lu had to help Sophie and Tyler in.

They crowded up the passage to the front of the wagon where kitchen and table stood.

There was a small...an acrid, faintly chemically smell that perked up Sophie and Tyler's noses.

Blankets and pillows were stacked to the sides. Tall sides with shelves filled with supplies. There were also any number of large boxes pressed to the side—cargo? The woman smiled at them. She said, "I am Golsa of the Elephant People. Sit. Water? Tiswin?"

Lu said, "Por favor."

The steady motion of the wagon was gentle and smooth, a bit hypnotic. The interior of the wagon seemed cut off, lodged in a dreamy elsewhere. But it wasn't stuffy or close. Tyler and Sophie sat on opposite sides, up against the wagon's walls, pushing in to pillows.

Lantine said, "We're going to the Great Machine."

Golsa said, "We're going to the zoo." She handed Lantine a bottle. Lantine took it, upended it, passed it to Lu.

Tyler said, "You worship elephants?"

Golsa pulled around a jug of water, then cups, began filling them. She said, "'Worship'?" She shook her head. "How do you mean? Pour que?"

Tyler said, "The elephant pulling this wagon is different from the one pulling the first wagon?"

"Yes," said Golsa. "We ride with Lux, the mastodon." She distributed cups. Lu and Lantine had each had a drink from the bottle. They didn't offer it to Sophie and Tyler. Now everyone drank. Golsa could see they were thirsty. "More?" she said. She retrieved the empty cups and refilled them. "Lux is a grandmother now. We will celebrate. Mucho tiswin." She shrugged and smiled, then: "Tres. Tres."

"I never knew my grandparents," said Tyler.

Golsa said, "That's sad." She took back her bottle and had a drink.

"You know how families are," said Tyler.

Golsa drank again, looking to Lu and Lantine for help, but no clarification came. She said at Lu, "You are Crot."

Lu nodded, smiled. "We love loxodonts."

Sophie changed the subject: "How do you know Peggy Dreiser is at the Great Machine? How do you guys stay in communication to know anything? Who is this Peggy Dreiser? She's like an engineer? Are you sure she will be able to help us?"

Lu smiled at her, reached for Golsa's bottle. She took another swallow. At Tyler, she smiled though he seemed far away. She had more water from her second cup. She said, "Drink. Drink up!"

Lantine said, "Peggy Dreiser is the point of the Circle."

Golsa said to Tyler and Sophie, "You are not from around here. Americans?"

Lantine said, "Je suis Americain. Merci!"

Golsa said, "Les enfants?"

Tyler and Sophie didn't know what to say. They were American, too. It had all been said so many times now, and it never helped. There was no explanation that brought relief. They were afraid. They felt a terrible sinking in their hearts, like falling down a well. What were they doing here? How would this help? At least, they had found each other, but so far it hadn't seemed to have helped much. They both felt different—uneasy, then queasy. Plus, they were realizing they would have to eventually take another sling ride back to Coltrane. They couldn't figure it. They didn't know not who to trust, but what to trust. Tyler had experienced war. Sophie had experienced the Butterfly Lords.

Lu said, "It's a story to end all stories. But, yes, we are going to see Peggy. You heard about the earthquake?"

Golsa nodded. She said, "The Great Machine is worried. Peggy Dreiser has been calming, talking it down since even before the earthquake. She's been walking it through its paces. Stretch. Resolution. There's talk of war with Mexico."

Lantine said, "The slings were strong. No problem there." She shrugged: "I guess, so far, the Great Machine is cooperating? We just came in from Coltrane."

Golsa went, "Ahhh."

Tyler said, "I saw war."

Lantine explained. Lu took Tyler's hand. Sophie glanced at their hands.

Sophie said, "Butterfly Lords told me we have to get back. Later, I mean."

Golsa said, "Then you will get back. What's wrong with you?"

Sophie didn't like her attitude, but she knew how easy it was to let go and rage up at the illogic of it all. The impossible is handled differently by each individual. Sophie knew to be strong, defiant, intelligent. But these people, their unquestionable assertion that Tyler and Sophie had to be here to see Peggy Dreiser first was getting to her. Which meant she couldn't help but feel angry.

Tyler said quietly, "We've been through a lot."

Lantine said, "In all the worlds people have ever known, there has never been this moment."

Lu continued, "It must be perfect. Necessary."

Golsa finished, "We are here. Celebrate! Together. No matter our outlooks or emotions."

"I don't believe in ESP," said Sophie.

They all looked at each other. The wagon swayed. They heard little from outside. They'd had their fill of water. They were hydrated. Lu and Lantine had some more from the bottle, then passed it back to Golsa. Sophie watched Golsa drink again, and realized what the chemically smell was, recognizing Golsa to be slightly inebriated.

Occasionally, a knock came at the front of the wagon, up high, and Golsa would knock back. Each knock meant they had passed a landmark. First, they'd crossed the river at what Golsa called the Bear Bridge. Then they'd passed the university and plastique center. Golsa explained they were moving near to the zoo. She said, it would be an easy walk for them from the zoo to the Great Machine.

Humans are never equal in ability. Some tend elephants and develop a rapport with them. Some excel in plastique, reading the codes like an open book. Others are journeyman carpenters or tanners or brewers. The mosaic of human diversity makes a tapestry of possibilities. Some farmed, some were artists. Some were organizers—leaders. Some focused so tightly on Natural Philosophy, whether metaphysical or practical, that they defined the possible. Some moved in and out, or back and forth between awarenesses of the lay and the ley, which were the same, just shifted. Everyone everywhere always knew there was more than meets the eye.

When she was a little girl, at the beach, Peggy Dreiser practiced this back and forth, which made sense, as the beach was the line between surface and below. She knew she went away for moments at a time, but she came back, and she came back wide open, different. What they called 'all eyes'. Peggy was beloved by family and community. And that community's culture provided guidelines or suggestions to Peggy. She certainly was never seen as freakish. One time a boy with a mustache kissed her on the beach. Who could blame the boy? There was such beauty, purely human, feminine beauty in the girl's precocious awareness and engagement. She tingled in it. People loved to be near her. She had the support of not only her community but her nation. People were excited to have in their midst such a conduit to knowledge.

Peggy's skills were used twofold: 1) in a leadership capacity that engendered intuition and creativity; and 2) in an adjuster, or fixer, mode, to act as Chichimeca's chiropractor aligning geophysical umbos. She had not earned this position. It was not her duty. She was the point of this Circle.

The control center of the Great Machine, its 3 half mile tall needles, was in chaos. The enhanced animals, there as tells, were literally chewing fur and feathers. Their bodies reeked of communications. Smells burned dire. The humans, enhanced and not, did their best to support their colleagues, ignoring the range of emotional aromas. The team was digging in. Perturbations! So far, alignments had kept the miniscule shift increments copacetic. But signals, the transfer of knowledge states, knew nothing other than exponential stress. Each micro-shift had extensive, expansive progeny. Control was exhausted and unraveled. Peggy worked it. They worried when Peggy worried. Peggy was everywhere at once, confiding, cajoling, making it work or hold on. This meant an unknown Peggy they hadn't envisioned.

The Great Machine consisted of 3 gigantic silver needles ascending a half mile above the city. They were crucial to eastern Chichimeca, located as they were on the most prominent geophysical umbos of the region. The silver needles were the inertial heart of the power system. From the populations centers of the capital in Santa Fe to the southern border city of Ciudad de Chihuahua, energy requirements came from the Great Machine. The Great Machine was an inertial machine. The lay of the land and the leys of the land fit here in a wonderful synchrony of geology and cosmology.

Western Chichimeca was powered through a series of smaller inertial needles in strategic positions near Prescott, Yuma, and Quitobaquito. A few other smallish needles were scattered throughout the vast spaces of

Chichimeca to facilitate power usage.

Inertial needles were always silver. Sling needles were white. An inertial economy is always aware of what's available. So there's no excess. Or waste. Everyone involved in the strategy, everyone was required to do his or her fairest.

Inertia does not dissipate. Power was up. But inertia can release or react...even against its will, or against Peggy's will. She and her team had been working at the site 72 hours. The first perturbations had occurred, it turned out, when the kids had first appeared by the Castor. Right about the time Jakes had contacted Peggy's people, Peggy was already on her way to Alburquerque to the Great Machine. Ever since, reports had been coming in from all over Chichimeca. Then from America and Califia. Perturbations seemed to center on the Castor, which somehow seemed to offset things at the Great Machine.

The most recent event in Coltrane, which people were calling an earthquake, had spiked processes, but clearly was connected to the Castor spot. All across Chichimeca people had sensed this. Peggy had surmised the event was not an earthquake at all. Instead, a crack, or break, in the intricate web of fields and forces had occurred. Maybe nothing like that had ever happened. Slight perturbations grew, adjusted, shifted. They amplified. They wailed. If there were more earthquakes (?), this key grid in Alburquerque, the 3 needles, could shift. Power would stumble. The Castor spot seemed the origin or original point from which all else followed. Would it expand? Would it contract? Viable answers plead for reason. Needles without efficacy was something the people had not considered. Some kind of breakdown. This was unheard of. Shifts typically occurred over millions of years, not in a few days. Which suggested that whatever was happening was cracking much more than an umbo or two.

"Slings holding," said Mark Pease, Peggy's key man, a slight fellow who tried to please. He knew all the ways in. Peggy had taught him chaos, and he had learned the locks, the valves, the regulators. He felt like a safe cracker, a code man, an escape artist. He knew what that meant: he was playing, and there was no room to buzz off to adventure now. He needed to fully focus, thus adding to Peggy's sensate.

Peggy began, "Gracias! If the slings are good, then power is not disturbed. We're not mining yet. But the needles are unhappy. We're keeping up. Focus folks!"

Mark Pease said, "Perturbations ample! We hold for now, our adjusts are sweet. But I don't know, Peggy. It seems new. Or different. When do we alert the commonweal?"

Peggy quipped, "They know! We're all worried, worn out now. Gnawing regret. Bug bites. Loose change. Kino adventures! We need to focus and make this specific. I was hoping we'd have a handle on things by now, so that I could know how to talk about it, what's happening. A bit of spoiled potato? Interesting. Itchy." Peggy sighed loudly, came out from her coffin board, a body fitting enclosure that aided access to parameters for her. She stepped away, stretched. She was covered in sweat. Her hair was pulled back in a ponytail tied with a yellow ribbon. She wore shorts and a baggy, short-sleeved cotton shirt. She was barefoot.

Mark watched Peggy unwinding from the coffin. He was dressed the same, shorts, short sleeved cotton shirt, bare feet. It was hot in control. When he knew she had caught her breath, he smiled to her, then: "Sling's in. They're here. The kids from Coltrane."

"Vraiment? Pour que non? Yes, yes," went Peggy. In an exercise of emotion, she stretched, she bent, she danced in place, feeling her charges resound. "Fortuitous, yes? Gladness. They had to be here, yes?"

The other members of the team, sitting at consoles, or in their own coffins, or adjusting the long ribbed calibrators, all smiled to see her excitement. A tiny moment of relief was allowed. The machines felt it, adjusted an iota, faintly quilled. Mr. Mittens in his rectifier jellyfish helmet muttered, "Now we shall see."

Mark continued, "They'll be here nowish."

"Aqui? Ici? Ahora? Maintenant?" went Peggy. "Should I go to meet— At the Circle? I should go to the Circle to meet them."

"No, they are here," said Mark. He looked away like he was embarrassed.

Mr. Mittens said, "Seems necessary to have them here. Very cute!" Mr. Mittens played with his jellyfish controls, then pulled off the helmet. He was an older man, dark skinned, with big brown eyes. He watched the others. He frowned, but his eyes were wide and bright. He said, "See what happens now. On all accounts. It's the right thing to do."

Golsa let the passengers off by the entrance to the Zoological Gardens. This gave Sophie and Tyler a chance to peek into the lovely landscape of open grasslands that sauntered into grottos and waterfalls and bizarre rock formations. The gardens included a system of enclosed boardwalks for visiting humans. At this zoo the animals were enshrined in freedom and grandeur, while the humans had to stay in cages. Humans couldn't keep themselves from interfering with animals. Of course, people with connections and duties could intermingle, but this was kept to a minimum to encourage the animals their own sense of a meeting place, their congress, their headquarters for animal input and righteousness.

Golsa waved goodbye and climbed up the elephant to the top of the wagon by the driver. The elephants sang out with upraised trunks. Answers came soon after. The Elephant People continued on into the zoo at an excellent pace.

Sophie said, "I know you can talk to animals. I met the Butterfly Lords. I guess I never realized how smart animals are."

Tyler said, "They know what they need."

"Which is what's best," said Lu.

Lantine said, "It's a walk but not far. See how close the needles are?"

"That gives me great comfort," quipped Sophie.

Tyler mustered his reserves and went over to Sophie and took her arm. "Me and Sophie have to talk. Just for a second." He led her aside to a walkway by the busy road. Passersby all called themselves to attention. Sophie thought, are they all drunk? Tyler went over each person nearby, taking in their features and clothing, as though he were judging a costume ball. Sophie and Tyler didn't know where to look first, so ended up staring at each other.

"Sophie!"

"Tyler!"

"All I know is these people are trying to help us."

"I know that. But they think differently than we do. That elephant lady was drunk. They're kinda spaced. You know I'm right. And that's fine. I'm not making fun. That's their choice. But our way of thinking, even if it's hyped and wrong a lot, is what we need in this kind of emergency."

Tyler nodded. "That makes sense. But I don't think you and I are smart enough to figure it out by ourselves. And we're the only ones here of that thinking."

"We see Peggy, we get back to the San Pedro."

"Agreed," went Tyler. Then: "You okay?"

Sophie grimaced. "What do you think? Of course I'm not okay. Are you okay?"

"I feel weak, like tired out, like I can't wake up."

"Well, have a drink! Just kidding. At least these people

have one vice." She snorted. "My anger keeps me up." She laughed. "I'm kidding! Okay. I'll behave."

"Lantine and Lu are nice. They're trying to help."

"Yeah, I see you and Lu being nice."

Tyler shook his head, but that started a tremor, but he didn't know what to say.

They rejoined the others, went on their way. The great silvery needles went up, up into the sky, and when Sophie and Tyler leaned back to find their tips they staggered.

Foot traffic and the occasional animal cart dominated the center of Alburquerque. People in all manner of dress and make up busied busied about. Hot air balloons hovered overhead. Sophie and Tyler both noticed right away: no ads, no advertising of any kind. The squat buildings with the silvery reflecting spires on tops were gaily painted on the ground levels. The stepped pyramids they learned were auditoriums for cultural events and social debates. What Lantine explained as 'administering the ministers'. She and Lu laughed at that. Sophie and Tyler looked concerned, not sure what that meant, but continued following Lantine and Lu down the paved avenues across squares and circles and gardens. They passed food vendors. Fresh fruit was on display. Drinks were offered for sale. Several vendors offered tiswin, others mescal. They passed a large fountain with 3 spires of white gushing water.

Lu could tell Sophie and Tyler were overwhelmed. She slowed to walk alongside them. She knew sometimes quiet was the best guide. They didn't want too many details right now. But they didn't understand the 'ministers', so how did they govern in their world?

Sophie, finally, allowed her a way in: "So Peggy is like a scientist? Or a priest?"

Lu explained, thinking she'd help them focus, about the ministers, "The best government is the least government. The Circle is divided into 360 degrees. Each degree has a role and place in Chichimeca governance. Trade, health, communications, banking, all of those things. Of course, the various groups of people and animals all have their own degrees. There are many degrees of Natural Philosophy, whether Metaphysics or tech. Then, research, applications. Plastique is very specific. Whenever so many people are involved in governance, then you have to have a group of people who monitor them. Yes? Then who monitors the monitors? It's a joke here, do you see?"

"Regulators?" went Sophie.

Lantine looked back. She said, "Odd word that."

"Bureaucrats," said Tyler.

Lantine huffed. "Of course. A good French word we use in America every day. But here in Chichimeca they prefer us not to use it."

They were close to the base of the gigantic needles.

Lu said, "Peggy is close."

Lantine said, "I feel her, too."

Tyler said, "This is the Great Machine?"

Sophie said, "But what does she do? Peggy? You didn't say? What's her position?"

Mark Pease let the party in. The whole team stopped what they were doing to watch. Animals hiccoughed and grunted and farted. Peggy had been discussing calibrations with their comfort zones. Adjusters knew not to interfere. Helmets and jellyfish were doffed. Control inhaled. Peggy smiled and ran over to greet them.

She felt it. She had to stop. She wavered. She thought she'd better sit down right where she was. But her strength came back. She had trouble seeing at first, lots of blurs and energy fields. She had to blink her eyes. She focused. The blue! The area by the door where the visitors entered writhed in a vortex of intersecting fields with overpowering blue light jetting from two of the visitors.

Fields of energy with plumes of blue!

Peggy managed, "Welcome, Lu and Lantine!" She

looked at the young people.

Mark was at her side, looking worried, staring at the young people too.

"You!" went Peggy. "You are not here."

Tyler said, "That can't be it."

Sophie said, "They said you could help."

Mr. Mittens called, "Peggy, right now, right now as I speak, the perturbations...the perturbations have vanished. Kaput. The needles show perfect alignment. High grade. Happy fields! Cogent pulses!"

Other techs and animals hurried to consoles and viewers and began confirming Mr. Mittens' news. They sang out with excitement. Mark went around from station to station to see for himself. He went back to the visitors and Peggy. He stood before Peggy beaming: "It's true!"

Peggy said, "They did it!" She collapsed into his arms and they hugged, holding on to each other tightly.

Sophie said, "You're Peggy?"

Lu said, "There was a problem. It's fixed?"

Lantine said, "Peggy, this is Sophie and Tyler."

"Of course it is! When they arrived on the Castor, the needles knew. Everything tweaked. Their presence seems...garish. But now—yes! yes! here we are, all of us. And now—look now what happens! When they visit here, it reverts back, re-ups, recalibrates. Re-constitution. Re-creation. Re-modern."

"Okay, Peggy! You're like a rapper," said Sophie. "Spoken word artist, right?"

Lantine said, "They think they should go back."

Peggy broke from Mark. She uttered sounds, smells, tweaks, taunts. She turned with a flourish and arms up, hands held high, sweat flying, said, "Thank you! Thank you everyone for seeing us through this!"

She came back from exuberance to focus on the visitors.

She was smiling broadly, nodding first to Lu and

Lantine. Then, her eyes settled on the other two young people, and her eyes got big, as she took them in. And, of course, they were taking her in.

Peggy said, "Can we touch them?"

Tyler said, "I don't think we're catchy."

Sophie said, "What just happened here?"

Peggy smiled to her. "The Great Machine was upset, unsettled, uncooperative. Now it is calm and self-assured. Intrepid. Diligent. Sagesse! Fine, fine. More than fine. Just as you came in."

Lu said, "We touch them." She demonstrated by taking Tyler's hand, then reaching out to Sophie. Sophie was reluctant but saw the point Lu was trying for, so she let her take her hand. Lu sighed. "We were at Whitewater."

Lantine said, "War, Peggy."

Peggy began to whirl and spin around, then she slowed, shook her head. She slowed enough to clearly speak to her team: "No one knows. Anyone know? No, no. Not us. Not yet, not yet. Robber, plunder, render. 'Ripeness is all!' I think Mexico suspects a new weapon. New tech that caused the perturbations." She started that whirling movement again, a slow dance of balance and blame.

Lantine said, "We thought we were bringing the kids to see you, but we were bringing the kids to see the Great Machine. Yes?"

Mr. Mittens called, "Indubitably!"

Tyler said, "The Great Machine—it knew? It knew something had happened? When we first came in?"

"It's like your power system?" asked Sophie. "Atomic? Doesn't seem very complex? What does it do?"

Tyler asked, "How could we have fixed it?"

Sophie stepped closer to Peggy, held her hand up, as though she was going to stop her, and said, "Can you help us? Can this big machine help us? That's what we gotta know. We gotta get back."

Peggy sighed. "Both of you! In blue light! Then 'catchy', 'complexity', we will have to work those. Language is power. 'Rapper'? It's true. We must get back. We all have to get back. Time is crucial. Chronoliths. Chronology?"

"We can sling," said Lantine, "to Coltrane."

Mark said, "I'll get word out."

Sophie said, "You folks never get adamant, do you? Know what I mean? Like really, really bold. Serious?"

Peggy said, "Ahh!"

Lu said, "They have this language in another language, Peggy. They don't mean offense. But we talk. We listen. Maybe they use language differently from us? Plastique would like to look at their codes, but right now—"

Peggy said, "No explain needed, Lu. You and Lantine have done splendidly! It's simple. Complex in sheer number of parts? Complex as in difficult? 'How many parts in the Great Machine,' is a question for school children. And the answer? 'How many parts in you'? it depends on how you look. Point of view. Filters. Systems— the process. Dynamics. Kinesthesia. Regulation. You define context, habitat, Umwelt; you filter you point."

"How did we fix it?" asked Tyler. "How could we do that?"

Sophie said, "Well, this is a lot of help. This is a whole lot of impossible. You know, Tyler, how when we first showed up we thought we were dreaming? Now we meet the great Peggy. Every question is answered with more questions. Makes no sense."

Peggy was now moving around Sophie and Tyler, sniffing at them, moving her hands up and down by them but without touching. She said, "Does anyone notice the intense blue of these two? Mr. Mittens?"

Mr. Mittens came over to the young people. "I can see what Old Duckbill meant. And the Butterfly Lords. Yes, you two must get back before it happens again. As for blue, as in leakage, or spill, or overlap slough...yes."

Peggy nodded. "I think that's right but I'm not convinced. I can understand and not."

Sophie couldn't resist: "So we will switch back to where we come from?"

Peggy said, "Overlap."

Mr. Mittens said, "Good palabra. Bon mot. Overlap? Yes."

Mark said, "I'm not following."

Peggy said, "I need to clean up, get some clothes. We'll need vehicles in Coltrane. Mark, I'm counting on you to set things up." Peggy smiled to Tyler and Sophie. "I know you know we mean well. Have you eaten? You must be exhausted. Loss of blue is loss of essence. Mark, see they get some food. I'll get over to my office and be back by the time you've eaten. Then we need to get to the slings."

"Slings will wait for you," said Lantine.

Peggy smiled. "So good to see you, Lantine. And you, Lu. The Crots are going to be called out that's for sure." She paused, gathered her thoughts: "It's depended all along on all of you showing up at the precise time you did. We make this happen. All of us together. Right now. Do you understand that?" She moved over to the visitors. She extended her hand and touched Lu and Lantine on the cheeks. She took Sophie and Tyler's hands.

Sophie said, "Not a word."

"I think so," said Tyler.

Sophie nodded, inhaled, hesitated, then: "You know what to do? That's what they told us. We just want to go home."

"'Know'?" went Peggy. "'Do'?" She smiled, squeezed Sophie's hand. "This is what it means: it works. What we have done 100s of years now works. Not for me, for Chichimeca. Maybe for the planet. But Mela and I both wonder: why should you stay close to the origin? Because the earthquake did? A beginning means there's an end?

The way you entered, the way you leave?"

Tyler said, "Where we came in?"

Mr. Mittens said, "Who's Mela? Peggy, restore yourselves!"

"It's logical. Isn't it?" asked Sophie. "That if we came through at that spot, we might go back at the same spot?"

"It was no earthquake," said Mr. Mittens, his jellyfish bobbing on his head.

Sophie said, "Nice jellyfish."

Peggy read the stories through their hands. "The universe makes sense. But why couldn't you go back from here? Unless that spot, unless it was an actual...tear? Rip?"

"It can't be impossible," said Mark.

A talking, big headed eagle, bobbed on its perch, and said, "Not an earthquake at all. Annihilation of space-time."

Mr. Mittens said to the eagle, "Ah, Mr. Virnig, You were always good at etiology."

"Like an A-bomb?" said Tyler.

Mark went, "'A-bomb'?"

Peggy looked startled. Her face dripped sweat as she said, "You know atoms?"

Sophie and Tyler glanced at each other. Sophie explained, "He's kind of a science nerd."

"Ahhh," went Lu. "What's a 'nerd'?"

Lantine said, "What's an 'atom'?"

Peggy danced again, this time speeding up. She sang, "Miniscule! Infinitesimal. Something that is not there but that is implied there. Infinitesimal! Infinitesimal as though a point, a perfect point of matter. A particle. Thing one. Thing zero. A monad."

Tyler burst, "You guys have space-time, you know about atoms. Quantum theory? Strings? The Big Bang? All that stuff?"

Peggy went, "Analyze! Discover! Examine! Explore—"

Sophie sang out with, "Conclude! Resolve! Defend!

Vanquish! Uproar! Classic! Blazed! Slayed! Supersize!"

Lantine inhaled sharply. "We need to get going," she said slowly. She glanced back and forth between Sophie and Peggy.

Lu said, "Moi, aussi."

Peggy slowed, stumbled, mumbled, "'Strings'? Tell me about strings. Tyler. Explain! 'Quantum'? Like yogurt? Like quanta pots? Ever since Karl Marx intuited field symmetries, field or point—well, points are imaginary but if you focus on the point, rather than the field, I can see how your culture might evolve. You know the monad. We focus on the field."

Tyler wanted to smile. He wanted to have hope in Peggy, but all he could manage was a garbled, "Ahh. I don't think I'm getting what you are saying, your *point* here." He nervously laughed. "And I don't know if I can explain."

Sophie interrupted in time, "What's a monad? A fad? A rad fad? You guys are tripping! And, Miss Peggy, what exactly do you do? What is your position?"

CHAPTER 12

It was one more than the recommended number of passengers, but Lantine knew they could do it. After all, no baggage. Sophie and Tyler had calmed about flying, and Tyler's stomach wasn't as queasy as before. He was determined not to throw up this time. He was pressed up to the window in the cabin's backseat with Sophie next to him. Luanna was on the other side of Sophie, pressed against that window. Mela was up front next to Lantine. Lantine went through her checklist. She made sure everyone was strapped in, seat belts shared as necessary. Once they were air borne, Lantine breathed a sign of determination, but she could tell right away they were heavy. They would be slow, floating, bobbing their way back to Coltrane.

Synchronicities and juxtapositions added support. She knew Kai was on it. He'd figure something. He depended on her knowing how to get in and out fast. Coltrane would be swarming with law enforcement. They'd be all over the roads and highways between Coltrane and Albuquerque. The school teachers who'd brought Sophie to Coltrane, Graves and Jakes, had heard talk of Albuquerque but not of an airplane. A very slight edge remained before they guessed the kids were flying.

Lantine knew the Crotalus people would not give her up. The authorities would not imagine they had access to an airplane—a lot teetered on this miniscule feather of an edge. She'd submitted her flight plan. She had to have permission to land in Coltrane. Otherwise, she maintained radio silence.

People from across the nation were alerted to what was happening in the American Southwest. Earthquakes in Arizona were unheard of, though historically they had been important. The vague or varying stories of what had happened were enough to keep the Internet popping. Soon theories began to unveil—

The noise in the small plane was deafening. Lantine was used to it and did have head phones. She glanced at her passengers. Mela was looking into the sky. The young people in back had pinched faces. She called, "You guys okay back there?"

Tyler went, "Again with the initials, 'O-K'? Pour que? Pour quoi? Warum?" But no one could really hear him.

Sophie called out, "Why is it so loud? Slings are silent."

Lantine said, "Don't know about that. This is fairly typical." She tapped on her headphones.

"That smell?" yelled Tyler.

Sophie nodded, yelling, "Like the S-U-V: internal combustion. C'est vrai?"

Mela turned to her. "C'est vrait!"

Luanna raised her voice, "Just quit hearing it. Hey, you guys, look at the bright side. I mean, we've been through so much and we're fine. We are doing it. Getting it done!" She whooped.

Sophie had eyes only for Mela and quickly shouted, "Do you know Old Duckbill?"

Lantine said loudly enough, "Cabin's not conducive to conversation. Old Duckbill may have to wait."

Mela stared into Sophie's eyes. "Blue. I don't know Old Duckbill."

Sophie yelled, "Old Duckbill said 'overlap'. Do you know what that means?"

Mela nodded. "Overlap. Yes. Overlap. Goes in many directions." But no one could hear her. She yelled, "Let's try this. I give overlap. We overlap."

It was unclear whether anyone heard what Mela said. Mela stayed twisted in her seat, so she could see Tyler and Sophie. She saw their concern, their worry, their unclear physicality. She said, "Peace."

Mela knew their parents were not at peace. Parents terribly confused and scared. Overlap? Prayers between worlds. How did that work? Did they affect each other? Praying with all their hearts for their children's safe return...in two worlds. Prayers received. Prayers sent out. This was a moment of great awareness.

Mela said, "Act. Choice? They have to get back. They have to get back to where it had started. The exact spot was essential." Could they hear her? Mela said, "Overlap." Sophie and Tyler watched her. Sophie smiled, but Tyler looked sickly. Mela continued: "The kids from here must have gone to where you came from. But how to understand the doubles? Two different types of overlap? Different circumstances? See, see. There's more see than meets the eye. Overlap."

Sophie pulled back as Mela turned away from the kids, to join the sky. Sophie tried to get comfortable. Now Tyler was tight to the window with eyes closed. Luanna stared into the bright blue sky on her side. Sophie moved her right hand over towards Tyler's. Nothing. No blue. No sparks. The Lise's had shown off their blue static. The static happened only between doubles. She needed to tell Mela this. But why had she and Tyler switched while the others doubled?

Sophie knew Mela was a sensitive. What did Mela see? Awareness brought sensitivity. We become aware of each moment's necessity: if there was some overlap between her world and this one, and she and Tyler had somehow switched to here, then the Sophie and Tyler from here had switched to their home. But if something from here, or there, had not switched properly? Was that it? Properly or appropriately? A balance? There had to be a balance? Was that the right word? A see saw affect? If the switch was not complete...some critical piece not switched? Could it have made for unbalanced overlap? What could that mean? Maybe a slight draw or tug or tension resulted? Then, that resulted in pulling in the doubles to here? So there, in her home, there must have been slightly more?

Sophie was exhausted. The thoughts were exhausting, too. She pondered, closed her eyes: she would not worry. She would meditate. All American kids learned to meditate at school. She grew quiet. She thought of her St. Louis. She remembered. The white noise of the engine lulled her to a still place of hope.

They all rested, slept, kept their eyes closed. Except for Lantine. No one puked. No one spoke for a long time. Lantine had been a pilot since she was a kid. She loved flying. She loved the sharp concentration it required. She felt she kept the plane up by sheer will power. It was a rush, a giddy fulfillment of who she was.

She liked when passengers settled down and quit their jostling. The hours went fast for her. Coltrane would be coming up, she realized, when she figured she was slowly coming into Arizona. The last few hundred miles were barren landscape in grays and browns, interrupted by bare, burned out mountains. Bleak: the 'after' shot of hundreds of years of water loss and over grazing. She could tell she was getting into Arizona because of the Chiricahuas to the south with their unique features. She could see Wilcox Playa ahead, to the west of the Chiricahua. Coltrane was not far. She began her descent.

The Coltrane airport was south and east of town within sight of the border. Border restrictions made her flight plan essential. The folks at the Coltrane airport would be expecting her. There shouldn't be any trouble. What if the feds showed up? The kids were underage. She could be facing kidnapping charges? Crossing state lines—but she'd brought them back! Wouldn't they take the two kids back to the river anyway? To be with their 'parents'? So the mission would be completed either way. Don't overthink it! She was hexing it. She'd just as soon not have to deal with the FBI or any law enforcement. But her fear spiral was getting a grip. She got focused, glanced at Mela. Yes, Mela!

Sophie interrupted with a loud cough, then gasp: "Hydrocarbons!"

Lantine twisted around, smiled at her. "Yes, gasoline." Lantine saw a face that was worried, tense, scared, sickly.

Luanna called, "Where are we, Lantine?"

"Coming in now," said Lantine.

Mela said, "The slings? Where are they?" but no one could hear her. Her voice so soft.

Lantine said, "Beginning descent."

Mela said, "We're on our way."

Lantine kept the descent gradual. She took her time, took it easy. They were skirting the Apache Mountains. They were going south around the mountains that contained the canyon which was Coltrane. The mountains were passed, left behind, and the view was now all white and gray desert flatland below them. Ahead, further south, the white air strip, like an unrolled bandage, tiny but necessary. Lantine circled, slowed, descended some more. They could see a few vehicles, cars and a truck, near the airport's office. The Coltrane airport was small. No state police or sheriff vehicles anyway. Lantine lined up for her landing. As she committed to the final stretch, they all saw the Border Patrol vehicles, lights blazing, at the airport turn off on the main road.

Tyler yelped, "What is it?"

Luanna said, "Wait for it!"

Mela said, "Diversion blue."

They made contact with the run way gentle as a kiss that stayed put. Lantine hit the flaps, the engine roared. She braked. They hurtled down the runway. Lantine let the speed slack, and she started curving around and back towards the office and hangers. She could see Kai standing by a big truck that was not the Crotalus truck. She stopped, turned off the engine. They all grunted in unison which made them all giggle.

"Thank you, Lantine!" said Mela.

Their heads echoed with the loss of the engine roar.

Luanna said, "That's Kai!"

He was coming towards them.

Lantine said, "Let's go." She opened her door, jumped out, turned and put the seat forward to let the passengers out. Mela did the same thing. Tyler got out on her side. The others on Lantine's.

Kai said, "Illegals! Big bust. The FBI agent here went over to help. Perfect timing. We're fine: we get in the truck, we head back to the river."

Lantine hugged Kai.

Mela said, "Ripe." She shook Kai's hand and said, "We've met."

"Yes," said Kai. "This is working."

Luanna wanted a hug too. Then, she said, "Crotalus?"

Kai smiled. "What could they keep us on? We don't know anything about what's happening. Anyway, wait 'til you see who's in the truck. It's dirty, a bit funky, but it'll do. Come on!"

Kai hustled them to the big, half ton. Its trailer had tall wooden sides, but it was open in the back. Lantine and Mela would ride up front with Kai. The others stared into the back of the partially filled truck. Where would they fit? There were burlap sacks stuffed with chiles in the back.

Kai came around to help. He said, "Habaneros!"

Sophie and Tyler and Luanna were delighted to see a small head peek out from the bags in the back.

Bishop said, "I wiggled a compartment back in here. Nifty as you please! Plus, I got water and fresh tortillas. All aboard!"

Sophie and Tyler and Luanna climbed into the back of the truck. Kai helped them get situated, then made sure the burlap sacks blocked them from view. Good thing Kai had backed into the parking space, so that prying eyes from the big bust would not see their machinations. The folks in the office were either gone or watching the bust. Kai went around to the front. He got in the driver's side. He got the truck going. He slapped the steering wheel wildly and said, "Mela, here's to beauty! Here's to you! Reality, here we come!" He moved the truck along the airport road to the flashing vehicles.

The 2 Border Patrol vehicles were pulled onto the shoulder off the road. Three Border Patrol agents had a group of young Mexican men sitting alongside the road. The Mexican men looked tired, dirty, but many had faces of incredulity too. As though they knew this was all a mistake. The Border Patrol men looked bored. A man in a suit stood talking to the Border Patrol, looking studious. The other Border Patrol agent was giving out drinks of water to the Mexican men.

When Kai stopped the truck at the road to make his turn, the man in the suit turned to look at Kai. Kai waved. Kai said to the folks in the cab, "He saw your flight plan and was curious, coming from the Duke and all. But we talked, and you know how friendly I can be. But I think," he swung the truck out into the road, turning west, and punched the gas to get out of there, "we are clear!"

He kept going. The Mexicans and Border Patrol were left behind. Mela saw the lined up sitting men finally as a line of pink bowls hanging in the air, receiving sprites from space.

Lantine said, "Someone must have called the Border Patrol at the exact time!"

Mela said, "Of course. We avoid Coltrane?"

Kai said, "We'll take the southern route that follows the border."

Lantine said, "And Tommy?"

"Apparently, he had some priors dealing with medicina verde. So they are keeping him right now. Their big concern was Albuquerque. Those other guys, the teachers, said Albuquerque too. The FBI wanted to know why the kids had to go there. They assumed the kids had a ride there—in a car, which seemed to indicate some kind of underground conspiracy. Trafficking? Smuggling? I don't know."

Lantine said, "The earthquake must have really freaked everybody out."

Kai said, "Local law enforcement are worried about Coltrane. Now there's talk it wasn't an earthquake at all. The river is going to be hopping that's for sure. We'll get in close as we dare. Then hike the rest of the way."

"Perfect!" went Mela. "The other kids? They're okay?"

Kai said, "Well, I guess you heard about the blue light sparks between doubles? How much do you know?"

Lantine said, "Mela's still learning."

"No one knew what was going on," said Kai. "That's why Bishop knew we had to get these two to you, Mela. That's the real reason for Albuquerque. How was the fair?"

Mela smiled a little, managed, "That sounds right. But I never made it to the fair!" She seemed studious, serious, or pre-occupied. Then: "When they showed up, it was wonderful. At the exact moment of our contact, everything changed there. I mean in Albuquerque."

They stayed on the state highway which followed the border the 20 miles to the river. As usual, not much traffic, and the sun was bright, and the sky was clear, but without summer intensity. They drove for several minutes watching the mirrors, checking the windows for signs of pursuit. No flashing lights, no helicopters overhead. Kai watched his speed closely, which was easy as the old truck could barely get close to the limit anyway.

Mela spoke up: "This earthquake—I heard about the earthquake. But a few days ago prior, I mean before that, I knew something was happening. I wasn't sure. I knew I was needed or called or summoned? But it seemed I should stay in Albuquerque. I was on this project to make a few beans to pay for my entrance fee, don't you know. Now I know why."

Lantine said, "A few days ago—that must have been when the first kids showed up. These two."

Kai said, "We'd heard about the project at Sandia. So you missed the psychic fair?"

Lantine said, "When we showed up at Sandia, at that exact moment, Mela said, the tests worked? Is that the right word? Just as we came in? I don't even know what you guys were doing. But that's what you said."

Mela said, "Clarified. Equipment clarification. Purgation. Lustration. All sorts of info was happy. It was upsetting for the electronics. Well, so, then, when Lantine called with the kids, at that exact moment, it was as if some great symmetry had re-set, some balance electronica pacifica. This was it. I knew they had had to come to Albuquerque to set things straight. But I'm not exactly sure what that means. I mean, the implications are at Sandia. Or here? Or at the river? I'm afraid those Sandia folks will be looking, too. For me."

Kai asked, "What happened when you saw the kids?"

"It was clear."

Kai said, "Wow. The doubles are weird. Wait until you meet them."

In the back of the truck Luanna and Sophie and Tyler

and Bishop huddled close. Enough air streamed through the slats of the truck to keep them from stifling. Bishop shared his water. He passed out tortillas.

As they ate and drank, Bishop said, "The story is real, the proverbial wild goose chase. First, you're at the river. Then you're with us. Then in Coltrane, we chance upon Sophie and Lantine. Now you jet setters are back from rendezvous in Albuquerque."

Luanna made a little sigh, tickling at Bishop, saying, "'Chance'? What chance, Homer?"

Tyler said from around a mouthful of delicious tortilla, "Mela said we helped her."

Sophie added, "She said when we showed up, her work clarified."

"Hmmm," went Bishop.

Luanna said, "These guys had to go to Albuquerque. Now we know why. And now we have Mela with us. It's all working fine. I'm glad they let you go, Bishop. I guess I'm worrying about Tom."

"He knows we'll get him back. It's his karma. He'll be fine. Crotalus will play again! There are stories to be told!"

Up front, Kai spotted the deer by the road first. "Wow! Looks like a mother and fawn." He slowed the truck.

Two white tailed deer, smaller than regular white tailed deer of the Midwest, these were the slim, smallish desert variety. The doe was standing by a tall yucca with waxy white blooms. Beside her, a young one, half her size, but no spots.

The truck slowed in its approach, and the deer didn't move. The doe raised her head, watched them with a very open, nonplussed look. She turned her head to the side. The young one kept touching her. Their tails weren't flicking like they did when nervous...but excited. The deer were on Mela's side so she rolled her window down as Kai slowed to a stop by them.

Mela said, "You need a ride?"

The doe sneezed and lowered her head. The baby watched its mother.

Kai said, "No one's around."

Mela said, "We'll have to help them into the back."

Kai edged the truck out of the road, then put the truck in neutral. Mela and Kai and Lantine got out of the truck.

Mela looked over the bags of chiles. She looked for the passengers. She smiled and sang, "You guys have company!"

Bishop called out from his hidey hole, "What gives?"

Lantine and Kai helped the baby into the back, the mother having jumped onto the truck at once.

Lantine called out, "Deer! Deer need a ride. It's okay!"

Kai and Lantine and Mela got back in the cab of the truck. Kai got it into gear and resumed their journey.

Tyler smiled, snorted, said to Bishop, "There those letters again!"

Bishop smiled.

Sophie pushed aside a bag of peppers. She made a window to their new fellow passengers. Sophie said softly, "How do you do."

Up front, Kai said, "Do I dare ask what's going on?"

A bit farther down the road, they came on a badger. The badger was sitting on its tail and back legs, front legs dangling sloppily, leisurely waiting on the shoulder.

Lantine said, "I wonder if it's the talking badger Sophie met?"

Mela said, "He knows us for sure. He's waiting for a ride too."

Kai said, "Super! No one will suspect we got the beginnings of an Ark here!"

Mela said, "It's perfect. Perfect diversion. Perfect intention. No one will see us now."

Kai stopped for the badger. They explained to the people in back what was happening. Lantine and Kai had to help the bulky badger up. The badger seemed embarrassed at needing help. Lantine whistled softly. The badger calmed, grumbled a ditty. The doe snorted once but the badger kept his distance, settling down among the bags of peppers, inserting himself between bags, so he was hardly visible. Sophie stretched out her hand to touch the badger's tail. The badger rattled a frisky rat-a-tat-tat then was quiet.

Sophie nodded, said, "They're here to help."

Bishop laughed, his eyes big, agleam.

Tyler sighed, said, "Old Duckbill?"

Sophie went, "Overlap."

Tyler said, "It makes me feel better, Sophie."

"That word again," said Luanna. "Can I touch him too?"

Sophie shrugged.

As Kai got the truck back on the highway, Lantine's excitement burst with, "What do you suppose is happening?"

Mela said, "The animals have a role here."

Kai said, "Border Patrol."

A Border Patrol SUV went by going the opposite direction. Kai waved, keeping it friendly. They started their descent now into the San Pedro Valley. In Spanish the form of the valley was called a bajada, which had to do with steep sides that broadened out into a wide, flat bottom land. They had an incredible vista of the valley, with the Huachuca Mountains forming the western horizon. The green belt of giant fluffy cottonwoods traced the river. A helicopter was slowly moving over the river, just a few 100 feet above the cottonwoods.

Lantine said, "Mechnico-dragonfly."

Mela asked, "How far to where the kids first appeared?"

Kai glanced at Mela. "Not far." He chuckled. "I know, not a good answer. We seek precision, right? Ha!" He said, "Security is going to be insane."

"I bet they want the kids back there as much as we do,"

said Lantine.

"Perhaps," said Mela. "But forces here, in this realm, as you know, get over heated. We humans, here, practice the great art of confusion."

"I hear that," said Kai. "That's why it's so easy to live on the side. No one suspects—"

"We have to be careful," finished Lantine.

"We're okay," said Kai. "We are."

Mela shook her head, the others glanced her way. "Funny how we use the letters so often. A person not used to them—what would they imagine?" Mela smiled. "Things are coming together."

Lantine said, "Are you worried? It's all happening so fast. Have you had time to really—"

"What? What more could we do? Worried about what?" Then: "Our language overlaps. Our meanings? Our actions? Right now? Not so sure. Maybe? Peut-etre?"

"No way!" started Kai.

Ahead on the road, over on the side shoulder was a big old desert porcupine. Kai slowed.

Kai said, "How will we get him up in the truck?"

Mela said, "We have no choice. No problem then. He can control his quills."

"If you say so," said Kai. He pulled the truck over on the shoulder ahead of the porcupine. Mela went to communicate with the others in the back of the truck.

But no one wanted to literally hoist the big golden porcupine up into the bed. Kai figured it out. He made a rough ramp of chile pepper burlap sacks. He had to get behind them to kind of hold them in place, as the porcupine scrambled and hauled itself on board. Big critter! Big rounded head, then a heavy tail that swept to the side in back.

Lantine whistled. Luanna yelped with joy and astonishment at the new passenger. There was not enough room now for the burlap sacks. This left the people in the back exposed.

Kai said, "Don't worry! Mela says we're pretty much invisible now with these guys. A masking, I guess. What do you think, Mela? How to explain it?"

Mela said, "Overlap has begun. It's happening now."

Lantine said, "We'll leave the sacks. Everyone fill your pockets. That should be enough. No big. Someone will stop and pick them up. Everybody in?"

Mela wondered what her 'double' might be doing or thinking or saying right about now. It made sense to think she was doing something very similar. Do we all have doubles, Mela wondered. And when the kids get back to their spot, what will happen? Mela thought but forgot to say to her double: 'Have you ever hitched across the west and come to a desert motel complete with tumbleweed, and you go in the tiny bathroom of the funky motor lodge and turn on the hot water all the way, then you wet your hands and arms and face, then soap them up, and the rush of scrubbing and rinsing, then doing it again, hands pressed tight to your eyes has you seeing everything at once.' Anyway, Mela thought: casual focus and I see all my pasts, all my presents, all my moments of water—splashing, hoses, squirt guns, the last desert motel room in the world flooding my own private, eternal graveyard.

Kai said, "They'll think it's pot."

"A certain symmetry," said Lantine. "I mean in terms of the chile peppers left here and the chile peppers that seem to have started this whole thing."

Sophie said, "They were like fire!" She stuffed her pockets with habaneros. The burlap sacks contained a mix of different peppers, but mainly jalapeno. Sophie took only the pumpkin orange ones.

Mela nodded, remarked, "That, I am unclear of." Everyone giggled almost, a slight titter through the back of the truck. Were the animals smiling too? Mela made eye contact with each of the animals in the back. Kai went around and got the truck in gear, calling out to Lantine and Mela. They went around and got in.

Sophie leaned over to Luanna. "The animals are part of this." She smiled wanly, nodded. "It makes sense. Makes me feel better."

Luanna smiled.

They were all feeling pretty good now for some reason.

Mela drank some water up front. Kai kept the truck moving west until they crossed the bridge over the river, where he slowed. There were a few homes around the bridge, some ranchers, some retired folks. They all looked empty. They couldn't see any livestock.

Kai said, "Too quiet?"

Lantine said, "Evacuated?"

Kai shrugged. "It's always quiet down here."

"We're invisible," said Lantine.

No one on the road. No other vehicle could be seen. The road was empty. Away from the river and trees, the blasted landscape was dry and pale, where the cows had eaten the little scrub left over. This was more than dust and erosion, this was the after shot of a battered landscape.

Then: Border Patrol trucks were parked in a cluster right at the turn off to the county road they were hoping to take. Kai slowed even more. No agents. Nobody. So he made the turn and saw Border Patrol agents leading a line of Mexicans through the desert. The agents were too busy to pay much attention to them. But, after all, they were simply an old truck loaded with peppers, that probably hadn't heard about any evacuation. They were invisible.

Kai said, "They don't trust their eyes!"

Mela said, "We're close."

Lantine gasped: "I mean, if they look in the back of the truck and see a porkie and a badger...know what I mean?"

Kai huffed, then said, "Overlap."

* * *

The sling back was accomplished in a caul of sound that did not seem to come from the slings at all. Nevertheless, Sophie and Tyler could hear, feel, sense a high-pitched vibration. They dealt with their terror and achiness, and made the passage much more—not easier, but at peace. Peggy insisted on it. She told a story to the group in the gondola, but all Sophie and Tyler would remember was a string of names—John Chapman, John Dee, Luther Burbank, George Washington Carver; and a string of terms like negentropy and activation energy. The peace came from the oddly appropriate fit of the story as some kind of underpinning to this world they found themselves in. Her story was simultaneously befuddling and explanatory? Tyler recognized when he was before a great teacher. Sophie knew when she was in the presence of a great pitch man.

In between needles, when he opened his eyes, Lu of the Crots took Tyler's hand and asked him if he needed a drink. He looked into Lu's eyes. He thought of centaurs and giant ground sloths. He remembered the Battle of Whitewater. He remembered his parents and his siblings. He looked away. How could she understand what he felt? He didn't want to cry. Somehow, she pulled his eyes back to hers. There was a warmth and generosity there he could not fathom.

Lu kind of whispered to Tyler, "We've come to see that the cycles of chaos in all our lives, those endless catch as catch can's—duties, errands, checkups—they go on forever. So what is important is what we do, what we *really* do, that is not part of that?"

Tyler, still in her eyes, reflected, fell back asleep, then shook himself awake to mutter, "You make sense, make me feel better."

Sophie seemed stronger than Tyler. Perhaps she was

more focused on knowing they would get back, so had convinced herself to pluck up. Opposite that, was the insistent thorn that kept on stabbing out: they were stuck here, which made her refuse—she was convinced their stay 'here' was a blip, with a quick trajectory and resolution, that inevitably ended with her back in the real St. Louis. They *would* switch back. She *would* go home to her St. Louis. No thorn! No bad, crazy thoughts!

Would she still pursue pre-med studies? That world, those words, seemed fantastic now. Beyond this realm for sure. What if they couldn't go back? And she and Tyler were here forever? She hadn't seen a single black kid in all her adventures here. Would she have to go to Africa here? That felt wrong. And stupid. She was slipping back to worry. She knew keeping at this would make her so mad she wouldn't be able to help. In her sling respite, she'd allowed doubt in. She didn't want to. She went back and forth between belief and worry.

Peggy was nice. Sophie couldn't help but like her. She was one of those adult types who set everyone at ease. Everyone kept glancing her way when she was in the room. They wanted to see what she thought, what she had to say. Sophie knew she had to trust Peggy. Hippy or not?

When they arrived at the needles in Coltrane, Kai was there opening the door. Sophie remembered him from Coltrane, when they'd gotten on the sling after the earthquake. Kai and Lantine were an item she thought. They were supposed to be 'American', too.

Tyler was glad to see Kai. He and Lu knew him from their trip to Coltrane from Whitewater. Tyler figured the big man an adventure type, besides a hunter. A man you could trust in a tangle. Tyler wondered how Tom and Bish were. How many had died at Whitewater? Peggy probably knew but he didn't want to ask her. She did seem calm, clear, smart, so she did make him—and the others, feel more certain. The oddest thing how this odd woman with her odd ways offered certainty to their very sense of presence. Like what they were, who they thought they were? Whether this had any bearing on understanding their predicament, Tyler could not tell.

After they had a moment to stretch and get their bearings, Kai escorted them to the trucks. Everyone they encountered knew Peggy and greeted her. The small, quiet needle complex they had left from was filled with people. The 2 trucks unlike any Sophie and Tyler had seen: they were open on top, with big wheels of wobbly balloons like the pods. Kai would drive their truck, with Sophie and Tyler, Peggy and Lantine and Lu. They also had 2 militia men, farmers from the Castor, with them on their truck. The 4 rows of seats could accommodate them all. Peggy sat up from with Kai. In the back of the truck were supplies and equipment. The 2 farmers had bangers. The other truck was driven by Ali, whom it was explained was a regional militia leader, and as usual a friend of Peggy. His passengers were all militia representing the different ethnic groups of Chichimeca citizens.

Food and water was distributed to the sling passengers as they got comfortable in their seats. Kai waited, got the word, set in motion as they headed out. He said Coltrane was a mess but help had arrived. Clean up and rebuilding already under way. Soon enough they drove through Coltrane, and the damage to the City of Waterfalls was evident where ever they looked. Buildings had collapsed. There'd been rock slides. Kai said it could have been worse. Three people had lost their lives. They took the main road through town that skirted the long canyon, so they ascended to the tunnel without interfering with all the work going on. The tunnel was safe, said Kai. Farther along, and they could see how rock falls had reshaped the canyon. But their road was clear. People were everywhere working, cleaning up, with equipment and vehicles. They made it through the tunnel. On the other side of the tunnel, they began their descent through the forested mountains. Overhead a balloon hovered. They passed trucks, pods, mounted Crots, and people on horseback. Kai said scouts had been sent ahead to watch for trouble.

Sophie called out, "Where are we going?"

Peggy turned to meet her eyes, stared. "We have to get you kids back to the river."

When they were coming out of the forest, and the road was not as steep, they accelerated. Sophie and Tyler remembered that Coltrane was not far from the river. It was so clear and bright, the wind in their faces so exhilarating, they felt tickles of energy working their way into them. The excitement builds, thought Sophie and scowled, wishing she had a hat.

Ahead, some horseback riders and mounted Crots formed a knot in the road. Kai, whose vehicle had been leading, slowed to see what was up. As he pulled up to the riders, the passengers could see that they were all heavily armed. Sophie and Tyler assumed that equipment was weapons but here one never knew for sure. Tyler did recognize bangers. The folks started whooping when they saw Peggy. She stood in her place, waved and smiled.

Kai stopped the truck, and leaned out to greet them. Then: "What do you know?"

A mounted Crot stepped forward, close enough to the side of the truck that he could rest a hand on Kai's door. "We got sign. Sign ahead. Incursions. Mexicans!"

A horseman clopped over on a big roan, and said: "Are we at war, Peggy?"

Peggy said, "Not if we can help it."

Everyone whooped!

Kai allowed the other truck to move ahead, to be first now. He waved them by. Peggy waved to them too.

Ali scooted his truck around. He knew, as did the militia, that this is what they were here for.

The Crot cried out, "Word's out. We should have

plenty of help."

Kai and Peggy thanked the Crot and rider. They proceeded along, holding back, behind the advance vehicle. They were in the valley proper now. The forest had receded, and it was all mesquite and creosote, yucca and ocotillo. The white gold brushy expanse of the wide valley. The road changed, to a white sandy and gravel base. They stirred up dust, dust that could be seen from far off.

Lu called out from her seat in the back of the truck: "I'm thinking we should go straight to Old Duckbill?"

Peggy had to turn around to answer. She said, "He'll know. Let's see what happens when we get closer to the river."

Lu said, "We can stop at my Assembly."

Kai called back, "Ali said that's where folks are meeting. Like the staging area. How are our two guests doing?"

Sophie called, "Fine!"

"Okay," snapped Tyler too fast, not wanting anyone to know how he felt.

Peggy whispered to Kai, "Those letters again. Et la blue! C'est vrai! Es verdad! Nueva azul!"

Kai said, "Blue?"

"Yes," went Peggy. "These kids' energy, the release, the releasers all over the place. This blue! This is the blue I think adjusted the Great Machine's infelicity." She shook her head slowly, eyes wide. "I don't know, I will have to study. But just as they came, the two switched kids, the Great Machine, perturbed, unlikely, petulant—yes, petulant, and it configured! Went all gladsome before our eyes."

"What's happened, Peggy?" asked Kai softly. "That was no earthquake, was it? Butterfly Lords, too, leaking energy all over the plenum! Leakage? Excess? Palpable!"

"Yes," said Peggy. "No unction in Chichimeca I'm

afraid."

Kai went on: "They're—everyone's worried, Peggy. Crots say the animals know, and they're fretting, vexed. You tell that? Do you know?"

"The animals? Yes," said Peggy.

Kai slowed a moment to let a doe and her half-grown deer clamber aboard in the back. They'd just been standing there at the side of the road. Sophie and Tyler didn't mind, helping the critters in. Kai chuckled and said, "Meanwhile, the American embassy announced that Americans in Chichimeca should be on the alert. We should render aid to our Chichimeca brothers. Or we should high tail it out of here. Back to America."

Peggy said, "America thinks it's war? Mexico thinks it's war. The animals? Not so much."

"I think the Americans think," said Kai, "the Mexicans have some breakthrough weapons technology. Bomb maybe."

Peggy said, "Mexico must think the earthquake-like event was a new weapon of ours."

Kai said, "If they only knew—"

"We have to tell them. They must know. No secret in any of this, with the children I mean. Otherwise, nerves fester, their imaginations and paranoia feather a monster nest. We must reassure them."

They drove in silence, coming down the bajada. They could see the line of green ahead, the wide banks of the Castor in their marshy, lush greenery. Then: special irrigated fields far to the west, and the bare range of wild Sacaton nearby. Aurochs grazing in small clumps, calves with cows. Bulls turned away feeding could be an outcropping of boulders. Tyler looked south, wondering if he could see all the way to Whitewater. Too far! The bajada was a bowl in white gold, mountains to the west in the Huachucas, mountains to the east and north surrounding Coltrane. With a big fat, green caterpillar running down the middle of the bowl, caterpillar of water and life. Space, expanse, distance! All at once Peggy knew the great love connection the families on the Castor had for their place.

The truck ahead, driven by Ali, was a couple hundred yards in front of them. They'd run to white silver flats of sand and gravel so not much plant life here. A wide open spot, no cover. Slightly twinkly because of all the quartz in the sand and gravel. Kai saw the other truck slow. Ali was pointing off to his left, to the south side of the road. Kai kept it steady, glancing over to see. The others in his truck caught it first. No threat! It had to be brethren.

Sophie called, pointing, "Porcupine!"

Tyler followed her point. "See how big it is!"

The long-tailed desert porcupine was as big as a dog, in a dirty golden brown color, lurching towards the road and the vehicles, its quills, flattened now, seemed wispy thick pelt. Kai stopped right behind the forward truck. Both vehicles had all eyes on the porcupine. From the rounded flattened head, there seemed to be grunts or chuckles emanating. As the creature neared, it could be heard to be making a chupping, nonstop babble.

Peggy called out, "The enemy of my enemy is my friend. We're heading into a trap, into an ambush. Just ahead. The porcupine needed to tell us. There, see where the brush comes back, in that tangle ahead. He wanted to make sure you—we knew."

The porcupine kept coming.

Ali stood, turned back to face her. "What is it? We can call for help."

Peggy huffed, then said, "Help's already here, Ali. We go on."

The porcupine stopped short of coming onto the road. It nodded its head, shook itself briskly, turned back, wobbling around to the back of the truck. No longer making the chuckling sounds, it was firm in its resolve to get on board. Sophie and Tyler managed to help. Peggy sang encouragement. The deer scooted up.

Ali got his truck moving. The balloon-like wheels started swelling and writhing as it got going. Kai gave him a lead, then followed. They kept their pace slow. Mesquite and creosote became more common. First, in clumps, then thickets of brush.

Ali and Kai both saw the tangle in question. The one Peggy had identified. A badger held back in the brush but watched them with dark eyes on a thick neck. Ali passed it. Kai inched forward slowly. On the far side of the road, up a little ways, sat the badger, casually watching them approach, waiting for them.

Lu called, "Visitors!"

Peggy turned to the people in her truck. "Messengers!"

Lantine went, "Peggy!"

Lu said, "Peggy's not in danger."

Kai called out, "Easy. Peggy? We take him too?"

Tyler called, "Badger on board!"

Sophie said, "Regular Noah's ark we got going here!"

Peggy stood up and raised her hands above her head. They were passing through thick brush now, mesquite and saltbush, that crowded the road. Mexican soldiers stepped from the brush and fired short range, noisy rockets over their heads. The rockets deployed nets that billowed out and fell gently, slowly towards the 2 trucks' open tops. Peggy got down, ducked. Some militia in Ali's truck twisted over the sides of the truck and out and away fast before the net settled.

Peggy called out, "Wait for it! Wait for it!"

Giant ground sloths appeared behind the Mexican soldiers in the brush. They were on all fours, humping noisily forward. They got up on their back legs. The Mexican soldiers scattered. But no one fired. No screams. It was a quite altercation. The giant creatures ambled to the trucks, reached up, leaning forward, two at each truck.

Their up thrust big forearms ending with long claws collected the net. They tore it to pieces, grunting a bit. Megatheria wept.

Some of the Mexican soldiers made it back to their vehicles hid in the brush. A few were captured by Ali's militia, to be held at one of the Assemblies until negotiations. The people in the trucks watched the ground sloths up close, then sniffing and huffing, they slow motioned away, back in to the brush. Tyler thought he could hear the pop of bangers close by.

Ali told the others he'd wait for his people, that they should go on. Kai got them going around Ali's truck and heading towards the river.

CHAPTER 13

Two at once. Two places at once. Twice as nice! One life not enough. A complete life embraced contingencies and personalities, the other half possibility integrated, conflated. Effectuate.

How much of getting to know your double meant forecasting the awesome options the meeting might take? The things we will do. The places we will go! Time travelers go in all directions and never leave their spot. Travel elsewhere, elsewhen.

Two at once: how many at once? Complete. Completed. Balanced. Symmetric. Negentropic. We are made of so many voices. I didn't know I could sing. I didn't know I could do maths. I didn't know I could run like that. I didn't know I knew these big words. If infants imagine themselves the center of the universe, maybe this extended to kids who imagine themselves the center of the universe, too—unfortunately. The best, then, for total kid ego tripping, centrality plus monomania, would be to have a friend who admired you as much as you admired you (not like a mother's love—egad!). Another uniqueness in the uniquity...impossible! Two things *can't* occupy the same space. Or can they? The mind, the soul, whatever you call it, does its slithering slide to heat death, chaos, and entropy, and says no. Their getting to know each other was officially global spectacular now. This moment essential in their lives, as no moment ever had been or ever would be, would now be essential to all humans.

Aurore, from there, who's going as here Aurore, thought, "C'est—"

Aurore, from here, who's going as there Noe, got scrambled and woke up. Focused. It was the middle of the night. She was in her bunk, stretched out under the covers, in her group's room.

The doubles had discovered another way to do this sleep and dream, nighttime body duty thing. They slept apart in different rooms, so as not to confuse the grownups. But they would *sleep together*—that kind of together, the other together. They didn't know how. Telepathy was impossible, the experts said. What it meant, or how they did it, was unclear, but no blue sparks, just tranquility. Coming together with your double was natural, composed, placed, sedate. One needed one's double. Amity ruled doubles. They didn't want to talk about it to the adults. And the adults didn't know anyway. Aurore quieted and fell back asleep.

Aurore, from there, thought, "Your thinks as though thoughts, cogitations, requisite activity, busy prep, you are always in prep—that's your word, preoccupying ruminations on what's next? Es verdad? As though you're writing it down for posterity. The great dictation?"

Two at once. Two places at once. Twice as nice! No separation!

Aurore, from here, went, "How considerate, your lucubration speculation makes me an abstraction, yes? I'm an abstract mess? You have—no, you *know* my secrets! My Kryptonite muse!"

Information streamed between the Aurores. Information had to be free, shared by all the doubles. But in varying formats, so for some of the kids imagery, for others logical precepts. Could it leak that way? Was there a danger? *Overlap?* Then all at once they knew at once: they're coming! There it was. They knew those faces. They were coming—

By morning, all doubles knew or thought or sent or received: *we will go to the spot.* Re-enactment. Rejuvenate. Resurrection. Reprehensible: Habaneros!

If it doesn't work!

Flip back? Double back? Switch back?

Annihilation?

Query: suppose I have to stay here? Does that mean red spectacles and blue flip flops forever?

Will we ever know what happened?

And if it does work, will forces recognize us in disguise?

Tell us apart? Flip us back wrongly? Doggedly blunder fallacious

Apocrypha?

Discern. Declaim. Threnody.

Mind is a community of mental floss. Aurore, from there, laughed mental, then dental, then twisted the rhyme to spinach!

Existence, a broccoli organism of knowing. A Brainiac with asparagus head! Or globular starry shell with tentacles coming out of the snoot. From the long ago to the long ahead, the sinews barge the news. Pale stench. Tentacled rhizomes.

Bacon.

Frühstück. Petit dejeuner.

Then the kids were ready.

Chile peppers had shifted the universe. But that makes piquant sense, Aurore from here mooned, thinking the universe of a trillion galaxies would be muy pimiento. Andale! The Aurore from there loved it—

The bed and breakfast breathed slowly and carefully in the wee hours. Before dawn, no monitors had picked up any activity of any kind. No handler or orderly or deputy noticed anything 'unusual' with the doubles. Caring for the little ones, pacifying the parents, had reached an end point. For right now, everyone was snug as bugs in a rug. Now even bathroom visits were monitored. They—the officials who claimed in charge, they, or everyone else, had decided what would happen this coming day: the doubles had to be re-located to the nearby army base, where tests and studies would continue. A security issue for sure—there were enough guards around so that no one could slip away here. But what if the earthquake-like blasts continued? What if the doubles were involved, were causing the explosions? Professionals were worthless when they ran out of ideas, which really meant running out of control: so they sought a semblance of control: let's move.

Adler knew security was most important when no one thought of it—when no one expected trouble. What did he expect? He knew he could change his tune. Think on your feet, adjust, adapt, go with the flow. That was official thinking. He wondered about un-official thinking. He knew to project this ideal of control and calm...no matter what. Taking care of business. He was tired of watching the professionals fall apart, while the doubles made blue sparks. There must be other—an other....

Aurore, from here, thought, the adults don't see...they think they're taking us away today. Odd, how they can be so dense.

The Aurore from there thought, odd, too, how our experiences do not match up.

Pas de tout.

You didn't see Sophie and Tyler from there coming in to here, etc.

I wasn't even near. Distance. Distance. Away. Perspective. Parallax.

Is this the adventure of our lives?

Forever coming to this crossroads?

We'll always wonder if we should have picked the other choice, the *other other other*?

Making us the excluded?

Because we were pre-occupied with 'difference', rather than figuring out? The whole world will know—

What a Diva. You love secrets! You love being found out! You think you're special!

Right now: Limbo. Nephelococygia.

Mr. Fort?

Don't you have secrets?

You should know by now.

Know the initial state of all bodies—

Then you can know any future position—

Everything solved so easy in books.

Don't be a text.

Macrocosm.

Microcosm.

Gravity quanta.

Extremely high leaking rainbow.

In a Lovecraftian sense.

Continuous laughter: you are funny!.

As above—

So below—

Overlap so dear!

Be real nearly—obliged? Caprice!

We are Poltergeist Girls!

I never quite—

You've never told me if you've ever seen a ghost.

* * *

Sophie and Tyler swore they saw aurochs in the dry, dead grass fields before the San Pedro River. Lantine, Luanna, Bishop, and Kai wanted to see them themselves.

Mela cautioned, "Beasts of the fields know their time,

their people, their end. All our energies now, all are needed. It's a build up? I feel so much more...solicitude—is that the right word? Worry, regard, for some break? As though we were on the verge, and even the aminals worry?"

They'd left the trucks and animals on a small dirt road that cut off from the county road. The animals were polite, nodding appreciative, moving off, knowing where to go. The humans'd taken water and pockets stuffed with habaneros. The road didn't go all the way down to the river. They were on the west side of the river. The Rio Vista Bed and Breakfast was across the way, on the east side. So far, since the Mexicans and Border Patrol, no sign of people. It was noticeably...not quiet, but full of expectancy, as was that part of themselves that rose and fell with excitement like a new organ. The guards were keeping folks in, so they wouldn't get out, not so alert about folks out, who wanted in—

Kai said, "Let's get across the field fast. Cover in the trees."

Kai led the way, single file, all seven of them. It was a fabulous spring day without a cloud in the sky. A blue sky, huge, a bit sparkly bright, so the approaching helicopter seemed to tackle that blue, a smudge, a dirty buggy splat in the blue. Blue was suddenly too open and easy. Splotches were real and gritty. So everyone hit the dirt, taking what little cover they could in the dead grass. A flock of black birds rose from the river and moved in an erratic collapsing sphere of wings. Was it crows? Were they moving towards the helicopter? The pilot must have been afraid the birds were getting too close, so the helicopter swerved north away from the open field. The birds followed, seemed to follow, maybe...maybe not?

Kai yelled, "Up! Let's go!"

They got to their feet and scurried to the trees and brush at the river. Tyler and Sophie, both, felt somewhat foolish sneaking around in their backyards. But so much had happened in the last few days that was plain absurd impossible: were they getting used to it? Absurd impossible to get used to absurd impossible! Finally, in the cottonwoods and brush near the river's eroding bank, they found waiting for them Special Agent Alan Adler. He was dressed in practical clothes and shoes. He had a water bottle in his hand and was using it to point to does to his left. Handful of feet away. The does tiptoed into nearby brush. Their big watery eyes did not seem scared or frightened. Their presence felt like now was opening up, reaching out. Inclusive. The does and the people bunched up in the trees around Adler. He looked them over; sighed, smiled. Everyone watched the does who gently wandered off. Adler's eyes found Sophie and Tyler. He looked them over. "You're back," he said.

Mela said, "You're here to help."

Adler reflected, "That some Jedi mind trick? Things are outlandish, so—" He shook with it, breathing lustily. "I knew you'd be back. This has got to be it. Our last chance, right? How did I know I'd find you? And right here? And with the deer?" He shook with it, but kept looking from person to person, making sure they were really there. He said, "Keep getting reports from the sheriff and his people about animals, just—I don't know, acting up? Coming out, right in front of people, behaving strangely. Listen, it doesn't matter right now. Right now, we get these kids to the spot. It's not far. Today is the day. How do I know these things?"

"You know exactly what to do," went Mela. "You always have." She announced with a slight quivering lilt: "Life rises up! Life! We're on, everybody! Overlap." She knew things, she sensed things, she felt things, she doubted things. She went back to simply knowing, trusting intuition, if that's what it was. Five senses? Six senses? How many were possible? She wanted so badly to seem confident and certain. She could tell the others...they were...but for herself as of yet—

Adler got ready to move, came around close to Mela, studying her. He had big eyes. She had big eyes He said, "You're not some hippy princess? You're the one the kids had to go to the Duke City for? Overlap, huh?"

She burst: "The animals! They're freaking."

Adler popped with: "The people back at the B and B, all those specialists, they're freaking! They want to get the kids away from here. This is our last chance."

"Chance," said Mela with a big grin as though she knew everyone expected some cryptic epigram. "No chance. This what we came for. Led here."

Tyler felt weak, energy dissipating. He whispered loudly enough that everyone heard, "Freak show?" Then, it was like he hit the bottom of weakness and confusion and found it lacking. He would have fallen, but some iota of energy and presence and fortitude bounced him back. Maybe because Sophie was with him. He felt exultant then. It was going to happen. He wanted to write a poem. He tried not to faint. He looked at Sophie and smiled.

Sophie said, "C'est vrai! It's her. We call her Peggy." The past few days to right now, thought Sophie, and we seem to be weakening. She would not give up. Tyler seemed weak. Sophie felt concern watching Tyler's physical rise and falls.

They were ready to head out. Kai said to Adler, "Who are you? There must be deputies and police everywhere. How'd you get down here?"

Adler said, "I don't think we've met. But I recognize you from your picture. Crotalus? I'm Special Agent Alan Adler, FBI. Don't worry, I've gone Cimarron. I took care of the others, at least the ones that stood in our way. No, I didn't hurt anyone. I figured you would show up. The kids from 'there' were certain you would too. They said Old Duckbill and Peggy made sense of it. See, I'm starting to talk like them."

They had to cross the river. They lined up along the bank, a line of people with shoes on or moccasins or boots or sandals. It didn't matter: the mud embraced them, soaked to their ankles. A bit slurpy and smelly too.

Bishop went, "I love mud."

Luanna said, "Uh-ho, mud story!"

Kia came up to walk alongside Adler. Adler met his gaze and said, "The kids will meet us at the spot. We gotta move."

Lantine said, "Glad to have you with us, Mr. Adler."

Luanna said, "Me, too."

Adler looked at Lantine. "Don't think I've seen your pic. But, you," he said, looking at Luanna, "I recognize you. You're from that circus, too." He glanced at Bishop. "You, too."

Bishop said, "Me three. We're here to help. This is our story now."

Adler said, "All of ours."

Luanna said, "It's going to take all of us. Isn't it, Mela?"

Mela smiled, walking fast now, moving up front to lead. "'Cimarron' is a good word, bon mot. A good story for today." She knew where they were going. She liked Adler. She liked them all. She felt the land, the people—animals wept....

They heard crashing nearby in the brush. It wasn't long before 2 horses with riders clattered into view.

Jakes said, "Rough along the bank. Hard on our guys."

Graves yelped, "Sophie! Good to see you! You're okay!"

* * *

On the other side of the river, but in another tense not past, present, or future, Kai and Ali parked their trucks around back at the Crot assembly. The visiting militia and specialists had set up a site there for equipment and vehicles. They left their trucks and went around to join the others. They'd let their passengers off in front of the assembly where a crowd gathered.

The spring blue sky was immense, a huge sky, like a stage, because the myriad peoples of Chichimeca, and talking dogs, were celebrating Peggy's visit. The parents of the missing children were eager, straining to hear every word—they craved news, and Peggy consoled them. Okla went from person to person, shaking hands, greeting, welcoming. Everyone wanted to touch and shake hands with Peggy. Hugs were bountiful. Sophie and Tyler hung back, both feeling fragile, unsure. They thought they knew what was happening. Lu ran among her people, smiling and laughing and hugging, asking of Bish and Tom. They were fine, she was told, but out on patrol. The militia joined their cohorts already there, and they went off to scout and set a perimeter.

Suddenly, the air high above was filled with crows coming in from the river. A big flock of them, cawing and cackling, fluttering, found a direction, started heading off. The people quieted, watched. Peggy held her head up and back, stretched out as far as possible. The birds were pointing to something she couldn't help but think. A mounted Crot and a militia man on a horse came pounding up from the river.

Fido called out to the assembly, "News! News! Ruff!"

The man on the horse shouted, "Take cover! Take cover!"

Sophie and Tyler knew those words, and with a jolt of adrenaline started talking earnestly to the people about clearing out, returning to their homes: cover meant get under something for protection from the sky. Ali and Kai understood and tried to help, too. Crots were taking up position, bangers in hand.

Ali talked with the Crot and the militia man, then called out to the dispersing crowd, "Everyone, return to your homes. Could be some new Mexican weapon. We don't know. Protection. Shelter. For right now. All eyes now! We got to get these kids to the spot."

Peggy let out a gasping cry and pointed to the southern sky. Kai yelled then, also pointing. A small white dot was moving through that southern sky, coming towards them in what seemed an arc. They were on the downward sweep of the arc. The dot left behind a white trail...of exhaust? The big blue sky was too open, too easy for this dot to pierce.

Peggy screeched, "They didn't!"

Okla cried, "Sky bullet!"

The Crot who'd come with the militia horseman said, "We don't know what it can do."

Kai said, "Can't be good."

By then, families and kids had disappeared. Others with weapons were taking up positions. Okla knew it was time as did Peggy. They had to get going.

The crows organized the sky to flock and space and dot, and they were swarming to the fast approaching dot.

* * *

When the helicopter exploded to the north, it was far enough away that the ten only heard it. No shock wave, no fire, no smell. They didn't feel it.

Mela said, "I can't believe that." They paused, formed up in a bunch for a few seconds. "Such a waste of life," Mela said.

Adler said, "Helicopters and birds don't mix."

Bishop moaned, "Death don't have no mercy!"

Birds called around them, a sudden, wild outpouring of songs or alerts. A bull frog started to croak. Unidentifiable chups and trills sounded from all sides. The ten exchanged glances. Their faces squinting up to hear better, see better, understand better. Mela and Adler led the way.

Adler said, "We're almost there."

Jakes and Graves were at the tail end of the group, leading their horses behind them. Jakes blurted: "Will it work?"

Bishop sang out, "I love mud."

Adler laughed. Mela said something about 'work working' and laughed herself. Or maybe it was something about the duty of work to work? Or maybe they were nervous enough to distract themselves with sillies?

Sophie said, "Will we return?"

Tyler said, "Will we switch back?"

Graves answered, "Only one way to find out."

Mela said, "The animals sure think so."

* * *

When the missile exploded in the sky, it was far enough away that no damage was done to the assembly. The crows on the other hand—

Peggy said, "Such a waste. Aminals."

Okla said, "We must get the children to the spot."

They were on their way. Militia trucks would get them across the open grassy fields, their floppy pod 'tires' streaming with puffy power. Peggy and Ali and Okla were in the lead truck. Sophie, Tyler, Kai, Lantine, and Lu were in the second truck. Lu held Tyler's hand. Sophie wished she had a hat. Sophie and Tyler knew their moment approached.

Pods came in from the river, joining up with the trucks, following alongside. Two mounted Crots led the trucks. It wasn't far. They'd have to get out and walk then. They had plenty of scouts around. People were scared because of the missile. Parents were scared they wouldn't get their kids back. Two men on pods came right up to the trucks to wave and shout. Sophie saw it was Graves and Jakes and called out to them.

Graves shouted with bubbling eyes, "Sophie! Tyler!"
Sophie said, "Bonjour!"
Graves called, "You are returning?"
Tyler said, "Will we switch back?"
Jakes said, "Peggy's with us."
Graves said, "Only one way to find out."

* * *

They splashed through algae and water cress that coagulated on the surface in gunk and foam along the banks of the river. Turtles and carp darted away from their tumult. Tyler saw a big softshell turtle with a snorkel nose. Sophie thought it was sad to see the river so oily. And those big yellow gold fish were not native she knew. When Adler had them bunch up again so he could say something, a kingfisher landed on an overhanging branch and let loose a wild laugh. Everyone saw the eyes flash, more eyes than any bird they'd ever seen. What did it see? What was it saying to them?

Adler said, "The animals know. I guess. I'm still learning. I guess we all are. But the kids, their doubles know to meet at the spot. The Aurores know exactly where it is. Remember, Sophie, Tyler, you stacked up some rocks? The Aurores said we'd need habaneros. We'll see if the kids can pull it off."

"We have habaneros," said Kai. They showed what they had in their pockets.

Adler laughed. "Should be enough heat."

Sophie and Tyler nodded, their tiredness and weakness eager to be forgotten.

Jakes said, "You're that FBI fellow."

Graves said, "It's going to work!"

Kai said, "So why are we lurking around like fugitives?"

Adler started to respond but Mela interrupted him:

"Animals are scared. People are scared. What's happening's too new. Perhaps never before experienced. They—all of us will have a hard time seeing it clearly like you do, Adler Cimarron."

Lantine said, "We could be walking into a trap?"

"No," said Adler. "It won't happen that way. Officials are stymied. Ask the Aurores what that means. All that's left right now is the kids' certainty. That's what we're going by. Push on! The so called experts, the so called adults back at the B and B are pretty worthless right now."

"Perfect," said Mela. "Then—"

* * *

Graves and Jakes left their pods by the trucks when everyone got out. They would walk the rest of the way. Here, lush green began. The ground become soft. Tangles of small blooming plants. Trees increased in size as they got closer to the river.

Peggy, Sophie and Tyler in front, led the way. Everyone thought Peggy was singing. Peggy thought she was voicing....

Aurochs were plentiful, heaps as big as hay piles in the near distance. Aurochs stopped their relentless grazing off sacaton to stare at the passersby. They looked into each other's eyes, humans and bests. Aurochs looking back, said they knew, or they were with them, or maybe they were just interrupted and wanted to get back to their grazing? Mounted Crots made 'tsk-tsk' sounds to remind them of their connections. A big bull auroch lifted its massive head, nodded briskly, bellowed.

Two giant ground sloths much closer, shy in the lush green, peeked at them from on high. Their heads, though huge, had a softness about them, a gentle heaviness. They uttered a swell of swallowing sounds, not quite burps, not quite utterances. They, too, were engaged with activities.

Big hairy arms flailed a bit, almost a greeting. Their eyes were big as avocados, Sophie thought. Were these the ones who had stopped the Mexican nets? The Mexican attempt to capture Peggy? Must be relatives then....

In a last patch of sacaton, they passed a big glyptodont puttering about, nosing through cholla skeletons, vaguely heading for the river, too. The rounded, armored head went up and down. At first like it was nodding, but then it was clear the great animal was scratching itself against the dried husks, before joining them. One look in its eyes convinced the people that he was on their side, ready to help.

Peggy recognized all of them and they recognized her. Could the very air be alive with life's recognition? The

greenery with small birds, the overhead skies with ducks and herons, the distance raptors high up, or in tree tops, their songs combined in to a song, an utterance that said they were alive, involved, part of the day. Raptors getting closer, moving in? All the birds were getting closer, raptors and small birds had a temporary peace treaty it seemed.

Was there gathering? Were they coming together? Joining forces? Something somehow coordinated?

Then, the humans noticed the invertebrates. Writhing counts! The six legged, the eight legged, the multi-legged said hello. Sounds rose! Wings thrummed. Sounds of vertebrates and invertebrates wove together, merged, became some new...force...presence? Pressure or gravity? An awareness of new sonics. Life views offered sensory experience.

Graves and Jakes moved up to the front when a dog faced bear loped in. Big toothy head. They were scary up close—and could be dangerous! Only a few had been planted here by the Crots. Everyone knew to stay away from them. Plastique couldn't change predators. At least, not yet. Jakes and Graves had talked it over with a dog faced bear a few times previously. They weren't sure if this was the same one. They had all shrugged in agreement to keep the peace, and to agree to disagree. The other nearby animals ignored the big predator so the people didn't worry. Peace treaty! The bear grunted, Peggy grunted back. The bear tagged along.

Jakes said, "We should be able to find the exact spot. It's marshy around here but—"

Graves turned to Sophie and Tyler, "Remember that auroch bull that startled you?"

Sophie said, "Graves! Of course! Yes, I remember."

"Yes," said Tyler.

Sophie said, "This is where it started. Near here."

Graves said, "A few days change everything."

Jakes said, "Even if the kids switch back, will there be war?"

Peggy said, "The Mexicans think so. They think it is war. The Mexicans think we have some breakthrough, so they're showing us their breakthrough. They will have a hard time seeing events clearly."

Ali Adler came over to join them. He said, "That sky bullet—whatever it was. They're serious that's for sure. But one thing at a time. Right now is our certainty. We take care of the kids. That's what we're going by."

"Perfect," said Peggy. "You see clearly, Ali Cimarron."

Adler looked to Peggy to see what she meant. She smiled and looked away, continued on their path. Butterflies all around them now. Flying critters near and high—air filled with fluttering wings, with gauzy wings. Feathers! Bats! Bats in the day time? Some clacked. Some made little twinkling sounds. Peggy led them to the spot. Bellowing throbs could be heard from amphibians.

Adler said, "I'm not blind."

Sophie said, "I don't like bugs."

Peggy smiled. "They like you, O child of the Butterfly Lords"

"Ah," went Sophie, and nervously laughed.

Tyler pretended to chuckle and managed not to throw up.

* * *

Jakes said, "We should be able to find the exact spot."

Sophie, who was near him, pointed ahead. There, through the mesquite and yucca spires, out of the thorny brush on the east side of the meager river, a parade of people marched in along a familiar trail.

Sophie called, "Aurore! Tu est ici!"

"Pourquoi pas?" answered Aurore.

Medea looked over the bunch coming in to join them. Her eyes settled on Sophie and Tyler. She looked like she hadn't slept in days. But the site of the two kids made her glad. "We brought your original clothes," she said. "Aurore thought it was tres importante. Bien?"

Sophie saw her parents and she ran to them, embraced them. They hugged and sighed and cried. Sophie said, "You have been wonderful. Thank you for everything!"

Sophie's mother, Winona, handed her 'other' daughter the clothes she had come in, the same sandals.

Sophie's dad sighed, touched her cheek, said, "You'll have to change in the bushes."

Tyler was surrounded by Gacks. The doubles, too, wanted hugs. But kept their distance from their double. The Campbells said together, "We're going back."

Lise from here snarled, "You are back, dodo-brain!"

Her Lise double cackled with laughter. "'Anger is an energy,'" she snarled.

Their mom huffed and humphed, but smiled at all her kids.

Special Agent Karen Connelly went up to Adler. "Found your note. This the spot?"

He nodded, smiled at her. "We've worked together

well. I appreciate that."

She said, "You did the right thing. I had to help. I wanted to help. I *needed* to help. With the kids. This is very important, and I needed to."

"I know," said Adler.

Noe came up to Adler. He nodded to her. She said, "The aminals are afoot!"

Adler said, "What's it about?"

Noe watched his face, his eyes...the way he peered intently made her realize he was up to no good with her. Then, she figured she had to trust him anyway: "They're considering nuking it? This spot? I know I'm right."

"You have the word 'nuke' where you come from?"

"After they get us out of here, you know what's going to happen. That's the best the contemporary adult world can come up with. Nuke it. Can you imagine now why kids don't like school or have much interest in anything but pop? Send a thermonuclear device down the rabbit hole!"

Connelly had been listening and came over closer to say, "Still—I mean," she snickered and had to rub at her nose a sec. She waved away flying insects. "What are the chances that a girl fascinated by—"

Aurore joined them, so finished, "Anomalies."

Connelly feigned surprise, then did it herself: "Anomalies. Ends up in the biggest anomaly of all time."

Noe said, "Something happened when those two bit the habaneros."

"Agreed," said Aurore. "But that is not an explanation."

Adler said, "Did you find any habaneros? Because these guys—"

Noe lifted a plastic bag of pumpkin orange peppers. "Delivered by the NSC!" Then, she said, "These 'plastique'...bags...so strange."

Adler looked at her funny. "I bet," he said.

Folks around them were calling out, pointing out all

the animals—cows, deer, a raccoon, then birds, that seemed to be gathering by them.

Noe said, "I was cogitating: kids from there had no plastic bag. We know this. But the kids here had one. Since their clothes did not change in the switch, I assume the kids here, Sophie, took the plastic bag with her in a pocket."

"You said the habaneros disappeared," said Adler.

Noe was so hot—sweating, blushing, ripening. She exclaimed: "Can you imagine the fate of the universe, its very integrity bound by the weight of a wisp of plastic bag?"

"And some chile peppers," said Adler. "What does it mean we have to do?"

Noe and Aurore came close to Adler. But not too close together. "We should join the others. Have you met Mela? The animals are—what are they doing?" The girls kept close, staring at him. Like a challenge?

They peered in to Adler, or at least he thought so, and it made him a tad uneasy, while he tried to figure what to say, what to ask for, what he wanted to know: "Tell me about hoaxes. "

Noe said, "Entropy is expanding."

Aurore said, "Lord Kelvin. Carnot. It never was a balance."

Noe said, "Bien sur."

Together they said, "Entropy is likely to increase rather than not." They both backed up when a family of skunks marched by, but with tails down. Then, ground squirrels, pack rats, tiny pointed nosed shrews came next. The Aurores seemed enthralled, enraptured by the lines of incoming animals.

Medea worked her way over to stand behind her girls. "'Aminals'! Right, my loves? Isn't that what you call them?"

Noe said, "Misspelling is fun? Free orthography!

Spelling? Invented spelling?"

Aurore went, "Poect. Tyler from there is a poect."

Medea said, "Don't gang up on me! Colloquialisms?"

Noe cried, "Vernacular!"

Medea reached out a hand to both girls, but didn't let them touch. As she made contact to grasp their hands, she lifted off her feet. That is, she rose a few inches above the ground, in a levitation spark dance that rose, then as she pulled her hands free, she was left to fall on her butt.

"Momma!"

"Mom!"

They held out hands to help her up.

Medea said, "I'm okay. Back off." She laughed. "You guys are—things are—both of you." She shook with it, a shimmy cascading through her frame. "How embarrassing." She looked so cute on the ground.

Mela came over to see. She smiled at the scene, mother and daughters, sisters the same, but they weren't. Medea got on her feet, brushed herself off. "You're the one they had to go see," she said.

Mela and Medea embraced.

Adler said to the two Aurores, "Share. For some reason you two have excelled through all this. Share what you know."

Aurore said, "Humans work against entropy."

Noe added, "Loschmitt Paradox: entropy increases in the past."

Adler said, "Lock what? You guys are playing? Still playing? There's no time. Share!"

Mela said, "Tell, sisters!"

Aurore and Noe began: "Two at once, two places at once. All sides now. But no contradiction. No canceling out like opposites might. It has to right itself. Like a teeter totter. O Poltergeist Girls, nacreous twists in a lemon sky."

In Noe's secret most dankness, hidden in stalagmites, a thought she didn't dare share: the difference between her and her twin was that they both knew what they should be doing, and she did it willingly, with pleasure, while Noe didn't do it. Couldn't be bothered. This was scary weak—

Adler said, "What are you guys—you're kidding. Okay, that was inappropriate. We're all a bit stressed here, waiting for the cavalry. But come on! 'Lemon sky'? Is that a Beatles' lyric? Do you know more you're not saying? Is there anything we can do? Any of us?"

But it was a lemon sky. Full of wings and bodies and floaters.

Doubles were all around them. Doris and Doris stood together but kept their distance from each other. Same with Catherine and Katerina. Thor and Terve did the same. Campbells had big smiles. Lises were sulky, glancing around nervously, as though looking for an escape route.

Their parents were around them. People in concentric circles, or in layers?

Aurore and Noe continued, "Dr. Jekyll, Ms. Hyde."

The doubles giggled, clapped.

The Campbells squealed out, "I know, I know!"

Aurore said, "I'm Dr. Jekyll. So that means you're—"

Noe sprang out with: "No way!"

Together they said, "Never that easy, simply opposites. Contraries are congruities. A person changes a person. People learn. They have to. To learn is to take it in where it becomes part of you. We have no choice. People change."

Mela said, "Everything changes."

Medea felt her eyes fill up.

Some of the parents were sobbing now. The doubles seemed okay.

The Lise from here commented, "You're pretty cool, my one and only."

The Lise from there said, "You are too. You are perfect,

even if you deny it; you just need to read more."

"You saying I'm the Dr. Jekyll of this dyad?"

Tyler from there said, "Sophie and I have learned so much. Change may be difficult. We thank everyone. A great poet from our home wrote a long time ago in a haiku: 'This world of dew is a world of dew. And yet, and yet.' His name was Issa. It means there's always more. In his manner, but not a haiku, my own: 'We went home the long way'."

Sophie from there grimaced, then chuckled, then said, "Perfect!"

* * *

A kingfisher showed them the exact spot, with the rock pile. This was a big guy, a bird with a spear for a beak, and his blue went from sky blue to azurite, depending on the angle from the lemony sun. Immediately, ants were everywhere, but organized as they are wont, making long march lines of black swarming movement, coming to the center of the life work. Red ants too. Orange ones. Big ants with blocky noggins, then small ones with thin ballerina legs. Teeny tiny ones. In lines.

Generations. Geometries. Species galore! They seemed to be moving in concert. On the ground, crawling forward, walking in, stumbling in, or sauntering over. Then the air was birds and flying insects. No conflict, no bumping into each other, no guile or defensiveness. Everyone was on best behavior. No snacking allowed. Peggy saw what we were doing.

Mela noted to the others the circles the ants were drawing around the doubles, who were around the spot. She pointed out how flying creatures were making the ground circles 3-D, in the air of living bodies. Sophie and Tyler would be in the center after they had changed into the exact clothes they had been wearing when they showed up. Their clothes had been cleaned. Everyone hoped the cleaning would not affect things. The parents formed the next ring of humans around the center. They were worried, though Peggy could make them feel better. The next ring, after the parents, had Lu, Bish, Jakes and Graves, other folks who had been involved with the kids. Luanna and Bishop, Kai, and Lantine.

When Sophie and Tyler came out of the bushes in their home world clothes, they witnessed swarms of life on ground and air, high tall circles of life, extending into the brush and into the sky. It all seemed precise, as though this was what it was doing, and there was no other way. Hovering, squawking forms, made a song, too, of life and urgency, fear and bravery, expectation and resolve. How far did the sphere of life extend underground with worms and nematodes and gophers? Yes, thought Peggy and Mela! All the way down to the center of the Earth, where we came right back up to here: we are the center, we are the edge of the arc.

Animals and humans, lined up between insect circles, termites, beetles, worms, maggots, lice, kept saying, "Watch your feet!"

Lines between lines, circles in circles! Giant ground sloths and aurochs and gomphotheres made the outer edges. Megafauna returned to the meditation of their come back, knowing it was for this.

Humans were close to aminals, the medium-sized animals
like turkey and deer stood with humans. Birds flew around them, sweeping in close. Insects everywhere. But the humans didn't mind them, and the insects didn't mind the humans. Reptiles and amphibians had a circle too.

Sophie and Tyler walked through the spherical mass of life to the center. The parents looked ragged and hopeful. Smiling at the 2 kids. The innermost circle spot was empty. No bugs. Waiting for them. Space and time ready.

No time for goodbyes. They were too busy watching where they put their feet. Sophie and Tyler took up position in the center.

Peggy and Mela stepped in, between them.

Lu called out anyway, "Vaya con dios, mes amis!"

Tyler and Sophie kept their eyes on Peggy, on Mela. She was Peggy, she was Mela. Ahh, they thought, neither really knew what that meant, but they didn't want to appear obtuse.

Sophie whispered, "Habaneros?"

Tyler shrugged. They both pulled them out of their pockets, then leaned over to make a pile between them. Then thought better of it and kneeled on either side of the little pumpkin orange peppers.

Sophie whispered, "What—don't think I can take any more cosmic lessons in hot sauce?"

Tyler shrugged. "See you back home."

Sophie said, "These bugs...they make me itch."

Then they bit down.

Everyone could see the blue light now.

* * *

When Sophie and Tyler came out of the brush in their home clothes, they joined an incredible spectacle. Swarms of insects made circles around the rock pile which marked the spot. Circles of species expanded into the brush. Sophie and Tyler saw the circles went in three dimensions: they formed concentric shells of flying forms, birds and flying insects in the air. Sophie and Tyler walked to the spot, stepping lightly around reptiles and amphibians. The concentric circles like shells of life nested together. Contain. Overlap. Not a sphere at all. A new or different geometry or merging, becoming, they hadn't imagined.

To complete the circles, animals and humans in

formation. Larger animals on the outer edges. A medium sized porcupine, apologizing profusely for being late, took up position next to a gossipy coyote. The humans in the inner circles were the doubled kids, then the parents, then their new friends and acquaintances. Sophie and Tyler walked through the mass of creatures to the center. Mela and Peggy joined them seconds later in the middle. Mela had her arms up, extended.

Lise called, "Watch where you step!"

Sophie said, "Invertebrates are out!"

Tyler said, "Everything that breathes shares our air?"

The parents of the doubles and a bunch from the bed and breakfast, including the Whitings and some of the scientists and technicians, clapped for a second then saw how that was not appropriate. The doubles waved and danced in place their gladness. Sophie and Tyler by the rock pile. Adler, Graves and Jakes, Luanna and Bishop, Kia and Lantine arranged among insects and reptiles and amphibians. Worms, too, lots of worms helped out in the arcs of the concentric circles.

Sophie and Tyler had to bunch up a bit at their spot. Doris from there cried, which make Katarina start. Lise from there bent to console them. Lise from here shouted out encouragement in French. Funny, but it wasn't that loud or bellowy with the beasts at all, so they could hear her. They could hear plenty here, for a soothing lively Earth thrum enveloped them all. The Lises waved to each other, eyes full of each other, babbling for a few seconds in their private babble language they had developed over the last couple days.

Sophie and Tyler took up position in the center, kneeling, smiling nervously at each other. Noe brought them the plastic bag of habaneros.

Lots of habaneros—were they all going to bite down at once? No one had really worked that out—

Luanna called out, "Friends!"

Tyler held the bag, standing next to Sophie. He couldn't resist: "We did it this way?"

Aurores called, "Yes."

Sophie whispered to him, "Do we really have to bite one of these?"

Tyler said, "You know what Aurores said. They saw everything. We'll do it just like *we* did before."

Everyone could see the blue light now.

What followed happened. Two at once. One is not enough. Duration. Adjustment. Shift—

Adler thought, 'paltry' for some reason. 'Paltry' came to Adler's mind, a word Aurores would savor, suddenly it was clear to him, or somehow he understood, the word came because words could not begin to come close to what was happening. So Adler thought about how he couldn't think about it. What was happening, he meant. Then: what had happened? It was over. No boom. No electric fire surge. No beacon of star light from the heavens! No jumping shock waves? Was Coltrane all right?

World settled back and down in the easiest way which was the best way. But is that all the time? Stability rules? But what of entropy, Noe/Aurore wondered. They put a pin in that for discussion next time. Because this time was over.

Events to events.

So Aurore from here was busted. They had not tricked the 'event' at all.

Adler had seen blue. Excellent! It wasn't 'paltry'.

No perturbations. No annihilations. As it subsided, whatever it was, his eager eyes settled on Noe and he knew it hadn't worked. But just for a split second, and then he understood. What of the others? The doubles? What about Coltrane? Had Coltrane suffered another bouncy earthquake?

Ah, a different set of Sophie and Tyler. Present! They

shouted, 'it worked'. Their parents shouted. Everyone shouted! They were back. They whooped it up. Except the left behind doubles: they wailed forlornly, missing their other halves. Adler went over to Noe...thinking he'd figured out...nothing—

Born in 1951 in the Ozarks, Chris Dietz is a writer, teacher, and a birdwatcher. Currently, he lives in Bisbee, Arizona, surviving a catastrophe.